WATERS OF REDEMPTION

WATERS OF REDEMPTION

CEDAR CREEK LEGENDS BOOK TWO

CEDAR CREEK LEGENDS
BOOK 2

JORDAN JACE

Print ISBN: 978-1-967657-57-5

EPub ISBN: 978-1-967657-58-2

CONTENTS

FOREWORD

Cedar Creek Legends, Book Two: *Waters of Redemption*

The town of Cedar Creek has always lived by its rituals. For generations, the river has carried its lanterns, the basin has blessed its people, and the bell at the fort has tolled dawn into every new day. But when those rituals begin to falter, long-buried secrets stir, threatening to break the fragile harmony of a community bound by memory, loyalty, and unspoken betrayals.

In *Waters of Redemption*, Miriam Adler—widowed newcomer and reluctant keeper of mystical gifts—finds herself at the heart of Cedar Creek's most unsettling mystery yet. At the opening ritual of the Rivers Festival, the ceremonial basin runs inexplicably dry before the entire town. Panic ripples through the crowd as an ancient symbol carves itself into the riverbed, shimmering with meaning too old for the present and too urgent to ignore.

Miriam's tentative bond with Julian Roth, Cedar Creek's earnest young historian, is tested as they search for answers. He clings to records, ledgers, and reason; she is haunted by visions and dreams that speak in chains, water, and silence.

Together they wade into the contested territory of the town's rival families—each quick to blame the others for sabotage, each carrying wounds from forgotten promises. As suspicion deepens, even the sheriff and pastor cannot keep hostilities contained.

Dreams lead Miriam to see the river not as a victim of sabotage but as a witness to betrayal. Whispers of an old oath broken during Cedar Creek's founding echo through her nights. Oral histories, ancestral confessions, and long-hidden ledgers reveal that the fracture at the heart of the town is not new—it has been waiting, century after century, for truth to be spoken aloud.

The deeper Miriam and Julian dig, the more their partnership sharpens into something more intimate. Vulnerability, conflict, and quiet confessions kindle a slow-burn romance at the very moment the town demands they carry the weight of its divided past. Each step forward means choosing between secrecy and exposure, safety and courage, silence and witness. And with every answer uncovered, the water seems to answer back.

When the truth of the old betrayal is finally spoken before the gathered families, Cedar Creek itself responds. The basin refills, lanterns flow downstream like absolution, and for one luminous night the town tastes reconciliation. But even as love and belonging take root for Miriam, a final twist refuses to let peace settle.

At dawn, the fort bell—faithful voice of Cedar Creek— refuses to ring. Its silence chills the town and casts a shadow across the green. For Miriam, the dream of the silent bride becomes prophecy. For Julian, the historian's doubt bends into something more personal and urgent. And for Cedar Creek, the hush marks not an ending but a summons.

Waters of Redemption is a sweeping blend of mystery,

romance, and myth woven into the fabric of small-town life. It is about what happens when a community dares to confront the truth it has hidden for generations, and what it costs to listen when silence speaks. With lyrical prose and unforgettable characters, the second volume in the **Cedar Creek Legends** series draws readers into a world where rituals are alive, history is personal, and the river itself carries the memory of every promise kept—and broken.

At once intimate and epic, *Waters of Redemption* is both a love story and a reckoning. And as the final pages close on the silent bell, readers will know with certainty: Cedar Creek's greatest mystery has only just begun.

PROLOGUE
THE RIVER'S OATH

The year was 1846, and the rivers ran high with spring thaw, their mingling currents swelling with a force that mirrored the unspoken tension among the gathered settlers. At the confluence where Cedar Creek joined the greater waters, men and women stood in solemn assembly. The fort loomed in the distance timber walls stained by rain, banners hanging limp in the damp air. It was a place of promise and precarious beginnings, where cultures, trade, and faith intermingled in an uneasy balance.

A carved basin, hewn from cedar and stone, sat at the river's edge. Its surface gleamed faintly with oils rubbed in by hands reverent and weary. The settlers had fashioned it together, each family contributing labor or resource, a symbolic vessel meant to seal their unity. Once filled with water from the river, it would stand as their covenant: to share land and resource, to bind their futures not to rivalry but to the flow of life itself.

The basin was lowered into the water with slow care. Voices murmured in prayer some in English, some in Spanish and more in French, others whispering in languages older still, carried from across oceans. For a moment the current seemed to pause, as though recognizing the weight of human intention upon it.

Among them stood Elias Adler, tall, broad-shouldered, with eyes that glimmered not only with faith but ambition. He had worked tirelessly in the building of the fort, his name whispered often when leadership was needed. Yet beneath his solemn expression, a restless desire stirred. He longed for more than unity; he longed for legacy. And in legacy, he believed, was power.

When the others turned their gaze skyward, reciting words of covenant, Adler bent low. From beneath his cloak he drew a stone flat, smooth, carved with his own initials entwined with a crude symbol of dominion. He pressed it beneath the basin, wedging it into the riverbed where currents might not easily dislodge it. The act was silent, almost invisible, yet it rang in his spirit like a tolling bell. He believed that in time, when the basin's place was remembered, his mark would be found. His descendants would inherit not only land but the right to say: it was Elias Adler who laid claim to these waters.

The prayer ended. The basin filled. Voices rose in gratitude. No one saw the hidden stone except the river itself. And the river does not forget.

The ceremony gave the town its anchor. Families shook hands, women clasped one another in tears, children splashed at the edges as if unaware of history's weight pressing upon them. Yet already, cracks had formed unseen fractures beneath the flow. One man had sought to shape the covenant to his advantage, planting betrayal at the very heart of their unity. And though generations would pass, though the basin itself would be polished, repaired, and placed at festivals as a sacred heirloom, the river carried memory deeper than any record.

The waters swelled, embracing the basin. For a time, all seemed well. But water has a way of revealing what lies hidden.

YEARS LATER, the memory of that day became legend. Covenant of Cedar Creek, a formless organization, spread stories of "The River's Oath," the covenant made by their forebears. The basin was carried forth at annual festivals, filled ceremonially to remind all that the river was their lifeblood and their bond. People believed the water blessing ensured peace and prosperity, and so long as it was observed, the town would flourish.

But beneath the surface, the Adler stone remained, eroded yet enduring, carved with a symbol that none but Elias himself had known. The river pressed against it season after season, its currents whispering secrets into the soil, its silvery fish darting past like messengers refusing to speak. The stone became a witness to every drought, every flood, every quarrel among descendants who claimed the riverbank as theirs by right of heritage. Rival families disputed boundaries, sometimes bitterly. They pointed to journals, to maps, to tales of who first tilled which patch of earth. Yet beneath all their claims, the river knew there was only one truth: that the covenant had been fractured before it had ever truly begun.

One autumn, a great storm swept through Cedar Creek. Trees toppled, fields flooded, and the fort's stockades were battered by winds that howled like judgment. When the storm passed, the river's course had shifted slightly, revealing new stones, swallowing old banks. For a moment, the Adler mark almost emerged, the current scraping its edge bare. But just as quickly, silt and branches buried it once again. The secret was not yet ready for unveiling.

Still, whispers stirred. Elders in the town muttered that the river had moods, that sometimes it reflected unity, and other times it punished discord. A woman named Esther LeClair herself a healer, daughter of voyageurs dreamed of chains lying broken in the riverbed. She told her children that the water longed to free itself from a hidden weight. They dismissed her as fanciful, but her words would echo down generations, resurfacing in the heart of another woman Miriam Adler who, nearly two centuries later of the Alder lineage, would inherit her same gift of seeing patterns in mystery.

For now, in the years after the oath, the settlers believed they had secured a future. But small slights festered: which family poured the first water into the basin, which claimed rights to the richest bend of soil, which daughter married across lines and brought dowry disputes. The basin was carried out again and again, but its presence could not mend what betrayal had already seeded. Like water seeping into a crack of stone, division widened slowly, invisibly, until it became part of the town's very foundation.

And yet, Cedar Creek endured. Babies were born, crops were sown, festivals lit the square with fiddles and lanterns. The fort transformed from necessity to relic, its walls aging into monument. The river kept flowing, outward toward seas unknown, carrying in its depths both blessing and curse.

But memory is patient. And waters, when stirred, bring hidden things to light.

. . .

By the dawn of the twentieth century, the original basin still existed, cracked but whole, its cedar sides darkened with age. It was kept in the fort museum, brought forth each year for the festival of rivers. Children dipped fingers into its water, laughing as if touching magic. Elders crossed themselves, murmuring prayers. Few remembered the true solemnity of the oath. Fewer still suspected that within the very riverbed, a secret mark still pulsed like a wound.

The Adler family had prospered. Their descendants were merchants, landholders, even mayors. They spoke proudly of Elias, of his vision and leadership. They did not speak of his ambition. Rival families particularly the Cavanaughs and the LeClairs resented their influence. Quarrels that seemed trivial over irrigation ditches, fishing rights, ferry tolls carried with them the bitter undertone of something much older, something not yet named.

The festival became both celebration and stage. Rival families presented floats brighter than the other, feasts larger, choirs louder. Beneath the laughter, beneath the dancing and courting of young couples, there was always an edge. A smile too sharp, a handshake too firm, a toast laced with rivalry. The basin, raised on its pedestal, was supposed to silence such discord. Instead, it became a mirror of what was unhealed.

Then, in the year 1902, an uncanny event unsettled the town. As the basin was filled from the river, its water vanished before the crowd's eyes. Some said the cedar leaked, others whispered of sabotage. Yet those who peered closest swore they saw, just beneath the basin, a carved mark glowing faintly before the silt swallowed it again. Panic flared. The festival ended in confusion. And though the basin was quickly repaired, the story of the disappearing water lingered like a bad dream.

Over the next century, the tale faded into half-remembered lore. Children dared each other to go to the river at night and look for the cursed carving. Elders muttered that the water held memory and would one day reveal the truth. Most laughed, dismissing it as quaint superstition. But superstition has a way of outlasting disbelief.

By the time Miriam Adler arrived back in Cedar Creek, widowed, searching for belonging, and maintaining the family's shop, *Solace & Sage*. Unbeknownst to Miriam, the festival was once more the crown of the town's year. Booths of honey and handwoven baskets lined the square. Fiddles played under lantern light. Children skipped stones by the river, while elders told stories of oaths and blessings. And at the heart of it all, the basin stood ready, gleaming with its promise of unity.

But Unbeknownst to the town, the river had waited long enough. Beneath its rippling surface, the stone still bore its mark. Elias Adler's secret still whispered in currents that had never ceased to flow. And in the year that Miriam first walked among the townsfolk of Cedar Creek, laughing shyly at Julian Roth's quiet wit, the river was preparing to speak again. Preparing to draw forth what had been hidden, to expose betrayal at last, and to test whether this generation would choose fear and division or healing and redemption.

When the basin ran dry once more, as it had a century before, all eyes would turn to Miriam. And though she could not yet know it, her gift would be the key to unlocking the water's truth.

The river, eternal and unforgetting, was ready to bring them out.

1

———

MORNING BY THE RIVER

Mist lifted from the confluence in pearled coils, unspooling from the water like breath. Miriam liked this hour best, when Cedar Creek was neither asleep nor awake when the bakery's first trays clinked against steel, when the cedar boughs held dew like beads, when the river's talk was louder than the town's. She followed the ribboned trail that stitched the park to the waterline, her steps unhurried, her palms tucked in the pockets of a soft wool coat the color of clover honey.

Belonging, she'd learned, didn't arrive with fanfare. It seeped in. It showed up in how the barista remembered her order without asking, in which neighbor waved first, in the question from the lavender farmer about which incense sold fastest in the shop as if her answer mattered to more than a sales tally. It was there, too, in the way her feet knew the route before she chose it: from the bench with the bronze salmon, past the sycamore whose bark flaked like paper, out to the railing where water gathered itself into a sheet of slate and ran for the sea.

She heard him before she saw him boot soles on gravel

in an easy cadence, and then his voice, warm and just a little surprised, as if the river had arranged the meeting on their behalf.

"You always beat me here," Julian said.

Miriam's smile came without effort. "Only on days when the river requests an audience."

He stepped beside her with a paper cup extended in truce or greeting or both. "Then the river and I conspired. One with honey, a reckless amount of milk."

"You've learned all my vices." She took the coffee, fingertips brushing his in a small, unhurried contact neither of them rushed to end. The warmth traveled her skin like a whispered yes.

"Not all," he said. The lightness of it skimmed the surface, but there was depth below. "But I'm a diligent scientist."

"Historian."

"Scientist of the past," he corrected, then tipped his head toward the water. "And outspoken admirer of mornings like this."

The fog thinned to gauze. Across the river, the old fort rose in its wooden geometry, watchtowers squared against the sky as if yesterday were something you could still fortify against. The museum windows caught the pale sun and flashed back a quick silver. Closer, the park unfurled in careful loops around native grasses and a few flagged beds where festival crews had tucked poles for lantern strung like bright punctuation. Miriam watched a cormorant arrow under and then surface with a startled fish, a tiny flurry of necessity played out in the shallows.

"They started marking plots for the food stalls," Julian said. "I walked the green before heading to the archives yesterday. You should see the chalk lines geometry masquerading as enthusiasm."

"Is that the curator's verdict on our week of revelry?"

"The curator's verdict is that everyone is already sleep-deprived and defensive of extension cords." He slid her a look. "But the citizen Julian is embarrassingly excited."

"Embarrassingly?"

"The Rivers Festival was my favorite thing as a kid," he admitted. "Those lanterns? The way they shiver in the air like a second sky? I thought the whole town was a ship."

Miriam turned so she could study him and the water beyond, two familiar things arranged in one frame. At forty-one, he carried himself as if he'd been toned by routine rather than vanity. He had the sort of steadiness that reassured skittish horses and distracted students quiet, observant, occasionally amused. But it was his curiosity she liked best, because it never pretended to be certainty. She'd learned to recognize how it lit him how he leaned forward, how he moved his hands without realizing it, how his questions were invitations rather than tests.

"Embarrassingly excited sounds useful," she said. "We could sell tickets."

"I'm already committed to a far graver performance," he said, adopting a mock-solemn tone. "The historical society wrangled me into co-hosting the opening lecture on water rites and regional trade routes. Which is administrative for 'please talk kindly to people who want stories more than footnotes.'"

Her laugh was soft but complete. "You can do both. You always do both."

He took that in as if the words were a gift he'd been permitted to open early. "Come with me," he said, then corrected himself, less abruptly. "I mean, would you cohost? You'd be better at the 'why it matters' piece. I'm much too loyal to ship inventories."

"Julian," she said, and felt the familiar tug between reluctance and the impulse to say yes for the sheer pleasure of building something together. "I'm not an academic."

"No," he agreed, and the gentleness in it made the single syllable an honorific. "You're the one people actually listen to."

"You mean the lady who sells candles."

"I mean the woman who notices things. Who makes them make sense." He half-smiled, then risked more. "Besides, I have a selfish motive. Standing beside you and sounding intelligent is good for my reputation."

She looked away so he wouldn't mistake the color in her face for the morning chill. Below them, the river ran its silver grammar. A set of ducks chopped the surface into commas. A barge horned somewhere upriver; the sound slid along the water, deep-bellied, patient.

"We could try," she said. "If you like."

"I like," he said, no hesitation, and she felt the word settle between them like a beam being set, some small architecture strengthened.

They moved on, at ease. He told her the archives had coughed up a ledger with a hand less tidy than the clerk's usual it might be nothing, he said, though he would look again. She told him the shop had a new line of soaps from a woman in Troutdale who swore by rosemary for memory, rose for courage. He rolled that around with comical seriousness before agreeing to be her test subject, on the condition that no one find out he smelled like rose courage, which sounded like either a poem or a scandal.

They spoke, too, of smaller things: a student who'd returned after five years with apologies and a toddler; the crows who had apparently convened a council over the museum's loading dock; how long the lilacs might hold on this year; whether cinnamon rolls counted as breakfast or dessert if the bakery sold out by eight. Their laughter found a consistent key. Between the notes, silences arrived and did not put them on their guard.

Miriam thought of the self she'd been when she arrived watchful, tender, not yet sure the bones of grief could hold a new house. She thought of the woman she was this morning, warmed by coffee and good company, alert to a day that wanted things from her she might actually be glad to give. She wanted to tell him about the dream last night, about the chain at the bottom of a river she'd never swum, about how it snapped and the sound was relief, but she filed it where she filed other intimacies that required the right hour and the right trust.

"Tell me your favorite part," she said instead. "Of the festival."

"Easy. The basin."

"The ceremonial basin?" She feigned scandal. "You are absolutely trying to impress me."

"It's working?"

"Tragically," she said, pleased at how the banter made room for something weightier without announcement. "Why the basin?"

He faced the river fully, as if asking permission to answer. "It's the moment everyone becomes quiet at the same time," he said. "It doesn't happen much. Not in a town. Not anywhere. We all attend to the same thing and agree, at least for a minute, that the water matters and so do we."

"Yes," she said. Her chest ached in the clean way. "I know exactly what you mean."

He glanced at her, something like recognition in the look

of the territory they shared and also the frontier they might cross. "Then you should absolutely stand next to me when we talk about it," he said, and his smile was unguarded in a way that told her this wasn't only about the lecture.

They reached the end of the path where a weathered bench held a plaque for a daughter who loved ospreys. Miriam rested her palms on the cool rail. Downriver, the surface roughened where the two bodies of water met Cedar Creek and the larger river exchanging unseeable volumes with the grave courtesy of giants. The difference in color was subtle one slate, one pewter but if you watched long enough you could read the seam where they braided. The town had been built on that seam. So, lately, had she.

"Morning, you two," called Mrs. Callahan. "You going to save me a seat for the lecture? I require a chair with a back. And a man to fan me."

Julian performed a courtly bow. "Name the hour, I'll bring a palm frond."

"Bring a sensible stool," Mrs. Callahan said, laughing, and was off.

"Belonging," Miriam murmured, more to the water than to Julian. It was both an observation and a prayer.

"Hmm?"

"Nothing," she said, but she didn't quite mean it. "Everything." She finished her coffee and took the last warmth into her hands. "Walk me through the green?"

He gestured like a man opening a door. "With pleasure."

They turned toward the festival grounds together, the river keeping pace at their side like a patient friend. The morning expanded. The light clarified. In the distance, on a stand where it would be polished later, the old basin caught the sun and gave it back in a wink quick, almost coy. Miriam felt the look land. Not a warning. Not yet. Just attention, as if the day had quietly cleared its throat.

BY THE TIME they reached the fort green, the place was already a hive. Chalked rectangles spidered across the grass to mark booth spaces, and a forest of slender poles leaned in stacks waiting for lanterns, their paper skins still sleeping in boxes. Volunteers navigated the polite chaos with clipboards and optimism, both in abundant supply this early in the week. The scent was a conversation of its own wet earth, fresh lumber, coffee, donut sugar, a hint of river brine.

"Watch your step," called Sloane from Public Works, lifting a hand in salute. "We're testing the power grid. If you see sparks, pretend you didn't."

"On it," Julian said. "Where do you want the museum table?"

"Under the cottonwood, between the honey guy and the historical fencers." She squinted at Miriam. "And if your candles catch a boy in chain mail on fire, you didn't hear that idea from me."

"Noted," Miriam said. She liked Sloane precisely because she understood that competence and mischief were not mutually exclusive. "I'll bring extra sand."

"Bless you." Sloane checked a box and jogged away, already answering three new questions.

Julian and Miriam cut across the field toward the temporary stage. A banner lay unrolled and weighted with rocks: RIVERS FESTIVAL - A BLESSING OF WATERS, a stylized current painted beneath the letters as if punctuation could flow. Two teens hammered in rhythm, a soundtrack to civic labor. At the edge of the green, the fort's dark timbers rose and the museum's side door stood propped open; from within came the smell of lemon oil and old paper.

"Before we're conscripted," Julian said, "come see something."

They detoured to the cool interior where the world narrowed to wood grain and glass cases and reverent light. Even without the visitors, Miriam could feel the room's attention a quality she had learned to recognize in spaces where the past signed its name. The docent desk sat empty, a sweater slung over the chair as if someone had just stepped out. In the nearest case, a parade of small domes protected beads, buttons, and a rusted nail whose label declared it had held down a roof in 1832.

Julian led her toward the back, where the special exhibit wall had been reconfigured overnight. A map of the confluence occupied the center, blue threads drawn in hand-tinted care, studs marking the old portages, the trading routes fanned like gull wings. To the left, under museum-grade glass, lay the ceremonial basin.

Even in the cool, faint lemon scent, the basin smelled of cedar clean, resinous, forgiving. Its sides had been worn by hands and water both. Faint carvings ringed the lip in a pattern of waves and vines, and there, near the base, a seam where a repair had been sanded smooth decades ago. To Miriam, the object felt less like a relic and more like a companion a witness that had missed nothing and would never gossip about what it had seen.

"It will be on the green by Friday morning," Julian said, looking not at the basin but at her. "But I keep it here until the last minute. Better humidity."

"Better protection from chain mail," she said, and he grinned.

He reached for the glass with a fingertip, stopped,

remembered himself, and let the hand fall. "Do you ever get the sense," he said, "that it's listening?"

She let the question ride the quiet before answering. "I think the people who built it meant to listen," she said. "They built an ear they could understand."

Outside, a forklift beeped. Inside, the tick of a clock shaped like a schooner counted something that wasn't quite time.

He guided her to a second case. "Ledger," he said. "Late entry. I told you about it earlier on the path." On the page, the clerk's practiced lines stumbled for half a dozen transactions shipments of lumber and molasses noted in a hand that leaned too far forward, as if running. A margin mark that was all but it had the feel of a thought interrupted. A smudged initial. A stray curl like a question.

"What do you see?" he asked.

She tilted her head and let more than sight attend. "Impatience," she said. "Decision, then second thought. Someone wrote faster than they meant to. Someone wanted to get on with it."

"On with what?"

"That's your part," she said, and he laughed, playful, but she watched him make a mental note, the way a man did when a stray detail stuck in the fabric and refused to be picked free.

They left the cool and reentered the haphazard symphony of the green. The mayor squinted at a flyer as if sheer glare would rearrange the type. The choir director paced off steps and muttered counts. Pastor Elijah whose sermons were gentle until they weren't stood with two organizers near the stage, hands in his pockets, nodding the way men nod when they intend to agree publicly and argue kindly in a back room.

"Mr. Roth," the mayor hailed. "You'll speak before or after the hymn?"

Julian's public voice slid into place so swiftly Miriam had to admire the turn. "After, if you please," he said. "Let the song settle first."

"Very poetical," the mayor said, approving what he didn't parse. "And Ms. Adler, your shop is donating candles for the lantern walk, is that right?"

"Unscented," Miriam said. "No one wants eucalyptus ghosting their ancestors."

Pastor Elijah's mouth tipped. "I wouldn't mind a friendly spirit of eucalyptus," he said, then lowered his voice for them alone. "We'll do a short blessing when the basin arrives on Friday morning. Not a sermon. Just a reminder of why we gather." He glanced toward the water. "We could use the reminder."

"We'll be there," Julian said.

"You're co-hosting?" the pastor asked Miriam.

"I am," she said, and found that saying it out loud felt like a seam aligned. "Try not to schedule me opposite the pie contest. I can't compete with cobbler."

"None of us can," he said, solemn. "Welcome aboard."

They walked on. The green was a stitched sampler of the town's trades and talents potter, blacksmith, beekeeper, bookseller, an elder whose knives cut paper-thin apple slices in a demonstration of patience. A group of middle schoolers rehearsed carrying lanterns, their line bending and laughing, light already moving through the air even without flame. Behind the museum, Sloane's crew tested the faucet on a temporary wash station; water spattered and gurgled into a bucket, bright as coins.

"Lecture at six on Friday," Julian said, more to himself than her. "Basin blessing after the hymn. Lanterns at eight.

Pie at nine, if the line moves. And somewhere in there I need to help Mack find the extra fuses."

"And breathe," Miriam said.

"And breathe," he echoed, then tipped his chin toward the river as if that were where his breath came from. "Do you ever imagine what this place sounded like two hundred years ago?"

"Two hundred minutes ago?" she said. "Quieter. Before we arrived."

He accepted the tease, then turned to the seam of water again. "I think about the first covenant," he said. "Not capital-C, just the practical kind. People agreeing to be bound to the same patch of earth. Agreeing to share the river. It sounds like a wedding vow when you put it that way. Or a risk."

"Both," she said. "Most promises are."

He looked at her as if she'd clarified something he'd been hoping would reveal itself. "Then that's what you'll say Friday. Keep me honest."

"Gladly," she said.

They made one more loop, their pace easing into the town's pulse. The festival wasn't a backdrop this year; it was the stage on which everything else would happen the talk, the blessing, the ritual with its brief hold on collective attention, the lanterns threading the dark. The green would be their commons and their crucible. Standing at its edge, Miriam felt the curious combination she always felt before a threshold: a readiness braided with a caution she had learned not to ignore.

They paused where the grass sloped toward the dock. Children practiced skipping stones and cheered for throws that walked the surface like small miracles before surrendering. One stone skittered farther than the rest and lodged on a shallow shelf near an exposed tangle of roots. The boy who'd thrown it grinned, triumphant, then frowned, cocking his head as if puzzled by what lay beneath.

"What is it?" his friend called.

"Nothing," he said, shrugging, already running after the next form of delight. But Miriam had watched his face sharpen and knew he'd glimpsed something he didn't have the words for. She let the moment pass. Not every thread needed to be pulled now. The week would weave what it would.

THAT AFTERNOON THE WIND TURNED. It came down the valley with a clean edge and blew the fog to memory, so that by evening the river was a polished length of steel under a sky scraped to a precise blue. On days like this Cedar Creek pretended to be a seaside town. The gulls obliged, inventing an ocean with their cries. The air tasted faintly of salt.

Miriam stood at the *Solace & Sage* shop counter adjusting a tray of votives unscented, as promised and felt the hum that meant the town had gathered itself into one conversation. People moved along Main in currents: festival volunteers in bright vests, couples arguing amiably about budgets and bunting, a teenage boy dragging a cart laden with paper lanterns and radiating an air of siege. Mrs. Callahan arrived for a book on regional birds and left with three sticks of cinnamon for "general morale." Mack from the hardware store came in for a candle to test the lantern holders; he left with two and a laugh at himself for calling it superstition when he meant tradition.

Late in the day, when the light slanted just so and turned dust to gold, Julian walked in with a thin folder and the expression he wore when he'd found a detail that refused to fit its drawer.

"Promise you won't say 'I told you so,'" he said.

"I will not," she said, "but I may frame it loudly with my eyebrows."

He set the folder on the counter and opened it to the ledger page they'd seen, now copied and annotated. "I checked the preceding week and the week after," he said, tapping columns with a pencil. "The hand returns to neatness. Even the clerk's decorative curls behave themselves. The

He pointed to the margin curl she'd called a question. "It's a habit in other entries. Usually it marks a note to himself pick up this shipment, double-check that weight. But here the note never got written."

"What do you think it meant to be?"

"I don't know yet," he said, almost cheerfully, and she loved him for that. "But I'll keep looking."

The bell over the door rung faint. The street's sound flooded in and washed back. "Walk?" he asked.

They closed up the shop together and let the evening draw them toward the river. The green had transformed in the hours since morning more poles up, more cord strung, a soft fretting over whether a row of lanterns would compete with the angle of the sunset. Sloane knelt by a junction box, muttering a prayer to the patron saint of fair weather and better contractors. Kids chased each other through the scaffolding of a half-built arch. The basin, Miriam noticed, was still in the museum. She was glad for that. Not every sacred thing needed to sit out all night.

Down at the dock, a small group had gathered for a rehearsal of Friday's hymn. Pastor Elijah stood among them with sheet music rolled in his hand, not conducting so much as anchoring. Their voices braided, and the river accepted their notes without complaint. Julian leaned on the rail. Miriam, beside him, felt the song find the tender places it always found, prized them open with gentleness rather than force.

She washed her hands in the sinking light and let a thought surface she'd been entertaining all day, as one entertains a guest in an anteroom before deciding whether to welcome them farther in. "Do you ever feel," she said, "that the festival this week doesn't just remember the water, it summons it? Not the liquid, exactly. The truth of it. The part that knows what the town has forgotten."

He didn't answer immediately. She liked that about him, too: the pause that took her question seriously. "I think remembering is a kind of summoning," he said finally. "We set the table. We leave a chair for what we think might come."

"And if what comes isn't what we expected?"

"Then we've still set the table," he said. "And we can still eat."

She smiled, and they fell quiet. Beneath them, the river worked. It always worked pushing against its banks, lifting silt, delivering fish and driftwood and whatever secrets it had agreed to carry. The current dimpled along the piling. In one of those dimples, something like an eddy formed and held no bigger than a plate, no more insistent than a persistent thought. It spun slowly, brushed a patch of rivergrass, then dissolved. In its brief life, its curve suggested a shape Miriam might have named if she'd been willing to be fanciful: not a petal, exactly, but the beginning of a pattern she recognized from dreams and old windows.

Her breath miscounted and then found itself again.

"You saw it," Julian said.

"I saw a circle become itself," she said, deflecting before she risked saying symbol aloud. When he glanced at her, she saw that he'd registered both what she'd said and what she hadn't.

The hymn ended, and with it the little spell that all singing casts. People spoke and laughed and checked their phones. A child dropped a pebble and stared as it sank, that attentive silence children know how to hold without instruction. The wind thinned to a whisper. Someone somewhere tried the faucet and turned it off again so abruptly the pipes knocked as if making their own opinion known.

"Come," Julian said. "I want to show you the stand they've built for the basin."

They cut back across the green where the stand sat on a tarp, a simple table built of fitted beams and dowels, handsome in its plainness. Miriam ran her palm a whisper above the wood without touching, an old habit and a new courtesy.

"They shaped a cradle." She nodded. "Good. It should sit held, not perched."

As if to answer her, the stand gave the barest tremor a carpenter checking a joint on the far side, a gust of wind worrying a tarp. It subsided as quickly. No one else seemed to notice.

"Tomorrow we'll measure height for the microphone," Julian said. "We'll need to live-test how loud the basin makes people's hearts."

"Do hearts require amplification?" she asked.

"For the folks behind the pie tent," he said gravely. "Yes."

They moved on. At the edge of the green, Mrs. Alvarez argued with a supplier about the price of berries; at the other end, the historical fencing club chuffed and thumped like an ancient kettle remembering how to boil. The ordinary life of a town, Miriam thought, refusing to be intimidated by omens.

Still, she couldn't quite shake the sense that the day had made a small, private announcement that hadn't yet found its crowd. She had learned to trust that sense without dramatizing it. A weight here; an ease there. A door in a hallway she hadn't noticed before. She filed the feeling and did not mistake storage for denial.

On the way back to Main, they passed the narrow street where deliveries backed in like leviathans. Water had pooled there in a shallow dip no one had bothered to fill. In the pool, a single leaf spun slowly, anchored to a twig submerged just enough to hold it. The motion was too regular to be accidental, too stubborn to be nothing, but not so unusual you'd mark it unless you happened to be the sort of person who watched water for a living, or for a calling.

"Tomorrow," Julian said, "I'll check the ledger again."

"Tomorrow," she said, "I'll order more unscented candles and, reluctantly, more cinnamon."

"And in two days," he said, "I'll stand on a stage and trust words to behave."

"And I'll stand beside you," she said, and the rightness of it clicked in her like a latch. "We'll talk about sharing a river as if it were a vow."

He looked at her, amused and earnest, two qualities that sat well together on him. "And we'll mean it."

They walked the last block slow, letting dusk locate them. The sky shifted to the color of dove wings. The river took on the shade of an old coin. The town laid its tools down one by one and decided it had done enough for the day. Miriam paused at the corner to watch the water one last time. It was doing nothing more spectacular than being itself, which, she thought, was spectacle enough.

Then small, quick, unarguable a fish broke the surface near the shallows, flipped once as if trying to erase a mark only it could feel, and was gone. The ripples ran outward in perfect rings. When the rings arrived at the dock supports, they met a counter-current and folded, and in the fold, for a breath and no more, Miriam saw the echo of a shape she had learned without a teacher. A curve, a stroke, a sign not yet named in the day's bright ledger.

She did not gasp. She did not turn to the nearest person and finger the elbow of alarm. She placed the observation on the shelf inside her where she kept other clean objects: a tune hummed by someone she loved in a kitchen at noon; a child's face when it realizes it can read; the look a man gives you when he wants you to know you are invited to the life he is building. Then she closed the shop of her mind carefully and said, "I'll see you in the morning."

"In the morning," Julian said, and if the phrase had been a plain goodbye before, it had gained weight now, due not to worry but to the generosity of repetition. They would say it many times in the week ahead. They would mean it each time. And the river would attend, as it always did, with indifference that wasn't unkind and memory that wasn't vindictive.

When she reached her door, she looked back. The basin still slept in the museum, cedar dreaming cedar dreams. The green held its breath. The river ran as it had run yesterday and would run tomorrow. And yet, if you watched the line where Cedar Creek slipped into the larger body and vanished, you might have said the seam brightened not the way a warning brightens, but the way a truth does when it finally thinks you're ready to hold it.

The festival would wake completely soon enough. The town would take its place, it would hum in that strong key it saved for shared tasks. There would be lanterns and pie and lectures and children midwifing light from paper. There would be, too, the moment when the crowd went quiet in the instant before the basin filled, when breath paused, and attention did the rare work of gathering itself.

And after that well. Miriam did not yet know what would come after that. Only that something awaited them at the lip of the ritual, as surely as the fish awaited the insect's shadow, as surely as the reed awaited wind, as surely as a promise awaited the mouth brave enough to speak it.

Night loosened from the trees and lay down on the river. The first star showed itself, small, scandalously faithful. She went inside, turned on the lamp, and set a fresh page on the counter out of habit more than instruction. Then she wrote three words she could pretend were notes for the lecture but were really a message to herself.

Remember the water.

2

FESTIVAL PREPARATIONS

By eight, the fort green sounded like somebody had set a kettledrum beating under the grass and invited the whole town to step in time. The day's first sun hit the timbers like a benediction; saws sang; hammers answered; cords snaked in hopeful geometry from generator to junction box to booth. Cedar Creek did not have a stadium, but if you stood by the cottonwood and watched, you could believe the green was an amphitheater built expressly for the music of getting ready.

Miriam arrived with a box of unscented pillars hugged to her chest and a basket of clothespins swinging from her wrist. Sloane from Public Works, ponytail already escaping her cap, intercepted her with a grin that said both welcome and help.

"You're an angel," Sloane called. "The kind with a tool belt. Put those by the lantern assembly table, and if you tell anyone we're using clothespins to dry test-wicks, I'll deny it publicly."

"Your secrets are safe with my reputation," Miriam said. She set the box down where Sloane pointed between rolls of twine and a coffee mug labeled NOT A WRENCH and took in the choreography. Teenagers in volunteer vests carted collapsible chairs in parades of ten. The historical fencing club tested sabers at a responsible distance, all swish and courtesy. The beekeeper arranged jars so the sun lit them from behind gold, amber, another gold, the spectrum of patience. The baker, Mrs. Miriam Levine, arrived with trays of hand pies and a teenage certainty that any adult giving direction must have it wrong. Mack from the hardware store unspooled extension cords like a magician producing scarves.

"Watch your toes," he warned cheerfully as a coil slithered past Miriam. "We're laying out the power like arteries. Wherever pie is, there shall also be electricity."

"Electricity and pie," she said. "The founding principles."

"Don't forget arguing," he said, winking, then trotted off to rescue a power strip from becoming a jump rope.

By the stage, the choir director sensible shoes, ferocious focus paced lengths, clapping three-four time and muttering, "No, not a march, a float, float, and stop grabbing your consonants like they owe you money." The mayor stood in a radius of clipboards, squinting at a printed schedule as if he could move events with the force of his gaze. Pastor Elijah shook hands with the man from the radio station and created a bubble of calm that followed him like an aura.

"Ms. Adler!" Mrs. Alvarez's voice cut the air like a festive trumpet. She hustled up with a clipboard and the accelerated heartbeat of a woman juggling four lists in her head. "You are officially the Candle Liaison. It's a made-up position, but the badge is laminated, so it's real."

Miriam accepted the badge with ceremonial gravity. "Will there be a sash?"

"Don't tease me unless you brought sequins." Mrs. Alvarez lowered her voice. "Also, Cavanaugh's people are trying to claim the east dock for staging. Again."

"Again," Miriam echoed. In Cedar Creek, again could be a liturgy.

"I told them we assign by safety and access, not family legacy," Mrs. Alvarez went on. "They heard: 'We hate tradition and puppies.' You're good at smiling people into reason. Do you mind...?"

"Point me," Miriam said, and Mrs. Alvarez pointed.

On the way she passed the potter hauling a crate of bowls in his hip like a toddler; the blacksmith fanning a sleepy coal for the demonstration forge; a pair of ten-year-olds arguing whether lanterns required wishes preloaded. "Obviously yes," the girl said. "They're like tiny boats. Boats need a destination." "They're lights," the boy said, "not mail."

Miriam liked that everyone, even the disagreement, felt threaded to the same fabric. The green hummed with mismatched melodies that somehow made one song.

Down by the river end of the field, two camps had formed without banners but with all the clarity of flags: on one side, the Cavanaughs, whose patriarch had been foreman on the dam rebuild thirty years ago and had never since recovered from the satisfaction of a properly set spillway; on the other, the LeClairs, descended from voyageurs and midwives, guardians of recipes and stories and the confident belief that the river returned affection when properly approached. In between stood a line of folding tables like a demilitarized zone waiting for casseroles.

"Morning," Miriam offered, stepping into the space a diplomat might call neutral and a local would call common sense. "I brought extra tea lights."

Mr. Cavanaugh square-shouldered, sun-browned, a hat that seemed issued the same day the American hard hat was invented tipped his brim. "We're fine," he said. "Just establishing our loading plan for Friday."

"By 'our,'" said Rosalie LeClair with honeyed precision, "he means Cavanaugh. Mrs. Adler, maybe you could explain to Mr. Cavanaugh that when a community ritual takes place on common dock, the concept of 'mine' gets politely retired."

"'Mine' is nine-tenths of 'ready,'" Mr. Cavanaugh replied. "And the Cavanaugh table's been at east dock going on forty years."

"And the LeClairs have lit the first lantern since before that dock had a post," Rosalie said. "Your grandfather lit our first wicks. He said it steadied his hands."

Miriam set the tea lights down and let silence widen just enough for breath. "What needs to happen," she said, "between now and Friday for each of you to feel the ritual is respected and safe?"

"Safe, see?" Mr. Cavanaugh pointed with a finger that had built more than it had broken. "She said safe."

"Respected," Rosalie repeated, as if the word were a balm she was applying to a bruise.

Sloane wandered by with a tape measure around her neck like a stole. "We can do two staging lines," she said without preamble. "Staggered by ten minutes for flow. East dock gets the basin's approach; west dock gets lanterns. Anyone with a complaint can rewire G9 to G12 for me."

Mr. Cavanaugh and Rosalie looked at each other, both startled into a brief, begrudging smile by the neatness of the fix. "Staggered," Mr. Cavanaugh said, trying the word like a tool's weight. "Might work."

"It will work," Rosalie said, because surrender voiced as

confidence preserved dignity. "But the blessing Father Elijah's words must be audible at the west dock as well. Last year half our line heard nothing but the generator."

"Done," Sloane said. "We acquired a second speaker. Miraculously, it's not broken yet."

"Then we're agreed," Miriam said.

They weren't, not entirely, but they were willing to behave as if agreement were the next step rather than a distant country, and often that was enough. As the two camps dispersed to good work Cavanaughs to measure the approach path for the basin's cart; LeClairs to fold cloth for lantern cradles Miriam felt the green's music reset itself around the newly cleared knot.

Julian materialized as if the air had requested him. "I saw you broker peace," he said. "Remind me to bring you to the archives when a map and a caption get into it."

"They'll forgive each other more easily if there's pie," she said.

"It's in the bylaws," he said solemnly.

They walked the perimeter so he could point to where the museum table would stand, where he'd set a small case with the ledger copy and a rotating display of artifacts trader tokens, a length of rope spliced expertly by a hand that had known wind and risk. He'd printed labels in a font the committee had deemed readable without being smug. "We're telling stories, not grading papers," he said. "And besides, any sign more than a hundred words gets ignored in proximity to kettle corn."

At the lantern table, volunteers were assembly-lining: insert candle, test wick, clip the paper lip, practice the gentle art of sheltering flame from wind. Miriam slipped into the rhythm for fifteen minutes, liking the small satisfactions the rightness of a centered wick, the whisper a paper shade made when you opened it. A girl in a denim jacket asked if wishes were better handwritten and tucked inside or spoken and blown toward the river. "Either," Miriam said. "Both. The river understands bilingual."

"That's not what bilingual means," the girl said, laughing, but she tucked the idea away the way people pocketed flat stones and old buttons.

Near noon, the food trucks arrived like modern caravans and chaos converted itself to lines and decisions. Mrs. Callahan bought two rice bowls and insisted one of them be for Miriam because "your face has that 'I forgot to eat' look about it." The choir director fell in love with a mango slushie and, briefly, with the man who poured it. Pastor Elijah accepted onion rings like Communion and gave out napkins the way some men handed out benedictions.

"Three more days," Julian said, surveying the green as a captain might survey a harbor. "By Friday we'll have invented a city."

"It's already a city," Miriam said. "We're just taking attendance."

A wind-shift brushed the river and tanged the air with metal. Somewhere under the hum she heard a softer rhythm a heartbeat, or the memory of one. She didn't tell Julian. She didn't yet have a name for it. Instead she pressed another lantern's paper collar into place and felt the day settle around her shoulders like a shawl: warm, useful, borrowed for work that mattered.

BY MIDAFTERNOON, the green had sorted itself into a temporary commons with lanes of travel and pockets of labor marked out not by rope but by the density of purpose. That was when the talk drifted toward the oldest recurring topic in town: who owned something no one could own.

It started, as such things do, with logistics. A committee sub-sub-meeting convened under the cottonwood to confirm timing for Friday morning's blessing. Rosalie LeClair, Mr. Cavanaugh, the mayor, Pastor Elijah, Sloane, and Julian who had tried to stand very still until someone forgot he was there formed a half circle around a chalked schedule. Miriam lingered at the edge with her laminates and the comfortable invisibility most people afforded a person whose role was called Liaison.

"Order of operations," Sloane said, wielding a pencil like a baton. "Hymn on the green at eight-fifteen. Blessing at eight-twenty. Basin moves at eight-twenty-five east dock staging to central stand. First pour at eight-thirty. Lantern rehearsal run-through at nine."

"Who carries the basin?" Mr. Cavanaugh asked, as if he didn't know.

"The committee," Sloane said. "Four on the cart, two each side spotters, and whoever is not currently arguing about it."

"In my father's time," Mr. Cavanaugh said, "Cavanaugh men were the arms under that basin."

"In my grandmother's time," Rosalie replied, "LeClair women lit the first wick, and the basin rose to meet our flame."

"In my grandfather's time," the mayor said, "we did both while a marching band played over us and everybody survived somehow."

Pastor Elijah set his pencil on the top of the schedule, pinning down the paper and the temperature both. "The ritual belongs to the town," he said. "Which is another way of saying it cannot belong to anyone. We need the people who remember to teach the people who don't. That's a kind of ownership, if you're desperate for the word. Stewardship suits me better."

"Stewardship," Mr. Cavanaugh repeated, like a man testing a step before trusting it. "Stewardship has rules."

"Stewardship has memory," Rosalie said. "Rules come after, if they must."

Julian cleared his throat. "If I may," he said, in the tone he used when coaxing a class from posture to curiosity, "there are notes in the museum files about this. Not law, just records. For the first fifty or so years, the basin was carried by whoever had been nominated by their neighbors the week prior. Mixed. Women, men, married, not. Usually people whose work interacted with water ferrymen, laundresses, the woman who boiled down hemlock for pitch, the boy who learned to swim faster than anyone and taught others. The first lantern was lit by the midwife that year, or the boatman, or a couple celebrating a birth. There wasn't a single family assigned."

Mr. Cavanaugh bristled, but less at the fact than at the surprise of it. "So when did it change?"

"Somewhere around the time we got more formal about leadership," Julian said mildly. "Committees became committees. Names calcified."

"The Cavanaughs never grabbed it," Mr. Cavanaugh said sharply, stung by a charge unspoken.

"Nor did the LeClairs," Rosalie returned. "We weren't thieves; we were volunteers. But over time, people stopped asking who wanted to lift and started assuming who would."

"And assumptions," Pastor Elijah said, "are how rituals become costumes."

Sloane tapped the pencil. "The rules we can write," she said. "What we can't write is manners. So here's the plan. We rotate. Four carriers, chosen for fitness and interest. The spotters come from two lines one Cavanaugh, one LeClair. First lantern lit this year by Rosalie and Mr. Cavanaugh's granddaughter together. In front of everyone, so everybody gets to see everybody be human."

Rosalie's mouth softened. Mr. Cavanaugh's shoulders set down an inch. "Done," they said, almost in chorus.

"Bless you and also me," Sloane said. "Now I'll go convince the sound guy that the second speaker is not optional."

As the committee dispersed, a cousin of Mr. Cavanaugh's lean, sinewy, wearing the purposeful scowl of a field boss stopped Miriam with an almost-accidental shoulder. "Stewardship," he said, low, as if tasting a bitter. "That word's a way to shame people who've done the work."

"I think it's a way to invite more people into it," Miriam said. "So you don't burn out and so the ritual keeps teaching."

He studied her with a frown that had nothing personal in it; it was the set look of a man who mistrusted soft words because soft words rarely lifted weight. "You're not from here," he said.

"No," she said. "But I am here."

He moved on with a grunt that meant neither welcome nor dismissal, and she let it be what it was. Belonging was made of many small pardons.

She busied herself a while with the lantern table and then with helping the beekeeper find a piece of muslin for an overbold sun. She fielded a question from the fencers about whether an exhibition bout could happen within sight of the blessing ("If your swords are a whisper and your egos are smaller than the basin"); she taught the two kids from earlier how to fold wishes like boats and slide them by syllable into the fold of a paper shade. "You can send a wish on a breath," she told them, "or you can tuck it in the light. Either reaches."

Around three, she slipped into the museum to refill her water bottle and set her hands near not on the glass that guarded the basin. The cedar held the light like a memory. She did not hear words; she wasn't that kind of mystic. What she felt was a pressure, gentle and even, the way a river presses, as if the air itself were testing the balance of the room.

Julian, who'd followed because he almost always did when she changed altitudes that way, stood a respectful distance off. "They're calmer out there," he said. "For now. Elijah's going to say something Friday about 'we' being larger than 'I,' and for a whole hour everyone will agree he's right."

"He will be right," Miriam said.

Julian leaned one shoulder to the wall not touching a single artifact and somehow anchoring the entire collection by posture alone. "Can I ask something that may sound foolish?"

"You can always ask."

"Is there a way," he said, selecting words like glass slides and arranging them under a lens, "for a place to inherit a wound?"

"Yes," she said. "In the same way it inherits a song. The wound changes how the song sounds until someone listens carefully enough to hear the original line. Then the music shifts. But it takes a while."

His mouth crooked. "You always make it sound manageable."

"It is not," she said. "But it is possible."

Outside, a raised voice carried in a man who had to be

Mr. Cavanaugh's cousin, arguing about the dock schedule as if it robbed him personally. Over it, Rosalie's voice surfed warmth braided with steel. Then laughter, then the kind of quiet that follows when a conversation returns to its correct size.

"It will be all right," Julian said.

"It will be what it is," Miriam said. "But we have some influence."

They stepped back into the afternoon and were instantly absorbed again into the undertaking: where does this go, how long should that wire be, what happens if it rains, how many pies are too many pies (there is no number; the choir director testified). A pair of boys in waders tested the shoreline depth and announced with the authority of scientists that "it's cold." The mayor affixed a poster reminding people to leave dogs at home during the night lantern walk, and three dogs wandered past, reading none of it.

As the sun tipped west, the green took on the look of a stage between acts. Everything stood where it ought to, but it was a standing that contained potential energy the way a bow holds song before the first pull. The unresolved question in the day wasn't whether the festival would come off; it would. Cedar Creek could build a celebration out of driftwood and disagreement. The unresolved question was who would stand where, who would say what, who would feel seen and who would feel slighted when the basin moved, when the lanterns opened, when the hymn rose and found throats and made them one instrument.

Miriam recognized the discomfort as the price of change and the opportunity of it. A ritual that had been assumed into inertia was being asked to learn again how to mean. That learning never arrived without protest. She stored the awareness where she kept other truths too large to hold in the palm and returned to folding paper into little moons.

EVENING BURNED DOWN SLOW, and with it the green's volume dropped from major key to murmur. The food trucks' generators clicked off one by one; lantern crates closed with the contented sigh of good work done; the volunteers' laughter thinned to those last strands that bind a day. The river, which had been backdrop, stepped forward again.

Miriam walked the edge of the dock with a bag of wicks over her shoulder and the sense that if she didn't stretch her legs she would carry someone else's tension home. The water below scrolled the day away greens to pewters to a darkness that was not absence but depth. Out beyond the pilings, an osprey skimmed the surface and rose sharp-fisted with its meal. The ripples it cut angled toward the place where Cedar Creek's own body merged with the wider river; there, as always, the seam made its quiet case that two can be one without ceasing to be themselves.

She reached the east staging area where the basin would travel and stopped. The stand Sloane's crew had built sat under a tarp, its feet fitted level to the field's slight pitch. She crouched to check the ground the way you check a bed for a guest, testing for lump or hollow. Flat, even, ready. She straightened and stepped to the river lip. The shallows there were scuffed a hundred shoes had pressed; a hundred stones had been tried for skipping; a hundred tiny decisions had been made about how close to stand to holiness.

A breeze came downriver, not chill but charged, and brought with it a smell like wet cedar and iron. It lifted the hair on her arms. She closed her eyes. The day came back in its pieces Rosalie's composed fury, the cousin's bruised pride, the choir's laugh, the patient honey, the musical argument of hammers, Julian's face when she'd said Yes. She placed those parts beside each other and listened for how they fit. The listening brought her to the river's under-voice, not louder than the sounds of evening, but older.

It presented itself not an image so much as an alignment and her body recognized it as a thing it had seen asleep: a mark half-known; a shape hinted at by currents; a curve that promised an answering curve. She held the impression in a loose grip so she wouldn't crush it with wanting. She did what she always did when the unseen offered its draft: she asked for permission to notice.

A footstep behind her. "I'm going to pretend I'm not interrupting a conversation," Julian said, soft.

"You're not," she said. "Or you are, but the other party doesn't mind."

He came to stand beside her with the care of a man entering a sanctuary he didn't own. They watched a cluster of minnows stipple the skin of the water. Downriver a barge shouldered the channel; its wake would arrive in a minute, wise and slow.

"They were arguing again," he said.

"I heard."

"Elijah says the right thing about we," he went on. "But the word ownership has a sweetness people can't easily spit out."

"Maybe we don't have to spit it out," Miriam said. "Maybe we can say we own the work. We own the effort it takes to be part of us. And we own the corrections when we get it wrong."

He looked sideways at her with that open, unguarded attention that had a way of moving the air. "You make honesty sound survivable."

"It is," she said. "It's denial that's lethal."

The wake reached the dock. The boards rose, settled, rose. In the second swell, the reflection of a paper banner down and to the left from where they stood broke and reassembled. In the break she saw, again, the ghost of a mark: a line becoming a loop, a curve seeking its completion. Her heart made a small, involuntary adjustment, like a compass needle shaking off distraction.

"Tell me," Julian said, not as a demand and not as a dare, but as a man asking to be admitted to an interior room he'd been near enough to respect.

She exhaled because that was the only way to say yes without speaking it. "Something is misaligned," she said. "Has been for a long time. We're brushing against the correction."

"Because of the arguing?"

"Because of the remembering," she said. "Arguing is one way of remembering. It's a terrible way, but it's honest."

"You think the festival will fix it."

"I think the festival is the table we set when we want truth to come eat with us," she said. "But truth doesn't always like the seating chart."

He smiled at that, then sobered. "Earlier you said we have influence."

"We do," she said. "It matters who carries the basin and who lights the first flame and who speaks and who stands quietly and who sings with their whole chest and who takes up less space than they could. It matters who sees what is happening under what is happening."

"You're talking about yourself."

"I'm talking about all of us," she said. "But yes. Also me."

They stood long enough that the river changed color twice. Volunteer voices ghosted up from the green and then away. A dog barked at a gull and lost. Mosquitoes executed small campaigns against ankles and were repelled by perfunctory slaps. Miriam felt in her body the exact moment when the day handed the field over to night and said, I'll see you in the morning.

Back on Main, the shop windows caught the last light and flared like brief fires before becoming mirrors. They walked slowly in that direction, as if the town would be offended if they hurried through its gloaming. She watched the faces they passed do the beautiful shuffle from public to private: the mayor with his tie loosened, Mrs. Levine, the baker, taking off her apron like a flag at sundown, the teen with the lantern cart now a teen again, relief softening his shoulders.

At her door, Miriam touched the key and then paused. "Do you remember," she asked, "the story about the first basin? The original oath at the rivers?"

"The bits the records hold," he said. "And the bits the stories embroidered."

"Do any records mention a mark? Not on the basin. In the river."

He thought, his gaze leaving the street and going inward toward shelves and boxes. "I've seen sketches of river stones. Not a carved mark. Why?"

"Call it a hunch," she said.

"I do, frequently."

She looked past him to the seam of the confluence. A light breeze slid its fingers through the surface and the water answered like cloth. The shape she'd seen twice today felt less like a threat and more like a promise the day wanted them prepared for. "Tomorrow," she said, "I'll help Sloane string the lanterns over the west path. Will you bring the ledger copy? I want to look at it again with better eyes."

"I will," he said. "And the font you liked."

"That was not a confession," she said. "That was a trap."

He stepped back and did a small, ridiculous bow. "Thank you for today," he said, straightening. "For making the unsolvable merely difficult."

"Tomorrow we'll solve it," she said.

"Tomorrow," he agreed, with a certainty that made her grateful and wary in equal measure, because certainty is a lovely thing to stand in and a dangerous thing to cling to.

After he left, she went upstairs and opened every window. The river came in a little just enough sound to name itself. She set a kettle on and sat with her notebook open, the page eager as a road. She wrote: ROTATE CARRIERS; FIRST FLAME SHARED; SPEAK WE. Then, under that, smaller: something misaligned asking to right itself.

When the kettle sang, she poured water and added a sprig of rosemary because sometimes courage needs to be reminded where the body keeps it. She took the mug to the window and watched the green, the fort, the line of the dock. In the half-light, the basin visible through the museum glass looked like a sleeping animal, sturdy and unafraid. She raised the cup as if toasting an old friend.

"I see you," she said into the room and the river. "We're getting ready."

The room didn't answer. The river did what it always did. And beneath its practiced surface, a patient intention drew breath and waited for the right moment to surface, the way a story waits for the sentence that can hold it without breaking.

Friday was coming. The hymn. The blessing. The first pour. The moment the whole town would go still, and if history has a favorite trick, it's to choose precisely that moment to teach. Miriam felt the tug again gentle, insistent, as if the water had taken her sleeve between two fingers and asked, politely, to be heard.

She closed the window. She left one lamp on. She lay down and, before sleep, decided to dream deliberately of a river made of every river she had known. When the dream arrived, it brought a picture that was not a picture but a motion. A line, a curve, a loop that had not yet met its other half. She reached toward it in the dream and felt her hand pass through water and touch cedar.

The tug did not become alarm; it became invitation. It said: remember. It said: bring us out.

She slept. The town slept. The river kept its watch.

And the basin, cedar dreaming cedar dreams, waited for the hands that would lift it into a morning that promised the ordinary miracle pie and song and children tripping over cords and the less ordinary one that happens when a community asks, without quite saying so: Are we brave enough to be told the truth in public? Are we kind enough to hold it together when it arrives?

The night did not answer. But it did not say no.

3

AT THE FORT MUSEUM

The museum opened like a careful book hinges creaked, light turned, dust rose and settled. Julian keyed them in before hours, the kind of privilege granted to people who had worn the path between home and work until the floor itself trusted their tread. He let the heavy door lean into his shoulder and held it for Miriam with a small bow that wasn't performance so much as habit, a courtesy he gave to rooms and people alike.

Inside, the air was cooler, citrus and wood polish overlaid on the old perfume of paper. The galleries were still glass cases like aquariums for time, labels standing at attention, the schooner-shaped clock on the far wall ticking the same calm it had ticked yesterday. Even quiet had texture in here.

"Come on," he said, and his voice did that change she'd learned to notice shoulders dropping a degree, vowels easing as if the work itself gave him permission to breathe differently.

He led her past the trading display tokens, beads, a brass scale whose pans found each other like reconciled siblings and past the case where a boy-sized blue coat hung next to a battered tin cup and the immodest caption: **From this cup two languages learned to drink together.** The floorboards creaked, not with complaint, but with recognition. Miriam always felt watched in the museum, not by cameras or guards, but by something like attention that belonged to the objects themselves, as if they knew their names and would say them if anyone asked correctly.

"In here," Julian said, and shouldered open the small door to Collections. The room beyond was windowless and neat in the way that reassures a surgeon and unnerves a poet. Flat files lined one wall; acid-free boxes labeled in a uniform hand lined the others. A single table waited in the middle like a dock.

He snapped on the task light. "I pulled the basin portfolio and the ceremony ephemera," he said, savoring the word *ephemera* like a candy that lasted longer than advertised. "You'll like the carpenter's sketch."

"You've already decided," she said, amused.

"You always like the carpenter's sketch," he said. "He draws the idea and the care at the same time."

He opened a drawer, slid out a linen-wrapped folder, and laid it on the table as if setting down a sleeping child. The ritual of it gloves from the little box, breath disciplined, the gentleness that came from muscle memory was a language he didn't translate so much as include her in. He undid the cotton tie and lifted the first sheet.

A hand-colored plan of the fort filled the page, the longhouse and the palisade and the river drawn in a blue that time had convinced toward smoke. In the margin, a smaller drawing three views of the ceremonial basin: profile, top, and a detail of the carved rim.

"There," he said, satisfied and almost shy, as if introducing a friend. "Our old companion."

She leaned in, palms on the table's edge, breath kept back. The basin in profile was as she knew it cedar staves, iron bands, a modest flare at the lip, nothing ornamental that hadn't earned its keep in repeated use. The top view showed a ring of wave carvings just suggestion, the sort of pattern you feel under your hand more than you see with your eye. And there, at the bottom of the page, the rim detail: a set of repeating curves interrupted by a small unfinished mark.

She had to look twice. The line began, curved, lifted, then stopped, a pencil's faint arrest mid-sweep, as if someone had lifted their hand not to rest but to reconsider.

"Do you see it?" Julian asked.

"I see a question," she said.

He grinned, delighted. "Same word I wrote in my notes."

She let her eyes learn the carpenter's hand the confident strokes, the few cautious ones. The unfinished mark was neither flourish nor error. It had the feel of a thought turning around itself, wanting to be drawn but unwilling to commit to being *this* instead of *that*. The rest of the page had been done by someone who knew how to finish. This little curve looked like a musician testing a note before bringing the bow down.

"Could be nothing," Julian said, because in history as in medicine you say it first to keep your heart honest. "A smudge. A child's hand. The paper was always folded on this line; that's why the discoloration. Still."

"Still," she said. Something low in her ribs recognized the shape, not as a picture but as a motion. Like the way last night's dream had moved. Like the way water had curled and then refused, twice, to complete the pattern in front of her. "Is there another drawing of the rim?"

He turned pages with the ease of a dealer pacing a deck. A bill for replacement bands. A note in a clerk's hand about humidity. An invoice for linseed and cedar oil. A letter from a woman named Esther LeClair complaining that in the previous year's ritual the basin had been "handled like a pail and not a vow," her complaint written with such moral music Miriam wanted to meet her. And then another drawing, perhaps a later hand cleaner, less tender but no unfinished mark there, the rim drawn as an unbroken set of curves with careful repetition, no hesitations.

In the second folder, a small watercolor: the Rivers Festival as it had been before anyone called it that, lanterns painted as soft moons, the basin lifted on a cart by four figures that could have been anyone because that was the point. The watercolorist, less skillful than the carpenter, had nonetheless captured the exact hush of a moment when a group neutrals itself into *we*.

Julian slid another sheet free: a pencil view of the basin from slightly below, as if the artist had knelt a reverent angle. And in the lower right, the faint remnant of a curve that began and stopped.

"This is the same hand as the plan," he said. "See the *R* in *rim*? That little bravado? Same bravado here in the *r* of *river*." He traced the letter without touching. "The mark repeats. It's unfinished in both."

"What would make a competent hand stop?" Miriam asked.

"A second thought," he said. "Or copying from a model that was marred."

"Or choosing not to draw what you're not supposed to see yet." She surprised herself with that.

"That is very Adler of you," he said, not unkindly, and straightened to fetch another folder.

She lingered over the rim. The incomplete line made her throat feel exactly as if she'd tried to sing a note without breathing for it properly no pain, just the warning hum that says: complete this or something in you will tug at your sleeve all day.

He returned with a small wrapped rectangle. "Two more things," he said. "A sketch in charcoal. And this."

He laid the rectangle down and unwrapped a mica sheet the kind used to face lanterns long before paper did the job its surface printed with a frieze of stylized waves and vines and, in one corner, a tentative pencil start that echoed the carpenter's hesitation. Not a symbol yet; a hint of how a symbol might move. Here and not here.

"It's so little," she said.

"They're all little," he said, and there was love in it the archivist's stubborn love for tiny witnesses. "All the big stories are stacks of small ones."

She nodded. Her attention had widened to include the room the wrapped boxes, the flat files, the lemon oil scent, the tick of the schooner clock on the other side of two doors. The museum felt, suddenly, less like storage and more like a brain that knew what it knew even when no one was asking questions.

"And the ledger?" she asked.

He slid a box forward with two fingers, as if pulling grace across a counter. "Here," he said. "I flagged the messy week and the neat weeks around it."

They opened to the page they'd studied yesterday: weights and shipments running in clean lines until they lurched for five entries, then straightening as if embarrassed. The margin curl his clerk's "remember" appeared here as an orphan, no note attached.

"Impatience," she said, and he nodded.

"Or interruption," he said. "The day the fort ran out of ink, the day the child cried, the day the ship came early. The day the clerk's own heart elbowed itself into the work."

She looked again at the faint, unfinished curve on the carpenter's page. A prickling ran along her forearms, not fear, exactly not even warning but the vertical attention she'd come to recognize as *pay attention now and without drama*. The mark had waited two centuries; it wasn't about to demand of her a panic. It asked for seeing.

"The museum is good at this," she said. "At letting the rooms calm you until you can see properly."

"That's the aim," he said. "And the challenge." His smile tipped. "Also, custody of the extension cords."

She laughed, and the sound slipped into the room and did not bounce; it lay down as if it belonged. Outside, the muffled clatter of the green continued its day hammers, teenagers, somebody politely swearing at a stubborn tent pole.

"Shall we look at the sketch under raking light?" he asked. "Sometimes a hesitation shows as pressure."

He flicked off the overheads, angled the task lamp low, and slid the beam across the page until the paper's tooth stood up under grazing brightness. The unfinished mark sculpted itself from suggested to undeniable: the pencil had pressed, lifted too soon and left the tiniest burr where the lead had dragged upward against the grain. Miriam could feel, in her hand, how the motion wanted to complete itself.

She didn't speak. He didn't either. The two of them leaned over the table like co-conspirators invited to a plan older than their joining.

"Whatever else," he said finally, soft, "he meant to finish it."

"Or meant to not finish it," she said. "Because to draw it then would have been to put it in a place it didn't belong yet."

He turned his head. "You think it belonged in the water."

"I think it belongs where it can appear," she said. "Not just be recorded."

He let that live without argument. In the doorway, the museum's light and the day's light braided together for a breath, and the carpenter's mark, no bigger than a fingernail, sat there between them like a patient seed, having always known it would one day have a good audience.

JULIAN LOVED the part of his job that involved evidence and order; Miriam had seen that. But there was a second love that came out only when he was certain his listener wanted more than data: the joy of showing. Not *teaching*, exactly it lacked that posture. Showing, as in: *Look what I get to see. Look what you get to see, too.*

He moved around the table with that particular attentiveness that museums train into their people sleeves off the paper, elbows gathered in, breath measured so as not to stir the work. Yet his voice warmed until the room felt less like a lab and more like a kitchen at midnight where a friend had produced a box of old photographs and a pie and said, Here, let's remember together.

"Hold out your hand," he said, and placed two envelopes in her palm weight enough to register as care. "Lantern orders. Same year. One before the festival and one after."

She opened the first. *Twelve sheets mica; three dozen cedar frames; six ounces fish glue; three sticks graphite.* The clerk's hand was content, the numbers unhurried. The second order had twice the frames and half the mica, as if the town had learned by doing that what it loved best was light traveling through paper.

"Trial and error," he said. "Sometimes you can hear it."

She looked at him instead of the paper because she could hear him how the day had been good already and would be better because he had someone to hand it to. "Do you ever feel," she asked, "like you live in more than one century, not as a tourist but as a neighbor?"

"Daily," he said. "Which is inconvenient when it comes to phone plans."

He set the envelopes down and turned the page in the basin portfolio. "Here. See how the carpenter numbers the staves? Not one through twelve, but one-next, two-next. It's a rhythm, not a math. He was thinking in rounds."

"And you love him," she said.

"Unreasonably," he admitted. "But not exclusively."

They laughed, and in the laughter a small current shifted nothing big enough to name, just the alignment of two people who had been walking parallel and for a step found the exact same cadence. He looked younger when he laughed, but not lighter; it was the kind of laugh that carried its own ballast, as if joy didn't need to be careless to be real.

He showed her how to read the paper's texture like topography "Here, feel the valley where the pencil lived" and how to tell when a label had been replaced "Different glue, see the shine, that's new." He told her the story of the docent who claimed the schooner clock counted slower when the basin was in the room. "I don't believe it," he said. "But I test it anyway."

"You test everything," she said. "Even what you don't believe."

"It's what I know how to do," he said simply, and she liked that as much as anything the confession of method without apology.

When he wasn't reaching for a box or a page, he tucked his hands into his back pockets, the posture of a long man reminding himself to occupy less space around fragile things. When he leaned over the table, the small scar near his left temple she'd noticed months ago picked up the lamp and made a pale crescent, a faint echo of the unfinished curve on the page. He was all frame and restraint and then, unexpectedly, the mischief of a smile that made her think of river light when the breeze first wakes it.

"Break?" he said. "Or do you want the scandal?"

"The scandal," she said, without thinking.

He produced a folded newspaper, the kind printed when pictures were new to news. Its headline scolded someone about a speech in Salem; lower down, a smaller column reported a Rivers Festival interrupted by "an unfortunate disturbance at the basin." The language was delicately outraged no gore, no names just enough anxiety to keep the town walking itself back to the calm side of the street. Someone had cut the column and pasted it into a scrapbook whose spine had failed and then been mended by the careful hand of a woman who'd done other mending.

He watched her read and then, not hiding the pride of a good host, said, "Now the break."

They retreated to the tiny staff room a kettle, two mugs, a shelf of tea that had cheerfully ignored sell-by dates, a container of almonds with a label in a docent hand: **Please eat these.** The windowless space held the amiable fatigue of people who do good work on purpose. He filled the kettle; she found peppermint; they conspired to ignore the jar of instant coffee.

"I saw you with Mr. Cavanaugh and Rosalie yesterday," he said, handing her a mug and sitting across, knees nearly but not quite brushing hers. "You make a circle where most of us draw lines."

"I move paper around," she said. "Sloane does the heavy lifting."

"Sloane moves mountains," he agreed. "You move weather."

She took that in, not smiling at first, because it's a delicate thing to receive praise for what is invisible. "You like this work," she said, nodding toward the closed door to Collections as much as to his face. "The showing."

He didn't bother to deflect. "I do. I love catching a person right at the instant they see that a small thing matters. You can watch it happen. The shoulders drop. The breath comes back. Their voice gets quiet without getting smaller."

"That's how you sound when you talk about the carpenter," she said.

"That's how you sound when you talk about the river," he countered.

They let the peppermint steep past any instruction on the box, because when a conversation finds its stride, water waits. He told her about the short list of objects he trusts more than others "The rope splice, because you can ask six fishermen and each one will say it's right. The spoon with the notch, because a child made that notch and it survived." She told him about the ways people decide to soften "It's never because you tell them. It's because they watch someone else be unafraid." He asked her whether a town could repent. She asked him whether a document could lie by omission and still be useful.

He enjoyed sharing his work and she enjoyed that he enjoyed it there was no other way to put it. The pleasure wasn't performance; no one else was watching. He trusted her to see what he saw, and the trust turned seeing into a joint craft.

"Will you say that on Friday?" he asked, as if they'd already agreed she would. "About watching someone else be unafraid."

"If you'll say that ritual is a table we set for truth," she said, surprising herself with the formulation and liking it. "And that we can't control the guest list."

"Yes," he said, bright with assent.

They took their mugs back in and set them safely away from the table. He slid a new page free and produced a loupe. "Now the indulgence," he said, grinning. "The pencil brand. If I can find it, I win a bet with myself about a supply shipment in 1845."

She bent to the task of looking too closely, of letting a fragment be entire for a minute. He bent beside her and the warmth of him was not an intrusion but part of the scene, like the task lamp and the ticking clock and the grain of the table. He didn't touch her; he didn't need to. The room itself held their proximity and made it simple.

"Do you know," he said, voice low because proximity makes language a finer tool, "that this is my favorite version of you?"

"What does that mean?" she said, startled and oddly unafraid.

"The one who is all attention," he said. "The one whose face changes when she feels the pattern click."

"Dangerous," she said, aiming for lightness because lightness was kinder than flight.

"To me?" He shook his head. "Not at all. To whatever stubbornness thought it could outwait you."

They let the remark stand without poking it. It didn't

require an answer, just the acknowledgment of a shared angle of approach. He loved showing. She loved being shown by someone who coveted no credit for the seeing.

For a while there was only the work pencil lines under a loupe, the soft slide of paper, the disposition of fragments into a story that never pretended to be whole but was honest about its edges. Then the museum's outer door gave its little metal cough as someone came in for the mid-shift. The spell adjusted, didn't break. The room had the look of a stage before the second act props arranged, players present, a collectively held breath waiting for the cue.

"Ready to look at the basin?" he asked. "One more time before we lock it for the move."

She nodded. He gathered the pages with ceremony and tenderness, as if the past, pleased, would agree to be moved forward a little by the way their hands behaved. When they stepped into the gallery, the cedar smell rose, distinct even against lemon and old paint. The basin behind glass didn't look trapped; it looked attended. Miriam stood close enough to see her reflection turn translucent over the wood.

"Hello," she said to it, not because she thought it listened but because she knew *she* did. Then to Julian, with the same feeling: "We're going to get this right."

"We are," he said, not as boast but as vow.

Outside, the green lifted a cheer at some small triumph of gaffer tape over entropy. Inside, the unfinished curve on the page they had left behind drew itself a fraction longer in the theater of her mind, then paused again, not coy but patient, as if telling her: Not here, not yet. Soon.

The afternoon slanted toward the hour when light behaves as if it remembers something and wants to tell you without words. Julian dimmed the gallery lights one notch for the sake of the cedar; the room softened, and with it the glass became less mirror, more membrane. The basin sat the most unassuming of sacred things built to hold, built to be carried, to be filled and emptied and filled again.

"Stand here," he said, and took her two steps to the left. "You can see the repair seam best from this angle. After the 1902 fiasco, they sanded the join. The texture's different."

"Fiasco," she said, smiling.

"Official curatorial term," he said. "We have a whole lexi-con." He pointed, not touching. "See how the grain stutters? Like a stammer."

She saw it. She also saw the line of reflection on the glass a white thread drawn by the task light's edge travel down, hit the curve of the basin, and arc. For a heartbeat, that reflection and the repaired seam combined into the suggestion of a sign she knew too well to be fooled by. She didn't startle; she held the sensation the way you hold a firefly without squeezing, and let it fly away rather than making it perform.

"May I...?" she asked, and he nodded, stepping back.

She closed her eyes and let the other senses attend: cedar and polish, the faint ion tang of the river through the building, the beeping of a forklift that memory provided though the parking lot was quiet now, the winged brush of someone in the next room. Beneath it, quieter than all of them, the attention she trusted like a needle, settling until the oscillation calmed and the indicator pointed. Not to a direction; to a question.

When she opened her eyes, Julian was watching not skeptical, not credulous present. That had become his greatest gift to her: staying in the room when she listened to what he could not hear. Not explaining it away, not performing belief. Just staying.

"The mark," she said. "It's not here for us to find today. It's going to show itself. Soon." She surprised herself by how certain she felt and how un-fragile the certainty was, like a chair you tested before sitting and found it held.

"On Friday," he said, a guess voiced as invitation rather than as trap.

"When everyone's quiet enough to notice the same thing at the same time," she said. "When the town is making its one voice."

"During the first pour," he said, because he thinks in event orders and spatial relations.

"Or as the basin empties," she said, and the word *empties* carried a riverweight that tethered itself to her ribs. "Water shows and water reveals. It isn't only for holding."

He nodded, folding the thought into his architecture of the day like a new beam test-fitted. "Then we prepare to look," he said. "And to help them see without panic."

"We don't prevent panic," she said. "We listen to it until it remembers what it is."

He huffed a laugh, not at her but at the accuracy of what struck him as impossible and therefore likely. "That's going on a sign," he said. "Next to the spoon with the notch."

They did the mundane things: checked the case locks; signed the movement log; verified the humidity reading with the suspicion of old friends who have been lied to by gauges before. He texted Sloane a picture of the casters that would carry the basin's vitrine to the lift; Sloane responded with a string of thumbs-up and a warning about a soft spot in the green near the cottonwood. They added one more thing to the list on the clipboard: **strap at two heights.**

"And now," Julian said, with the exaggerated sigh of a man who knows the next hours belong to emails and chairs and arguments about microphone levels, "the romance of gaffer tape."

"I thought this was the romance," she said, and made a small gesture that included glass and cedar and him.

"It is," he said, and the answer landed between them with the ease of a pebble tossed into a pool you've both already decided is yours to share.

They stepped out into the corridor. A docent greeted them the sweater from the empty chair now on her person, her hair pinned with a pencil. She had the particular kindness of people who know that strangers are just pre-friends. "Oh good," she said. "You're here. Someone on the green wants to know if the basin will be offended by tulips."

"It has a long memory but no grudges," Julian said gravely. "Tulips are fine."

"Thank you," the docent said, accepting the tone as much as the content. "Also, a child has left three smooth stones in a row on the front step. Is that you or the universe?"

"The universe," Miriam said. "But we can thank it."

They walked toward the front. On the step, the stones gray, pale brown, a blue that only shows when wet sat obedient as offerings. She touched one with a fingertip as if to bless it back and then stood, something in her widening an aperture she felt during the better prayers and in rooms where people had agreed to tell the truth.

"Ready?" Julian asked.

"For chairs and gaffer tape," she said. "For people who will insist that the microphone hates them personally. For Pastor Elijah's patience. Yes."

"For Friday?" he said, more careful.

"Also yes," she said. "But yes the way you say it to a

mountain you plan to walk. Not the way you say it to a door you plan to open."

"Understood," he said.

They crossed the green together, and the work of the day resumed around them, a theater company building the set in sight of the audience that would later applaud the miracle as if it had arrived out of nowhere. At the edge of the dock, two teenagers practiced lighting lanterns with a butane wand they treated as if it were a dragon. They laughed too loud and immediately shushed themselves, as if the river had scolded.

Sloane appeared, tape on her wrist like a bracelet, radio clipped to her hip, a strand of hair refusing conscription behind her ear. "We're moving your glass in the morning," she said to Julian. "Two carts, four humans, no heroics. The soft spot is flagged. I have sand for the stand feet. We're not improvising this."

"Bless you," he said.

She tipped her chin at Miriam. "And you your lantern people are artists. They want the west path hung in a fan pattern. I told them we could try if we keep the center clear."

"Fan and center clear," Miriam said, tucking the words away where she kept stage directions.

"Good," Sloane said. "Also, Rosalie and Mr. Cavanaugh's granddaughter came together to ask about wick length. I'm taking it as a sign. Don't ruin it for me."

"I won't," Miriam said. "The universe left three stones on the step. That counts too."

Sloane looked at her for a second with the affectionate exasperation she reserved for people who spoke fluent metaphor. "Great," she said. "Then tell the universe to sign for the generator delivery."

They laughed. The green flexed. People lifted, carried,

argued, conceded, solved. The river threaded through it all with the patience of something that had seen many of their festivals and would see many more.

At dusk, when the breeze returned and the light did that evening trick of softening hard edges, Miriam and Julian walked back once more to the museum to make sure everything was as it should be. On the gallery floor, the last wash of sun made a long bright shape. It slid across the glass and up the basin's side. In that moving bar of light, the seam and the reflection, just for a heartbeat, made that almost-mark again the curve that wanted its other half.

She didn't point. She stood very still and let the experience have her, rather than trying to have it. When it ended, it ended without ache. Promise is like that, she thought. It's only painful when you mistake it for its fulfillment.

In the foyer, as they turned to lock up, the schooner clock ticked its tidy, uninterested measure. The docent's sweater lay on the chair again, abandoned for an errand in the front garden where tulips would not offend cedar. Julian held the door; she stepped out. On the step, the three stones remained. They had not moved, because stones do not go in for theatrics. Still, she felt thanked.

"Tomorrow," Julian said, that word they kept spending and finding renewed.

"Tomorrow," she said, and added, because the shape in the light had taught her how to leave a sentence open where it belonged, "and then Friday."

He touched the door frame, a private blessing for wood and hinges and the labor of keeping time safe, and then they went down the steps into the near-dark. The river ran with the sound of a thousand small things agreeing to go in one direction. Over their heads the first lantern strings crossed the path, unlit still, patient as stars staging.

Somewhere beneath the dock, a current pulled silt off a flat stone and set a small carved edge free of its coat. The river kept the secret in motion, not hoarding it, not flaunting it. It would tell when the town was assembled and quiet, when the basin sat where the oldest hands had intended and the youngest eyes could see.

In Collections, under linen, the carpenter's unfinished curve waited on its page the way a lamp waits on a match. Not longing. Not restless. Ready.

And in Miriam's chest, the same. A room readied for a guest, a table set for a truth that had sent its RSVP two centuries ago and was finally, audaciously, on its way.

$$4$$

THE BASIN RUNS DRY

The morning arrived like a promise the town had practiced saying together. By eight, the green thrummed at a frequency that turned individual heartbeats into a shared tempo choir lined at the edge of the stage, lanterns sleeping in their strings, vendors smoothing tablecloths with the seriousness of altar guilds. The river kept its patient counsel alongside, slate and pewter braided at the seam.

Miriam stood beside Julian at the lectern, paper in her hand that she might not need. They had decided the shape of their words and then given themselves permission to let the room this green under a wide Pacific Northwest sky alter the rhythm. Pastor Elijah waited near the basin stand, palms loosely folded; Sloane did a last tour of the cordons with tape on her wrist like a bracelet; Rosalie LeClair and Mr. Cavanaugh's granddaughter stood shoulder to shoulder, first flame ready between them like a lesson someone had decided to teach by doing. The carriers four neighbors nominated by other neighbors for strength, steadiness, and a willingness to be part of a *we* gripped the handles of the basin's cart, breaths even, knees set.

Julian opened his mouth, and the green obliged with quiet. "We gather," he said, and Miriam felt the words take their place like planks laid over a wet stretch of ground. "Not for spectacle alone, but because water lets us rehearse belonging. We carry together what none of us owns."

She spoke next, resisting the urge to repeat what he'd said because the river did not need an echo; it needed a harmony. "Rituals are tables," she said. "We set them for truth and for mercy. We don't control the guest list. We only promise to listen when something comes we didn't expect."

The choir rose on the hymn. It wasn't a showy piece, and that was the point; it was one the town could find without practice. The notes made a lane in the air. Children fell quiet the way they do when a room's attention aligns; phones lowered; the dog that would later ignore the lantern-walk poster lay down and sighed like an amen.

Pastor Elijah stepped forward. He did not preach. He named the river with courtesy, named the people who had lived here before the fort and after, named the ones who carried, the ones who built, the ones who keep. He said *we* in a tone that did not exclude *I* but asked *I* to bring a dish to the table.

Sloane lifted her chin: ready. The carriers pushed; the cart rolled; the basin cedar staves, iron bands, a thousand handled mornings in its history came forward in a hush that felt earned. When it settled into the cradle, the green exhaled as one. Rosalie and the granddaughter leaned in, struck the flame, and warmed it between their palms. The first light touched the day and did not look small. Miriam watched that moment the handoff between tinder and tinderbox and it bent something inside her to the right shape.

Then the water.

Julian took the pitcher from the table, lifted it with the form of a man who knew his task mattered more because it was ordinary, and began to pour. The first sheet hit cedar, shivered, pooled. The second, the third cool, clear, caught and held. The sound the basin made pleased the ear the way certain words always do *enough, welcome, stay.*

Miriam heard it change.

She couldn't have said at first what shifted. A fraction of pitch; a thinner sound; the water's refusal to deepen in the body of the basin. She saw, too how the surface failed to climb to the mark inside that told old hands when to stop; how the gloss dulled as if something had opened beneath it. She looked at Julian. He had felt it as well. His brow flicked, not with alarm but with attention sharpened like a knife's edge tested with a thumb.

He set the pitcher down. The choir's last note fell away into that unsettled space you get when the room hasn't yet decided what to be next. Pastor Elijah stepped closer, palms still, voice low enough to remind the day how to breathe. "It's all right."

Water slid. It vanished not over the lip, not through a found crack in cedar, but down, as if toward a drain the eye could not see. It went with a sound Miriam had heard only once before: in sleep, when in the dream a river she did not know made a door for itself in the ground and walked through.

The green reacted in the only way a crowd knows how when the practiced becomes strange. A ripple *what?* ran through the bodies. A child said, too loud, "It's leaking!" and then cried because it wasn't. Sloane was already at the stand with a wrench and three contingencies, cursing softly at physics that refused to consult her. Mr. Cavanaugh's cousin, who believed everything mechanical obeyed the same set of rules if you glared at it properly, glared. Rosalie adjusted her grip on the first flame as if protecting it from a draft no one else could feel.

The water went out. Not all at once; almost politely. What had been a small pool became a skim, the way a bowl looks in a kitchen after the last soup has been ladled and you are deciding whether to scrape or soak. The cedar was wet, but the basin did not hold. It offered itself and was refused.

"Back," Sloane said quietly, because she trusted volume less than tone. The carriers stepped away on her count. The cart did not move. Miriam realized with a start that the refusal wasn't to the basin; it was to the idea that the basin belonged up here and not there.

"There," because the river had made its case in the only language it has.

A sound rose a different sound, deeper and farther, like a voice below a stage. Those nearest the stand turned toward the dock without deciding to, bodies following attention. The surface at the shallows had a look Miriam recognized. Not agitation. Formation. The river arranged what lay upon it. A branch turned, released silt, lifted, and drifted aside like someone stepping from a pew to make room. The light found a place to hold.

She saw the stone then. Not large, no bigger than a bread plate. Its face, newly cleared by the move of water and the patience of centuries, showed an incised mark. Not the neat rim pattern from the carpenter's drawing; not a flourish; not decoration. A line that began, curved, hesitated, and met its other half *this time* meeting it, not retreating the loop completed in a shape older than the town's argument and simpler than any alphabet. The current kissed the groove; the groove answered with shadow.

It was, impossibly, beautiful.

Miriam didn't gasp because she had spent years learning not to perform for revelation. But she felt her chest answer as if two notes had finally found their third and the chord had resolved into a thing you didn't know you were missing until you heard it. Beside her, Julian made a sound low in his throat that she had heard once before when he found, in a letter hardly legible, a footnote that threaded three years of research into clarity. Pastor Elijah's eyes brightened with the kind of wet that does not ask to be called tears.

The basin, emptied, sat uninsulted; it looked like what it had always been a carrier between positions. The water moved where water wished to be. The green held its breath because breath, too, is a tide.

"Friends," Pastor Elijah said, and his voice found its calm. "We will step forward and look, together. Slowly. Kindly. We will not decide what it is before we see it."

Sloane lifted her hand. "We'll set a rope," she said, already in motion. "Two at a time near the edge. No one gets foolish on my watch."

Rosalie took the first flame and covered it with her palm as if to keep it from the wind that was not there. She looked not at Mr. Cavanaugh, not at the crowd, but at the river with an expression Miriam wanted to paint and keep near her bed: reverence without surrender. The child who had cried a minute ago hiccupped once, twice, and stopped. The choir director, on instinct, hummed a single note. Not grief. Not triumph. A key.

The town leaned as one toward the edge. The stone waited where it had waited for longer than anyone knew, the carved symbol no longer shy. The first major manifestation had not been a thunderclap or a storm or a rending. It had been a refusal to hold what wanted to be shown, followed by a hand if water can be said to have a hand lifting a cover away from a face.

Miriam, who had dreamed of chains snapping on a river bottom, stood within the ease that comes when the unseen stops hiding. She knew two things at once: that none of this was for spectacle, and that all of it needed witnesses. She took Julian's hand because her body wanted to and because witness work is easier done linked. He squeezed once, as if to say: *Yes. I see it, too.*

THE FIRST MINUTE HELD. Then the second. In the third, somebody decided they were being patient enough and asked a question too loudly.

"What did you do to it?" Mr. Cavanaugh's cousin called toward Sloane, toward Julian, toward anyone official enough to be a target. "That basin never emptied like that in my father's time."

"Then your father wasn't standing here in 1902," said an elder at the rope, voice dry as cedar bark.

"Back," Sloane said again, gentler this time because a gentleness you can count on is stronger than a shout you can't. The rope line breathed; the town tried again to decide on a single body temper. For a beat they almost managed it, until the second question rose and found allies ready in old habits.

"Is this what you wanted?" a woman asked Rosalie, not cruelly and not kindly, either only with a suspicion shaped over decades of hearing that a ritual had been handled incorrectly by the wrong hands. "You and yours keep talking about change. You got it."

Rosalie did not blink. "The river is no one's *got*. It does not take orders from my family or yours."

"You'd be surprised," the cousin muttered. "Some people think they own tides."

Pastor Elijah lifted both his palms in that way that often makes people remember they, too, have palms to lift. "We will not give ourselves to fear," he said. "We will not give ourselves to blame."

"We will give ourselves to caution," Sloane added, practical as breath. "Two at a time. See with your eyes before you decide with your mouth."

Sheriff Mayhew arrived at the green's edge with deputies who looked startled to be summoned to a hymn and a puddle. He took in the basin, the stand, the rope, the stone, the symbol. He was a man made for incident reports and de-escalation, not for carved marks touched by current, but he had lived here long enough to know what power pays attention to. "No one in the water," he said mildly, and when three teenagers groaned as if robbed of glory he added, "Today," because the wisdom of *not now* is still wisdom.

The mayor, who talked too much when nervous, began to talk too much. "We will be putting out a statement," he said into a mic no one had turned on. "We will be forming a
"

"We already have a committee," Sloane said to no one in particular, stretching rope between two temporary stanchions. "It's called town."

Julian's hand warmed in Miriam's. His eyes were on the stone, but he was cataloging, she could feel it the order of events, who stood where, the exact minute the basin refused, the temperature, the way the moss along the dock newel had briefly lifted as if in greeting when the symbol appeared. He was not armoring himself against the weird; he was giving the weird a chair and a pad of paper.

"Take pictures," he said softly, and she nodded because she'd already pulled her phone. She wanted record enough to keep the later rumor honest. She took shots wide and then near: the curve completed; the depth of the incise; a pair of minnow shadows crossing as if to sign the bottom of the page. She resisted the impulse to name the thing aloud. Names would come; better late than early.

At the rope, people filed and peered, and in the peering you could read the lay of old ground. The Cavanaughs stood like men who'd been accused and were trying not to accuse back; the LeClairs held themselves like women who'd been told reverence was a performance rather than a profession and were not, today, accepting the note. The choir, clustered together for comfort, tried not to hum and failed beautifully. The beekeeper handed a jar of honey to a child without charging him because some mornings require sweetness not accounted for in the spreadsheets. Mack from the hardware store did what good men do when panic looks like it might spray he went around quietly telling people they were doing great, and somehow they were.

"Someone drilled a hole in the basin," the cousin announced, because a problem ought to obey the sort of solution he had tools for.

"Show me the hole," Sloane said with a briskness that often prevents meetings. She ran her hand along the cedar as a farrier handles a hoof palm sure, thumb testing, eye unflicking. "No hole," she said. "No leak. You could drink soup from this and not lose a drop."

"Then the stand," he tried, unwilling to befriend mystery.

"The stand is plumb and true," Sloane said. "Ask the level and the two men who leveled the level. If you want to be helpful, hand me that bag of ties."

He handed them, and by the time he did he had helped, and when you help your mouth learns humility faster than any sermon can teach it.

The talk returned, as if on rails, to ownership. The ritual, the dock, the river, the right to carry, the right to light all the conversations the town had learned to disguise as logistics when they were, at their root, about a wound older than any of them. The 1902 elder spoke again, voice carrying just enough. "It happened before," she said. "Ask your grandmothers. Ask the women who stood at the edge and said *be gentle*. Ask the men who pretended they hadn't heard and still were."

The mayor finally realized the mic was off and put it down. Pastor Elijah had not moved much his power was to create stable gravity, not to chase comets but you could see people's shoulders drop a degree and their elbows tuck in when they happened near him. The choir director, abandoning quiet, chose a note and held it under her breath like a shelf. Rosalie's flame never faltered.

The rumor mill spun hard, as rumor mills do when someone forgot to throw the switch at dawn. Sabotage. Curse. Nature. Judgment. Trick. Miracle. The labels didn't matter to the stone. The symbol lay in its groove and accepted light without changing itself to fit the town's need for quick categories.

Julian eased his hand from Miriam's and moved toward the stand to ask the carriers for their account: the weight, the feel under their hands, the pressure before the decline. He would write it out later in a notebook whose pages were full of words arranged like lumber to frame a house that could hold weather. Miriam let him go and, in the space his body had filled, felt the wind thread her sleeve as if to remind her the day was not only human.

"Ms. Adler," Sheriff Mayhew said, stepping close as men step when they mean to be economical with their calm. "I don't pretend to understand your ah skill set. But if your sense says we should keep people back, we will."

"Keep them near," she said. "Near and slow. It isn't here to be hoarded. It's here to be seen without us breaking it."

He studied her the way a cautious reader studies a book that has surprised him twice in three pages. "All right," he said. "Near and slow."

On the rope, a small boy asked Rosalie if wishing on a carved rock worked better than wishing on paper. "They are different doors," she said. "Both open if you use the handle gently."

Mr. Cavanaugh came to stand beside her granddaughter, who held the lighter with steady hands. He looked older than he had yesterday. "Your great-grandfather lit mine," he told Rosalie, not loudly. "When I was seven. I spilled wax on my shoe and cried." He managed a smile that painted itself well on his face despite disuse. "He told me, *we forgive shoes.* Maybe we could forgive...more."

"We could," Rosalie said, and she did not make him work for the mercy of the agreement.

Miriam watched the symbol hold. The town hadn't broken; it had shifted into its familiar storm argument as comfort, accusation as remembered choreography. But below the choreography lay a possibility she had not yet seen Cedar Creek permit itself at scale: to be told something in public and to accept the telling without turning it into a weapon or a proof. It was work. It would always be work. But the work felt closer than it had been at dawn.

Behind her, Julian returned, eyes bright and task list forming like condensation. "We'll need to record the mark's exact orientation," he said, "and ask Sloane for stakes farther out so no one steps where the current keeps the silt clear. I'll bring the ledger page to the table so people can see that sometimes our records stutter before our rituals do."

"Good," she said. "And maybe we move the rest of the speeches to this afternoon. The room has changed."

"This is the room now," he said, with no complaint. "We live here."

They looked at each other the way you do when you both hear a sound and you both know, without talking about it then, that the survival of the next week will depend on the quality of your listening. Then the choir director, recognizing that the green needed a friend, led the town in a verse that did not pretend to know what had happened but did know what to ask for: *Make us one.* The shape of the vowel on *one* carried over the rope, over the stand, over the dock, to the seam. The water accepted the note without changing any of its own plans. It does that; it is not offended by us.

Panic did not take the day. Panic tried. But the town had built too many tables in too many storms to let panic run the whole meal. Instead, unease set a chair and sat down like a relative you don't trust and can't quite disinvite. The symbol floated a fraction clearer as the sun lifted. Sloane finished the rope run and wiped her hands on her jeans with the air of a woman who knew good work is the only comfort worth trusting when the universe reschedules your morning.

Miriam, who had felt the tug beneath the bright for a week, felt now the tug become direction. It pointed backward as much as forward toward the people who'd dreamed before her and toward the paper she'd kept at the bottom of a drawer because grief had made her cautious with inheritances. She did not, yet, say the name she had for the curve. Saying it would make it smaller than what the river meant. Better to sit with it until it told them how to speak.

By ELEVEN, the green recovered its balance like a person who has stumbled and declined to turn the stumble into performance. The food lines formed nervous chewing is still chewing and the kids rehearsed the lantern walk with a seriousness that saved the rest of them from having to. Sheriff Mayhew loitered within eyesight without looking like surveillance. The choir split to ferry casseroles to elders who insisted on staying at the rope. The basin remained where it was, not punished by its refusal, only resting until Sloane and the carriers decided what to ask of it next.

Julian went to the museum and returned with the ledger page in a protective sleeve, a copy of the carpenter's drawing, and the small mica panel with its tentative pencil start that had felt like a message when they first saw it. He laid them at the museum table with the humility of someone arranging a family photo for a visitation. People drifted through, peered, whispered, asked him to tell the story again, asked if he thought it connected to the mark in the shallows. "We don't know yet," he said, scrupulous as you have to be when a story has started telling itself in several directions. "But the carpenter stopped his hand twice. And the clerk's neat lines stumbled here." He let them see without forcing them to agree.

Miriam excused herself and walked to her shop. The river had set her a task, and the task required a key. She climbed the stairs to the apartment, an air quieter than the green receiving her without complaint, and knelt at the trunk under the window where she kept what had come to her from her great-aunt a tangle of ribbons and letters and a blue shawl that still smelled faintly of someone who had taught her to say the blessing over candles before she could spell *blessing.*

She knew the letter she wanted. It had a water stain that perfectly matched a day two summers ago when grief and rain had visited together without appointment. She slid the paper free, unfolded it along the old crease, and read words she already knew by mouth: *When the town forgets its first promise, the water remembers. It will empty what we fill until we see what we buried. Do not be afraid when it does. The point is not punishment. It is repair. When the sign appears, stand near it with kindness and with a voice that knows how to speak "we."*

Her great-aunt had written in a hand that respected curves more than corners. In the margin she had drawn not the symbol, not exactly, because she had never claimed to be a seer but a line that began, curved, paused. A hesitation made into counsel. *Say less,* the tiny script said below it. *Listen more.*

Miriam pressed her fingers to the page the way you do when you greet the dead who have also, somehow, arrived early. She felt her chest echo the river's motion breathe in, breathe out, and in the second breath find room to add a truth without choking on it. She folded the letter back, slid it into its envelope, and carried it with both caution and ease, the way you carry a cup of something that can burn if you rush.

When she returned to the green, Julian saw the envelope and did not ask. He waited the way good men wait when love is required to do two jobs at once: guard and serve. Pastor Elijah drifted near on a vector calculated by long practice; he had a talent for being useful without being in the way. "We will move the speeches," he said. "This afternoon, in the shade of the cottonwood. No microphone. We'll speak into a circle and see if we can mean it."

"We can," she said. "If we remember why we came."

"We came because the river is good at reminding," he said, and smiled a smile that didn't pretend to have answers, which made it the most pastoral thing he'd done all day.

They walked together to the rope. A woman Miriam recognized only as someone who knew how to choose plums stood and cried without making noise. Miriam handed her a paper napkin because paper is sometimes better than hands. "It's beautiful," the woman said, embarrassed by her own honesty. "And frightening. I don't know what to call it."

"Don't call it anything yet," Miriam said. "Tell it what you felt. It can use that."

The woman nodded, reassured that experience counts as currency in economies where names are not legal tender.

Mr. Cavanaugh approached, hat in hand in a way that rewrote three weeks of posture. "Ms. Adler," he said, then cleared his throat and faced Rosalie because that was the correct vector for apology. "We will do better at listening before we lift. The way you held that flame well. It taught me. I act like lifting is the only work there is."

"It's one of them," Rosalie said, not softening the words and not needing to. "We've got others."

"Teach me," he said simply, and the town's air changed by a degree you could not register on a gauge. You felt it, though. You always feel it when an old rivalry unclenches long enough to pass a cup.

Julian joined Miriam at the rope with a quiet that meant he had moved one set of tasks forward and was ready to put his shoulder to the next. "The ledger's crowding with fingers," he said, amused and watchful. "But people are reading the notes. You can see them love the idea that a clerk got interrupted. It gives them permission not to get it right the first time."

"He didn't," she said. "We aren't."

The symbol lay in its groove, lit now in a more perfect angle by the sun that had decided to help. The completed curve was not ornate. It was almost stubborn in its simplicity, the kind of line a child might have drawn and a master might have left alone. It could have been an initial, a sign for *and*, a piece of a larger pattern. It could have been a letter in a language the town had once spoken and forgotten how.

Miriam let her eyes go unfocused so the scene layered itself the stone, the water, the reflection of the rope's line, the faint shimmer of silt making up its mind to move or stay. In that softened gaze, she saw again what she had seen under raking light on the carpenter's page: *almost* wanting to become *is*. She heard, clear as the voice in her kitchen that tells her when bread is done, the phrase her great-aunt had written: *When the town forgets its first promise, the water remembers.*She understood in her bones the difference between threat and invitation. This was invitation. It said: *Bring out what you hid, not to shame it but to set it among us correctly.*

"Chains," she murmured, without intending to speak. "Breaking."

Julian's head turned toward her, question asked by eyelids rather than mouth.

"In the dream," she said. "And now here. The first expression." She rarely reached for overt theology in public spaces because she had learned that for some people God is a cudgel, for others a bruise. But the words rose and did not hurt anyone. "*I will bring you out.* It isn't always a hand pulling you. Sometimes it's a door opening where you never thought the wall would soften."

"From what?" he asked, not pressing.

"From the story we've been telling that protects us from the true one."

He received it like he received artifacts: no rush, no cult of certainty, no need to make it less strange than it was. "Then we'll need more chairs," he said. "A true story draws a crowd."

She smiled, grateful for his way of translating mysticism into logistics. "And better bread."

"Always better bread."

They stood long enough for the symbol to become ordinary and then, because that is how you keep a wonder from being cheapened, they turned away to do the work that keeps a town able to hold both wonder and lunch. Miriam took the lantern volunteers to the west path and taught them how to fan and leave the center clear. Julian walked the green to ask nervous old men to tell nervous young men about the time the river flooded the bakery and everyone learned how to make loaves in the neighbor's oven. Pastor Elijah gathered small circles and said out loud the sentence *We do not have to finish deciding today.*

By late afternoon the basin had dried completely. The cedar did not warp; Sloane blessed it in her practical way by oiling a seam with a rag and a mindfulness that looks, in public, like maintenance and, in private, like prayer. Sheriff Mayhew signed a paper that said in stern language what Miriam had said kindly: *Near and slow.* The mayor stopped talking and fetched folding chairs without being told which way the seat should face and did not get it wrong.

As the light left, the symbol held. It would hold through

dusk and into a night when paper lanterns, each with wishes tucked or spoken, made their patient parade along the seam. Children would point and whisper and, occasionally, test the strength of the rope because bodies are designed to test boundaries for both safety and fun. Elders would sigh, some with relief, some with recognition, a few with the ache that comes when a pain you've learned to carry asks to be set down where others can see it. The choir would carry the softest verse over the water like bread.

Miriam went home just long enough to wash her hands and touch the blue shawl and tell the empty room, "Thank you for the warning," because gratitude is a discipline that makes room for the next day's surprise. When she came back out, Julian was at the museum table, the mica panel catching the last stripe of sun. He lifted his head as if he had felt her across the grass and smiled in a way that said nothing performative out loud and everything sustaining under it: *We're in this together.*

They walked toward the dock as the lantern walk began, four abreast, slow, quiet, faces turned toward light the way plants do even when no one has told them that's what they were made for. When the line passed the rope, the symbol took their glow and did nothing with it but accept. That acceptance was more moving than any miracle she'd been taught to look for as a child.

At the very end, after the last child had whispered a wish and the last father had picked up a dropped paper shade and returned it to the team without getting credit for saving the world, after Sloane had turned off the generator and the moon had decided to show up for its shift, Miriam and Julian stood a minute longer at the edge. The water was very dark. The stone was very still. Somewhere, a heron made the sound a hinge makes when it works.

"What do we do tomorrow?" he asked.

"We do what we always do," she said. "We look. We listen. We lift together. And we go where the water shows."

"And we find who put the rock there," he said, because history has its own appetites.

"And we find why," she said, because meaning does too.

She reached for his hand again and found it easily as if his hand had been there in the air a second before hers decided to close. In the joined quiet, she could feel the town thinking. It was not a comfortable thinking; comfort comes later if at all. It was a thinking that sounded like ropes tightening the right amount, like chairs opening without pinched fingers, like a committee remembering to be human, like the first dough ready at dawn because somebody had risen before the sun and decided to tend what fed everyone equally.

The river moved. The symbol did not dim. Her great-aunt's warning had been less about danger than about readiness; less about being spared than about being summoned to participate. *Do not be afraid when it does. The point is not punishment. It is repair.* Miriam took that into the place inside her where she stored instructions for living that had proved themselves in both storm and quiet. She would need it for Chapter 5 and for every chapter that followed, because what water begins, a town must learn to continue.

Behind them, the basil in the planter outside her shop released pepper into the night. Ahead, the seam shone where two bodies made one without erasing themselves. She and Julian let their hands fall and walked back across the green to where Sloane waited with a list and Pastor Elijah waited with a story and Rosalie waited with a flame balanced like a promise. The basin emptied to teach them shone a little with the oil where Sloane had blessed it with cloth.

"Tomorrow," Julian said.

"Tomorrow," Miriam answered, and the word did not feel like postponement. It felt like consent.

Above them, the lanterns found their gentle sway. Below, the carved curve held its quiet. Between those two, the town rehearsed how to be brave and kind in public. The river approved in the only way it knows how: it kept moving and made room.

And Miriam, who had felt the tug for days, felt it again not warning now, but invitation pulling her toward the work already laid out under the lights, toward the ledger and the letter and the stone, toward the long labor of bringing out what is truer than the stories that have kept us safe and small. She nodded to no one and to everything and went to join the others in the ordinary magic of putting away chairs.

5

WHISPERS IN THE SQUARE

By midmorning the square had turned into that particular kind of newsroom only small towns know how to staff no desks, no masthead, just clusters of people standing in half-shade, trading versions. The bakery chalkboard, usually devoted to scones and the moral superiority of cardamom, had surrendered its top line to Sloane's clear print: **BASIN NOT LEAKING. PLEASE BE KIND.** Someone added, smaller: **Try the pear tart anyway.**

Miriam came in sideways the way you come into a conversation already in progress paper cup warming one hand, the other free to carry what the day pressed into it. She didn't intend to correct anyone. You couldn't fact-check a feeling, and what was moving through Cedar Creek wasn't an absence of information; it was a surplus of fear trying on voices to see which one would carry farthest.

"You can't tell me it wasn't sabotage," a man at the coffee cart was saying, loud because certainty runs on volume. "Why else would it drain *during* the blessing? Timing like that isn't natural."

"You mean sacred?" the barista offered without sarcasm.

She had the bone-deep calm of a person who had witnessed the full human catalog before noon shifts. "Or you mean suspicious?"

"Silly," his companion said, affectionate and annoyed in equal measure. "Everything's suspicious to you. It's a sign."

"Of what?"

"That we're all being watched."

"By who?"

She sipped and moved on, letting their ping-pong exchange do its familiar labor of turning anxiety into banter. Two teenagers on the bench by the fountain pushed rumors toward currency. "My uncle says in 1902 a preacher cursed it because his fiancée broke the engagement." "That wasn't 1902," the other said with authority borrowed from nowhere. "It was 1899, and it was a lumber strike." Across from them, Mrs. Alvarez's clipboard conducted traffic like a wand, checks blooming next to boxes as if reassurance could be written into existence.

At the green's edge, the beekeeper sold honey with the air of a woman who had read Ecclesiastes and taken it to heart. "If you want the clover, you'll have to give me back last year's jar," she told Mack from the hardware store. "That's how we remember we live here by returning what isn't broken." He obliged, shaking his head. "Town empties a basin and the economy shifts to a glass-jar standard."

Sheriff Mayhew, eternally twenty minutes into a nap he would never take, stood close enough to the rope to read mood but far enough to let it be. He'd pinned a sheet to a cork board that said **NO WATER CONTACT TODAY NEAR & SLOW** and answered the twentieth variation on *Is the river safe?* with the same steady tone that made dogs love him and drunks resent him mildly.

The museum had set out a portable lectern and a pair of

framed copies: the ledger page with the stuttered entries, the carpenter's drawing with its half-curve like a thought you could almost make out. Julian fielded questions with the patience of a man who had walked students back from more cliffs than the public knew. He told the 1902 story not as a relic but as a reminder that the long song sometimes repeats a bar when the choir forgets their place. He did not name the mark. He did not need to.

Miriam took the square as a map and walked its intersections: the north corner where the choir director was hushing herself by humming; the bench where two elders traded memories about a flood and found themselves forgiving each other for something small and old; the pop-up radio booth where Confluence FM aired a live segment titled *Rivers Unscripted* and Pastor Elijah said exactly what you say when you know any adjective will be misquoted "We'll go near. We'll go slow."

Whispers, she noticed, had families. One line ran through curses and old vows and a sense that the river had been insulted. Another threaded practical suspicion holes, valves, the municipal water intake that a man insisted had "gotten uppity." A third drifted toward inheritance: *our family always* and *their family never*. The fourth made a straight road to shame and parked there, engine idling if the town had failed its promise, what else were they failing without knowing?

She didn't try to braid them. Braiding made pretty things and she wasn't in the market for pretty. She gathered them the way you gather river stones one from each bend, slick from their own running and set them where she could feel their weight without turning them into weapons.

"Ms. Adler!" The call came from the vintage store owner who curated nostalgia with the zeal of a monk and the hustle of a talent agent. "Do we cancel the lantern rehearsal for tonight?"

"Not unless the wind tells us to," she said. "And we'd better ask the wind nicely."

"Good," the woman said, relief visible in her shoulders. "People need to carry light when the day confuses them."

"They do," Miriam agreed.

Near the fountain, someone had scrawled in sidewalk chalk: **LET THE RIVER DECIDE** and below it a child hand had added **NO RUNNING** because rules, like hope, are a habit learned young. Rosalie passed with a bag of votives and the particular dignity of someone carrying light for use, not display. Mr. Cavanaugh's granddaughter walked with her, jaws set in that brave teenage determination that grows when adults make an effort at repair.

At her shop, Miriam propped the door open and carried out a tray of unscented candles and a hand-lettered sign: **TAKE WHAT YOU NEED. LEAVE WHAT YOU CAN.** People obeyed the spirit more reliably than the letter; some left crumpled bills, one left a small river-polished shard of blue glass signed on a Post-it "For brightness." She put the glass in the window where the sun could make it practice.

Her phone buzzed. *Museum line doubling. Docents doing triage. J.* She slid it away. He had joy in his work even today. That joy wasn't frivolous; it was a craft. He could shepherd a crowd toward attention without raising his voice or his pulse and still make room beside him at the table he set for the past. She would join him later. For now, the square needed ears.

By the hardware store window, two men took turns being certain. "You know they've been hinting at changing the ritual for years." "Who's *they*?" "Don't be willfully naive."

"I'm not willfully anything. I'm tired." "Well, that's where they get you."

"Where who gets who?"

He flapped a hand in the universal gesture for the permanent enemy who shapeshifts to match your suspicion. She walked on. Not every knot needed her fingers.

At the coffee cart again, an elder stood aside while a young mother negotiated both stroller and latte and failed at neither. "You were a child during the last one," the elder said to no one in particular. "Do you remember?"

"I remember being told never to tell," the man behind her said. "That it upset the water to talk about it. That kind of forgetting grows mold."

The barista turned to Miriam as she passed, raised her brows in a question that carried several sub-questions and a hope that a friend could answer them. Miriam shook her head no certainties, yes presence and the barista nodded back and set another cup down with the gentleness you reserve for fragile things and mornings after.

At the county table, Sheriff Mayhew had begun collecting names for an informal "tell me what you saw" list with the promise no one would be dragged into anything they didn't consent to. "I just want records," he said into his clipboard to a woman who needed to be reassured that record-spells didn't turn into interrogations. "I don't make them testify."

A pickup rolled by, loud muffler telegraphing opinion. Its passenger leaned out just long enough to shout, "Put it back in the church!" and then they were gone, leaving behind an exhaust cloud that turned to a smell and then to nothing. The shout prompted three people to agree, two to argue, and one to ask the question quietly: "Would the church do a better job at listening?"

"The church is the people," Pastor Elijah said later, with a smile that gave the sentence more grace than a scold would.

Noon came and made choices: half the town lined up for tacos, the other half argued in line for tacos, a subset of both turned their attention to the symbol in the shallows because it demanded a kind of looking that made you breathe slower and, eventually, say less. Miriam bought two hand pies and, on impulse, three jars of honey: clover, blackberry, wildflower. "Insurance," she told the beekeeper, who nodded gravely as if invited to co-sign a policy on collective sanity.

She ate one pie sitting on the courthouse steps and read the text from her great-aunt again, not the words on the page she kept in the envelope in her pocket, but the sentence that had moved into her like lodger-kin: *When a town forgets its first promise, the water remembers.* The second part of the sentence, unspoken in the letter but clear in the day's behavior, added itself: *and then it makes us remember together or not at all.*

By the time she crossed back to the museum table, Cedar Creek had taught itself the morning's news in a dozen dialects. The first draft was messy. It was also honest about its edges. That counted. That would count more later.

"Reporters called," Julian said when she reached him. "From the city. I told them the town will say its own name before anyone else does." He'd put a sheet out for people who wanted to bring family letters or diaries to scan. "If the water is remembering," the sign read in his careful block print, "maybe our boxes will, too."

She touched his forearm in thanks. Their eyes agreed on a handful of things at once the beauty of the mark, the ache in people's throats, the work ahead that was not just research or ritual but the long practice of letting a community be found telling the truth in public. Then she went to stand in the line at the rope and listen to the rumors sing their scales.

THE FIRST FLARE came with lunch: a man with a clipboard and the confident body language of a petition pressuring signatures for *RETURN THE BASIN TO THE CHURCH STEPS*. He positioned himself between kettle corn and lemonade for maximum foot traffic and a steady sugar supply of righteousness. When Pastor Elijah passed, he didn't scold; he bought a lemonade and added a polite footnote. "The basin was built to travel," he said, "and we would do better to travel with it."

"That's not a signature," the man said.

"It's a suggestion," the pastor said, and moved on.

Twenty minutes later another petition sprouted a dozen yards away: *KEEP THE BLESSING AT THE RIVER SHARE THE CARRY*. Rosalie refused to sign either and taught two middle-schoolers how to say no like a blessing. "Thank you for asking," she coached, and the children practiced until the word lovely sat in the space where the word annoyed had wanted to stand.

The rumor mill shifted into high gear. Accusations sharpened. "Of course it happened when *they* were in charge of the flame." "We weren't in charge; we were involved." "Same thing." At the hardware store, a man announced that the rope had "mysteriously slackened" and then had to accept Sloane's calm correction that ropes sag at noon and would be retightened at two because physics doesn't care about human drama.

An alderman floated the word *postpone* for the evening lantern walk and caught so much pushback he backpedaled in a clumsy tap dance that resembled apology. "Safety," he insisted. "We like safety, don't we?" "We do," Mrs. Alvarez said sweetly, "and it's safe to say our children need the walk more than you need to feel heroic canceling it."

Someone started a group text titled *Basin Truths* that immediately filled with pictures, exclamation points, and a misplaced enthusiasm for labels. A newcomer from downriver posted about a chemical leak upriver last fall and ignited a flurry of outrage that Sheriff Mayhew extinguished in thirty seconds with a printed statement from the county water board: **INTAKE NORMAL NO IMPACT PLEASE STOP EMAILING US AT 3 A.M.** The official sarcasm made people laugh, a useful pressure valve.

A thin spiral of outsiders drifted in two paranormal enthusiasts who wanted to rent a kayak; a history blogger filming b-roll of the fort; a podcaster whose tone suggested he hoped for tears. Julian intercepted with the softest version of museum authority he possessed and folded them into the "near and slow" instructions without using the word *no.* Watching him give curiosity a place to sit without letting it crash the table, Miriam thought again how much of love is simply making room for what might arrive without letting it burn the house down.

By two, the museum looked like a kindly DMV line snaking, numbers called, docents triaging. The scanning station Julian had improvised from two lamps, a wool blanket, and a copier feeder began to collect family papers as if the act of carrying them into the square could lean the town toward cooperation. A woman handed over a bundle tied with faded ribbon. "My great-grandmother wrote down recipes and births and one story I never understood," she said. "Maybe it belongs here now." A man brought a tool casually at first, then with reverence when Julian recognized the rope splice and asked permission to display it beside the photograph of the boatman who had taught the knot. "He was my grandfather," the man said, a little stunned to hear himself say it.

The mall of opinions hummed at the courthouse steps. "Form a task force," the mayor said to anyone with a pulse, and the square sighed like a room whose furniture had been moved one too many times. "We already have one," Sloane said later when asked privately. "It's called *literally everyone,* and fortunately it doesn't report to you."

On Cedar Thread, the town's digital gathering place, threads proliferated. **Basin hoax???** got ratioed into oblivion by grandmothers with the rhetorical gifts of appellate lawyers. **We need to protect our kids** ran a long course that ended in an actual plan with names assigned: crossing guards, extra lantern shepherds, a lost-and-found table. **If this is a curse, how do we lift it** spun toward the practical. "If the curse is fear," Miriam typed gently from the staff room while her tea steeped unattended, "we lift it by telling the truth together and deciding to be kind in public even when we're frightened." The thread went quiet in the way threads do when you've said the sentence people were trying to remember.

The friction did what friction does: it threatened to burn. In the line at the taco truck, a Cavanaugh cousin and a LeClair aunt squared off and then, at the exact moment the salsa ladle hovered over both plates, decided neither of them was in the mood to spoil lunch with inherited anger. "You can go ahead," the aunt said. "No, after you," the cousin said, and the salsa became, briefly, sacrament.

That small mercy held long enough for a larger one to set. Pastor Elijah, true to his morning promise, moved the afternoon speeches into a circle under the cottonwood. No microphone, no dais, just people standing when they had something worth the square's time, and sitting when they'd said enough. You could feel the square's shoulders loosen. Even the petition man drifted closer and listened hard enough to forget to collect signatures for a while.

The circle didn't fix anything; it isn't what circles do. What it did was mark a boundary around what the town agreed to hold: facts where they had them, feelings where they didn't, questions that would not be rushed into shabby answers. Julian spoke once short, clear, putting dates to stories. Sloane spoke once practical and funny, announcing that anyone who tried to unclip the rope would be recruited to *reclip the rope twelve times a day for the rest of their natural life*. Rosalie spoke once tender and firm about how ritual without humility turns to theater. Mr. Cavanaugh spoke once carefully, unhandsomely, with a sincerity that improved his posture. Miriam did not speak. She would, later, when the moment asked for her voice. Today, the square had enough voices trying to do good work. Her contribution was to keep listening until the sound under the sound resolved to a note she trusted.

By late afternoon, escalation had found its ceiling. The square had learned how loud it wanted to be. The petitions thinned, the taco line shortened, the rumor threads cooled into neighborly debate. The river kept its patient counsel. The symbol in the shallows loop completed, stroke sure took the late light and gave it back as shadow. Even panic, faced with the town's refusal to make it the day's star, gave up and wandered off to nap.

IN THE HOUR between bustle and lanterns, when shops switch their lights from fluorescent to flattering and the air cools just enough to make you remember your shoulders, Miriam sat on the lip of the fountain and let the square pour its last run of whispers through her. She had learned, over the years, to hear beneath words the small percussion of motive the muffled drum of fear, the fragile tambourine of hope, the wooden clack of habit, the oiled hinge of a new thought deciding to open. Today, four distinct rhythms had kept time.

First: the fear of being erased. It wore many faces petition man and teen bench, a grandmother's sigh, a cousin's glare but the music was the same: *If we change the ritual, we will lose our part in it.* Tradition can be the cloth that keeps a table warm; it can also be the table someone uses to keep others standing. People were not wrong to want to keep their seats. They were wrong when they mistook seat for belonging.

Second: the fear of being exposed. She'd heard it in the way some voices kept asking *who?* as if a name could plug the hole through which discomfort seeped. If someone could be blamed, perhaps the water's refusal would be less a mirror and more a target. But the stone hadn't given them a villain. It had given them a mark. The town's craving for a culprit was a way to avoid the older conversation: *What did we bury and why?*

Third: the fear of incompetence. Not in the sense of "we are clumsy," but in the deeper sense of "maybe we don't know how to be the kind of people this moment requires." That one she felt in her own bones, too. The cure for it was never mastery. It was consent to learn in public.

Fourth: the fear of punishment disguised as piety. This one braided shame and scripture and would, if left alone, convince a town to grovel before a river instead of learning to listen to it. Miriam could feel that old temptation moving through Cedar Creek like a fog that some personalities loved to live inside: *We are bad. That's why this happened.* That was a story that made sense because it made pain useful. The harder story asked: *What if we aren't being punished? What if we're being invited to repair?*

She stood and crossed to the museum table. Julian had been fielding a steady stream of "does this matter?" and finding ways to say yes that were both true and generous. He slipped her the pen to sign a stack of permission slips and, when their hands met, the square receded to a low hum. "How are you?" he asked, not as a greeting but as a reading.

"Listening," she said. "They're scared of being erased, exposed, incompetent, and punished."

"Four chairs," he said, not missing a beat. "We set them out so we know who's talking."

"We add a fifth," she said. "For curiosity, so it doesn't have to sit alone on the curb."

He tipped his head, smiling in that way that made his eyes confess the exact measure of his pleasure. "You going to say that under the cottonwood?"

"Not today," she said. "Today the square needs to hear itself. Tonight, maybe, we ask it to hear what's under that."

"Tonight," he said, as if he were saying *amen.*

The lantern walk gathered like breath and then released itself onto the west path, four wide, then two, then a string, then a slow, quiet river of faces lit from within and without. Miriam walked near the rope with the other shepherds and watched the town choose to be gentle with itself. You could call that romance and you would not be wrong. You could call it civic hygiene and you would not be wrong either.

At the rope, a boy tugged her sleeve. "Is it a letter?" he asked, pointing at the symbol, hushed as children are in the presence of older things. "It looks like it wants to spell something."

"It might be the part of a word that means *and*," she said. "The part that ties two things together."

"Like me and Ashlyn," he said, scandalized and thrilled by his own courage, and the girl next to him punched his shoulder in the exact ratio of delight to denial. Behind them, a pair of elders stood arm in arm and said nothing and said everything.

The square's psyche, if such a thing can be said to have a shape, felt less like a crowd today and more like a single body practicing a new posture. The old muscle memory accuse, defend, retreat had raised its head, snorted, pawed the dirt. But the day had taught it another option: hold the tension without choosing a lie to relieve it. Cedar Creek could be brave like that for an hour. Could it be brave like that for a week? A month? Miriam didn't know. People's courage tended to arrive in bursts, then set down to pant and look for water. She hoped the river would be kind to the town's stamina. She thought it might. Rivers prefer steadiness over spectacle.

At the cottonwood, when the lanterns had found their sway and the food trucks had shifted appetites from hunger to dessert, Pastor Elijah asked for three minutes and got silence without a gavel. "We are going to practice a thing," he said simply. "It's called *we will not decide too soon*. We'll tell what we saw. We'll name what we fear. We'll remember what we promised each other when we built this town by the place where two bodies of water agree. Then we will sleep and try again."

He nodded to Miriam not a summons, not a stage cue, just a permission. She stood because the square had reached that point in its song where another voice could braid in without tangling the line. "When I was a child," she said, "I thought promise meant keeping a thing exactly the same forever. Now I think promise means staying in the room when the truth arrives."

There were no applause lines built into the sentence and no applause followed, which pleased her. People stood still, a better response. They needed that steadiness more than they needed the relief of noise.

After, she drifted to the edge and took the long way back to the rope. On Main, her shop's window held the shard of blue glass in the last light. Upstairs, in the trunk, her great-aunt's letter waited with the patient weight of bequeathed work. She felt no urge to quote it to the town like scripture; the page wasn't a spell. It was an instruction to pay attention without dramatizing the attention a subtle craft most communities struggle to learn because someone's always trying to get extra credit for noticing first.

Julian found her on the dock stairs and sat, leaving exactly as much space between their knees as the week could afford. "I've been thinking about that ledger," he said. "About the clerk who almost wrote a note and then didn't."

"He wasn't ready to say it out loud," she said.

"He was ready to write it down," Julian countered, and she loved him then for being the kind of man who trusted ink to teach people courage. "Maybe he figured someone downriver would read it when the room could bear it."

"The room can bear it," she said. "We can bear it."

"We can work for it," he said, correcting the tense like a historian guarding against hubris.

They watched a lantern try to lift, fail, and then succeed because a pair of hands cupped it against the breeze. That was the lesson, probably. Not that miracles were disallowed.

Not that ritual was a game. Just that help is not the antonym of holiness.

Behind them, in the square, petition man had fallen into a conversation with the woman who'd cried without noise and they were, against all odds, laughing together at the way toddlers like to throw bread at ducks not from cruelty but from an unshakeable faith in sharing. In front of them, the symbol held. If you squinted, you could imagine the stroke had thickened by a hair, but that was likely the sun's last trick.

"What do you hear under it now?" Julian asked. He didn't mean the crowd; he meant the town's quieter instrument.

"A memory waking up," she said. "Not a curse. Not a show. A memory asking us to stop pretending we can be a town without telling the truth in public."

"And the truth is…?"

"That we made a promise and buried part of it," she said. "That we can dig it up without destroying each other."

He let the hope sit between them like a match not yet struck. Hope, too, thrives on oxygen and consent.

When the walk ended and the children trailed home smelling like paper and sugar and the river's particular damp, when Sloane began her late shift of checking ties and gathering trash and answering the same four questions one more time, when Pastor Elijah escorted two tired grandfathers to the same car by mistake and made it funny, when the choir director finally allowed herself a slice of pie and the gift of one small expletive said into her napkin when the square exhaled its long day into night, Miriam slipped back to her shop and wrote four words on a page she would tuck into the trunk beside the letter: **We will stay present.**

Then she turned out the light and went downstairs and

stood one more time where the river had pulled them all to stand. The mark held its easy dignity. The basin, newly oiled by Sloane's cloth, gleamed like a tool put away without resentment. She could feel, in the dark, that the town had turned a small corner. Not the corner. A corner big enough to count.

Tomorrow there would be investigations and interviews and fresh annoyances. There would be practicalities permitting, signage, porta-potties, pies. There would be more versions, some kinder, some less. The square would continue to teach itself the news. But tonight Cedar Creek had remembered, at least a little, what work it was for. Not only making a festival. Making a *we* that could endure its own history and choose to repair it with something other than blame.

On her way up the stairs she looked back once, not to fix anything with her eyes but to tell the night she was paying attention. The river didn't answer. It rarely does. It simply made room, as if to say: *Bring it out when you're ready. I'll keep moving.*

6

COFFEE WITH JULIAN

The chalkboard over the counter had been revised twice before eight. First it said **TODAY: PEAR TART RETURNS.** Then someone added **BASIN NOT LEAKING. PLEASE BE KIND.** By the time Miriam pushed the Riverlight Café door with her shoulder, another hand had scrawled **CARDAMOM BUNS SOLVE 65% OF PROBLEMS** in a hopeful curve.

The bell made its small confession. Morning gathered around the low tables in incarnations of Cedar Creek contractor boots; a toddler distributing sugar packets like communion; the choir director with a pen behind her ear; the radio host from Confluence FM nursing a drink he called tea and everyone else called water with an alibi. Light came in from the square and divided itself on the floorboards. The café smelled like mercy.

Julian was already there. Not at their usual table by the window too visible today but at the back, under a hook where someone had hung a wool coat that kept forgetting winter was over. He stood when he saw her, then remembered old habits weren't necessary and sat again, awkward enough to make something warm unfurl in her chest.

"Thank you," he said when she reached him. As if she'd rearranged the weather.

"For what?"

"For being the person I thought of when my stomach invented new ways to complain."

"Good," she said. "Let's feed it reasons to be quiet."

He smiled quickly and then not at all. This was a different version of him than the public curator who had moved like water through yesterday's questions. He looked not wrecked he wasn't the wrecking type but as if his edges had rubbed thin on something he hadn't seen coming.

The barista arrived with the ease of a person who'd been told exactly what to bring. "One reckless-milk with honey," she said to Miriam, "and one grown-up black for Mr. Roth, who asked me to be brave on his behalf." She set down a plate of cardamom buns, because solving 65% of problems was still forty points better than most committees managed by noon. "I can run interference for ten minutes if you need it. After that, the town will remember this door is not, technically, a portcullis."

"We'll take ten," Miriam said. "Bless you."

When they were alone again, or the closest thing to alone the Riverlight Café ever allowed, Julian pressed his palms flat on either side of his cup and stared into a black that did not blink. "I'm embarrassed," he said. "I am the historical society called it 'featured in regional media' and I am embarrassed."

"For ?"

"For enjoying my work," he said, frustrated by himself most of all. "For liking the artifact table and the scanning station and the part where a story catches and people lean in. For liking it while the river did a thing we don't comprehend and the square did a thing we know too well." He huffed a laugh without pleasure. "History became scandal on my watch. I don't know why that feels like a failure, but it does."

"It feels like exposure," she said. "We're trained to believe the good kind doesn't exist."

He looked at her finally, eyes darker than coffee. "You mean vulnerability."

"I mean honesty that happens in public," she said. "It's allergic to tidy. It still counts."

He slouched back enough to be a different shape. "My mother would disagree," he said softly, the words like a long-handled tool he hadn't used in years. "She believed the world is better for ironed shirts, arranged spoons, respectable mysteries. Her gentleness was discipline. She told me once that other people's discomfort is never the point, which in practice meant we avoided it at all costs." He touched the small crescent scar near his temple, that familiar pale comma. "I learned to catalog what I could and keep quiet where I couldn't. I liked that version of the world. It looked a lot like order."

"And yesterday didn't," Miriam said.

"Not at all."

She broke a bun and pushed half toward him. "Then it's a new practice. You can like order and still stand next to a thing that refuses it."

"It refuses me," he said, a confession he hadn't meant to make but trusted her with. "The river, I mean. It chose a morning when I had notes and a lectern and a plan. I looked like a man surprised in his own house."

She pictured him there palm on cedar, mind already outlining a paragraph for the museum log when the water began to leave. Courage, she'd decided years ago, had very little to do with being ready. Courage belonged to the person who stayed. "You stayed," she said.

"I had tape and docents," he said. "That's not heroism; that's inventory."

"It's one kind of heroism," she said. "Paper, tape, a willing spine. You kept people near and slow. That's what the square needed."

He shook his head, embarrassed again but this time at the compliment. "I felt performative. Like one of those TV historians who narrate disasters with very clean hair."

"You are impossible to film," she said gravely. "You squint at truth until it confesses. Cameras hate that."

He laughed then, the sound releasing something from his shoulders. "I'm worried I dragged you into it," he said. "Into the glare. Yesterday people kept looking at me and then at you, like we were cause-and-effect. You were good with them and I was "

"You were good with them," she said. "And if the town saw us as a pair, it may be because we stood next to each other on purpose."

He didn't look away this time. "We did."

"And the work is easier when we divide it," she said. "You keep the notes on paper. I keep the notes in people. When the room needs both we stand shoulder to shoulder and hope it's enough."

"It might be," he said. "If we get to keep this table."

"We don't," she said, nodding toward the door where silhouettes were already accumulating like weather. "We have eight minutes left."

He lifted his cup, drank, and winced the way men do when they refuse to admit they like milk better than bravery.

"Then tell me something true," he said, like a dare he wanted her to win.

She considered telling him about the envelope in her pocket, her great-aunt's letter, the sentence that had become a spine. She considered telling him about the dream two nights ago the chain at the bottom of a river, the sound of breaking that wasn't violence but release. She considered telling him that when he speaks about rounding out a story until it is sturdy enough to stand, she thinks of his hands on her shoulders. She told him something adjacent. "It isn't going to get quieter," she said. "Not soon. The square will keep singing its versions. The symbol will sit there and ask us to be people who can be told a thing together. The worst thing we could do is pretend we know more than we do."

"And the second worst?" he asked.

"Pretend we know nothing," she said. "So we can avoid the work."

He looked down at the half-bun he hadn't touched and tore off a piece like repentance. "I can do work."

"I know," she said. "That's why I'm here."

They ate then, in the small meaningful silence that falls over people who have agreed to the next hour. The barista angled herself like a human windbreak between their table and the square because kindness is architecture, too. For nearly the whole allotment of mercy, the town obeyed the implied velvet rope. Then the bell announced a change in barometric pressure, and the door became what it always becomes when fear remembers its manners are optional: a portal.

"Mr. Roth?" A woman in a windbreaker stepped in and kept stepping. She had a microphone with a foam cover the color of warning. "Do you have a minute for Confluence FM? Our listeners are..."

"Curious," he said, standing with the practiced warmth of a man who refuses to add rudeness to a day already packed. "We all are."

"And Ms. Adler," said petition man from yesterday, arriving in the wake of the microphone as reliably as driftwood after rain. "Since you were up there with the pastor how long before you and your friend admit the basin's compromised?"

"Sixty-five percent of problems solved by cardamom buns," the barista intoned, sliding the plate into the wedge between microphone and table with an expression that might have gotten her canonized in a slower century. "The rest require beans and time." She glanced at Miriam. Time was up.

Miriam touched Julian's sleeve a hello, not a goodbye and stood to face the day. They had made a little room together. Now they would widen it and see if the town wanted any.

THE CAFÉ SHAPE-SHIFTED in the way Cedar Creek's rooms do when a conversation reaches critical mass: a few degrees louder; chairs angled toward the new center; the sound of cups touching saucers like punctuation. Miriam had a congenital allergy to turning tables into stages, but today the choice wasn't hers.

Confluence FM's host smiled into the mike with the faux-casual tone of a man who'd learned his voice in a mirror. "We're here with Julian Roth of the Fort Museum and Miriam Adler of well everywhere, after yesterday's startling events. People have questions. We appreciate you two taking the time." He aimed the mic at Julian. "First: did the museum stage this?"

"No," Julian said, no heat in it. "We're not that creative."

"And not that reckless," Miriam added. "No one drains a public ritual to drive foot traffic."

A woman near the pastry case raised two fingers the way a student volunteers when she's also sure the teacher is wrong. "If it's natural," she said, "explain the timing."

"I can't," Julian said. "Yet."

"'Yet' implies you will," petition man said, halfway into the interview by sheer force of volume. "By when? People want to know when you're putting the basin back on church steps."

Pastor Elijah, who had come in for a cinnamon roll and a portable prayer, lifted his cup without approaching and somehow added ballast to the room. "The basin is built to travel," he said. "Today it sits by the river because the river has something to show us."

"That symbol," the radio host said quickly, smelling ratings. "Mr. Roth, Ms. Adler what does it mean?"

"It means 'and,'" the boy from last night blurted, one table over, brave with caffeine and proximity.

"I love that answer," Miriam said. "We're cautious about naming. The moment we stamp it with certainty, we'll stop listening for what else it says."

"So you know and you won't tell," petition man concluded triumphantly.

Miriam kept her face a friendly shape. "We know little and we're telling all of it. That's the practice."

A woman with a stroller cleared her throat. "Is it safe?" she asked. "To walk the path tonight."

"Yes," Sheriff Mayhew said from the doorway, because order, too, has good timing. "Near and slow. Rope stays. Lanterns stay. Panic stays home."

The host pivoted, sensing he'd lose control if he let the

sheriff be definitive. "Mr. Roth this ledger everyone's passing around in copies. Is it legit? Some say the messy week is forged to build a narrative."

Julian's public voice settled into its gentle rigging. "Yes, it's legitimate. We'll be scanning it in front of anyone who wants to watch. The clerk's hand stumbles there; the week is not forged. The stumbling, to me, is human: interruption, hurry, a thought bigger than the margin."

"A thought like 'let's sabotage a basin'?" petition man said.

"No," Julian said. "A thought like 'something changed and I don't have a neat sentence for it yet.'"

The host switched targets. "Ms. Adler people say you 'feel things.' Did you " He groped for a word not required to pass a fact-check. " *sense* this?"

"I thought the room would get interesting," she said. "I wasn't wrong."

He grinned, too charmed to hide it. "That's not very quotable."

"It isn't," she agreed. "It's still true."

Sloane shouldered in, ponytail ragged, tape bracelet replenished. She took in the half-circle around Miriam and Julian and breathed out through her nose the way you do when you arrive at a cluttered garage with a truckload of shelves. "Okay," she said. "Ground rules. If you're going to ask them to answer fresh mysteries between sips, you have to give them room to breathe and you have to bus your own table." She picked up two abandoned cups without breaking eye contact with the radio host. "You can keep your mike. You can't forget your plate."

"I... of course," he said, flustered into humanity.

"Thank you, Sloane," Miriam said, meaning it with two layers.

"We've posted a schedule," Sloane continued. "Two o'clock: scanning session at the museum, open to anyone with patience. Four: circle under the cottonwood, same as yesterday, shorter words. Tonight's lantern walk stays. Petitioners, you can petition, but if you block the stroller line you will apologize with pie."

"Yes, ma'am," petition man said, uncharacteristically meek in the presence of equipment he did not understand.

Rosalie appeared beside the condiment station and set a bag of tea lights down like a peace treaty. "We'll be at the rope by six," she told anyone who needed telling. "I'll trade one candle for any rumor you'd like to stop telling yourself."

The radio host, jolted into the old-fashioned duty of actually reporting, tried again. "Mr. Roth, there's talk that the mark in the shallows matches a family symbol." He glanced at Miriam. "Theories implicate Adler, Cavanaugh, LeClair, a couple of others. If a family is culpable, will the museum "

"Culpable for a stone?" Julian said, amused despite himself. "If a person carved it, they're dead. We're not in the justice business. We're in the meaning business."

"Meaning includes responsibility," petition man muttered.

"It does," Pastor Elijah said from his post, "which is why we'll ask not who gets punished but who is called to repair."

A teenager in a hoodie one of the lantern shepherds raised his hand. "Could someone," he said, "just tell us a story? Like, the short version. Not of who to blame. Of what we do now."

The café went quiet the way rooms do when the right question gets air. Miriam and Julian looked at each other and found a chord.

"We keep our promises out loud," Miriam said.

"We write down what we know and mark what we don't so we don't pretend," Julian said.

"We touch the river with our eyes, not our feet," Miriam added, nodding toward Sheriff Mayhew, who nodded back.

"We share the table," Julian said, tipping his head toward the door where daylight waited like one more audience they were ready to face.

The radio host lowered his mic an inch. "That... plays," he said, almost disappointed not to have made a villain and relieved he didn't have to. "We'll be there at two. Live."

"Bring a clipboard," Sloane said.

Outside, the square resumed its busy hum petitioners circling like moons, children negotiating the ethics of extra cookies, elders holding back tide and time with easy chairs. Inside, the café exhaled. People remembered their drinks. Chairs scuffed. The barista topped off cups and quietly put a cardamom bun into a paper bag that she slid toward the petition man without ceremony. He took it. Mercy accumulates by inches.

When the microphones improvised themselves back into pockets and the crowd redistributed its curiosity, Miriam sat again because her legs had become something approximating stone. Julian sat, too, forearms on his knees. "I didn't say anything I regret," he said, surprised.

"You won't," she said. "You're too careful for regret; you leave yourself a path."

He looked up at her with relief that threatened to wring her in a way she did not permit in public. "I keep wanting to ask your permission to be relieved."

"You don't need mine," she said. "But you have it."

They let the quiet be. Their cups had gone cold again, and they drank anyway because ritual sometimes matters more than temperature. The bell rang three times in a minute with minor variations; none of them were for their table. They had a pocket of room again. A small one. It might be enough to name what had danced at the edges since she sat down.

"I wish," he said finally, unable to leash the sentence any longer, "we had one day where nothing was asked of us. Where we got to be " He ran out of nouns.

"People who like cardamom buns," she supplied.

"Those," he said, grateful, and the smile was not strategic; it was a field finding sun.

The bell rang a fourth time. The mayor stood awkwardly near the pastry case as if he'd discovered it was not in the budget to buy doughnuts. "Mr. Roth," he began, "Ms. Adler. A word?"

"We have many," Miriam said brightly, because kindness that protects is still kindness. "Which one do you need?"

"Discretion," he said. "The city paper is circling. Tourism is well. Could we agree to keep the ledger and the sketch in-house? Until we form a message?"

"No," Julian said, so gently it took a full second for the mayor to register denial. "That's not our practice."

"The town should see what we see," Miriam said. "Even if it means they see our not-knowing."

The mayor pushed his mouth into a sympathetic fold that didn't fit his face. "You must understand the optics "

"We understand the people," Pastor Elijah said from behind him, having materialized the way men of the cloth often do in rooms with bad acoustics and good intentions. "They can bear it."

The mayor sagged politely and took his leave without doughnuts. The radio host held the door for him like an old friend, which they were not. Sloane, who had not stopped moving since she woke in 1998, ticked one more box on a list no one else would see and pointed at the clock on the espresso machine. "One hour until scanning," she said, to the room at large. "If you're coming, bring patience. If you're mad, bring your inside voice. If you're confused, welcome."

Miriam and Julian glanced at each other as if they'd just found the same line in different books. The romantic tension hadn't disappeared under town business; it had sharpened. The table between them felt like both sanctuary and occasion. He reached for the cardamom bag. She put her hand over it at the same moment. His fingers paused under hers. The contact was unremarkable by any legal standard and very important to both their pulses.

"I " he started.

"I know," she said.

"You don't."

"I do," she said, and took her hand back because the room allowed them a small grace but not indulgence. "Two o'clock."

"Two," he said, and they stood into the work again, together by practice even when they walked through separate doors.

At one-fifty-five the museum's multipurpose room looked like a garage sale for ghosts. People carried in boxes tied with the past letters, recipe cards, photographs, a handful of stones someone had mistaken for artifacts and was not altogether wrong. The table lamps that Julian had appropriated for the scanning station cast a light that made paper look like skin. Docents lined out a queue with tape and calm.

"Here's how this works," Julian said to the room. He had rolled his sleeves not for performance but because paper forgives forearms and hates cuffs. "You hand us what you're willing to have copied. We scan in view. Your original never leaves your hands unless you want it to. We post the copies on the museum site and a bulletin board out front. If something seems sensitive, we talk, and you decide. No surprises. No secrets."

"What about privacy?" someone asked, the tone reasonable.

"We blur names on request," he said. "We redact when asked. We don't bury."

"Burying is what got us here," an elder said, not to him but to the air. Several heads nodded because some sentences arrive ready for ratification.

The first bundle belonged to a woman who had introduced herself as "nobody important, just the one who inherits junk." She untied the ribbon and revealed a ledger of her own household, 1880s, kept by a woman who did arithmetic like a form of faith. Tucked in the back was a note in a shakier hand: *We have been asked to keep quiet about the first basin. I will do so until the water says otherwise.*

"The water said otherwise," the woman whispered, half in awe, as the scanner hummed. "Didn't it?"

"It might have," Julian said. "Let's give it witnesses."

A man brought a letter from a Adler descendant Julian showed no surprise and even less appetite to make a headline. The letter mentioned land disputes and the use of stones to mark claims. It did not confess to carving anything in any river. It did not need to. The words *we took more than our share* had a way of changing weather without the help of tools. Julian scanned the sheet and handed it back with a nod that contained neither absolution nor indictment, only welcome to the work.

A teenager produced a napkin on which his grandmother had drawn a version of the symbol. "She called it the 'loop that makes neighbors,'" he said proudly. "She wrote it in the church cookbook in 1969."

"We'll scan the napkin," Julian said, eyes smiling. "And if she'll loan the cookbook, I'll bring it back with a pie."

The line moved, and with it the room's temperature changed. People stopped whispering. They did not stop caring about their own versions; they started caring about their neighbors' versions, too. It is a small miracle when a community becomes curious about each other in public without the prurience of gossip. You can hear the difference: the questions slow, the eyes soften, the urge to collect stamps *aha, proof* gives way to the desire to understand where to place the next chair.

Miriam moved along the line like a conductor who believes the orchestra can tune itself if given a minute. She carried a basket for the skeptical to hold while they waited there is no more disarming object than a basket meant for nothing in particular and she asked people, quietly, what they hoped the day would do for them. "Make us less angry," a man said, surprising himself. "Make me less scared for my kids," a woman said without embarrassment. "Make my grandmother feel like she can tell her story without the old men correcting her," someone else offered, and the grandparents in the room smiled in the way grandparents do when they forgive something they had not yet admitted they wanted to hold.

At three, the mayor poked his head in and saw a line of residents handing over family papers for copying. You could watch him recalibrate his version of leadership in the time it took to inhale. "This is good optics," he said accidentally, then flinched when Sloane, passing with a coil of extension cord, said, "It's not optics, it's us."

The radio host from Confluence FM set up a microphone unobtrusively and, in the first mature decision of his on-air life, chose to narrate without provoking. "We're seeing Cedar Creek bring out boxes," he told his listeners. "We're seeing a town talk to itself in the daylight. There's a symbol in the shallows, and perhaps it points to a sentence we're writing together."

"Cut the poetry," his producer hissed from the hall, and he ignored her, because sometimes conversion sneaks up on people wearing the face of good prose.

In the corner, away from the lamps, Miriam slipped the envelope from her pocket and took out her great-aunt's letter. She read the lines again, then again, not because she doubted them but because they did what good sentences do: centered her in the room where she was needed. When she turned, Julian was there, a respectful distance, eyes asking before his mouth did. "May I?"

She didn't hand him the letter. She handed him the message. "It says the water empties what we fill until we see what we buried," she said. "It says not to be afraid. It says the point is repair."

He let the words settle like tools on a bench and reached, without touching, for a piece that matched. "I found a margin note in the carpenter's hand," he said. "Faint. Almost erased. It says *not yet* next to the rim drawing with the unfinished curve." His mouth tilted. "It might be a list for the next morning. It might be a theology."

"Both," she said. "He didn't finish it then. We are being asked to finish it now. Not to complete the symbol. To complete the promise."

They stood together in the non-romantic light of office lamps, which has ruined many kisses and improved many decisions. He put his hand on the table's edge; she mirrored.

It was not a touch. It was a brace. The gesture said we aim to build a public thing that will still stand when we have the luxury of being private.

"What do we tell and what do we keep?" he asked, the question honest enough to make the air sharper.

"We tell anything that keeps us from pretending," she said. "We keep what isn't ours to give."

"And how will we know which is which?"

"We'll ask the people who are holding the stories," she said. "We'll ask the river by watching if we get calmer when we speak or more agitated. We'll ask our own bodies. When we're hiding, my chest tightens. When we're protecting, it widens."

He gave her a look that told her he believed that because he had watched it happen on her face. "All right," he said. "Tonight, after the lanterns, I propose an 'Evening of Records and Remembrance.' No speeches. No dais. Just a table in the square with what we have and three chairs one for anyone who wants to read aloud, one for anyone who wants to listen, one left empty because it feels right to leave room."

"And bread," she said. "And honey."

"And the mayor's folding chairs," he said, allowing himself mischief. "He'll be delighted to be useful."

They both laughed, and in the laugh their shoulders did the same thing: they let down the part that had been holding the room and picked up the part that knew how to be two people in a hallway after a hard day. He touched his scar without meaning to. She noticed with the gentleness of a person who will ask later. The moment was theirs, ephemeral, true. Then the next person stepped up with a stack of postcards and the room returned to its job.

By four, the scanning table had become a kind of secular

altar. People placed their offerings ink and paper, sweat and memory on the glass, and the light made a record as precise and as forgiving as anyone could ask for. Outside, the river kept doing the thing it has always done: moving forward without explaining itself. On the shallows, the symbol took another hour of watching without growing bored.

They closed the station at five with apologies to the last three in line and promises for the morning. Julian took the new copies to the board out front and pinned them with clothespins the same ones that had dried test wicks a day ago. The wind did not argue. The square gathered and read and read again. The words made one kind of weather; the presence of neighbors made another.

At dusk, Miriam walked the west path with the lantern shepherds and took her post at the rope. The first paper moons lifted, then the second, then a hundred more. The symbol accepted the light. It did nothing but accept, which turned out to be everything.

After, under the cottonwood, they set a table with the copies and a loaf of bread and three chairs. People sat. A teenager read a paragraph from a diary about a woman learning to swim in a dress and refusing to be told no. A man read a note from his grandfather about how they moved the basin after a flood and said it was heavier when they carried it without speaking. A woman read the list of names of those who had taught children to float. No one used the empty chair. That was the point.

The mayor brought the folding chairs without instruction and set them facing the right direction. He did not speak. Sloane lit two lanterns and hung them from the lower branches. Pastor Elijah stood nearby and kept his hands open. Sheriff Mayhew leaned against a post and looked relieved to be bored. The petition man sat, ate bread, and said "thank you" to the person who passed the honey. Rosalie held a match for Mr. Cavanaugh's granddaughter, who lit it with a steadiness that made three grandmothers hum involuntarily.

Near the table, Julian stood with the comfortable posture of a man who has decided to stop performing and start apprenticing. Miriam stepped beside him with the posture of a woman who has chosen truth over drama so many times she no longer worries about applause. They watched their town be brave in the humble way out loud about what it fears, generous about what it loves, stubborn about staying.

"Scandal," he said quietly, without bitterness or self-pity. "It's just another word for when truth forgets which door it was supposed to use."

"Then we'll open the one that fits," she said.

"And keep it open," he said, eyes on the square and then on her. "If you'll stand here with me while people walk through."

"I will," she said.

"Even when it's messy," he said.

"Especially then."

He nodded once, approval of a plan they hadn't exactly written down, and they took a breath together the way people do before lifting something heavy. The breath didn't make them heroes. It made them ready. That would have to be enough.

Behind them, the museum's lamps glowed like second stars. In front of them, the river finished another day's work and did not require thanks. Between those two, under paper light, a town made room for its stories in public. The symbol held in the shallows, loop complete, stroke sure, neither a curse nor a crown. It was an *and* a hinge big enough for a community to swing.

They stayed until the last chair folded and the last lantern dimmed and the last person said, "Good night," like the practice it is. Then they walked home by separate streets, carrying the same sentence without needing to say it: *We will tell the truth, and we will keep what is not ours, and we will know the difference because the room will breathe or it won't.*

In her kitchen, Miriam set her great-aunt's letter back in the trunk and whispered thank you to the air the way she always did when she'd asked a dead woman's words to go to work again. In his apartment, Julian washed his hands and wrote three lines in a logbook that had never lied: **Public scanning. Evening of records. Town stood the test today.** He paused, then added, **We did, too.**

7

____

THE FIRST CARVING

Miriam woke with the symbol still in her hands, though she hadn't touched the stone. In the lamplight she folded a grocery receipt in halves and quarters, then took a pencil and drew the curve as her body remembered it: not decoration, not alphabet, an *and* made of river. The first attempt looked too polite, the second too sharp. On the third her wrist found the pressure it had felt at the rope, the moment when light fell at an angle and the groove in the stone answered. She left the end open, then drew the completing stroke with a breath there. The loop closed and made the rest of the page irrelevant.

She slid the receipt between two pages of her notebook as if tucking in a child and went downstairs. The town had not yet chosen its volume for the day. The square held its first coffee and its last shadows. A gull's cry sounded like an untested theory.

At the museum, the door clicked and admitted her to lemon oil, old paper, and quiet. Julian was already in Collections with the lamp low and the portfolio open, tie slung over the back of a chair like a concession to morning. He looked up and his face did the new thing it did now when she entered relief visible without apology.

"I brought what my hand remembers," she said, offering the folded receipt.

He did not smile at the medium. He took it like an artifact and laid it beside the carpenter's rim drawing. For a moment they just looked. The unfinished mark on the old page, the completed mark on the slip, two versions of a thought waiting a century and change to speak.

"Let's try it," he said, already reaching for a transparency sleeve and a pen that understood circles. He slipped the receipt into the sleeve, traced both the carpenter's fragment and Miriam's whole, then set the overlay over the rim detail and nudged, tilted, nudged again. The curve that had stopped on the old page now met the one she'd completed. The line completed itself in layered ink.

Julian didn't exclaim. He exhaled. "We're not imagining the kinship," he said softly. "They share a hand. Or a grammar."

"Look here," she said, tapping the point where the stroke thickened on the stone her muscle memory had made it heavier for an instant, the way a hand presses when the body commits to finishing. In the carpenter's start, the pencil burr had lifted at exactly that angle.

He adjusted the light and brought the loupe. "Same squeeze," he murmured. "Same hesitation. It's not that he didn't *know* how to draw it. He did. He chose to stop."

"Not yet," she said, thinking of the faint margin note he'd found.

"Not yet," he repeated, and the words sounded less like caution and more like instruction.

He fetched a protractor and a length of thread, the kind of measuring tools that made him feel at home. "Humor me," he said, and laid the transparency over a photocopy of the photo he'd taken yesterday symbol in the shallows at noon, the dock piling like a sundial. "If we assume this is a pointer yes, yes, I can hear you laughing, but pretend we can measure orientation. The completed loop aims here." He tugged the thread from the loop's throat toward a landmark: the old cottonwood, and beyond it, the museum's south window.

"Which used to be a door," Miriam said, surprising herself. She had not lived when the fort was still a fort. But standing there, arm braced near Julien's, the memory arrived with the certainty of a scent. "The carpenter's scale sketches show a door in the south wall. It was boarded when "

"When we added the second gallery," Julian finished, brow furrowing as if recalling a relative's birthday from a family tree. "Yes. The 1930s remodel. What was that door in the 1840s? Not decorative."

"Utility," she said. "Or ceremony." She pulled the portfolio toward her and started turning with care, the way you turn a stranger's pages without sounding like you're riffling a purse. There: a small plan, not the public one in the front case, but a draft with smudged footprints near the south wall, a note in the carpenter's hand: *south threshold procession.*

Julian's fingertips hovered as if in benediction. "We might be chasing meaning into places it didn't intend to go," he said, honest about the historian's allergy to apophenia.

"We might," she said. "But it keeps going there."

He reached for another folder the one with the mica panel, the penciled start in the corner like a note a hand failed to write loud enough. He placed it under the transparency. The edge of the half-mark paired with the arc of her loop more neatly than chance should permit. He didn't say *aha*. He didn't have to. His eyes had already.

"Missing history," he said, not as accusation, not as romance, only as the weather report that it was. "Not in the sense of hidden treasure. In the sense of a piece removed because it made someone's day less tidy. Or never recorded because the room couldn't bear it then."

She thought of the ledger's messy week. "There are other ways to hide," she said. "By not finishing the sentence."

He angled the raking light again. The pencil burr on the carpenter's start glinted like a tiny compass needle. "Let's overlay the whole," he said. Together they lowered the clear sheet over the old drawing and watched the curve align. The line completed the rim's repeated wave pattern in a way that made sense and didn't at the same time as if the basin had been speaking in a motif around its lip, and this mark was the word that bridged motif to meaning.

"What is it?" he asked, not expecting an answer.

"A door," she said, then shook her head. "No a hinge. The thing that lets a door be a door."

He smiled sideways. "That boy in the café called it *and*."

"He's not wrong," she said, feeling the relief of an object that refused to be an idol. "*And* is where a community begins."

They marked the angles, distances, relations: loop to piling, piling to cottonwood, cottonwood to south threshold. Julian penciled a small map, a clean skeleton on which flesh could later hang. He made a list on the yellow pad he loved: check the south wall records; hunt the 1930s plans; look for references to a procession no one remembers; ask Sloane for a line-of-sight measurement from the rope to the old threshold; scan for any replacement of rim carving or repairs that might have sanded a symbol into discretion.

"Do you see the crack?" Miriam asked suddenly, pointing to the basin's repaired seam in the gallery beyond. From here it was only a difference in light, not visible to anyone not devoted to the object. "The way the repair sets your hand a hair off when you touch it through glass."

He went to the case and stood where she stood. He saw it, because he trusted her and because he'd trained his eye to agree to see once invited. "You think the mark may have been cut shallow into a stave that later needed repair."

"Or the opposite," she said. "The repair respected the rim and avoided the mark. Either way, the basin isn't the only sentence. The riverbed is the other."

"The river's the long version," he said, and something like joy rose in him, fresh as if he hadn't been embarrassed yesterday at all. "We get to read both. Parallel texts."

Miriam lifted the transparency to the light and watched the overlayed lines make a third thing: neither old nor new, exactly, but a reconciliation. "Then let's not translate too soon," she said. "Let's listen."

He tucked the receipt into the portfolio the way he tucked every living person's offering carefully, with respect. "We'll note it as *Adler sketch, day two*," he said, and the tone simple naming was as intimate as anything he'd said to her that morning.

They both looked at the door that used to be and then at the south window that replaced it. The space held quiet like a held note.

"Let's go look at the wall," Julian said. "I want to see if the plaster lies."

They crossed the gallery. Under the south window the paint had a slightly different sheen, and in the far right corner the trimboard misaligned by the width of a thumb-nail. The sort of detail only plumbers and long marriages catch.

"Boarded from the inside," he said. "Curator's choice in the thirties, probably control light; prevent drafts."

"Or prevent processions," she said.

He smiled. "You're incorrigible."

"I'm hired," she said.

He didn't argue. He put his palm flat on the plaster as if greeting an old animal. The museum resulted to the touch: cool, steady, withholding and kind. "We'll find the plans."

"We will," she said, and they stood with a door between them and the people who had walked it across generations, the old mark and the new one making a hinge where the wall pretended there wasn't one.

THEY POURED coffee from the staff room pot that had been new in another era and carried the mugs back to Collections like contraband. The transparency lay on the table with a look of completed thought that made Miriam both relieved and shy, as if she'd brought a guest and the room had agreed to like them.

"I want to tell you something," she said, sitting, hands around the cup because warmth is permission. "If you promise not to make it smaller than it is, or bigger."

"I can promise not to perform with it," he said. "And not to make you perform."

"That's the promise I needed." She took a breath that felt like stepping into cold water and let it become the sentence. "When I say I 'sense' things, it's not " She gestured, trying to shoo away the idea of crystal balls and spangled shawls, their tidy clichés that made people either scoff or kneel. "It isn't a show. It's a way of listening. Rooms have weather. Objects have attention. People carry a note even when they aren't singing. The river has memory. It's not God; I wouldn't be so presumptuous. But it has a long mind. Sometimes I can feel where it's looking."

He didn't write anything down, which was a kindness. He didn't widen his eyes in the easy flattery that turns trust into theater. He said, "Okay," because consent is the first tool you put in someone's hand when they put one in yours.

"I have dreams," she added, because hiding them would turn the partnership into a lie. "The chain at the bottom of the river. The sound when it breaks. The breath afterward. My great-aunt left a letter that reads like a field guide: *When the town forgets its first promise, the water remembers. It will empty what we fill until we see what we buried.* She wrote it not to make me special. To keep me helpful."

"She succeeded," he said, and the words worked on her bones like a tonic.

"I don't know what to do with it when rooms get full of microphones," she confessed. "I don't want to be a channel. I want to be a citizen."

"You are," he said simply. "We can build a method that honors your sense and my discipline and protects the room from both our worst instincts."

She laughed lightly. "My worst instinct is to apologize for seeing."

"Mine is to insist on proof too soon," he said. "So: what do we do? We write a rule."

He pulled the yellow pad closer and wrote **Adler–Roth Method** at the top without irony and with just enough mischief to keep the air kind. Beneath it he numbered five lines.

"Rule one," he said. "We don't name what the symbol

means until we have at least three independent witnesses: object, record, community memory. A triangulation."

"Rule two," she said. "We don't hide the not-knowing. We say *yet* out loud."

"Rule three," he said. "When you sense, we test. Not to disprove. To find the edges."

"Rule four," she said. "When you find a fragment, we ask the room how it moves. Does it widen? Then we keep going. Does it tighten? Then we set it down."

"Rule five," he said, warming, "we make all this public enough that no one can accuse us of hoarding the story, but private enough that we don't invite spectacle to trample it."

He looked up. "I want one more," he said. "Rule six: we tell each other the truth even if it makes us look foolish."

She considered the small, practical courage that sentence required the kind of courage that does better in paper light than under lanterns. "Agreed," she said. "But if I'm going to tell you when the room moves, I should show you what it feels like."

He hesitated only long enough to be human. "All right."

"Stand there," she said, pointing to the corner where the portfolio met the table's edge. "Close your eyes if it helps."

He did not close them. He let the eyelids half-lower the way people do when they want to hear a violin better. She moved to the south side of the table and placed her palm just above the transparency. The air changed the way it does when a storm considers the valley and decides to see more. "Do you feel that?" she asked.

"Yes," he said, surprised at the ease with which the answer arrived. "It feels like a room leaning."

"It's attention. Not mine. The room's. It moves when our thought aligns with something old. It's not mystical when you get used to it. It's like hearing the undertone in a choir. It tells you if you're still in key."

He let the metaphor do the job of saving him from smart questions. He didn't ask for measurable units. He didn't demand replication. He looked at the south wall again. "The procession," he said. "People walked a line from door to water."

"Or from water to door," she said. "Or both. A hinge."

"And the symbol is the hinge's sign."

She nodded. "Not power. Permission." She lifted her palm. The feeling thinned. "Now listen at the ledger."

He crossed to the cabinet. She didn't touch the book. The old paper had a dignity that discouraged fingers. She spoke instead, softly, like you speak to a child who wakes not wanting to be alone. "Messy week. Interrupted thought. The curl that should have been a note. The clerk wrote *remember* and then didn't."

"It's an ache," Julian said, startled at his own choice of noun. "In the page."

"Yes," she said. "He wanted to finish the sentence and didn't. The carpenter wanted to draw the line and didn't. The basin wanted to hold the water and didn't. The river wanted to show the stone and did."

He leaned his shoulder to the case, as if choosing to trust a piece of furniture were a way to begin trusting the greater dare. "I'm in," he said.

"Into what?"

"Into believing that if we are gentle with the unseen, it will be gentle with us," he said. "Into building a practice where your listening and my keeping can avoid turning into performance."

"Into suspicion of missing history," she said. "Not conspiracies. Decisions. Men who thought they were protecting the room when really they were protecting themselves from it."

He didn't flinch. "My profession has done that," he said. "We can do better."

She took his hand because there are moments when *we* needs skin. He held back just enough to ask permission; she tightened enough to answer. Then they let go, because the work was the point and the room was already curious.

"Next step?" she asked.

"We go find the thirties plans," he said, eyes bright now, not to impress, but with the delight of a man who has found in the present a door to the past that requires company. "And we ask the south wall what it's been holding back."

"And we ask the river," she said. "Tonight. Without putting our feet in. The light will show us where to look."

They wrote the plan on the pad beneath the rules like a grocery list that could feed a town.

SLOANE GAVE them a grin and a crowbar, which in her vocabulary counted as a blessing. "You're not tearing anything," she said, "but you can knock the trim with your knuckles and see where it lies. And I'll bring a stud finder because I have one and it likes attention."

They spent the next hour marrying intuition to carpentry. The stud finder warbled in three steady places and went shy in a section the exact width of an old door. The trim's nail pattern changed there two nails, then three, then a void where a hinge might have sat. Miriam felt the room breathe and said nothing. Julian used the calm voice of a man wooing a grant and asked Sloane if, purely hypothetically, a small exploratory removal twelve inches by six might be permitted with a reversible patch.

"Not today," Sloane said, which they'd expected. "But I'll pull the building file. If the thirties plans are in our archives, I'll find them between my lunch and my fifth conversation about porta-potty placement."

"Thank you," Julian said. "For everything you're always doing."

She shrugged. "I like being useful," she said. "Also, I like a mystery that requires tools I already own."

They left the south wall intact and their impulse to pry satisfied by the stud finder's shy song. Outside, the square ran its noon errands without starting a fight. Sheriff Mayhew nodded at them in the way men nod when they've seen you control your curiosity. Pastor Elijah, passing with a brown paper bag that looked like a marriage between grace and cinnamon, lifted two fingers in benediction. Rosalie had a map of the lantern route in one hand and a list of names in the other the next generation of carriers was full of will and elbows.

Back in Collections, Julian set the Adler–Roth Method in a folder labeled with a piece of blue tape and a date. He wrote **hinge** in smaller letters in the corner of the page without noticing. Miriam noticed and decided to like the word.

"Let's test the boy's theory," she said. "The *and*. If the symbol is a tying mark, who or what was it tying?"

"Land and water," he said. "Door and river. Families and ritual. Trade and blessing."

"Past and present," she said. "Museum and square."

"Record and memory," he said. "Proof and story."

"Truth and mercy," she said, and the room admitted a

small wind, enough to lift the edge of the transparency by a fraction, as if in assent.

They began to sleuth like people who enjoyed both paper and people. Julian wrote down every instance of the carpenter's hand in the files and marked them with a red tab. Miriam wrote a list of elders who had that particular way of talking around a subject you only learn when your grandparents told you never to say a thing out loud. They divided: he would live in the building file, the 1930s minutes, the correspondence with the state historical society; she would live on porches and in kitchens, at the rope and under the cottonwood, where the unofficial minutes of Cedar Creek gathered themselves into sentences when someone who knew how to listen sat down with a slice of pie and a pen that made small sounds.

At two, the scanning station opened and the town brought more boxes. This time people came ready to be part of the plot. "We found a sketch," a teenager said, holding up a page her grandmother had tucked in a cookbook. The curve on it mirrored the one on Miriam's receipt, drawn in ballpoint and labeled *river sign? don't forget*. An old man with a crumpled hat brought a spool of twine and said, "For your measuring," as if donating a kidney. A LeClair cousin produced a strip of cedar with knife marks practice cuts, wave pattern, and one hesitant start. "My great-aunt carved to think," she said. "She stopped here and said, 'Not yet.'"

Julian scanned, cataloged, and displayed with the joy of a man who had found a way to be responsible without becoming a gate. Miriam watched faces as much as paper. The symbol had begun to teach the town how to be curious without being cruel. That alone felt like rebellion against the way rumor likes to run.

In the late afternoon, he closed the cabinet with the

tender finality he reserved for days that had earned their rest. "If the south wall used to be a door, the procession must have traced a line from river to threshold," he said. "Which means the basin's place at the blessing isn't ornamental. It's cartography."

"Then the first carving is a map legend," she said. "Not a destination."

"We suspect missing history," he said.

"We suspect missing honesty," she said. "Embarrassment layered with good intentions, then with dust."

He hesitated the way you do when offering a piece of yourself you'd prefer to keep until you're sure it won't be mishandled. "There's a rumor in my own family," he said. "That my great-grandfather argued to 'sanitize' the exhibit in 1934. He called it protecting donors. My grandmother called it cowardice when she was angry and prudence when she was tired."

"That's a kind of hinge, too," she said. "The one between motive and consequence. We can honor motives and still repair consequences."

He nodded, and you could see him shift a long-standing weight to a better shelf. "I'll check our board minutes," he said. "If there's a vote, I'll read it out loud under the cottonwood."

"Thank you," she said. "For not treating your people as a museum that only you can curate."

At dusk they walked to the rope together and took their places two posts at a makeshift sanctuary. The symbol waited in the shallows with the patience of the unafraid. The lantern shepherds made their first pass, and light laid itself along the path like intention. A child pointed and whispered, "There," the way children call stars.

"Tonight," Miriam said, "I want to try something with

the light. If we stand not here but three paces left, look at that seam, the stone gives its depth. It's like the river's cut encodes a second stroke you can't see head-on."

"Parallax," Julian said, delighted to have a word. "A long word for 'move your feet and you'll see it.'"

They moved their feet. The second stroke appeared and then vanished. He measured the angle with the kind of joy people reserve for seeing a bird they only knew from a book. "I want to make a grid," he said. "Stakes in the grass. Sloane will hate it until she loves it. We'll mark coordinates where the symbol reads clearest at different hours. We'll invite the high schoolers to chart changes over the week. Give curiosity a job."

"And give fear a seat," she said. "So it doesn't have to pace."

When the walk ended, they stood with Pastor Elijah under the cottonwood and told the square the part of the truth that had ripened enough to be shared. He held up the transparency, the carpenter's start under Miriam's completion under a lamp that made no promises larger than illumination. They didn't call it a revelation. They called it a rhyme.

"Missing history isn't erasure alone," Julian said to the circle. "It can be care gone sideways. We're going to read the minutes from 1934 when we find them. We're going to ask the south wall what it holds. We're going to look at the stone and the basin and admit when we've reached the limits of our eyesight. And we're going to do it together."

"And we're going to repair," Miriam said. "Not accuse first. Repair first. If accusation comes, it will be an honest tool to loosen a stuck board, not a hammer to break a table."

The town didn't cheer. It breathed. That was better. Sloane drew a chalk X where Miriam had stood to see the second stroke; Sheriff Mayhew wrote **NO STEPPING HERE** beside it with the air of a man who knows his audience. Rosalie handed Mr. Cavanaugh's granddaughter a match and a lesson in patience. The mayor produced a stack of folding chairs in the correct orientation and did not make a speech.

Walking home, they passed the south wall's outside face the cedar siding dark as toast, the window that used to be a door reflecting a sky losing blue on purpose. Julian touched the sill as if signing in. "Partners?" he said, not because he doubted, but because some vows deserve their own air.

"Partners," she said, and they stopped there, where the hinge of the old door met the hinge of the evening, and let the word fit.

"Truth and secrecy," he said, testing the theme they'd been orbiting since coffee. "How do we hold them?"

"As neighbors," she said. "Secrecy becomes the one you forgive but don't let run the HOA. Truth becomes the one you invite to dinner even when you're tired. Neither gets your keys. Both get your time."

He laughed, then sobered. "We'll disappoint someone," he said. "Probably several someones."

"We will," she said. "That's how you know you're telling the whole truth and not auditioning for a side."

They reached her door and didn't rehearse a goodbye. The work had made them fluent in a softer grammar. He lifted his hand, not quite a wave. She touched the jamb again the way he had touched the sill, a little private rite no one had taught her and everyone would recognize if she told them. He turned toward the museum. She climbed the stairs.

At her table, she took out the receipt and the letter and the page where he'd written their rules. She added one line in her own hand under the six they'd agreed on: **7) Ask the river for mercy, then offer it to each other.** She tucked the slip back beside the carpenter's ghost of a curve in her mind and felt the day finish clicking.

Down by the rope, the symbol slept without sleeping. In the south wall, a door remembered being a door. In the portfolio, an unfinished mark finally had its partner. Cedar Creek, awake to itself, made a list without writing it down: repairs to attempt, stories to fetch, chairs to set out, apologies to practice, bread to bake, lanterns to tend. The river, which had never needed lists, kept moving. It always does. But for once it felt if feeling were a thing rivers admitted accompanied.

RIVAL FAMILIES

They started with the Cavanaughs because it would have been taken as disrespect not to. The ranch house sat where the cottonwoods gave out and the pasture began, its porch piled with rubber boots like punctuation. A coil of rope hung from a nail. On the rail, a coffee can held nails that had forgotten their original purpose and were ready to audition for the next.

Mr. Cavanaugh himself opened the door and let them in without ceremony, as if hospitality could be a truce that didn't require a speech. His kitchen was the same color as the fort museum's oldest filing cabinet, but it smelled like bacon and oak soap, which improved the paint by forty years. His cousin sat at the table with his chair tipped back and his jaw set the way men set it when they have already decided the day needs a fight.

"Coffee?" Mr. Cavanaugh asked Miriam, then, as an afterthought powered by decency, "Mr. Roth?"

"Please," Miriam said. Julian said yes, too, because it was easier to accept the rules of a room than to write new ones on someone else's floor.

They sat. A wall calendar showed a photograph of a dam that had been a boast and then a cautionary tale. On the refrigerator, a magnet shaped like a lantern held a coupon for feed.

"We're making a record," Julian said, and the cousin snorted softly at the word. "Of what people saw and what they think " he paused, choosing the less-inflammatory noun " happened."

"What happened," the cousin said, leaning forward, chair thumping to level, "is that someone bled the basin. You can put dates on it and call it history if you want, but it's sabotage when it happens on purpose."

"On purpose to whom?" Miriam asked, mild as table salt.

"To us," he said. "Our line was set on east dock. Our carriers had the handling. The town was watching. Then " He spread his hands. "Gone."

Mr. Cavanaugh set the coffee down and stayed standing as if neutrality required altitude. "The river isn't a valve, Lou," he said to the cousin. "It did what it did. You could accuse the weather just as well."

"I have accused the weather," Lou said. "It never answers."

Julian made a small note on his pad: *tone: grievance worn smooth by time.* "Can we ask about 1902?" he said. "The elder on the green mentioned a similar event. Any family memory?"

"Old stories," Mr. Cavanaugh said, uncomfortable with ghosts at his table. "My grandfather said it ran out once, yes. Said the men argued and the women told them to hush so the river could talk. Said it was about a promise."

"What promise?" Miriam asked. She kept her voice light,

like you do when coaxing a skittish animal toward an open hand.

"That part changes every time," he said, unhappy with the slipperiness. "Sometimes it's about who carries. Sometimes about who lights. Sometimes about the Adlers." He shot Miriam a look that wasn't accusing so much as hungry. "You heard about the Adler claim?"

"We're hearing about many claims," she said. "We're also hearing about many promises."

"The LeClairs are making promises none of them intends to keep," Lou said. "You show up with a bag of candles and you think the river's on your side. We built the stand. We've been steady. If somebody wanted the town to see us fail, they picked the perfect trick."

"Trick requires actor," Julian said. "Who would risk the town's safety, reputation, ritual, to make a point?"

Lou didn't flinch. "Ask Rosalie."

Mr. Cavanaugh shot him a look he reserved for men who walk on ladders wrong. "We will not accuse Rosalie," he said. "Her grandmother lit my first wick after I spilled wax on my shoe and cried." He turned to Miriam, and if she squinted she could see the boy he had been, a little raw around the eyes, a little proud about being seen at all. "We argued too long," he said. "We always argue too long. When a thing is shared, you learn to argue shorter."

Miriam nodded, and the cousin, irritated by harmony, stood abruptly. "The Adlers," he insisted, as if the family name itself were a pry bar. "They always thought the river was a ledger they could balance by shouting columns into it."

"Thank you for your time," Julian said before accusation could harden into posture. He stood to let the visit end on the good note of asking to leave rather than being asked to go. "We'll be reading board minutes from the thirties, too. If there's anything that belongs in the circle under the cottonwood, we'll bring it."

"Bring it," Mr. Cavanaugh said. "And tell Rosalie I said we forgive shoes easier than we forgive stubbornness. Maybe we could switch that around."

They took the side road to LeClair House next. It wasn't a single house so much as a set of allied kitchen tables. Rosalie's aunt was on the porch shelling peas with the ferocity of a woman who did not intend to be caught idle. The smell of lemon oil and yeast rose from open windows like proof of life. A ribbon of river could be seen from the steps if you tilted your head just so.

"Come to make a list?" she asked without getting up.

"To listen," Miriam said.

"Listening's the secret ingredient," the aunt said drily. "Everybody wants to switch to announcing when the recipe calls for listening." She squinted at Julian. "You the museum boy who refuses to call the mark a miracle?"

"I'm the museum boy who refuses to call it anything quickly," he said, and she barked an approving laugh.

Rosalie arrived with flour on her hands and a set to her shoulders that suggested the morning had already tried to borrow more from her than she could loan. "We're not sabotaging our own flame," she said. "If the Cavanaughs sent you, you can send them back a pie with 'no' written in crust."

"They didn't," Julian said, and handed her the same sentence he'd handed Mr. Cavanaugh: "We're making a record."

Rosalie's aunt emptied a bowl of peas into a pot with the air of someone settling a matter. "My grandmother said once that the basin is a teacher," she said. "When the town lies to itself, the basin refuses its assignment until we correct the homework. That isn't sabotage. That's a lesson plan."

"Who's the liar?" asked a cousin from the doorway, bruised by yesterday's petitioners, jaw set in the same direction as Lou's.

"We've all been," Rosalie said, without the softness that spoils medicine. "We keep telling the short version because it's easier on the throat."

"Did your people ever carve a mark?" Julian asked. He waited to see if the question would be taken as admiration or accusation.

"Of course we carved," the aunt said. "We carve bread, do we not? We carve spoons, boats, time. Any family worth its salt cuts wood when wood needs cutting. If you mean that mark " she lifted her chin in the direction of the river " no one I loved took a knife to that stone. But I know a thing when I feel it under my hand. That groove is older than my grandmother's temper."

The cousin snorted. "Ask the Adlers."

There it was again, the third name invoked like a spell.

"We intend to," Julian said.

"Ask them why their ledger pages get tidy when the town gets messy," the aunt said. "We keep our messes on the table. They file theirs under donors."

"That's unkind," Rosalie said, and then, because she had a conscience that kept her posture honest, she added, "It's also how it looked, some years."

They traded thanks and left with a paper packet of biscuits because declining a LeClair carbohydrate would have been taken as metaphysical insult. Back in the truck, Miriam kept her eyes on the road and her attention on Julian. "You all right?"

"I don't like being a courier of distrust," he said. "But it's useful to see the shape of it."

"The shape is triangular," she said. "Cavanaugh, LeClair, Adler. Each one points at a different tip and insists the other two are the problem."

"We need the fourth point," he said, looking past the windshield at the seam where their creek met the river. "The one labeled *we*."

They drove to the Adlers by the longer road as if politeness could be measured in miles. The Adler place had winched itself into respectability a generation ago and never let go: clapboard white, shutters navy, hedges squared as sentences. Mrs. Adler hair that didn't dare misbehave greeted them with the smile of a person who cannot imagine her own family ever being the subject of a messy anecdote and therefore has never learned the pleasure of surviving one.

"Of course," she said, when Julian introduced himself, "we support the museum. My father-in-law used to say history is only as good as its labeling."

"And its receipts," Miriam said pleasantly.

Mrs. Adler blinked. "You're the candle person," she said, as if naming a minor seasonal deity.

"Among other jobs," Miriam said.

They were ushered into a parlor that had never forgiven children for existing. The chair cushions had the same scold in them that lived in the kettle on the tiny, chemical-clean stove. Framed along the stairs: certificates, dedications, a picture of a Adler shaking hands with a man in a ribboned sash no one could immediately identify as useful.

"We hear," Mrs. Adler said, underlining *we* as if *we* were a limited club, "that there's been a... complication."

"A symbol in the shallows," Julian said. "And a basin that emptied."

"Tragic," she said, and Miriam felt the little electric flicker that comes when a person lies without believing they are. "The Cavanaughs must be mortified. They do so enjoy carrying things."

"Do you have any family record," Julian asked, "of a similar event? Or of adjustments to the ritual? A hedge next to a promise?"

Mrs. Adler's smile steadied. "We've preserved minutes from several board meetings in the thirties," she said. "It was a delicate time. Donors were scarce; the stories were... curated. I imagine your files already reflect that."

"We're pulling them today," Julian said. "May we scan copies of yours if they differ?"

"You may scan what we provide," she said. "But understand, Mr. Roth: the role of history is to keep a town from reliving its worst instincts. Your *public circles* " her voice weighted the phrase toward misgiving " risk inciting."

"Repair requires accuracy," Miriam said.

"Repair requires discretion," Mrs. Adler returned. "Otherwise you call in a storm to fix a leak."

"We've already got the storm," Julian said, kind because he couldn't bear to add rudeness to an overburdened day. "We're trying to read its clouds."

Mrs. Adler placed a thin folder on the table between them. "These are ancestors' deeds," she said. "You'll see that water rights were acquired legally."

"Legally is not the same as ethically," Miriam said before she could stop herself.

Mrs. Adler's chin tipped. "We were instructed by men who built institutions," she said. "If you wish to scold, scold the men who built institutions."

"We wish to read," Julian said. "And to bring what we read into the same room where people can hear their own voices next to the paper."

Mrs. Adler's expression softened in the way of people who cannot decide whether they're charmed or threatened. "You're very... serene for a young man," she said. "You must forgive me. I was raised to keep these matters *in* the house."

"Some of them will stay there," Miriam said. "Some of them have to come outside for air."

They left with the thin folder and a promise to return copies. In the truck Julian did something he didn't do in rooms where people could see him he swore, just once, as if letting air out of a tire before it burst. Miriam laughed, not at him but with him, because profanity, when used for relief rather than harm, is another kind of prayer.

"Three houses," she said. "Three versions of the same ache."

"Which is?" he asked.

"That the first promise keeps showing up and asking to be remembered," she said. "And every family thinks remembering it will cost them more than it will."

He nodded and, pronouncing a verdict he would later put in less elegant words for the circle, said, "We have suspects. We don't have villains."

"Good," she said. "Villains make lazy stories."

Word traveled faster than trucks. By the time they crossed Main, chairs had been dragged into alignments that suggested debate disguised as errands. The square itself had learned yesterday how to hum at a helpful frequency, but the alleys still hosted little theatres with sharp scripts.

At the hardware store door, a Cavanaugh cousin and a

LeClair nephew sparred over sandbags who bought them, who placed them, whose method wasted less time. "If you'd stayed out of the staging area " "If you'd listened when we said the lanterns needed three feet clear " "If your aunt stopped treating prayer like a permit " "If your uncle stopped treating permits like prayer "

Julian angled himself so Miriam had space to pass between them without getting shoulder-checked by inherited grudges. He didn't touch her; he didn't need to. Bodies protect other bodies by the way they choose to be in a room.

"Gentlemen," he said, with no sarcasm at all. "We'll need both your skills at four when we mark parallax points: sandbags to hold stakes, lantern clearance for sightlines. Will you bring them to the river instead of using them up here?"

The cousin's mouth jerked toward a smile. "You're a menace," he said.

"I have a schedule," Julian said.

The nephew, saved from a fight he would've regretted in front of his grandfather, deflated into useful. "Fine. We'll bring both," he said. "Tell Sloane not to put me on trash pick-up again as punishment for existing."

"I have no influence over Sloane," Julian said, which was both true and a good policy sentence.

At the café, petition man had graduated to a banner and a small entourage. **RETURN THE BASIN TO THE STEPS** the fabric announced in a font that suggested decisiveness. Opposite him, a newly minted coalition had chalked **RIVER FIRST, SHARED HANDS** in letters that looked like they had been written by six women who had practiced taking turns before their coffee.

"Ms. Adler," petition man called, discovering the power of a name shouted in a small space. "Is it true the LeClairs admitted to carving on the river?"

"No," she said. "And if you keep saying it, I'll charge you a candle a sentence."

"I'll cover his bill," Rosalie said, appearing at Miriam's shoulder like a well-timed angel armed with receipts. "If I can bill him for our rope."

Petition man blinked, calculations interrupted by a woman's audacity. "You can't bill me for rope," he said.

"You can't bill us for river," she said amiably. "We'll call it even."

Julian leaned toward Miriam, low enough that only the rim of her ear caught it. "With your permission," he said, "I'm going to monopolize petition man for ten minutes and introduce him to our scanning queue. If I can put him in charge of handing out numbers, he might forget to shout."

"Sheer genius," she murmured, and watched him peel the man away with kindness weaponized into logistics.

He returned with ink on his fingers and a look that said he had survived something that had started as a conversation and tried to mutate into outcry. "He knows where the stapler lives now," Julian said. "I think that means we're engaged."

She looked at his hand, at the line of tiny black dots the stapler had tried to tattoo across his thumb. "Come with me," she said, and led him to her shop where she kept a medicine drawer for men who told you they were fine while bleeding in small, meaningful increments.

While she fished out a bandage, an Adler niece walked in with her mother's face and her own shoulders less stiff, more capable of carrying the weight of a sentence that begins *I was wrong.* "Ms. Adler," the niece said, "if we bring the board minutes from the thirties, will you read them out loud in the circle? Not to shame. To... end the rumor before it becomes legend."

"Yes," Miriam said. "Thank you."

The niece looked at Julian's thumb, at the quiet camaraderie between them, and smiled, relieved at the sight of adults who could stand near each other without requiring a calamity to justify it. "I'll bring cookies," she said, and left, the bell confessing the relief of a day that had decided not to avalanche.

They tried, once, to take five minutes with coffee and failed twice. The sheriff called with a request to inventory who had handled the basin cart that morning and whether any wrench marks looked new. "We'll come down," Julian said, neutral as a level. "We'll bring what we know and what we don't." Pastor Elijah texted that the elder from yesterday who'd spoken about 1902 had remembered a name and wanted to speak it without microphones. "We'll come," Miriam wrote back. Sloane sent a photo of stakes and tape arranged like a geometry lesson and a caption: **if this turns into performance art I refuse to clap.** "Understood," Julian replied.

At the river a pair of teens in waders stood too near the rope, eyes bright with the thrill of being allowed to assist and the terror of messing up in front of the entire town. "We'll mark where the symbol is clearest at three," Julian told them, "and again at four, and again at six. You get to write the numbers. This is a job."

"Can we name it?" one asked.

"No," Miriam said, smiling. "But you can teach your friends how to be quiet."

They stood side by side while the first measured points were placed. The breeze came up the seam; the symbol did what it had done since showing: accepted light and lent it back with kindness. Miriam felt the mood of the green tilt toward argument again a stir near the food trucks, a rising and falling near the court steps where the mayor had against advice decided to hold a mini-press update with a cardigan and a set of phrases no one had asked for.

A voice sharpened behind them. "You people," a man said neither Cavanaugh nor LeClair nor Adler, just a man with a mortgage and the urge to punch the nearest symbol to make his fear behave "you people are going to get someone killed with your rope and your... mysticism."

Julian moved by instinct half-step forward, half-turn, one hand slightly out not to block but to receive. "We can talk," he said to the man, calm as night. "But we won't shout. Not here."

"You think you can stand between me and my river?" the man demanded.

"No," Julian said. "I'm standing between you and a mistake."

Miriam put her palm lightly on Julian's forearm permission and praise and a warning to herself not to drag them both into a theater. Sheriff Mayhew materialized from the left with the bored competence of a man who removes hornets from kitchens. "Let's take a lap," he told the man, steering him with a professional gravitational field. "You can try your sentence on me first. If I survive it, maybe it's safe for the square."

Julian's breath came back slow. He didn't look at Miriam, but his arm eased under her palm.

"You didn't need me," she said later, when the man had been walked into kindness and out of volume.

"I needed the part of me that remembers to be generous when I'm frightened," he said. "You carry that for me sometimes."

The romance of it wasn't in the tone it was in the consequences. He moved closer without making a show. The town pressed in without meaning to. The day asked for more than two people could carry, and somehow they carried it anyway by dividing it between them, the way you carry a basin when you don't want to slosh.

By late afternoon, the list of suspects had grown not by names but by motives. It wasn't just families it was anyone with a story to protect, anyone with a parent to defend, anyone with a ledger entry that would look ugly in a bright room. The square contained all of that and managed not to burst. Love does that. So does shared work.

AT THE NIGHTLY circle under the cottonwood, the fractures showed the way hairline cracks do when the sun hits the glaze. No one broke. Plenty of people flexed.

A LeClair uncle asked to speak first and did with uncommon succinctness. "If you think we cut the river," he said, "you don't know us." He sat before the sentence could be collected for use by people who thrive on collections.

A Cavanaugh aunt stood and admitted her family had demanded first place too often. "We lift well," she said. "We don't share the lift well. I'm sorry." The air around the apology changed like a room that has learned to open a window. "In 1934 the board voted to move the blessing closer to the steps. In 1937 the board voted to move it back. In neither vote did we ask the people who did the work to answer first. We should have." He handed Julian a folder. "This belongs with you, not with us."

Murmurs rose some relief, some resentment that the record could be so tidy when the feeling had not been and Pastor Elijah, who had developed a sixth sense for detonations that could be prevented by song, lifted a hand. "We will not grade each other's grandfathers in public," he said.

"We will bring the papers and the memories to the same table and let them work on each other."

The sheriff spoke briefly about keeping tempers shorter than rope. Sloane announced that the high schoolers would be in charge of tomorrow's measuring and that anyone who argued with a seventeen-year-old in a reflective vest would be sentenced to clean every extension cord in Cedar Creek County. Laughter helped. It always does when the world is trying to turn your throat into a closed fist.

Then the elder who had survived 1902 raised a hand and everyone, as if taught, stilled. "We promised each other once," she said. "When the fort was a fort and the river decided if we got bread. We promised not to take more than was our share. A man took more. We forgave on paper and kept the score in our bones." She looked at Miriam as if reading off a page only the two of them could see. "You're going to bring it out. Don't be frightened when you do. We lived. We'll live again."

After, the circle dissolved into clumps that looked like ordinary neighbor talk until you listened: all the appeals and retorts and hesitations of a community trying to learn a new skill in public holding two truths at once without using one to kill the other. The fractures were not shattering lines. They were hinge pins that had gone a little rusty.

Miriam and Julian walked the perimeter with a clipboard that carried a to-do list disguised as three questions: *What did you see? What do you fear? What do you hope happens next?* Nearly everyone answered the third. Most people surprised themselves with the size of their answers.

"Hope is treason in some rooms," Miriam said, checking off a line where a man had said he hoped his grandson would learn to carry without being told who to hate.

"In this one it's currency," Julian said, and she loved him

for using financial language to describe mercy. "We can afford to spend it."

They slipped away for ten minutes because even the diligent need a pocket of dark. On the dock, the lanterns made their gentle map and the symbol in the shallows rested like it had been certain of this night for a hundred years. He leaned on the railing, forearms touching wood that had learned to hold the weight of people who were almost ready to tell the truth.

"We have suspects," he said, listing as if preparing a label. "Motive across three families, plus pride, plus fear, plus the ancient human habit of wanting to be right more than we want to be whole."

"And a mark," she said. "That refuses to be a cudgel."

"And a town," he said. "Cracked but not broken."

"And us," she said.

He turned toward her then, the square's song behind them, the river's patience in front. It would have been so easy to let affection draft a speech, to turn the moment into blush or flourish. Instead he did the thing that would keep the room steady. He stepped nearer and said, "I'm going to walk on your left when we go to the Adlers again, so the front door doesn't box you when she opens it."

She laughed, startled; then her eyes warmed the way cedar warms under oil. "Thank you," she said. "I'm going to speak first when we see Lou, so he wastes his glare on me."

"Deal," he said.

It was intimacy in the form of strategy two people drawing a map that made future rooms safer. The romantic heat wasn't an interruption of the work; it was the work, the way sharing weight is the most ancient foreplay in the world.

On their way back up the path, they passed two

teenagers practicing what to say to a grandfather who insisted the symbol was a hoax and the river a faucet. "Ask him for a story," Miriam called softly over her shoulder. "Not an opinion. Stories break less."

They reached the square in time to see petition man hand a stapler to the Adler niece so she could post the scanned minutes, and if that wasn't an omen for repair, Miriam didn't know what was. Sheriff Mayhew took off his hat and scratched the place in his hair where his patience lived. Sloane rewound a cord the way a sailor makes a bed. Rosalie blew out a test flame and nodded to Mr. Cavanaugh across a lane of folding chairs like a pianist acknowledging a drummer after a good run.

Later, at her table, Miriam opened her notebook and wrote down the names they had heard, the phrases that belonged to this day: *door/hinge; not yet; forgive shoes; ledger as weather; remember in public.* She added a private line for herself: **I will bring you out doesn't mean without pain. It means with company.** The page took the ink and made a quiet place for it to live.

Across town, in his apartment over the museum, Julian put the Cavanaugh coffee under the sink because he could not bring himself to drink it after seeing Lou's jaw, then wrote a line in a logbook that he would later share in the circle: **Suspects: habits, histories, pride, fear. Missing: villain. Present: neighbors.** He stared at it, then added, almost shyly, **Present: partnership.**

Cedar Creek slept the way towns sleep when they've used their bodies to resist the old gravity and succeeded for a day. In the shallows the mark kept its loop and refused theatrics. In the south wall, the old door remembered being a door. In three kitchens and one parlor, family names practiced letting go of the breath they'd been holding since someone first wrote *remember* in a margin and then failed to finish the thought. The basin, oiled and silent, waited for hands that would lift it with less entitlement and more care.

Morning would bring new rumors, a sheriff's notebook, a board folder with a date that mattered, a dream with chains in it and a sound like a hinge in good repair. But tonight, under lantern light and the hum of tired men stacking chairs correctly on the first try, the fractures looked less like a map of breaking and more like a guide to where the hinge pins went places to oil, places to check, places to bless.

9

THE DREAM OF WATER

Sleep, when it finally came, arrived like weather: not obeying her request so much as deciding her house lay beneath its current. Miriam drifted, the kind of drift you get when the body keeps a little vigil even while it agrees to go off duty. She knew, as you sometimes do while dreaming, that she was in two places at once her bed under the window where the shawl hung like something faithful, and a bank beside the wide dark seam where the creek and the river stitched themselves together without asking anyone's permission.

Night had shed its surface: no paper lanterns tonight, no hum of neighbors at the cottonwood, only the raw sound of water doing its oldest work. She stood on the dock in bare feet that did not feel cold. The moon wore no drama; it kept to its business. Downstream, the bend went black and then not, like something breathing. She waited, because waiting had turned out to be the only useful skill the last few days required waiting without deciding what the waiting would produce.

The river ran harder in the dream than it had yesterday

in noon light. It had the force of questions asked with sincerity: not angry, exactly, but unwilling to pretend. The surface pleated and unpleated as if hundreds of invisible hands smoothed a sheet and wrinkled it again, testing for proper fit. She heard, far under the sound, a separate tone as if stone itself hummed. She tried to place it. The note had a human register. It wasn't grief. It wasn't triumph. It was the hum you get when a valve opens after years of rust and says *oh,* a word made of metal.

The water changed. Not because anything above it commanded, and not because the moon asked, but because something underneath decided. The rush separated, not with violence but with a kindness that startled her like a friend parting a crowd with a forearm and a smile. A channel showed where no channel had been. The seam unwove itself and then rewove, leaving a strip of riverbed uncovered and shining in a light that didn't come from the moon or from any lamp. She didn't think *Red Sea* until later; in the moment, she thought, simply: *space.*

And there they were. Not the delicate ironwork her mind would have supplied if given the task of set design. Not the cartoon shackles of plays that teach children to hate, safely. These were working chains links thick as a wrist, dark with a history of silt, grown into the river's bottom as if the water had decided long ago to keep them from air. Their geometry had been warped by years of weight and pressure; places meant to pivot had fused. Some sections had become almost organic with the slow accrual of grit and shell. The river had made them furniture.

A hand if water can be said to have a hand moved along the length. Miriam didn't see fingers. She felt pressure: attention with weight. It tested each joint. Here a rock lodged. Here a knot of wire. Here rust had performed its slow mercy, turning implacable into friable. Here, though here the link still held what it had been forged to hold, tight as a mouth refusing an apology. The hand stayed. The pressure increased, not as force but as patience acquiring muscle.

"Whose?" Miriam asked, and the sound dissolved. Dreams don't offer you microphones. They offer you posture. She closed her mouth and watched, the way she had watched the cup yesterday pass from Rosalie's hand to the child with the steady wrist, the way she had watched the symbol receive sunlight and refuse to spend it cheaply.

When the first link broke, it didn't shatter. It cracked along a line you could have predicted had you been the one to forge it and the one to maintain it and the one to neglect it and the one to repent it if you had been all those people in succession. A soft sound soft not because it lacked strength but because the river absorbed it like a mother absorbing a child's first shout rose. The second link gave easier, as if permission had been granted by the first. The third required a little argument. You could feel the river grin at the chance to argue kindly.

She knelt then, in the dream, without deciding to, and put her palm flat on the dock's gray board. The wood under her hand felt like a friend's shoulder. The river's patience flowed through it into her bones. She thought of the ledger's messy week. She thought of the carpenter's pencil stopping on purpose. She thought of the basin that refused and the stone that accepted. The chain's fourth link sighed. The fifth let go like a held breath. The sixth clung out of habit. Habit is not nothing. Habit built chairs and rules and beloved recipes. Habit also built prisons.

A flash on the link's outer curve caught her eye: a mark. Not the river's loop symbol exactly, but kin to it a bend, then hesitation, then completion scratched with a knife by a human hand into metal, the way men sign their work where only weather will see. A maker's mark? A warning? A prayer disguised as proof? The river's attention rested there and, in resting, increased. The link cracked, and the sound this time was not soft. It was a report, a little like laughter.

Miriam wanted to ask *Who put you here?* She wanted to ask *Who did you keep?* She wanted to ask *Who did you protect?* because chains sometimes keep people from being dragged by currents they cannot fight alone. She stayed quiet, because questions that large are better asked with the whole body, and she was only one person kneeling on a dock in a night that might not even exist.

When the last remaining link surrendered, the chain didn't leap. It lay. It had been a tool. It would now be a story. Water moved over it, around it, touched its empty sockets and discovered they were not empty at all they held a different use. Not lock. Hinge.

That was when she heard it, clearly, in the part of the dream where meaning travels better than language. *I will bring you out.* Not as thunder. Not as politics. As instruction. The sentence landed in her chest like something you hang on a nail you installed for that purpose months ago without quite knowing why. The tone carried no threat. It carried a promise that included work. The words did not say *I will carry you.* They said *I will bring you out,* which implied movement you are asked to participate in.

The river rebraided. The seam closed its opened lips. Light returned to doing its small honest job on surface. The dock decided to be wood again instead of a stethoscope. Night regained its ordinary size. Miriam stood, and the perspective of the dream tilted the way dreams tilt when they're finished with you and decide you can be returned.

She woke with her palm still pressed to the mattress as if the dock had followed her upstairs and the house had agreed to let it. The window showed gray beginning to fade into blue. The shawl on the chair looked like a tide retreated and left folded witness. She lay quiet and listened to her blood. The chain sound remained faint as an aftertaste, sure as a signature.

Her first impulse was to put the dream in a box labeled *nice.* Her second stronger was to sit up, swing her feet to the floor, and write. She reached for the notebook and found, tucked where she'd put it last night, the receipt with the completed loop and the page where Julian had titled their rules. She sketched, quickly: dock, seam, chain, links releasing in order, small knife line where a maker had claimed his sin or his craft. She wrote the sentence twice *I will bring you out* once like a heading, once like a request. She circled the word *will,* then circled *out.* She underlined *you.*

The house hadn't warmed yet. She wrapped the shawl around her shoulders and felt ridiculous for an instant in the way you feel ridiculous when you wear an heirloom on an ordinary morning. The ridicule passed. She went to the kettle, lit the flame, watched the smallest blue triangle catch. The day hadn't decided on its tone. She could help with that only by telling the truth at breakfast and then again at lunch and then again at dusk when the lanterns came. A weaver's work of hours.

On the counter she laid the notebook open and, without ceremony, wrote a small prayer she would pretend later she hadn't written: **If the chains are ours, show us where. If they are our parents', let us repair without breaking their hands. If they are the town's, make us strong enough to lift together.** She added a line for herself: **If my gift is to hear this, let me use it like a tool, not a crown.**

Steam began. The kettle sang like a distant cousin to the river's hum. The dream stayed in the room, not as a movie but as a blueprint.

SHE MET Pastor Elijah because he was the only one awake who would hold the dream without turning it into either a sermon or a circus. He was sweeping the church steps at an hour that suggested either insomnia or service beyond sense; with him the two were regular cousins. The morning had gone linen-white. The square would arrive later with its versions. For now, the broom made the only public sound.

"Morning," he said, then looked up, then really looked. "Do you want to be asked how you slept?"

"I want to be asked if you have five minutes," she said, and he made five look like a loaf.

They sat on the top step. She told him the dream like a woman reporting weather observed from her porch, not like a prophet descending a hill. Chains. Linking. Release by sequence. A maker's mark on an outer curve. The sentence lodged in her chest like a nail hung for the future.

"'I will bring you out,'" he repeated, rolling the words as if checking each for cracks. "Not 'I'll bring you back.' Not 'I'll bring you up.' Out." He smiled at the preposition like an old joke between friends. "Do you want me to bless it? Or do you want me to hold it until you are sure it's not trying to make you bigger than you are?"

"The second," she said, relieved to be understood that quickly. "I don't want to be the town's... funnel."

"You are the town's ear," he said. "Ears aren't thrones." He rested the broom across his knees as if it were a staff, as if the staff were a broom, as if he had given up long ago needing his tools to announce themselves. "The sentence is good news with a job attached. The bringing out, Miriam it requires feet."

"Whose?" she asked.

"Ours," he said. "That's the hardest part. People want deliverance to arrive like mail. It arrives like work with a map."

They sat with it. A gull stitched the air. Somewhere down the block the baker negotiated with dough in a language that shouldn't have been as holy as it was. Pastor Elijah said, after a minute, "Chains are odd in Scripture, aren't they? Sometimes judgment, sometimes folly, sometimes literal. We're so used to reading texts as metaphors that we miss that there were always people under them. The Exodus is glory, yes, but it is also logistics. Sandals, water flasks, their children's moods."

She laughed. "Our people are moody."

"They are," he said. "And beloved. Consider this: if the river shows chains, perhaps it wishes us to remember both sides what bound and what kept from drifting. My old teacher said once that vows and vows broken look similar from a distance." He looked at her with the half-teasing expression he used to break the danger of over-seriousness. "You are not allowed to singlehandedly interpret the town's dream, and I am not allowed to hide behind procedure. We shall consent to both."

"Consent to both," she echoed. "That's the only way the 'we' works."

He leaned back on his elbows, allowing his body to relax in a way she rarely saw in public. "Say the sentence again."

She did: *I will bring you out.* There again the part of her chest that had felt tight for days let go half an inch. The words felt less like marching orders and more like a hand at her back reminding her how to stand.

She walked from the steps to the museum, where Julian would be making his early rounds the private tour he did for the building when no one watched. She found him in the south gallery, not touching the old plaster but looking at it the way men look at a friend's face that won't yet tell them what hurts. He turned, and his relief at seeing her landed like a soft thing on a table made of work.

"Morning," he said, his voice lower, the way that happens when a room is holy and you haven't told it it is yet.

"I had a dream," she said.

"Do you want me to be glad, skeptical, or both?" he asked, smiling a little, testing their method as if they'd built it for this very hour.

"Both," she said. "And protective."

"Always," he said, and she told him the river parting, chains, the sequence of release, the small knifed mark, the sentence.

He listened the way good men listen when they refuse to turn women's seeing into a show. He asked two questions not to poke holes but to help the picture sharpen: "Which link held longest?" and "What did the river do after?" She answered. He nodded. He reached for the yellow pad and wrote **dream: chain / link sequence / maker's mark / 'bring you out'** in his careful block letters that made everything look ready for a dossier. He drew a small rectangle for the dock and a curve for the seam and then almost laughed at himself. "I'm making a map of your sleep."

"Maps are welcome," she said. "It helps me not feel like I'm trying to move the town with a sigh."

He reached for the mica panel without being asked, laid the transparency with her loop over it, then set the receipt beside his schematic. "The maker's mark," he said. "We'll add it to the list things to look for on the stone you saw last night when the light did that trick at the rope. If it exists in metal, maybe the carver imitated it on cedar or on river rock. Or the other way around."

"The river argued kindly," she said, remembering the give of the fourth link. "Not violent. Firm. It felt like consent engineered from two sides inside and outside both wanting the same thing."

"Then our job is not to drag," he said. "It's to align."

She could have kissed him then for the word alone *align,* so sensible, so kind to mystery without making it magic. Instead she said, "I went to the steps. Pastor Elijah blessed the sentence without smothering it."

"And what do you need from me to bless it without turning it into policy?" he asked, half-joking, wholly sincere.

"I need you to keep asking for the proof that teaches the room how to trust itself," she said. "And to ask me to tell it once in public not as performance. As record."

"Tonight, then," he said. "Under the cottonwood. Not as a *thus saith.* As a *this is what I saw in my sleep, and this is what it gave my body back when I woke.*"

He moved a fraction closer without making it about closeness; his nearness felt like the mayor bringing chairs facing the right direction. "Say the sentence again," he said, and when she did he closed his eyes, unembarrassed by faith when used respectfully. "It sits right," he said. "In the way a well-driven nail sits right."

They called Sloane and told her the least sensational version. She didn't flinch. "It tracks," she said. "Chains show up where people don't think through load. If the town over-loaded a promise a century ago, no wonder we're hearing snapping sounds." She added, because she was Sloane,

"Also if you tell this to anyone with a YouTube channel before we get our electrical inspected I will replace your coffee with decaf for a week."

They brought the sentence to Sheriff Mayhew, too, because he'd asked for anything that might help keep people from turning into matches in a dry season. He listened and thought for a long time, head cocked the way a dog listens to a frequency humans rarely admit exists. "I don't know what to do with it as law," he said finally. "But as practice: near and slow, even with our mouths. That fits."

By noon, the dream had stopped being a bright object and had become a tool. Julian set the high schoolers to look for maker's marks in photographs of the basin under raking light while he wrote a simple brief labeled **Chain Imagery in Cedar Creek Sources** two citations, three questions, one caution against overreading. Miriam carried a folded card in her pocket with five words to remind her not to inflate: *report, not proclaim; invite repair.*

The sentence began to do its work in her as well. When a LeClair cousin spoke harshly at the rope, her chest tightened and then widened *bring you out,* it said, not *bring you under.* When a Cavanaugh aunt pressed a rumor into her palm as if it were currency, Miriam held it, saw it, and then, gently, refused to spend it. When Mrs. Adler's niece brought the board minutes and said, "Please tell them my grandfather wasn't a villain," Miriam nodded. "He was a hinge," she said quietly. "We'll oil the pin, not break the door."

She did not float through the day on a mystic cloud. She fetched stakes; she lost her pen twice; she answered the same question fourteen times with slight variations in vocabulary to prevent boredom from becoming contempt. But the dream mapped her patience. The sentence gave her breath something to aim for.

· · ·

EVENING. The square had learned, surprisingly quickly, a cadence that reduced the day's chance of self-harm: scanning, work, walk, circle. Miriam felt the minute arrive when the town would be best able to receive a story without weaponizing it. She found Julian's eyes across the green, and he gave her the smallest nod on purpose. Sloane had somehow adjusted the angle of the temporary light under the cottonwood so people's faces looked like their faces and not like villains in cautionary tales. Pastor Elijah held the room with his hands open and his sentences shorter than the line for pie.

When it was time, he didn't introduce her like a prophet. He said, "Miriam dreamed and brought it to a kitchen table and then to us," and he sat.

She didn't stand on anything. She didn't seek the center. She simply turned, so the circle could see her face, and spoke with the plainness she saved for people she refused to perform for.

"Last night," she said, "I dreamed the river parted not like a show, but like a friend making room. I saw chains on the bottom. Not everywhere; one length, like a sentence laid down to be read. Links broke in order. Some gave easily. One held longer because habit kept it shut. There was a small knife mark on an outer curve like someone's name where only weather could read it. When the last link let go, the chain lay quiet. I heard a sentence in my chest that felt older than our town and kinder than my fear: *I will bring you out.*"

She let silence do its job for a full breath. You could hear forks. A child whispered to a child. People do that fill in space on your behalf. She kept it open.

"I'm not telling you what to believe," she said. "I am telling you what my body brought back. It did not feel like a threaten. It did not feel like a trick. It felt like permission to do the work in front of us without pretending we are heroes or victims."

Julian stepped to her right but not *in front of,* which would have been theatrical and held the transparency up the way he'd held ledger pages, as if saying *here is another record.* He spoke once. "We will look for the maker's mark in wood and stone," he said. "If you have objects in your homes with that small curve scratched in, bring them to the table. We'll scan, return, and make the copies public."

Mrs. Adler's niece lifted a hand. "If the chain held someone," she said, trembling at the door between metaphor and confession, "will we say who?"

Miriam met her eyes. "If the chain held a habit," she said, "we already know its name. If it held a person, we will treat that name like a wound and a responsibility. Either way, we will not use it to break each other. We will use it to repair."

Pastor Elijah said, eyes crinkling, "Amen to repair," and the circle breathed. Sloane distributed notecards and tape like votives. Sheriff Mayhew, who needed everything grounded in a job he could point to when asked by people whose relationship to control was litigious, posted a simple sign he had written himself: **IF YOU BRING A THING, WE'LL SCAN IT; IF YOU BRING A FEAR, WE'LL HOLD IT; IF YOU BRING A RUMOR, WE'LL TEST IT.**

After the circle, a woman Miriam didn't know pressed a tiny brass charm into her hand. "From my grandmother's sewing tin," she said. "We never knew what it was. It looks like a link without ends." It did. A little oval, open. Miriam didn't keep it. She put it in the scanning bowl with the same care she would have used for a letter or a loaf. "Thank you," she said, and meant: thank you for risking the making public of private weather.

She found Julian at the table with the mica panel and a small line of high schoolers combing photographs for signs their town had left itself breadcrumbs. He had ink on his wrist and the patient smile of a man whose favorite sport is consistency. "You were exactly right," he murmured when she reached him. "Report, not proclaim."

"You were exactly right," she returned. "Proof, not bludgeon."

He tilted his head toward the river. "Will you come sit by the rope for five minutes? I want to listen with you. Not for a show. To calibrate."

They walked. The lantern shepherds were halfway through, and the symbol kept its habit of grace. Miriam sat on the very edge of her chair, leaned forward, and offered the river the most sincere kind of attention she knew a willingness to hear no answer and still be grateful for the conversation. The current touched the stone. The groove held. Between them, their shoulders aligned without effort.

"What do you hear?" he asked finally.

"That we'll find the mark," she said, surprised to feel a certainty that wasn't smug. "And that the ledger we need will feel like an apology written by a man who never learned how to apologize in public."

He nodded once, not because he shared her exact sense but because he had learned to trust the way her sentences opened rooms where his could hang maps. "Then tomorrow we live at the archive until the dust calls me by name."

"Tomorrow," she said, and the word contained the quiet joy of people who have finally chosen to let their gifts stop fighting and start multiplying.

Walking home, she found she was not ashamed of the dream. She had expected shame: for needing extra senses, for bringing old language into rooms where people wanted all their nouns measurable. The shame wasn't present. In its place: a wary ease, the knowledge that some mornings the work would be to carry a word into the square and set it on the table without insisting anyone eat. If the word was right, it would feed someone by accident.

In her kitchen she lit two small candles the way her great-aunt had taught her, not as magic but as habit, and the room brightened in a way that made the refrigerator's hum sound like a cousin to prayer. She took the letter from the envelope and set it beside the notebook. She added to the page where her rules lived: **7) When given a dream, test it against kindness, then against courage, then against the room. Keep only what passes all three.**

She made tea and, while the water turned dark, reached for her phone and typed a text not to Julian but to the Adler niece, who had looked like someone holding an heirloom that had a sharp edge. *If you want,* she wrote, *I can come by tomorrow and listen to the story your grandfather wouldn't tell. We can decide together how to set it down.* The three dots appeared, hesitated, vanished, and then: *Please. Morning? I'll bake.*

Miriam smiled, because healing sometimes sounds like that *Please. Morning? I'll bake.* She put the phone face down and sat in her small chair by the small window where the shawl swung slightly in a draft. Her body, that stubborn recorder, felt more like a tuned instrument and less like an antennae someone else controlled. The gift wasn't a performance. It was a job, and she had partners.

Across town, in his room over the museum, Julian added one line to the logbook that had started to do more than inventory objects. **Public dream shared. Circle held. Work continues.** Then after a pause in which he allowed himself to be a person and not only a curator he wrote: **I believe her.** He didn't underline it. He didn't need to.

The river kept moving. It always does. But that night, if rivers are capable of satisfaction and who is to say they aren't? it moved with the contentment of a thing seen truly and carried rightly. In the shallows, the loop accepted starlight and whispered its single articulate word to any body willing to hear it as both instruction and comfort: *and.* The chains, wherever they lay on the bottom of the river, in the hollows of families, in the ledger that waited in a file the thirties had tried to teach the fort to forget felt pressure that was not coercion. The first hairline cracks widened a hair more. The town dreamed its own dream: walking out together, not back, not up, *out.*

10

THE HISTORIAN'S DOUBT

Julian had paper spread like a low tide. The archive table took it well, oak accepting maps, minutes, photos, the yellow pad with their rules at the top: **Adler–Roth Method.** In his blocky hand he'd added a new line beneath the six: **7) Pre-register questions before looking for answers** a historian's version of tying his own hands kindly.

"Sit," he said when Miriam stepped into Collections. He sounded like a man trying to be courteous to a fire.

She sat. The room kept its museum hush, the kind that has nothing to do with reverence and everything to do with paper being old enough to deserve a stable temperature. He didn't reach for her hand; he reached for a stapled packet.

"I wrote up the chain brief," he said. "Four historical uses in town records logging, ferry mooring, mill wheel lock; three metaphorical uses temperance meetings, a sermon in 1923, a school essay inexplicably titled *Freedom is a Bridge with Chains,* which I am choosing to forgive because adolescence; and two physical sightings that could matter: 1891 flood inventory lists 'one chain length seized by sheriff pending dispute.' And a 1934 ledger note that might be about securing the basin cart during the switch to the steps."

Miriam scanned, grateful for the way his lists quieted the room. "It's good," she said. "It's careful."

He didn't smile. "Careful is the point today."

She looked at his mouth. Careful had tension in it. "Say what you need to say."

He took the breath men take when they don't want to be mistaken for cruel and don't want to start apologizing before they've told the truth. "Your dream," he began, then corrected himself. "The dream you reported to the square. It's doing what dreams do spreading by retelling. Three people have already 'seen' chains before breakfast."

"Or three people saw chains," she said softly. "And were relieved someone else said it first."

"Maybe," he allowed. "And maybe we lit a fuse we didn't mean to. I have a responsibility to keep this room from becoming a church for one story no matter how good that story sounds. I need something to triangulate against. Objects, documents, memory our rule. I can't let a vision be promoted to fact because it arrived with poetry."

She let the word **church** sit between them without picking it up. "Do you think I want that?" she asked. "To turn generosity into doctrine?"

"No," he said quickly, and the speed told on him. "I don't think that. I think you underestimate how hungry we all are for sentences that spare us work. *I will bring you out* sounds like someone else is going to do the lifting. It doesn't say *we will carry*."

"It didn't sound like that to me," she said, and there was nothing injured in her voice, only the steadiness of a woman who'd already argued with herself before breakfast. "It sounded like permission. And it gave me the detail of a maker's mark on an outer curve. That's not doctrine. That's a test we can try to run."

He leaned on his elbows, the paper beach under his hands making a small soft sound. "Confirmation bias exists," he said quietly. "If we go looking for a scratch shaped like your loop, we might see it everywhere. Our eyes are devout, Miriam. They will bow before whatever we train them to love."

"And yours are devout to caution," she said with a little smile that made space for his habit to be respected. "Which is why we don't go alone. Which is why we wrote the rules."

He rubbed his thumb over the pad's edge like a man needing the feel of a boundary. "Rule one: three witnesses. Right now we have two your dream and the community's appetite. We have a symbol in stone, but not proof that it speaks the same sentence as your river. If we start to hang meaning on it, and later the documentation doesn't hold, this room will have taught the town to distrust itself."

"What would proof look like for you?" she asked. Not challenge. Inventory.

"A ledger entry that names a link or a person chained at a blessing," he said. "A letter complaining about a mark carved into a stone during a dispute. A tool with a maker's mark matching your scratch. Minutes recording that 1934 moved the basin to the steps in order to avoid a procession tied to a promise." He exhaled. "A plan that makes a prediction before we go hunting and makes us stick to it."

"Then we can draft one," she said. "Prediction: if the dream's maker's mark exists, it's repeated men sign their work. Maybe on cedar. Maybe under the repaired seam of the basin. Maybe on a stone they pulled and set back. And if the betrayal is about water rights, the missing ledger will not accuse with thunder; it will apologize in the margin and call that prudence."

He lifted his eyes. They were serious, save for the small flare there when he found a sentence he liked. "You think cowardice writes like that."

"I think love does," she said. "Love that wants to stay in a room with men who feed your family and pay your bills and also broke your town's first promise."

"I want to be that kind of love," he blurted, surprising them both.

"You are," she said, quieter now. "You also want to be a good steward of paper and of rooms. So tell me your line. Where do I go too far?"

He laughed, without mirth. "When you ask me to treat what you feel as equivalent to what I can hold," he said. "I need to keep them different until they shake hands."

"And where do I go too far?" he asked himself, because he knew this game, too.

"When you act like what you can hold is the only way truth shows up," she said. "You need to make a seat for what is older than our filing system."

He turned the stapled packet so the staple faced up precisely. He took the pen from behind his ear and wrote on the yellow pad: **8) Feelings ≠ facts; feelings → hypotheses. Facts ≠ only truth; facts → shared ground.** Then, without irony, he underlined both arrows.

"You know what frightens me?" he said.

"That you'll become your grandfather," she said before she could varnish the sentence. He didn't flinch.

"And you?" he asked, almost tender.

"That I'll become a funnel," she said. "A person the town uses so it can postpone being brave in its own voice."

They sat with the admission and the affection grew in

the space between fear and the table. The affection didn't fix anything. It made them bolder.

"All right," he said. "Here's my plan. First, we pre-register two testable predictions on the museum board: **a)** we will find a repeated mark on wood or stone matching your dream's scratch; **b)** we will find in 1930s or earlier ledgers a dispute over water usage that changed the ritual's geography. Second, we blind the hunt as best we can two volunteers will examine surfaces without being told what to look for, then we compare notes. Third, we keep bringing the town into the room."

"And fourth," she added, "we promise not to use our argument to keep from touching each other's work."

He smiled then, real and wrecking. "Fourth," he agreed. "Signed."

Sloane slid in, as if she'd been waiting to pick her moment like a lock. "I heard the word *blind* and assumed someone needed tape," she said, tossing a roll on the table. "I also have your permit to open twelve inches of the south wall after lunch if you promise to treat dust like it's sacred."

"Bless you," Julian said.

"Don't make me your liturgy," Sloane said. "Also, the mayor just told a reporter he has the 'full confidence' of the situation. Someone please give that sentence a seat outside."

They laughed, not because it was funny but because the room needed oxygen. Julian turned back to Miriam. "I want you at the wall," he said. "But I need you behind the drop cloth. Dust isn't good for lungs, and I like yours."

"You like mine," she said, annoyed and warmed in the way affection shows up to complicate irritation. "You also like control."

"That, too," he said bluntly. "Come anyway."

She came.

· · ·

THEY SET the drop cloth with the solemnity of people who know a wall can become a memory you regret touching. Sloane handed Julian a utility knife as if it were a narrative they were about to revise. Miriam stood just behind the cloth, eyes on the corner where the trim board changed its nail pattern two nails, three, void.

"Here," Julian said, tapping twelve inches south of the seam where her hand had warmed the paint yesterday. "Rule seven: cut where the plans suggest, not where we like."

"Rule eight: listen while you cut," she said.

"I am listening," he said, and he was ear to the wall, to the way old plaster speaks when you ask it to move. He scored, shallow. The blade sang the quiet song of gypsum. Dust rose and Sloane's shop vac started its low patient purr. The first rectangle loosened easier than pride does. He set it aside. Behind it: lath. He pressed gently and felt air rather than dirt. He looked at her over his shoulder, the grin involuntary.

"Hello, door," he said.

"Don't flirt with architecture," Sloane muttered, though her eyes were lit.

He slid his fingers into the gap and a chunk of lath splintered in his palm. "Damn," he said softly, not about blood but about the part of him that hated breaking any sentence the old room still wanted to speak. Miriam moved without deciding to, the way bodies do when they've rehearsed saving each other. She grabbed his wrist, turned it palm up, and wrapped the cut while managing not to scold or coo.

"You're allowed to be careful with yourself," she said.

"You're allowed to stop stepping in front of flying objects," he said.

"It wasn't flying," she said. "It was surrendering."

"And you weren't frightened?" His eyes did a small fierce thing.

"I was," she said. "That's not illegal."

He laughed, short. The air around them warmed. Sloane, who had the social graces of a cat with power tools, lifted the vac hose toward the ceiling. "I'm going to pretend I heard none of this over the noise of responsible custodianship," she said dryly. "Also, Mayhew is coming. Smile like people who planned this."

They widened the opening until there was no mistaking it: a threshold hidden by a generation that valued light control and donor nerves over processions. The trim on the buried jamb had a line of holes where hinge screws had once bitten. Julian touched the empty circles with his knuckle, reverent.

He glanced back at Miriam, dust in his hair like another century's dandruff, and everything about him his devotion to paper, his ridiculous caution, his sharp tenderness that hated to be caught in public knocked gently against her patience like a boat asking to tie up. Anger threaded with want; want threaded with the desire not to turn a fight into foreplay because the room was watching. That balance is a grown skill. They tried to keep it.

"You hate this," he said suddenly, reading her face as if it were a ledger. "Me cutting before we find your mark."

"I hate pretending that science and care make us safe from hurting," she said. "We hurt the wall. That's the price of knowing. I hate that it's always your hands."

"They're good hands," he said. "They've practiced."

"Stop making me love them while we're arguing," she

said, wrecked and fond and frustrated. The heat between them cracked something that had needed cracking for a while: the illusion that their restraint was only virtue and not sometimes a way to keep from admitting how much they wanted to be on the same side of the drop cloth.

Sloane snorted lightly. "If you two could time this to not coincide with the sheriff's arrival, that would be swell," she said.

Mayhew stepped in with a look that said he had seen worse in kitchens at 2 a.m. on holidays. "Looks like a door," he observed.

"It was," Julian said. "We'll patch."

"Patch later," Mayhew said. "Right now I need two responsible sentences to give to a man down the block who thinks holes are metaphors for anarchy."

"Tell him," Miriam said, "that we are making room for a story the wall wanted to tell."

Mayhew blinked, considered, nodded. "That'll play," he said. "As long as you also say 'permit.'"

Sloane waved a clipboard like a talisman. "My favorite word."

They covered the opening for the moment no one would pass through it without a plan and a blessing. Out by the rope, the light shifted toward evening. The symbol in the shallows readying itself, as always, to do nothing dramatic and everything necessary.

They walked there because that's where the arguing had to end by the water that insisted neither of them owned the right to define it. The teens doing the parallax grid greeted them with casual competence. A boy had drawn the loop clean in a notebook and labeled it **and** without irony. That steadied them more than any sermon.

Standing by the rope, Miriam stepped too close to the

edge with the focus of a person tuning an instrument. Julian's hand shot out automatic, gentle, stupidly attractive in its insistence gripped her elbow, tugged. She turned on him, both grateful and salted.

"Don't pull me," she said. "Ask me."

"Please don't step farther," he said immediately. "I can't think straight while you're risking your balance."

"Your thinking straight isn't the only thinking necessary," she said, anger cooling into its useful form clarity. "You are not allowed to keep me safe by making me smaller."

"I am allowed to want you alive," he said, voice a notch above whisper, because some truths refuse to be whispered. "I am allowed to stand between you and a mistake."

"I am allowed to decide what my mistakes are," she said, and then, because she could feel him about to apologize out of reflex, she touched his wrist where the bandage sat. "And I am allowed to admit that today I didn't want to make one. Thank you."

He looked at the wrist she held, and when he lifted his gaze the want in it had been educated by humility. "I keep treating proof as the only safety," he said. "It isn't. You are."

"You keep treating caution as love," she said. "Sometimes it's fear in a suit."

"Then teach me the difference," he said.

"I am," she said.

The lanterns came. They did the work they always do lowering voices without silencing them, giving the square an indoor feeling under an outdoor sky. The conflict between them didn't disappear; it integrated, threading itself into their stance in the way bodies do when they've agreed to tell the truth without turning it into theater. Passersby saw two people by a rope doing a job. Neither could see the way heat argument's, affection's made a small weather system between them and kept this edge from freezing over.

INTEGRATION STARTED, as their best things did, with a pad and a promise. Back in Collections, the wood dust tucked into their cuffs like a leftover century, Julian wrote a title large enough to be read by anyone who walked past and felt the itch to be included: **The Hinge Protocol.**

Below it, six lines that looked like common sense made brave.

1. **Make predictions in public.** Miriam writes what she "hears" before evidence is sought. No changing adjectives afterward.
2. **Pre-register searches.** Julian logs which boxes, shelves, surfaces they will check and in what order. No adding "oh we also looked there" without labeling it as afterthought.
3. **Blind volunteers.** Two teens (or one teen and Sloane, God help them) examine surfaces for marks without being told the shape. They sketch what they see. Only then do we compare to Miriam's sketch.
4. **Three witnesses or we wait.** Object + record + community memory. If we have two, we don't force the third. We keep listening.
5. **Report not proclaim.** The phrase that had carried them through the circle went on a line with a weight it had earned.
6. **Hold each other's worry gently.** If Julian says

"proof," Miriam hears love. If Miriam says "river," Julian hears work.

He set the pad by the south window the one that used to be a door and looked at her with the face he made when he'd built something serviceable and hoped she would use it.

"I will," she said. "And I'll make myself do the part that feels like math. Predictions. Here." She took the pen and wrote beneath his six: **A)** *Mark on cedar under basin repair or on a carved training stave in a family drawer.* **B)** *Ledger in 1930s box 'B' contains a note acknowledging overuse of water rights by one man; language avoids blame; mentions 'temporarily moved ceremony'.* **C)** *South doorway was used for a procession; term 'threshold' in carpenter's hand lines up with 'bring you out' in town memory.* She capped the pen and didn't move away from him. "If I'm wrong, I'll say it out loud."

"I will, too," he said. "I am wrong about tone as often as I am right about facts."

"You are not wrong about me needing the rope," she said, letting generosity be specific.

"And you are not wrong about me needing the sentence," he said.

They worked. He took the 1930s storage box that had been moved three times since the last intern mislabeled it. She took the community map and made appointments: Mrs. Alvarez at ten, the elder who remembered 1902 at noon, the Adler niece at two with cookies. They met in the middle at eleven-thirty when Sloane sent a text that read **south jamb = hinge ghosts, bring your polite faces** and came down together to trace the screw holes and the dirt shadows of a worshiped threshold.

At one, the teens reported from the parallax grid that the symbol read clearest from a point thirteen feet west of the rope and that, weirdly, a fish kept hovering at the loop's throat whenever the light swung low. "Does that matter?" a boy asked, trying to sound like a scientist and failing charmingly.

"It matters that you saw it," Julian said.

"It matters that you asked," Miriam added.

At two, Mrs. Adler's niece didn't tremble when she put her grandfather's pocket notebook on the table. "He wrote in pencil when he was ashamed," she said matter-of-factly. The paper was onion skin, the hand small and tired, the entry dated six months after the 1934 vote. *We agreed more than shares; who will tell? Move the blessing until tempers cool. Returning later will require contrition unpopular.* There was no thunder. There was apology, and the kind of prudence that has saved as many towns as it has delayed their healing.

Julian looked up at Miriam the way you look up at a person who has not only loved you but has also loved your job. "You were right about the tone," he said. He made a copy and wrote in the log: **predict → pencil; found → pencil.** He didn't underline anything. He didn't need to.

At three, Rosalie's cousin arrived with a cedar strip from her great-aunt's tool chest: wave pattern practice cuts and, at the far end, a hesitant scratch a bend, a pause, and then the beginning of completion that had been stopped on purpose. It wasn't proof; it was kinship. They scanned. The teens sketched it blind. Both drew a curve with a hesitation in the same place Miriam had circled. "Okay," Julian said, like a man agreeing to be convinced not by poetry but by pattern.

At four, Mayhew read the hinge protocol in the window and said, "If you two were cops, I'd put you in charge of things involving diaries," which, from him, counted as benediction. Pastor Elijah stopped and, without fuss, tapped Rule Six and smiled like a man whose favorite kind of religion is the kind that makes two particular people kinder to each other.

They still argued. At five, Miriam wanted to draft how she'd speak the sentence that night in the circle; Julian wanted her to improvise so it would stay honest. At five-thirty, he wanted to seal the south opening with board and she wanted to leave it breathing. They compromised: board, but not screwed, just braced. At six, she started toward the water too fast for his stomach; at six-oh-one he apologized for making a face a man makes when he believes he might lose something he could spend the rest of his life needing.

At the circle, they took separate chairs for once. He wanted to feel his own back. She wanted him to see her from the outside and decide he still chose this. The square listened better than it had any right to after a long day.

Julian spoke first history, not sermon. "We opened a section of the south wall with permission and dust, and we found a sealed threshold. The hinge screws left ghosts. The carpenter's plan, which some of you saw yesterday, labeled that side *procession*. In a 1935 pocket notebook, a man wrote that the blessing had been moved 'until tempers cool.' We will post the copy."

Miriam spoke next report, not proclamation. "We looked for a maker's mark blind. Two sketches from two sets of eyes saw the same hesitation. It may be nothing. It may be kin to the loop we've all learned to see with more patience. And my dream " She didn't look at Julian and also, somehow, she did. " it continues to be a tool, not a rule. If it is mercy, it will keep making us kinder to each other and truer with our paper." She held up the teen's blind sketch the way you hold up a small clean thing. "The town is learning to listen to itself."

A woman asked if the chain meant a person had been bound. Miriam felt the old urge to soften, to promise an answer that would save the town the hard work of nuance. She didn't. "We don't know," she said simply. "If we learn it, we will decide together what we do with a name."

Sloane announced, to no one's surprise and everyone's relief, that she had put the hinge protocol in the window because "nothing terrifies nonsense like transparent procedure." Mayhew asked for fewer rumors and more objects. Rosalie asked for volunteers to teach the toddlers that 'and' is a nice word. People laughed and signed up and brought pie.

When the circle eased and the lanterns took over, Miriam and Julian didn't retreat to the dock. They took the longer path under the cottonwood and stood at the south wall outside where the dark made the sealed door into a rectangle of not-yet. He set his palm there; she set hers beside it. In the quiet her shoulder touched his. They didn't move away. The friction of the day had left a warmth that felt like agreement, not truce.

"I don't want you to be my source," he said, the words careful and correct. "I want you to be my partner."

"I don't want to be your miracle," she said. "I want to be your method."

He laughed, relieved. "Do we get to kiss when the ledger turns up?"

"We get to keep working when it does," she said, and because the evening had made her generous and brave in the way integration does, she added, "We get to kiss when we don't need it to prove anything."

"Deal," he said. He didn't move. Neither did she. The

door in the wall said nothing. The river said the word it always says to people who have finally decided to bring both of their tools to the same table: *and.*

11

SABOTAGE SUSPECTED

Sheriff Mayhew asked them to meet at the municipal building's basement conference room the one with the flickering ballast that made everyone look like a suspect under aquarium glass. He'd chosen it on purpose, Miriam decided. There's a tone a room sets before anyone speaks, and this one said: write clearly, sit straight, don't waste the oxygen.

On the table: a brown evidence box with a number scrawled on blue tape, a stack of incident forms, a cheap recorder in a plastic bag like a goldfish. Mayhew's hat hung on the chair back as if to reassure them he hadn't turned into a different species of man just because he had paperwork.

"Appreciate you coming in," he said, voice in its morning register, which was two notes lower than his afternoons. "I want the cleanest account you can give me. No embroidery. No omitting from kindness. I'm building a sequence; that's the only way out of the rumor fog."

"We wrote a chronology for the museum log," Julian said, setting a folder on the table as if he were docking a boat. "Times, witnesses, actions. We can read it into the record."

"Please do," Mayhew said, tapping the recorder. He glanced at Miriam. "And Ms. Adler, after Mr. Roth reads, I want what you would add that paper can't carry."

He switched on the machine. Its little red eye made the air feel official. Julian read curator voice, steady as a level. "Commenced lantern walk at 2000 hours," he said, and then stopped, smiled at himself, and switched to human. "At eight, I was at the rope with two student volunteers. Sheriff Mayhew at the south post. Pastor Elijah at the cottonwood. Miriam Adler midway along the line, with Rosalie LeClair. Symbol visible as of 2006 hours from parallax point thirteen west."

Mayhew nodded, jotting. "Proceed."

"At 2017," Julian continued, "two individuals crossed the rope: male, mid-30s, later identified as Craig Thurber; and his brother Mark, early 20s. Sheriff intervened. Five-minute walk. They returned calm. At 2029, water in the ceremonial basin set on the river rock per tradition began to drop. No splashing, no visible siphon. Within two minutes, bottom dry. Crowd murmurs. Miriam moved to the rope. I secured the basin cart with Sloane Trieste. Pastor held the circle. Sheriff kept perimeter."

Miriam added, "At 2037, as the last of the water slid away, the symbol's loop was clearly visible. The town went quiet on its own. That rarely happens."

Mayhew's pen didn't stop. "At what point did you observe possible tampering with equipment?"

"Next morning," Julian said. "Sloane noticed wrench marks on the basin cart's rear brace new scuffs, not there at our last maintenance. The caster lock had been loosened. We logged it at 0915."

Mayhew lifted the lid on the evidence box and set a clear bag on the table. Inside: a brass plug the size of a walnut, threaded, a washer ringed with silt. "Found this near the east dock piling, seven feet from the basin staging area," he said. "Could be from an irrigation line. Could be nothing. Could be something. Did either of you see anyone near the pilings after the move from the steps? Anyone with tools?"

"Everyone has tools these days," Miriam said. The attempt at humor missed the table by an inch. "I didn't see a wrench."

"Sloane keeps three in her apron," Julian said. "But she was with me. If this was a deliberate drain someone inserted a plug, opened a stop, or used siphon principle. I have a list," he admitted, as if confessing to a vice. He turned to a page he'd printed: **Possible Mechanisms of Unauthorized Drainage**. Siphon hose concealed in floral garland. Hidden valve under river rock. Temporary gasket bypass. He sounded not excited afraid of being right.

Mayhew's mouth moved in a shape adjacent to a smile. "I like lists," he said. "They give my people a fair shot at a day."

He slid two photos across. "Second issue," he said. "Someone cut the rope at the west end at 2300 last night. No one crossed. But the cut was neat. Knife with a serrated belly. We're canvassing hardware stores. Meanwhile, Confluence FM ran with the 'Sabotage' word before breakfast. The Cedar Creek Observer newspaper wrote the mayor would like this to be an 'isolated incident.' The county water board would like 'controlled demonstration.' The insurance adjuster would like 'act of God' or 'unforeseeable.' Pick your poison."

"Rumor has already picked for us," Miriam said.

Mayhew looked at her, not unkind. "That's why I need

your account to be boring," he said. "The only thing rumor fears is boring."

He clicked off the recorder and leaned back, hat brim scraping the wall. The posture said: now we speak without stenographers. "I'm not here to make you doubt what you felt," he told Miriam. "And I'm not here to make you doubt what you can prove," he told Julian. "I am here to keep this from turning into a proxy war for a century of grudges."

He pulled a small notebook from his pocket. "Three calls before nine accusing the LeClairs of 'trickery with candles.' Four accusing Cavanaughs of 'rigging the cart.' One accusing the Adlers of 'financing mischief.' You can see how helpful this is."

"Like blaming weather on whichever neighbor hung laundry first," Miriam said.

"Exactly," Mayhew said. "So: I'm going to ask you both three questions and then I'm going to tell you a thing you won't like." He held up a finger. "One: do either of you believe a living person intentionally drained the basin?" He waited.

Julian stared at his list and at the brass plug and at his own fidelity to method. "I believe it's possible," he said. "I do not have evidence."

Miriam felt the shape the dream had left in her chest. It did not argue; it asked. "I believe the town is being shown something," she said. "I don't know if a hand helped the showing."

Mayhew lifted a second finger. "Two: are you willing to give me names of people who had opportunity? Not motive opportunity. People with access to the cart, to the staging, to the rope."

"Yes," Julian said at once. He read from his log. Sloane. Himself. The teen volunteers. Pastor Elijah. Rosalie. Two custodians. Sheriff's deputies. The mayor who hovered near the ribbon with a look that always made the tape nervous.

"Three," Mayhew said. "Will you commit to not announcing hypotheses as truth in the square for forty-eight hours while I canvas and check the pilings and see if anyone bought hose at midnight?"

Miriam felt the tug: transparency versus prudence. Their rule report, not proclaim helped. "We can tell the room what we *don't* know," she said. "We can say we're letting the sheriff do his work."

"Good," Mayhew said, satisfied because he liked to leave rooms with jobs. He stood, put the hat back where it belonged. "Now the part you won't like: I'm going to set temporary boundaries. Lantern walk stays. Rope stays. Scanner stays. But the basin stays in the museum until we sort the cart."

"The town will be livid," Julian said, and the idea hurt him more than he let on. "They've held themselves so well."

"They'll be livid at me," Mayhew said. "That's part of the job. Better they aim at one hat than at each other. I'll take my lumps at the microphone."

Miriam stood, the chair legs making a small apology. "If people come to me for certainty, I'll hand them your boring."

"Do," Mayhew said. He glanced at her again, a small private kindness. "If the river is telling a story, it'll keep telling it tomorrow. I need to see if any human hands tried to add a chapter."

They stepped out into the courthouse hall where light came through thick glass like a good idea slowly arriving. The mayor was already there in a sweater vest the color of mashed peas, consultant at his shoulder like a second spine.

"Ah," he said, relief spilling like coffee. "Narrative partners. Tell me we're going with valve malfunction."

"We're going with investigation," Julian said pleasantly.

"Unhelpful," the consultant murmured.

"Accurate," Miriam said. "Which helps more by noon."

They left them there, calibrating their statements. Outside, the square lay in that precarious early hour before the day decides its script. Two people were already arguing by the bakery door. Confluence FM's van idled by the curb like a rumor with a license. Miriam tucked her chin into the shawl she'd forgotten to forget and braced for the weather.

By eleven, the square had achieved critical mass. Banners went up without permission **RETURN THE BASIN** at one corner, **RIVER FIRST, SHARED HANDS** at another. Someone chalked **#StopTheSiphon** in a script too pretty for outrage. Across from it, a rival hand wrote **#NotAnAct-OfGod** and drew a tiny loop symbol that was either solidarity or blasphemy depending on your morning.

Mayhew stood on the courthouse steps with a mic he hadn't asked for. "The basin will remain in the museum today," he said, and it was remarkable how fast sound can move. A ripple of **boos** from the east, a ripple of **good** from the west. He kept his hands open. "Two reasons: we have evidence of tampering on the cart; and we're checking the pilings for any devices. This isn't forever. It's for now."

"Convenient!" someone shouted Lou Cavanaugh, of course, jaw in its usual mood.

"Cowardly!" from what sounded like the Adler porch club.

"Wise," Rosalie countered from the lantern table, and a slice of the square exhaled on her behalf.

Mayhew took it. "If you came to be told whom to hate," he said, voice steady, "I'm going to disappoint you. If you came to help, we have jobs: calm the toddlers, hold the line, bring your objects for scanning, and drink water. It's hot." He stepped back and let the square argue with itself for a minute. People who understand crowds understand fatigue; it's as good a tool as a whistle.

Confluence FM's host sidled up to Miriam and Julian as if he'd been invited. "We're live," he said. "The word 'sabotage' has traction. Can you confirm evidence of a plug?"

"I can confirm the sheriff is investigating," Julian said. "And the museum will publish today's findings at five."

"So that's a yes," the host said, turning to the mic, married as he was to inference.

"It's a *process*," Miriam said, and if she'd been holding a candle she would've put it in his hand to occupy it.

Rumors bloomed like algae. The LeClairs had been seen "late near the rope" true, because they cleaned wax spills. The Cavanaughs had been "conferring over the cart" true, because they maintained it every year. A Adler grand-nephew had "shouted at a deputy" true, because the deputy had called his sign ugly. Every fact softened into cudgel if you repeated it at a pitch.

By noon, the mayor's consultant had erected a podium near the cottonwood. Sloane took it down with her eyebrows and the force of her personality. "No podiums," she said. "Chairs in a circle. If you need height, stand on a crate like a carpenter."

"Messaging," the consultant whispered, horrified.

"Neighbors," Sloane replied.

The high schoolers soldiered on with the parallax grid while taking on the accidental job of de-escalation referees. "Sir, if you shout at Miss Rosalie you have to hold this stake for exactly four minutes," one of them told a red-faced man, who miracle held it. Two kids chalked a hopscotch near the rope with the loop symbol as the safe square; adults played while pretending to supervise the game. Pastor Elijah distributed lemonade with the air of a man who knows sugar can save marriages.

Still, the town drew lines. The bakery closed its back door to Adlers for an hour, then opened it again after Mrs. Levine remembered how many times Mrs. Adler had paid for Christmas rolls she couldn't stand to eat. The hardware store refused to sell hose to anyone without a driver's license; five men took offense on principle and then bought hose elsewhere and felt unvictorious about it.

A scuffle started near the museum steps when a man declared the basin should be reclaimed by "traditionalists." Miriam arrived in time to see Julian step between shoulders and shame and catch the arm that might have landed. "Not here," he said, not stern but disappointed. Shame has no defenses against disappointment; it sat down.

"Mr. Roth," the man muttered, "with all due respect, your job is to curate, not to "

"Keep going," Sloane said, appearing like a bouncer caught between resentment and glee. "Finish that sentence so we can all hear if it's as foolish as it sounded in your head."

The man didn't. He walked away. He would come back later with pie because Cedar Creek preferred that kind of arc to the other.

At one, Mayhew returned from the river with a muddy pant leg and a face that said: progress, not victory. "Two anomalies," he told Miriam and Julian in the lee of the cottonwood. "One: scrape marks on the east piling at a height consistent with someone bracing a hose. Two: a tether line under the third rock, cut clean. No device present. Might be old. Might be last night."

"Chain?" Miriam asked, thinking of the dream, and he shook his head. "Twine. Newer than chain. Older than this morning."

Julian's pen was already writing. "If there was a siphon," he said, "we'd expect water stains in a line from basin to river, but last night was dark. Our volunteers were watching the crowd. A person could have set it, left it, let gravity do the rest."

"You're not helping my blood pressure," Mayhew said, though the undernote in his voice admitted gratitude for minds that would do the unglamorous work of method in a town that loved drama.

They agreed to widen the rope by two feet and to ask the teens to point their attention up-crowd during the pour. "We are not turning a blessing into a police line," Pastor Elijah insisted, and Mayhew nodded. "We're turning it into a slower line," he said. "Slower lines spill less."

By three, Confluence FM and the Cedar Creek Observer had their headline: **SABOTAGE SUSPECTED; SHERIFF INVESTIGATES; BASIN PULLED FROM RIVER.** The square repeated the words as if repetition could turn them into proof. That's how rumor works it uses cadence the way hymns do.

At four, the Adler niece who kept finding new stores of courage the town didn't deserve but gratefully used brought out the pocket notebook page with its pencil apology and stood beside Miriam to read it aloud. The reading did not solve anything. It softened three men's throats, and that mattered.

At five, the museum posted the day's boring: hinge holes, parallax points, Sloane's permit number, the evidence of tampering logged without exclamation points. People read. Some calmed. Some burned hotter. By six, the square was a choral piece sung in rounds: accusation here, defense there, children running a loop in between like a counter-melody that kept the piece from becoming unlistenable.

They weren't going to win the day. You don't win days like this; you outlast them without letting them change your shape. Miriam watched the river; it did not scowl. It kept offering the same truth it had offered since it made the town possible: move forward, carry only what you must.

Evening cut the heat and turned breath back into air. Lanterns lit. The rope glowed like the outline of a lesson. The town's arguments softened to murmurs visible as hands moved, faces turned, brows loosened. That was the window Miriam waited for.

She stepped away from the circle before anyone could ask her to speak. She found a patch of grass near the south wall where the threshold slept behind board. She sat, back against the building, the wood cool as a calm thought. She closed her eyes and tried to hear what remained once slogans ran out of battery. The day left a residue silt of accusation in the chest, grit of caution in the teeth. Under it, though: the steadier hum she'd woken with since the dream. Not trumpet. Tool.

She took out her notebook and wrote a list with no poetry at all:

- **Mechanism.** If siphon: where concealed? If plug: source? If valve: who accessed? Map routes and hands.

- **Motive.** If present: embarrass a family? Force a return to the steps? Prove a pet theory? If absent: did the river act alone and we're mistaking its lesson for a trick?
- **Means.** Who had tools, time, proximity? Cross-reference with Mayhew's list.
- **Memory.** Whose story gets quieter when sabotage shouts? Who benefits from noise?
- **Mark.** Find the maker's scratch in wood or stone. If found, compare to chain dream. If not, admit absence.

The list calmed her. Lists are humility on paper: they admit you can't carry the whole thing in your head and shouldn't try.

Footsteps approached and stopped at an angle she recognized without opening her eyes. "You're not avoiding me," Julian said, "you're avoiding microphones."

"Also you," she said. "But not personally."

"I deserve it," he said mildly. He sank down beside her, back against the same wall, careful to leave a gap that wasn't a rebuff, only a courtesy. "Mayhew is stretched. The mayor is inventing new synonyms for 'manage optics.' Rosalie is three kindnesses past human capacity. I am sitting here until my spine agrees to be on my side."

"We're losing the room," she said.

"We're holding the room," he countered. "It just doesn't look like winning, which is deeply offensive to our need to feel useful."

She laughed, then sobered. "I'm going to the riverbank after the circle," she said. "Low side by the willow, where the old ferry tie-off was. If there was a siphon, it would have fed there. If there was a plug, it'll have left a scrape trail. If there was nothing, I'll take off my shoes and listen, and maybe the water will tell me which edge to look at tomorrow."

He turned his head. He did not say *no*. He did not say *I'll come, because I must.* He said, carefully, "Do you want me with you?"

The question felt like the right kind of love. "Yes," she said. "But I'm going whether or not you can. This isn't " She searched for the word that wasn't melodrama. " delegable."

He nodded, and in the motion she watched a man decide to trust a future where he wasn't the only one with a plan. "I'll bring a headlamp and a magnifier," he said. "And Sloane's grippiest gloves. And I'll text Mayhew so he doesn't think we turned into raccoons."

She smiled. "Text Mayhew that we turned into raccoons with permits."

"Rule nine," he said, pretending to write on his knee. "Never do anything useful alone."

They sat a minute more, listening to a town try to remember the harmonies of most of its better days. The circle swelled, then gentled. Pastor Elijah's voice came across the green like a note you can rest on. Mayhew spoke the smallest possible set of rules to make the night responsible. Sloane stored a coil of rope with sailor accuracy and a mother's fatigue. The teens closed their notebooks and remembered briefly how to be young without jobs. Miriam breathed, deep. The gift was there, not loud. She did not resist it. That was new.

They met Rosalie by the lantern table. "We're taking a walk," Miriam told her.

"Take a deputy," Rosalie said.

"Take my stubborn," Miriam replied, and Rosalie put a small first-aid kit in her hand as if to bless the project and the people and the river with the same object.

Down by the willow, the air cooled two degrees. The old tie-off post leaned in the water like an elder who'd sat too long at a reunion. Julian's headlamp made a clean cone that Miriam tried not to interpret as theater; it was a tool. He crouched at the bank and scanned the stones. "Here," he said, quiet. "Scrape along the old line. Fresh. Something dragged. Parallel marks two lines, an inch apart. A hose clamp could do that. Or a small ladder. Or a mind determined to see too much."

"Let's assume the unexciting answer first," she said. "Then see if the river contradicts us."

They moved slow, palms on rock, knees wet. Two crawdads floated enormous in the headlamp beam like tiny gods offended by human hypotheses. Miriam closed her eyes for a moment and listened for the pressure that had accompanied the dream. It wasn't there, and she managed not to be miffed. Gifts aren't faucets; they're weather. When she opened her eyes, she noticed something purely physical: a thin thread of fine gray clay, out of place among the usual brown. She put a finger to it. "Not our bank," she said. "Wrong silt. Downriver, near quarry runoff."

Julian touched it, testing the grit like a jeweler. "If a plug came from an old valve, it could carry clay like this," he said. "Especially if handled with wet hands."

They followed the thread, small and unglamorous. It led to nothing cinematic only to a scuffed place under a flat stone and a single zip tie, cut, tucked in the grass for the next wind to claim.

"Human hands," Miriam said, not triumph but gravity.

"Maybe sabotage," Julian said. "Maybe an experiment that got out of hand."

"Either way," she said, and felt the sentence settle: **Either way, uncover it.** She didn't feel righteous. She felt busy in the best sense called to small exactness that would make the next day less susceptible to lies.

He bagged the zip tie with museum neatness. They took photos with an old phone that had never learned to be a camera but tried. They noted, dated, indexed because that is how you love a town the dull ardor of keeping track so neighbors don't have to guess.

On the walk back, he took her hand for balance over a slick patch. She didn't let go when the ground leveled. It wasn't ceremony. It was load-sharing.

At the edge of the green, the circle had given way to cleanup. Folding chairs made their old metal complaint. The cottonwood shook itself like a dog dismissing weather. Mayhew stood by the rope with that face men get when they've thought three days into their future and none of the options are a nap.

"Sheriff," Julian said, holding up the bagged tie and the photos like modest spoils. "Old tie-off. Fresh scrape. Wrong clay. Cut zip."

Mayhew took them without comment and did the thing that made people trust him: he wrote down exactly where and when and who and how, and he didn't say what it meant. "Thank you," he said. "I'll check at dawn when the river brags less." He tipped his head toward the willow. "You two keep being raccoons with permits."

Miriam nodded. Her resolve had sharpened into a shape she could carry. She wasn't going to solve the whole thing no one could. She was going to find the next small true piece, and then the next. She would listen and test and carry and refuse to make any single thought a weapon unless the patient work of evidence turned it into a tool.

Back at her table, she dried her knees with a dishcloth, made tea she'd forget to drink, and wrote three lines in her notebook that were both vow and map: **We will not be ruled by the loudest version. We will not be rushed by the hungriest. We will bring out what is hidden, gently, even when it embarrasses our favorites.** Then, near the bottom right corner, as if leaving a light for herself she could find in the morning, she wrote the sentence that had changed the air in her chest without removing its need to breathe: **I will bring you out.**

She closed the book. Outside, Cedar Creek kept its old promise the water moved, the river listened to itself, and the town, wounded and alive, rehearsed a better way to be a "we." Tomorrow they would seek the hidden ledger. Tomorrow someone would start a newer rumor with older words. Tomorrow the hinge in the south wall would remember how to swing. And tonight, in the small quiet that follows a day you didn't win but didn't lose either, Miriam let the gift sit next to her ordinary resolve without demanding precedence. She would uncover the truth. She would not do it alone. She would, at last, let the work be both river and record.

12

———

CARVED STONE UNEARTHED

They went before the town woke enough to argue about it. Sloane met them at the willow with a coil of climbing line, a canvas tarp, and the particular look of a person who has decided to be brave on purpose. The willow's drape made a green room around the old tie-off post; the bank there stepped down in shelves where boots made sense until they didn't. Mist hung low thin cloth over a table set for trouble.

"Pre-registered," Julian said, holding up the yellow pad like a permit. He'd written their predictions in big letters so even the river could read them: **A)** *Find maker's scratch on wood or stone.* **B)** *Carving oriented to south threshold.* C)*Evidence of allocation (tally, measure, mark).* Beneath, he'd added the duller lines that make adventures survivable: *two tugs = come up, three = light, four = stop; no heroics; Sloane calls Mayhew if we find anything shaped like a weapon.*

"You left out *don't drown*," Sloane said, tying the rope around Miriam's waist with a competence that turned worry into job. "Add it with a star."

"Don't drown," Julian said, writing. He checked the

double fisherman's knot, then checked it again. His hands were calm in the way you practice for years.

Miriam shrugged out of her jacket and stood in the shallows a moment letting the cold learn her. She wasn't equipped like a diver Cedar Creek had waders, not wet suits but she wore old clothes, a borrowed mask, Sloane's grippiest gloves, and a bandanna the color of caution. The rope at her waist made her feel, oddly, more part of the room than less. "Two tugs," she said, rehearsing.

"Up," Julian and Sloane answered in unison.

"Three?"

"Light," Julian said. "For the stone. We'll angle the headlamp."

"Four?"

"Stop," Sloane said, the word like a benediction.

They had chosen the willow because last night's thread of wrong clay and the cut zip tie had led them here. Downstream of the rope, tucked in an eddy the town forgot except to fish quiet. Miriam went in slow, the way you treat a friend's threshold. Water closed around her shins, then her knees, then her waist with that first bright sting that makes you honest. She put her face under once and came up because her breath wanted to be reminded how. Then she went.

The river made a different voice under the surface quieter, more intent. The light from Julian's headlamp found a lane of stones and made them into objects instead of the pattern her body had learned by feel. She moved with her palms reading, not her eyes rock, root, the slick language of algae. Past the old tie-off post the bottom stepped down again. She slid forward and the silt took her hands like flour.

There. An edge that wasn't just an edge. A rectangle's corner where a river's geometry usually rounds. Miriam set her fingers to it gently and felt the line continue under silt. She brushed like an archivist with a toothbrush. The river accepted the help and lent its own: a little current whisked away the cloud of brown. She saw stone: pale, not the usual river-dark, like a thing meant to be read in a dim room. A groove cut shallow and deliberate, not the gouge a rock makes against its neighbor. Her chest did the small, traitorous thing joy does when it arrives in the middle of duty.

She tugged twice up only to take air and measure her greed. When her head broke the surface, Julian was there like a sentence you know by heart.

"What do you have?" he asked, voice very even.

"A stone," she said, laughing once at the absurdity of the obvious. "Carved. The line is shallow. It might be the loop. I need to uncover more."

"Three tugs when you want light," he reminded her, and the care in that reminder made her warmer than the sun could.

She went down. Three short pulls on the rope. The beam slid over her shoulder in a moving square. Under it, the groove grew itself further: a bend, a pause, the beginning of the completing stroke she'd seen in the dream and on the carpenter's start. She felt for a maker's scratch with the pad of her thumb. Not yet. But the groove's walls had that matte patina that told on age in a language she didn't speak but recognized: mineral that had had time to talk to water.

The rectangle extended, a hand's-breadth by a hand's-breadth. She followed it until her fingers met lichen slicker than the rest old growth holding. When she brushed, a pale tally mark revealed itself a notch perpendicular to the loop. Then another, farther down. She swore a little through her nose and felt the river grin. Notches. Count a thing. Mark a turn. Share.

Two tugs. Air. She described what she saw in short nouns like she was calling out a recipe to someone at the oven. "Loop, shallow. Tallies. At least two. Stone is rectangular. Might be set, not loose. Feels older than the cart."

Julian had the pad ready before his mind finished the sentence. "Orientation?" he asked.

She found the south in her skin like all locals learn to, then matched the groove she could see to the seam of the river and the memory of the museum's south window. She went under, laid two fingertips along the loop's throat, and pointed with the other hand where the groove aimed when it completed. Up. "South-southwest," she said. "Toward the threshold. It's not exact this isn't survey grade but it's not random."

Sloane made a little sound that was neither surprise nor triumph, only acknowledgment: a puzzle piece deciding to agree with the table.

They worked. Miriam uncovered more of the stone with her gloves doing the patient work fingers do when the rest of the world wants glamour. Julian kept the light steady and let his breathing be a metronome. Sloane, who believed in things you could put back together later, opened the canvas tarp and weighted its corners with river rocks for a cradle if and when the stone came up.

"Edge," Miriam said on the third pass. "Mortised into the bank. Someone set this here a long time ago. It wasn't dropped."

"Can you see tool marks?" Julian asked, not to rush, only to collect vocabulary. He loved vocabulary. He loved when vocabulary saved a day from the tyranny of mood.

"Chisel, not knife," she said. "Not machine. Narrow. Like a spoon gouge but harder." Under the beam the groove's floor showed tiny parallel lines, even now under silt. She passed her thumb over a corner and felt the sharp language of a mason who intended legibility to outlast weather.

The town woke somewhere upstream the square clearing its throat, a truck grumbling, a child with a bicycle practicing bravery. Down here the willow held the sound back like a woman cupping her hand around a candle in wind. Miriam reached further under and her fingers found emptiness at the stone's base. Not a hole; a deliberate channel. She followed it. Her heart misstepped with the cold and the newness of thinking with the palm of her hand alone.

Two tugs. Up. "A drain," she said, breath short with the way a discovery both widens and tightens the chest. "Or not a drain an outlet. A notch under the stone. It would have let a little water pass under the slab and over a mark. Like reading through running water."

Julian closed his eyes just once. When he opened them, he looked not excited so much as steadier. "An allocation stone," he said. "The loop not as decoration but as legend. Tallies as measure. 'We take this much, and no more.'"

"And the man who took more cut a seventh notch," Sloane said softly, not as accusation but as hypothesis trying not to jump the gun.

Miriam went down again to be sure her breath wasn't inventing patterns. The loop had aged into its purpose. The tallies she could make out three for certain, perhaps a fourth. The under-notch made the water itself part of the device: as the creek ran low, the trickle would name the measure. She felt along the lower edge for a maker's scratch. There. Small. Not the main loop merely a tiny bend, a pause, a nick. It could have been anything. It felt like signature. She pressed her thumb to it as if to say *someone's hand lived here once.* The river didn't argue.

Two tugs. Up. "We're not moving it today," she said, already bereft at the thought of any removal. "But we need a rub. And a photograph with scale. And to convince the town not to make this stone into a national crisis by lunch."

"Rub first," Julian said. "Then Mayhew. Then Pastor. Then we decide how to teach the room to listen without trampling." He looked at Sloane. "You brought graphite?"

"Do I look like a person who would come to a river without graphite?" she said, already laying the plastic over the waterline and taping it neat. Miriam went under once more, guided the edge, smoothed the sheet, and felt the river consent. Above, Julian ran the graphite short, side, and the loop rose on the paper like breath fogging glass.

They stood knee-deep, studying the rub in the willow's shade. The loop's throat aimed right where they thought it would. Three tallies sure, a fourth possible. The tiny scratch hung on the lower margin like a whispered initial. The stone's rectangle squared, unnaturally square for creek geology.

"Well," Sloane said. "The river kept a receipt."

"And it's older than the basin," Julian murmured, touching the graphite with his cleanest finger as if that could tell age. "Older than 1902, likely. Older than the 1870s cedar practice strips. Not prehistoric the tools say nineteenth century. Early. First promise time." He looked up toward the museum as if through the bank he could see the south wall. "We've been using the wrong dictionary."

The mystery didn't narrow. It thickened new strata over old. Which felt, perversely, like relief. It meant sabotage or no sabotage, the story had a spine older than this week's tempers.

· · ·

MAYHEW CAME by nine with his deputy and a thermos and
the face of a man who had hoped for boring news and didn't
get it. Pastor Elijah came with a towel and the expression he
used when the room needed to be kept sacramental without
anyone using the liturgical word. Sloane posted a hand-
lettered sign at the top of the path that read: **ARCHIVE
WORK WALK QUIET.** People understood words when you
gave them a job.

Julian presented the rub, the orientation sketch, the
prediction sheet, and the bagged zip tie with the courtliness
of a man giving evidence and a neighbor giving bread. He
didn't sell. He reported. Miriam stood a little back under the
willow, arms wrapped around herself because her body was
still considering being wet, and watched the stone receive
men who were not her.

Mayhew crouched at the edge and peered under. "Allocation stone," he said, without pretend expertise, only a
working man's willingness to learn a new tool by its intent.
"Marks look old. Not a prank." He glanced up, met Pastor's
eyes, then Miriam's. "We're not announcing this until we get
security and a plan. If you tell the square too early, someone
will chisel a selfie into it by dinner."

"Agreed," Julian said immediately. The speed helped.

Pastor Elijah took the rub like a page the church had
misplaced. He ran a finger a quarter inch above the loop, the
way he blesses without touching. "Legend, not ornament,"
he said. "'And,' not 'mine.'" His throat moved, once. "The
river remembers the promise better than we do."

Miriam stepped closer and knelt, jeans wicking cold that
made her aware of each joint. "There's an under-notch," she
told them. "It makes the water a measuring line. If the creek

ran past this much under the slab, you were allowed this; if not, you waited. It's kind, in a way. It keeps a hungry year from turning into theft by mistake."

"And a cruel year from excusing theft as survival," Mayhew added quietly. "Which is the sheriff's language for the same thing."

Julian flipped to a fresh page and wrote **allocation stone (nineteenth c.?)** and **under-notch aquatic measure** and **maker's scratch (lower margin) compare to training stave.** He looked up the bank, imagining the procession from the south threshold to this slab and back. "The carved loop inside the basin," he said, "if it ever existed completed, would have rhymed with this one. When the basin refuses, the river is asking us to read this first, not itself."

"Which is to say," Pastor Elijah offered, "repair the promise before you pour the blessing."

Mayhew stood, pocketed his thermos cap, and peered upstream to where the square would be dragging its chairs out. "And which is to say," he added dryly, "good luck with that at noon on a festival week."

They laughed, quietly. Laughter kept panic from borrowing a chair.

The link to betrayal arrived not as thunder but as the kind of detail you see when you decide to wipe your lenses. On the rub, below the tallies, faint and almost not there, lay another line short, vertical, then diagonal a ">" shape nested where the under-notch would drip. Miriam turned the paper, then turned it again. It was not tally; not loop. It was a wedge. She felt in her hands what the water had done once it ran low: the drip would darken that wedge before it darkened anything else. A warning. Or proof.

"Show me the ledger," Pastor said suddenly, smile like a

man who had just remembered a phone number without looking. "The one from 1935 the pencil apology. Does it say *moved blessing until tempers cool* or *until levels rise?*"

Julian flipped. Read. "Moved until tempers cool," he said. "But the line after here *'harvest first, water after '* then scratched out, replaced with *' water first, then harvest.'* The order matters. The man was confessing the order had become convenient instead of covenant."

Mayhew whistled softly. "So the crowd is arguing about who touched the cart when the stone says the fight is older: who took water first when they'd sworn to measure second."

Miriam thought of the elder's voice the night they'd stood at the circle: *We promised not to take more than was our share. A man took more. We forgave on paper and kept the score in our bones.* The stone's wedge and the ledger's scratched-out line made a handshake.

"Connection to family names?" Mayhew asked, because his job required nouns people could understand at lamplight.

"Careful," Julian said, reflex sparking. "We don't have an initial on the stone. The maker's scratch might match a carver in a drawer somewhere, not a settler. The ledger's pencil belongs to a man in 1935 embarrassed by a vote in 1934; the theft could be 1860s. If we rush to a surname, we turn a community lesson into a courtroom."

Miriam added, "But we have a shape. A man changed the order for his benefit and called it prudence. That's the betrayal." She touched the rub again, the loop like a throat clearing. "If we teach the town to see that, names will matter less than repair."

Pastor Elijah nodded. "And once we teach it, we can say the name if it keeps us honest, not if it gives us a villain."

Mayhew made a note she couldn't read and then made a

decision she could. "We'll post guards here," he said. "Volunteer, not badge, plus one deputy at night. Sloane, can you rig a screen so people can't see the exact spot from the path until we're ready? Julian, you and yours do your scans. Miriam " he hesitated the way men do when addressing a job that has no job description " keep listening and keep not making it a show."

She nodded. The directive relieved her in the same way it burdened her. The listen part she could do. The part where her restraint had to be stronger than the town's curiosity she could do that, too, but only if she kept sharing the work. "We'll bring the rub to the circle," she said. "Not the stone. We'll say what we saw and what we didn't. We'll ask for stories about the old weir and about years of taking turns."

"Say 'turns,'" Pastor advised. "Not 'rights.' It lands better on mouths that have been yelling all day."

They left the willow by twos, turns, like they were practicing the thing they planned to preach. On the path up, Miriam passed the high schoolers coming down with clipboards and stakes. One of them had written **and** in the corner of her page and drawn a tiny hinge next to it. The sight steadied Miriam more than all the grown-up plans combined. Kids who can draw hinges on purpose are hard to lie to.

Back in Collections, Julian laid the rub beside the transparency of her loop and the carpenter's unfinished mark. The three curves made a chord that didn't resolve yet, but promised it would. He wrote **allocation stone older than basin** and underlined *older* once. Under that he added, almost shy: **dream, hypothesis, evidence** and then, in smaller letters, **not proof of everything, proof of this.**

Miriam stood with her palms on the table, head bent as

if listening for something the wood might say back. She didn't call the moment sacred. She didn't need to. When you've been trusted by stone, the air knows.

By late afternoon the town heat climbed into its old unhelpful habits. The sheriff held the line. The mayor tried to hold a narrative. Sloane held the extension cords. Miriam held her mouth. Julian held his lists. It worked, mostly. At dusk, as the lantern shepherds lit their first row, the grid at the rope hummed to life like an instrument tuning.

"Fifteen minutes," Julian murmured, leaning close enough that the back of his hand brushed her sleeve. "Fifteen to speak the rub and the rule what we know, what we don't. Then we walk to the willow and post the screen."

She nodded. "Then we go back in after," she said, and he stilled. "To secure the stone better. I want to place a wedge so the under-notch doesn't erode while we delay. Just a smooth shim. No chiseling. A mercy."

"You want to get in the water at night," he said, every line of his body at war between sense and trust.

"Not alone," she said. "With you at the rope, Sloane on the line, Mayhew on the bank. We do it quiet. It's what the stone would ask if it could ask."

The circle received the rub the way you hope a town will receive delicate news: with hands still and mouths learning to be. Miriam held the paper in both palms and said what she'd promised loop, tallies, under-notch, orientation. She did not say allocation stone. She said the slower words: "a way of measuring fairness." Pastor Elijah said, "turns," and a woman repeated it as if swapping vocabulary could keep her marriage from using the wrong tools this week. Mayhew explained the screen and the guards, and the room did not turn on him. It turned toward its better self.

At full dark they went. Sloane carried the rope as if it were an heirloom. Mayhew walked point, no hat, the better to stand in the same light as the rest of them. Julian carried the wedge a slice of smooth cedar, too pretty for the job but the only thing at hand. Miriam carried nothing. Her job was to look and to not let wanting to be useful make her reckless.

They set the line. Two tugs, three, four rehearsed in the hand. Mayhew posted a deputy at the path. Sloane stepped into the water up to her knees and said, "All right, family," which she says at cookouts and disasters. "Let's be smart."

Miriam went under. The night made the stone closer, the light narrower, the world simpler: this groove, this notch, this measure. The river's chill bit harder now, and her ribs negotiated the rate of their opening like a contract. The under-notch had collected a tiny braid of leaves and silt since morning. She teased it away with a gloved finger. The loop's throat gleamed under the beam like a calm eye.

She signed with the rope: *light at base*. Three tugs. The headlamp brightened the notch. She reached for the wedge. It did not arrive in her hand. She felt it instead against her shoulder as Julian eased it down the line to her. Not throwing, not tossing offering. She took it. Her hand shook once, hard. She breathed it away.

She slid the cedar into the under-notch, not to alter, to cradle so the trickle would keep its line without eating the very edge that taught it. The wedge fit as if the stone had left room for it. She almost laughed. You shouldn't laugh with river in your mouth.

That's when her foot found the old tether loop of iron under the silt the one she hadn't cleared that morning because the current had tucked it away. Even with Sloane's gloves, even with the rope, even with every plan, feet find old iron when you'd prefer they didn't. The loop caught her boot lace and cinched. She tugged once, twice, uselessly. The current decided then to answer a wind the town couldn't feel and pushed harder along the bank. The world tilted just a degree, but enough to make panic think it had an argument.

She sent four tugs down the rope. Stop. The line went taut in a breath Sloane already braced, Julian already leaning his weight backward. Miriam did the arithmetic her aunt had taught her: *You have thirty good seconds before fear chokes useful. Use twenty for work, ten for air.* She put both hands calmly on her boot and tried the lace. Silt made blind fingers blinder. The iron edge rasped. She felt the wedge still in her left palm and had an absurd wish not to drop it because kindness matters even when panic tries to declare bankruptcy.

Three tugs came back up the rope light, aimed exactly where she needed it. The beam found the loop. She saw the knot. Saw the frayed end. Saw the uselessness of untying. With her right hand she reached for her pocket knife. It was not there; they'd left blades topside because they made poor headlines. Useful, she scolded herself, is sometimes a bad word.

A shadow moved in the cone above Julian, fully clothed, sliding in to his waist, then chest, then shoulder, rope around him, face set. He did not come for gallantry. He came like a coworker walking across a shop floor to lend the tool you forgot. He reached under slowly, gloved hand finding her ankle by permission alone. He placed Sloane's shears where had she conjured those from? into Miriam's palm. Miriam cut the lace. The boot loosened, then stuck because suction likes drama. She pressed her heel down and toward the loop, then bent her knee and slid the foot free. The boot remained, claimed by river. She didn't mourn it. She kicked once, gently, to be sure her toes could obey instruction. They could.

Two tugs. Up. She broke the surface laughing and coughing in the same syllable a ridiculous animal of relief. Julian was there, not gone cool at all, breath high from the shock of cold, eyes wrecked with a kindness that refuses to call itself that for fear of becoming sanctimonious.

"Boot," she said, as if it mattered. "Wedge's in. And I didn't drown."

"Two of those things are excellent," he said hoarsely. "Give me your hand."

She did. He walked her in the last two steps like people walk each other out of hospital rooms after minor surgeries the kind of walking that says *we're pretending this was ordinary because we prefer you alive to the story of your bravery.* Sloane wrapped her in a towel that smelled like trucks and sun, then smacked Julian's shoulder with the flat of her hand affection disguised as admonition. "You owe me shears," she said. "The good ones. And new rope."

Mayhew had not moved from the bank. He took the wedge's existence as a report, not a miracle. He nodded, not as approval for rule-breaking, but as endorsement of field medicine. "You two are going to give me gray hair where I can't see it," he said. "Next time, tether the chest, not the waist."

"Next time," Miriam said, teeth knocking as her body rediscovered the idea of warm. The adrenaline drop made the willow's leaves look briefly too green. She breathed through it. Julian draped his jacket over her shoulders without asking. She didn't refuse. He shivered in his shirt in the breeze and didn't try to make it seem like nobility. Sloane handed him another towel and rolled her eyes like a blessing.

They walked the path back to the square slow to avoid turning into a parade. Lights in the museum's south window made a gentle rectangle on the grass. The board behind it **Hinge Protocol** caught a little glare and made the words harder to read, which seemed correct: the town had learned enough for one day.

"Thank you," Miriam said when they reached the porch two syllables that tried to carry sixty. "For bringing the shears. For not trying to rescue me faster than I asked."

"I wanted to," he said, honest. "But I wanted you to want me to more."

She laughed, nose red, towel a cape, hair wild. The heat between them wasn't melodramatic; it was competent and specific. He touched the ridge of her knuckles under the towel and left his hand there exactly long enough to make both of them sure they weren't inventing any of this. "We are not kissing on a museum step," she said, which contained within it all the other sentences they were saving for a room that wasn't tiled in public.

"Agreed," he said. "We're cataloging."

They did. They logged the wedge, the shears, the lost boot, the zip tie, the wrong clay, the under-notch. They added a line to the protocol: 7) **Night work requires the same daylight rules + one more light + one more adult.** Sloane initialed it with a flourish. Mayhew appended: **8) Text me.** Pastor Elijah, arriving with two mugs, wrote beneath in tiny letters: **9) When fear speaks, answer with the job.** He handed the mugs across as if passing the peace.

Back at her table, Miriam set her bare foot on a folded towel and examined the crescent the iron had left across her instep. It would bruise by morning. She didn't mind. She wrote three lines in the notebook while the room remembered how to be hers.

Found: allocation stone with loop + tallies + under-notch. Older than basin. Orientation toward south threshold.

Kept: wedge to protect measure. Work before show.

Given: a gift that doesn't rescue me from risk, only makes the risk worth taking.

She closed the book. Outside, the town bickered more softly over pie. The willow shook its green like someone shrugging off a story they'd told too often in the wrong tone. At the river, the stone lay with its wedge in place like a splint you put on an old fracture to keep it steady while the body remembers how to heal. The loop, dark now, took starlight and returned nothing the eye could use, which was exactly right. The scandal could wait. The river had waited longer. And upstairs, pressed warm between towel and shawl, Miriam allowed herself the smallest private vow: **I will bring it out but gently.**

13

———

ANCESTRAL SECRETS

The morning after the stone, Miriam made a map with coffee rings for compass roses and went calling. History is not a genre; it's a neighborhood, and you don't drive through one of those with the radio up and the windows tinted. You slow down. You wave. You accept whatever people hand you, even if it's a story wearing a coat of rumor. Especially then.

Her first stop was at Cedar Lodge, where the hallways smell like lemon oil and oatmeal and the wall clocks keep time in three towns because the residents' bodies do. The director had set aside a little room with a square table and a vase containing the sternest zinnias in the county. Pastor Elijah came with her for the first hour to soften the air and to show this was not an interrogation. He took the seat in the corner that makes old men tell better jokes.

Mr. Pike went first, ninety-two, eyes like flint and a laugh that had not come for free. He wore a tie clip shaped like a wheat stalk and a cardigan that looked like it had officiated several arguments and a christening. "Your great-aunt used to bring candles here at Christmas," he said as soon as he sat. "Had a trick for lighting the stubby ones without burning the tree. I assume you inherited the trick and the stubborn both."

"Guilty," Miriam said, clicking her pen like a confession. "Tell me what your people said about the river when you were little."

"That it had a better memory than the rest of us," he said. "My grandfather used to take me to 'read the stone' his words, not mine. In years when the blackberries soured early, he'd say, 'let's go see what the river thinks.' He'd lay his hand flat on the big pale slab by the willow, and the trickle under it if it made the wedge mark shine, we had to cut our pumping in half, even if we didn't like it."

"The wedge," she said, careful not to teach.

"You know the wedge," he said, pleased. "There were tallies, too, of course old ones. He'd count them like a baker counts rolls. Sometimes spat. Sometimes laughed. 'We forgot we wrote our own rules,' he'd say, 'and put them somewhere we cannot argue with.'"

"Did anyone ever... add a tally?" Pastor Elijah asked, as if he were checking for a bad tooth.

Mr. Pike's mouth went thin. "We don't chisel the river," he said. "That's what was said to us. My mother believed it like she believed breath. But there was a story, yes. Whispered. Before my time, before theirs, even first years. One settler ran a siphon late one night and claimed the river had given him permission. The next morning the tallies looked like they counted more. Maybe they did. Maybe we taught ourselves to see what we had already taken."

"Name?" Miriam asked, voice the neutral tone dentists use for 'swallow now.'

"Not from me," he said. "From Jade June Hollis. She

keeps names like people keep peppermints in their hand-bags: for when the throat needs help."

June Hollis lived two streets over from Miriam's shop in a house the color of library paste and pride. She answered the door in a sweater with thirty winters stored in its wrists and the kind of lipstick that once intimidated dance halls. "You're the candle girl," she said, which in Cedar Creek counted as a greeting and a résumé. "And the boy from the museum isn't with you. Good. Bring your own courage."

"I did," Miriam said. "And a recorder, if you'll allow it."

June Huffed. "Put it in the sugar bowl," she said. "I've always believed machines behave better near sweetness."

She made tea the way women make tea when they mean to talk much and say things they were told to forget. The living room had two chairs that still knew how to hold men after layoffs and a third that had learned to hold women who pretended layoffs didn't affect them. On the wall: a photograph of the 1947 lantern walk, skirts like bellflowers, boys too conscious of themselves to smile.

"My grandfather was small," June said without preface, stirring a cup she would not drink. "Not in the heart. In the height. Had to climb onto a crate to speak at the fort, which he did not mind. 'Makes the words travel further,' he used to say." She jabbed the spoon toward the wall where the south window of Miriam's mind waited behind plaster. "He called that door 'the gate.' Said it should never have been shut. Said shutting it was like telling the town to whisper."

"What did he say about the oath?" Miriam asked.

"That it happened twice," June said, and the old room adjusted itself around a sentence it had heard before and refused to get used to. "Once at the river, once at the ledger. The river one counted. The ledger one endured." She set the untasted tea down so the cup wouldn't shiver in her fingers.

"When they first took the basin to the stone, they said the words everybody says 'we'll take turns,' 'we won't cheat,' 'we'll let the river shame us before our neighbors do.' And then a man one he got his people on side, he turned the order. He said they'd check the stone after the pour, not before. 'Weather swings,' he said, like weather is an accomplice."

Miriam sat very still. History requires stillness; you can nod and ruin the record. "And your grandfather?"

"Spat," June said, pleased with his ghost. "Into the weeds where I was not supposed to be listening. He said, 'we just learned how to lie to the river.'"

"Did he say a name?"

"He said initials once, when he couldn't sleep," June said. "He said an 'A' and a 'B' and then he drank water and said, 'it's no use making enemies of all the families who fed me, Junebug.' He said, 'we forgive on paper and keep the score in our bones.' He said, 'do not let us become the kind of town that only tells the short version.'" She looked over the rim of her cup and sipped finally, grimacing; the tea had cooled. "He also said whatever you say under open sky counts more," she added, practical. "Which is why you better be careful what you say in that circle, Miriam Adler."

"I will," Miriam said, which was both a promise and a life.

She went to Mrs. Alvarez after lunch at Pastor's suggestion. Mrs. Alvarez kept a tin of buttons that could clothe two centuries' worth of coats in absolution. She also kept a ledger with lists of who borrowed casseroles and who returned them. "My grandmother wrote names in pencil," she said, laying the thin book on her lap with the weight we give to babies and sin. "Not because she meant to erase them. Because she didn't trust ink. She told me: 'hard things need forgiving over and over; if you write it once in pen, you will pretend it is done.'"

"Do you remember a story about moving the blessing to the steps?" Miriam asked.

"I remember my mother using the word 'convenient' like a curse," she said. "And I remember visiting day at the fort school when they showed us the exhibits and skipped the south side. My father said, 'that's where the door used to be.' I said, 'used to be what?' He said, 'honest.'"

Between houses she scribbled phrases that would later sound like poetry and were, in the moment, inventory: *read the stone; wedge shines; two oaths; don't chisel the river; initials swallowed; pencil is for forgiving.* She alternated water with coffee with a lemon candy some aunt had pressed on her in high school when she was trying to quit rescuing boys who loved excuses.

At dusk she sat with the elder who had once raised her hand in the circle and said *we lived; we'll live again.* Her name was Alma Trigg, and her bones still believed in chores. She kept her Bible by the window and a hammer by the door. "You found the slab," Alma said, not a question. "The one that listens."

"We did," Miriam said. "We're trying to decide how to bring it to the town without letting the town break it by loving it wrong."

"You will fail a little," Alma said, kind. "That is how towns learn."

"What did your parents tell you?" Miriam asked.

"That the man who first changed the order stood with his back to the stone like a man standing in front of a mirror he had polished and didn't want anyone to see the scratches," Alma said. "He told jokes while the men waited. My mother said the jokes were funny and rotted the floor under him." She folded Miriam's hand into hers, warm and astonishingly strong. "Don't go building gallows, child. Build a table, set out water, and make people drink it next to the promise they made to share."

On the way home, the willow looked the way willows do when your body has asked too much of it and your mind wants a confirmation that you are not inventing hinges. The river said nothing out loud. It didn't need to. The stone kept its mouth under water and its purpose above it.

The map on Miriam's kitchen table became a quilt bits of language pinned to corners, arrows between corners that refuse to live alone. In the corner where she'd drawn Cedar Lodge she wrote: **Don't chisel the river.** Next to June's living room: **two oaths.** Next to Mrs. Alvarez: **pencil ≠ erase; pencil = repeat.** Next to Alma: **table, not gallows.** In the center she wrote the sentence that had stopped being an ornament and turned into a tool: **Bring you out.** Not in, not up *out.* The preposition did a lot of load-bearing work in a town that had learned to store weather indoors.

JULIAN READ her notes with the tenderness of a man who loves paragraphs and the correction of a man who fears them. "We're threading needles with gossip for thread," he said, tapping the margin next to June's initials. "We need something that does not fray when we tug."

"We have a stone," she said.

"And a ledger page from 1935," he said. "But the betrayal everyone is waiting to hate is older and harder to prove. If we speak too soon, we make villains out of hungry people and saints out of sturdy liars."

"Sturdy liars," she repeated, because the phrase would

be useful later when her better self needed a nickname for the versions of herself she disliked and forgave.

He poured her a coffee and set it down on her side of the table the way he'd learned to: near enough to be kind, far enough not to jostle her hands. They were both practicing new habits with each other. The discipline of not saying things they'd been learning that since the south wall turned into a confession.

Pastor Elijah named it plainly when he joined them at the museum window where the hinge protocol hung like laundry the town had consented to see. "Confession is for what you did," he said. "Not for what your daddy did. Truth is for everyone."

"Do you think we are supposed to say the name when we find it?" Miriam asked.

"I think you are supposed to say the name only if you have learned how to say it without wringing doing out of it," he said, eyes kind and intractable. "Otherwise you will practice a cruelty you will call courage."

They practiced the discipline of not saying things that day, which only works if you do other things instead. Sloane hauled the screen down to the willow and rigged it with tarps so that gawkers would see a tent and assume boredom. Mayhew posted a deputy in a lawn chair with a paperback and the capacity to be uninteresting in a way that makes teenagers forget to mock you. Rosalie baked a pan of lemon bars and put them on the table under a sign that read: **BARS ARE FREE; PATIENCE IS EXPENSIVE; PAY WHAT YOU CAN.** People paid.

Miriam made appointments with three more elders whose stories hooked into the earlier ones like paper clips. Mr. Wagner said when he was a boy he'd been taught to walk the circuit south door, stone, square and touch each post. "So my body would know the route," he said. "In case my head someday forgot." Ms. Dubois said her great-aunt had a necklace shaped like a tiny loop and wore it only on days the river ran thin and then hid it under her collar on the years the town pretended abundance was a personality trait. "She thought God was practical," Ms. Dubois said, and the remark sat on Miriam's page like a sentence she would someday need to say back to herself.

By midafternoon, Confluence FM had managed to find the story without finding the stone. **FOUNDATION SLAB DISCOVERED? TOWN MUM.** The anchor tilted his head and did the dance reporters do when they want to be angry about "lack of transparency." The comments went predictable places: cover-up, conspiracy, copy of a story from a larger town that had built a dam where a river once ran and called that thinking. The square weathered it with less drama than the morning before; the rumor engine was sputtering for lack of better gas.

What did not sputter was the old reflex: families taking inventory of slights. The LeClair aunt who had admitted greed the day before found herself boxed at the hardware door by a woman wanting theatrics. "Say it louder," the woman demanded. "Say your men stole." The aunt lifted her chin. "We broke pace," she said, not backing up. "We are learning to count out loud." That sentence kept a dozen bad arguments from learning to walk.

In the late light, Miriam returned to June Hollis not to shake more names loose but to practice the discipline again spiral back and see if the story had changed under its own weight. More than once in the last year she had learned that silence, when asked respectfully, will cough up an extra detail. June met her on the porch with her lipstick set to war and her sweater accommodating another memory.

"You want the part my grandfather almost told?" June said, before Miriam could ask. "We called the oath the *water promise,* but the old men called it *the counting.* They stood at the slab and read the tallies and then they lit the basin and they said words under the open. The man who changed the order had beautiful hands. My grandfather always hated that. He said, 'beautiful hands can lie pretty.' He said the man learned to tell jokes so people didn't notice where his thumb sat. That is what betrayal sounds like, Junebug. Not thunder. Applause for the wrong part." She touched Miriam's wrist the way women do who have suddenly found their daughters again in other people. "Write that down," she said. "Applause for the wrong part."

"I will," Miriam said, because she already had. "And the initials?"

June looked at the sugar bowl where the recorder sat in its candy disguise. "I'm going to say them," she said, "because this town kept me alive when my husband died and it has a right to watch itself be brave. But you may not make those letters into a weapon. You may make them into a hinge, if you can. Can you?"

"I can try," Miriam said, which was the exact size of promise honesty allows.

"A," June said. "H." She waited. "In our house we whispered them as *A Hand* not because that was his name, because he used his to distract our eyes."

"Adler?" Miriam asked, not because she wanted to, because the letter asked, and June shook her head with a ferocity that came from something older than argument.

"Do not pounce," she said. "Names jump around our families like old stories and clothes. It might have been *Ackers* or *Abner* or a name we stopped using because it made soup taste bitter. The ledger will tell you. And when it does, promise me you will not let it make you lazy. Tell the whole thing."

"I promise," Miriam said, and meant it and dreaded it and was relieved to have said it.

Silence and secrecy: you could feel them turning in their places the bad kind unclenching its fist, the good kind patting your shoulder and saying, *now,* as if it had been waiting under the floorboards for this day. She thought of Book 1's winter, of her great-aunt's letter, of the way bricks in that season had carried heat nights after the fire in them went out. A town can stay warm on old secrets. It can also burn itself down on them. The difference is what you're warming: a room you're inviting others into, or a room where you admire the fire alone.

She wrote at her table until the page's edges curled and the ink turned glossier from the oils on her hand. The discipline of not saying turned into the joy of writing down accurately. It fed instead of starved. She slept without having to trick herself into it.

THE NEXT MORNING FELT HIGH-SHOULDERED. You know those days the ones that walk into your kitchen before you do and put their hands on their hips and say, *are we doing this or not?* Mayhew texted at six: **we're doing this,** and included a photo of two volunteers in lawn chairs at the willow smiling like people whose brand of heroism involves thermoses and a willingness to be bored.

At nine, Miriam met Julian under the south window. He had a folder marked **FOUNDING DOCUMENTS (possible).** It contained a copy of the deed with the creek boundary written in the language of men who pretend they invented direction and one page of the 1871 meeting minutes where someone had drawn a rectangle and written *proces-sion* in a looping hand. "There's a gap," he said, annoyed not at the people of 1871 but at the way holes carry themselves with entitlement through time. "Between this and 1883. Letters exist somewhere. The ledger Mr. Pike's cousin thinks is in their attic might be the bridge."

"We'll get it," she said, because sometimes hope needs a little arrogant friend to get out of bed.

They had not planned to present anything in the circle that night beyond the rub, but the town had a way of promoting afternoons to evenings if you set the chairs in a certain way. Word got out the good kind. *Miriam is collecting someone's grandmother's version. Julian is scanning door labels from when the door was not a wall.* People brought more than objects. They brought sentences their parents had started and never finished and asked the two of them to finish them kindly.

An old man named Tris stood under the cottonwood and said my mother told me not to marry a woman from the steps because your people don't listen to stone, and then he cried because he had, and it turned out she did, and he wanted his mother to apologize. An old woman named Ruth put a folded scrap into the scanning bowl that said simply: *He bent the order with a joke.* And Pastor Elijah, God help him, told a story about his own grandfather stealing peaches and returning one a year later with a note that said *interest* and how sometimes that kind of humor costs more than it buys.

At noon, the Nadia Reeves came forward with a box she had guarded like a lover for two days and set it on the table in front of the south window as if she were setting down her father's head after carrying him home. "He kept this in his closet," she said. "Don't make my grandmother a liar. Make her a woman who ran out of bravery some years. I have more. Here."

The box held a small ledger smaller than Miriam wanted, bigger than a man hides when he intends not to be found. Onion-skin pages, a hand that tried for elegance and landed on habit. Julian opened it with the ritual that keeps hands from shaking they turn into curators. Midway through: 1872, *meeting adjourned for water counting.* Then a jump, three blank leaves, then 1873, *moved blessing to steps this year; returns to river when weather fair and temper also.* In the margin, faint, someone had written *A.B. insisted* and the rest had been rubbed blank by a thumb.

Miriam didn't realize until then how much she had been bracing her body to be the one to say it first. Relief is not always a fountain; sometimes it's just an unclenching. Even so, the room tightened. June Hollis, who had taken her good chair out into the sun like a queen who had made peace with the possibility of bad news, released a breath Miriam could hear from across the green.

Mayhew read the line, then closed the book because sometimes that's what you do to keep a room from going off its rails. "We are not doing names today," he said in his sheriff voice, which isn't louder than his man voice, only lower and with less apology. "We will confirm. We will check another source. We will not let any single letter turn into a pitchfork."

The discipline held. The square miracle held with it.

But the stakes rose anyway, because that's what truth does it does not ask permission to raise stakes. It sees a ledger and says *more chairs.* It sees a slab and says *more light.* The young couple Miriam had counseled in spring slipped in at the edge of the circle and stood holding hands like people trying to hold a bridge up with their bodies. He was a LeClair; she had an Adler. Their faces had that look engaged people get when the future's table seating plan and the past's seating chart have started a fistfight.

Miriam went to them quietly. "I know," she said. It was not enough. It was the exact size of a sentence that would make the next one possible.

"We fought last night," the girl admitted, chin stubborn with shame that hadn't earned the right to set up shop in her. "He said my people moved the blessing because we couldn't stand the stone. I said his people never met a line they didn't cross and call a dance. We didn't sleep. I don't want to be the kind of town that uses the wrong words to be right."

"You won't be," Miriam said, and believed it exactly enough to hand it to them. "We're going to tell the whole story. It will embarrass the dead and free the living."

"Will it free the dead?" the boy asked, earnest.

"Possibly," she said. "But I can't be in charge of that part. My jurisdiction is among the breathing."

They both laughed, which is how you can tell repair is possible.

At twilight, when the circle put its chairs in their now-familiar ring and the lantern shepherds cheated the darkness into a useful texture, Miriam asked permission with her eyes and then stood. She didn't mention the initials. She didn't show the ledger. She held the rub and the sentence about temper and weather and the knowledge that someone had used jokes to move an oath. She said:

"We have found, in the river, a way our town once kept itself honest: a stone with a loop and tallies and an under-notch that makes the water part of the reading. We have found, in a book, evidence that in a year of temper and weather a man changed the order. We have not found his courage in ink yet; we have not found whether he confessed. We will look. Meanwhile, we are going to practice a discipline. We will not build gallows. We will build a table. We will speak the name when we can carry it without using it to avoid our own repair."

She let the quiet work. Someone cried. Someone clapped before stopping himself. Pastor said, "amen to tables," and Sloane yelled, "and to wedge-shims," because her good humor had been holding the town's roof up all day and sometimes needed to hear itself say so.

When the lanterns were half-spent and the air had that hour's decency, June Hollis raised her hand. "My grandfather said the betrayal wasn't a man taking more one night," she said. "He said it was the town learning to tell a shorter story. You going to bring us out of that?"

Miriam looked at Julian. He had dust at his collarbone again; he had ink on his palm; he had a face people had learned to trust in rooms where they could not afford melodrama. He nodded, once. She nodded back. "Yes," she said to June and to the rest and to herself. "Out of that."

Stakes are not only threats; they are also pegs you tie a line to so you don't lose the tent in a wind. The town had a slab, a ledger, a threshold, a protocol, a sentence with a preposition, a couple who wanted to marry each other more than they wanted to win, a sheriff who had chosen boring as a strategy, a pastor with a broom, a carpenter with good rope, a niece with onion skin, and two people who had learned, blessedly, to turn their argument into procedure.

Upstream, the river ran like it never learned to be tired. Under the willow, the wedge held the under-notch as if it had been expected all along. In the south wall, the old door remembered every palm that had pushed it open and said, *today?* and this time the town answered *soon.*

Back home, Miriam wrote three lines and let herself be done:

Oral history: two oaths; the stone remembers better than we do.

Silence: not hiding; holding until we can carry.

Betrayal: not thunder; applause for the wrong part fracture from the first pour.

Then she added beneath, almost like a child practicing the letter she wanted to forge in herself: **We will bring you out. We will not leave you there.**

14

A FAILED ENGAGEMENT

The first alarm came not from the couple but from their mothers, who arrived together like twin weather fronts that had decided to share a sky. They stood in Miriam's doorway exactly half a pace apart, wearing coats the color of intention.

"Do you have a minute?" the Adler mother asked, already certain the answer would be yes.

"We brought lemon bars," the LeClair mother added, already setting them down like an apology that hoped to get eaten.

Miriam did have a minute. She also had a kettle and a table and the impulse she reached for when a situation wanted drama: chairs arranged in such a way that people had to turn toward one another to speak. "Where are they?" she asked, meaning the children, though the children in question were twenty-three and twenty-four and had learned to repair boat motors and crabby uncles.

"In the parking lot," the Adler said. "Arguing in separate cars, which is an advanced skill and a terrible sign."

"Bring them in," Miriam said. "One at a time if you must."

They brought them in together because habits prove stronger than insight around nine o'clock in the morning. The young woman, Nora Adler, wore a sweater that had once sat on her grandmother's shoulders for picture day and a stubbornness that had sat on no one's. The young man Evan LeClair wore a jacket with sailing rope burn at one cuff and an expression that insisted on being gentle even when offended. They took chairs at two corners, which is where people sit when they haven't decided what shape their argument is allowed to have in public.

"We're calling off the wedding," Nora said, before anyone could set down a mug.

"We're postponing," Evan said, at exactly the same time.

Miriam considered the two verbs like tools laid side by side on a bench. "You're both telling the truth," she said. "You just haven't agreed on timing."

Nora's jaw moved. "My family's name is in a ledger," she said. "Or near one. Or next to it. Or written in a handwriting that looks like us. We're the ones everyone looks at when the word *steps* gets used like a slur. I am not bringing that into his house and calling it a casserole."

"It isn't an indictment," Evan said, aimed at Miriam as much as at his fiancée, as if asking the room to pick sides before noon. "We don't know anything in ink yet. And even if we did, it's a hundred and fifty years old. We cannot make a new promise if we let old men's fear run our wedding."

"Old men's skill with jokes," Nora corrected, a little savage, remembering June's sentence. "Applause for the wrong part. My grandfather used to say that. I didn't understand it until this week."

Miriam poured tea unceremoniously. People remember

what you said better when their hands are doing something they've done since childhood. "Tell me how last night went," she said. "Use nouns."

"We ate at my mother's," Evan said. "She made stew like a blizzard was on the way. We were cheerful."

"We were pretending," Nora said. "We made it to the part where people tease each other about who will wash the bowls, and then his uncle made the joke about *your people and the steps,* and I put the ladle down and said I would wash nothing until he stopped saying *your people* with that mouth."

"And I should have said something sooner," Evan admitted, shame in his shoulders. "I waited to see if my mother would, and by the time I remembered to be brave it was too late for the easy version. I said it badly. She was already " He looked at Nora. "You were already walking out of the good room."

"It's always the good room," she said, not looking away. "The one with the old photographs and the silence. You can hear the old fights in the frame moulding."

Miriam let the silence expand. Silence is dramatic when used badly. It is medicinal when used correctly. She folded a tea towel on the table so her hands had a job that would not turn into instruction. "When did the wedding start to fail?" she asked finally, soft.

"When Pastor said *turns,*" Nora answered, surprising herself. "It was the right word. It made me cry. It also made me mad that we hadn't used it before. It felt like the room was relearning manners, and we were expected to sit quietly and clap while our grandparents' sentences got rehabbed."

"Mine when the stone turned out to be older than the basin," Evan said, trying to name his fear without dressing it up. "Because then I knew this fight wasn't seasonal. And I thought, *I should be as old as this to marry her,* which is not reasonable and also true."

"We made lists," Nora said. "Of things we could promise without lying. We got to *I will not let my family belittle yours,* and that one was easy. Then *I will not use your name to get out of telling the whole story,* and that one made me feel like crying. Then *I will not make you the room where I store my town's weather,* and I hated that one because it felt like marriage was going to steal our air."

Evan's eyes went hot and bright at the same time. "And I said I would build another window," he said. "And she said she didn't want to have to keep rebuilding it with me."

"Then you drove here," Miriam said. "Good choice."

The mothers had taken the back row like choir members who knew when to keep quiet. One had her hands folded and lips thinned and eyes wet. The other had her arms crossed in the posture of a person trying to keep an argument inside her coat. Miriam looked at them and then back at the two at her table. "If you do not marry," she asked, "what happens next?"

"I go to the city," Nora said with the speed of a plan she had used to keep herself from drowning. "My aunt's shop needs a manager. I can forget how a square feels when it thinks it's a courtroom."

"I don't go anywhere," Evan said. "The river is rude that way. It stays. So do we."

"You could both stay and not marry," Miriam said. "Or both go and marry. Or marry and learn new words for your houses. Or not marry and build a bridge anyway. There are more than two options. The trick is not to turn a wedding into a referendum on whether Cedar Creek deserves you."

Nora's laugh had steel in it. "And does it?" she said.

"It's trying," Miriam said, without spin. "So are you."

They talked for an hour in the prose of people who would rather not be poetic because poetry tends to legalize pain if used without supervision. They named five things the wedding was not allowed to carry: the ledger; the initials; the under-notch's old shame; two uncles' pride; the county's need for a story with a villain. They named five it must: *turns*; *no gallows*; *stone before steps*; *tell the long version*; *and.* They wrote them down on a card Miriam slid across the table like a receipt.

At the end, Evan said the sentence you wish men would say sooner in more rooms. "If postponing is what keeps us from lying," he told Nora, "then let's postpone and not punish each other for it."

Nora stared at him long enough for a life to grow up and move away and send postcards. "I'm not punishing you," she said. "I'm refusing to be a museum piece."

"You're both refusing to be artifacts," Miriam said. "Artifacts don't get to change. You're changing. That's the work."

Nora wiped her eyes with her sleeve and caught herself immediately, mortified at the smear on her grandmother's sweater. She laughed in a way that sounded like something breaking and something repairing. "Fine," she said. "We will tell the room tonight together and disappoint the six people who like certainty more than cake."

The mothers exhaled so forcefully the zinnias on the table shivered. "We'll make more lemon bars," the LeClair said. "It's what we can do."

"And I'll bring the photographs we don't show," the Adler said, daring herself. "The ones with the door open."

"Good," Miriam said. "That will help."

When they left, the shop felt like a bell that had been rung and was still, inside, ringing. Miriam sat and wrote, because writing is how she empties the air back into the room. She wrote **postpone without punishment; stone before steps; no artifact marriages.** She underlined **and** because some habits, it turns out, are healing.

JULIAN ARRIVED as noon light spilled over the museum steps like an apology that had learned to be on time. He carried the folder with the onion-skin copy and a bag of bolts for the screen at the willow and, like always now, a small kindness not wearing a name tag. "I heard we're officiating a postponement," he said, wry and unpanicked.

"We're officiating accurate expectations," Miriam said. "With lemon bars."

He put the bolts down and did that thing he does when rooms feel combustible looked for the places that would hold weight and then moved himself there. "I can tell the circle what postponement means from the vantage point of a man who once dated a person who thought it was a synonym for *later when I have changed you.* It is not that," he said.

"What is it?" she asked.

"Respect," he said simply. "And appetite management."

"Say more," she said, because when he is right she likes him to have to explain it to himself.

He leaned against the counter because his body knew this posture now near without crowding, ready without presuming. "Respect, as in: refusing to write vows with pens we haven't earned. Appetite management, as in: not letting our need to make things better by five p.m. become the thing that breaks them."

"You're flirting in policy," she said, smiling and wrecked, because the heat of it didn't need metaphor; it lived in the grammar of his sentences. He flushed and chose, deliberately, not to retreat a step, which was its own kind of progress.

"I am," he said. "I'm also terrified."

"Of?"

"That this will become our story," he said, instantly honest. "We postpone. We curate. We never risk the moment the thing might become a mess."

She heard what he didn't say: *we never kiss, we never merge houses, we never carry anything heavier than paper.* The day before she would've cut it with a joke. Today she didn't. "We're going to risk," she said. "Just not as a performance."

The square broke into small scenes and minor theater; the town was getting good at being dramatic without needing to be tragic. The young couple and their mothers set a small table with index cards and photos at the edge of the circle where people could pause and practice taking in a longer story. Pastor Elijah chalked **AND** on the pavement next to the hopscotch, and two children started playing a game that involved stepping into the loop only when your partner said *now. Mayhew* pretended the radio in his ear was listening to him and not the other way around.

At the willow, Sloane had wedged two stakes into the bank and strung a neat canvas to suggest boredom. "It's a curtain," she told Julian and Miriam. "Not because we want to hide. Because the river deserves an intermission while we learn our lines."

Julian set the bolts and tightened, then tightened again, then realized he was doing that and handed the wrench to Sloane, who smirked and tightened a third time. "Men," she said, fond. "With your feelings left-handed."

He looked at Miriam over the canvas edge. The romantic tension between them had changed shape since the south wall and the night wedge: less like spark, more like heat from a disciplined stove. She stepped closer and touched the edge of his wrist with the back of two fingers the briefest inventory. "Tonight," she said.

"Not as leverage," he returned.

"As appetite," she said, and because she could, she added, "As respect."

He made a sound that could have been a laugh and could have been a prayer.

They returned to the square to find the couple at the table, facing outward together. Evan said "postponement" in a voice that didn't apologize for it. Nora said "no artifact marriages," and six old women nodded like the line had returned them to an earlier version of themselves they'd liked better. The mothers stood shoulder to shoulder. People approached and practiced not handing them blame in casserole dishes. When a man asked "so whose was the initials?" Nora said "we're telling the long version," and he had the decency to look chastened. The town practiced the discipline Miriam had named the day before. Practice might not make perfect. It made different.

Miriam felt the part of her that always wanted to step in and translate relax because translation was already happening. She walked the circle with a stack of index cards labeled **what we can carry** and **what we cannot.** She invited people to write fear on one and hope on the other. They did. Fear put down **the ledger will blame my house** and **if we say the name no one will come to my bakery** and **she will leave** and **he will stay angry.** Hope wrote **turns** twice and **I will not die of embarrass-ment** and **the door will open** and marry anyway, later, better.

She handed the stack to Pastor Elijah, who stood on no podium and read neither the worst nor the best out loud.

He summarized the room the way a good man summarizes a meeting without showing off what you trusted him with. "We are afraid of loss and eager for honesty," he said. "We will accept postponement that releases us from lying. We insist on cake later."

Julian added the thing that had become his portion of the ritual. "Here is what we know and what we don't. The stone is older than the basin. The order matters. The ledger suggests a change in 1873. We do not have the name. We are not making room for weapons. We are making room for repair."

"And," Sloane called from the lantern table, "we are keeping the shears in the drawer unless someone's boot needs saving."

A ripple of laughter. It helps, laughter. It oils hinge pins.

Late-afternoon sunlight turned the square's edges the color of documentation. The couple packed the table. The mothers hugged without pinning blame to the other's coat. Mayhew let his shoulders rest for twenty minutes. The mayor tried to name the day and Miriam refused to supply him with adjectives, which probably saved his career.

Under the museum's south window, Julian stopped beside Miriam the way people stop by wells. "I have an idea," he said.

"I'm listening," she said.

"After the circle," he said, "come with me to the south wall. Not to pry. To open the board and stand in the old threshold a minute. You and me and " he nodded toward the couple " them, if they want. To let their feet know where a door once was. Bodies learn what minds forget."

She felt the suggestion go through her like bread. "Yes," she said. "Yes, that."

"Good," he said. He looked like a man who had just

allowed himself to say the right thing out loud and not run from its consequences.

THE CIRCLE CAME GENTLE, as if the town were tired enough to accept useful words. They told the truth about postponement without turning it into theater. "We're waiting because we like each other too much to lie," Nora said, and somewhere at the back of the ring a man who had promised too soon and too often flinched, then smiled, wrecked. "We're waiting because we want a marriage that isn't working off our grandparents' tab," Evan said, and three grandparents grunted an amen in private.

When the lanterns warmed the faces, Miriam shepherded the four of them Nora, Evan, their two mothers toward the museum's south wall. Sloane had left a neat note **Hinge Protocol in Progress** and a screwdriver on the sill. Julian lifted the board, careful as prayer. The opening wasn't dramatic; it was reasonable a rectangle that had remembered being useful and was trying to be again.

"Step through," he told the young couple. "And then come back. That's all."

They did. Evan first, then Nora, then both together, and then again this time with Nora leading because order matters. The mothers watched with faces that betrayed their training eyes wet, mouths trying to be sturdy brims. Miriam and Julian stood like thresholds themselves present, not ornamental.

"What is this supposed to feel like?" Evan asked, because men are allowed to ask this and ought to more.

"Like you didn't invent leaving and returning," Pastor Elijah said from the hall, having appeared without fanfare. "Like your bodies know the move in and the move out."

"It feels like a hinge that needs oil," Nora said, smiling for real. "But not like it's going to break."

"And like you don't have to force it," Miriam added.

"And like you don't have to perform it for the square," Julian said.

They closed the board. They wrote **stood in the threshold: Nora & Evan** in the log. They dated it as if it mattered, because it did. The mothers exhaled in a different key than the morning, a little lower, a little freer.

After, on the dock, the lanterns made their map and the symbol in the shallows kept its patience. Julian and Miriam took the two chairs nearest the rope, the way they do when they don't want anyone else to have to remember the edge exists. The air was soft enough to forgive the day its clumsiness. Shipments of fireflies made the square look like it had learned code.

"You didn't fix them," Julian said, gratitude in it.

"I gave them less to carry," she said. "That's all."

"That's everything," he countered. "I keep wanting to be a repairman. And then I remember: curation is also repair. You teach a room which objects deserve light."

"You taught me that," she said. It was not flattery. It was inventory.

"You taught me the other thing," he said. "That some rooms are not rooms unless someone says an old sentence out loud first."

They sat with the humility that follows a day that asked too much and you gave it more than you intended and no one died. Below them, the river wore the night like a shawl. The stone kept its wedge. The under-notch held its line.

"Do you want to hear what I didn't say today because I'm practicing restraint?" Miriam asked, close enough that the question could have landed on his shoulder like a hand.

"I very much do," he said.

"I wanted to tell the couple that postponement is a sacrament," she said. "But then I remembered ten-year-old me, being told a hundred grown-up words without anyone explaining them in groceries." She smiled. "So I didn't. I told them to sleep. That feels like a sacrament and doesn't need a choir."

He laughed, low and real. "I wanted to tell the circle that I love you," he said, calm as if naming the weather. "But then I remembered eighteen-year-old me, turning every declaration into a project." He smiled sideways, wrecked. "So I didn't. I told them what we know and what we don't."

The word hung between them. It was not a proposal. It was not a performance. It was an inventory item on the right shelf.

She looked at him without fleeing. "Good," she said. "Keep doing that."

"I will," he said. "And " He stopped himself, not out of cowardice, out of care. "And I will ask you to go to breakfast with me tomorrow, early, before the town discovers we're human."

"Yes," she said, laughing. "Breakfast is not a sacrament. We can handle it."

"Everything is, a little," he murmured. "But yes."

Sloane walked by with a coil of rope and, without breaking stride, muttered, "finally," which is the kind of friend she is. Mayhew followed, tipped his hat, and didn't speak because some men are better when they don't use up your air at the end of a long day. Pastor Elijah sat on the step behind them and hummed a hymn quietly enough not to claim the scene. The town stayed, the way places do when they've decided not to go home angry.

Later, Miriam went home through streets that recognized her shadow. She took off the shawl and the day and left both on a chair. She made toast because toast is an apology and a celebration and an edible metaphor for processing. She wrote three lines in the notebook where she keeps the sentences that will have to carry tomorrow:

Parallel: their vows and ours stone before steps; turns before cake.

Symbol: threshold practice = slow burn order matters; we step in and we step out.

Depth: postponement as mercy; telling the long version heals both the living and the rooms we keep them in.

She emptied the pockets of her jacket: a piece of river clay, a bolt, an index card with **I will not die of embarrassment** in unfamiliar handwriting, a lemon bar wrapped in wax paper. She laughed at the inventory and then ate the lemon bar because days like this need sugar more than philosophy.

And upstairs, under the open window where the night did a decent job pretending to be harmless, she said the sentence to herself that had stopped being a banner and started being a practice: *I will bring you out.* Not up. Not back. *Out.* Out of short versions. Out of weaponized history. Out of rushed weddings. Out of the habit of telling love it must arrive like weather. Out of pretending you can't be frightened and honest at the same time.

Tomorrow would carry its own weather: a ledger page; a meeting with the woman whose grandson had a rumor about a valve; a breakfast cup at a table that would have to learn new manners. Tonight she let herself be a person who had done a day's work and done it more gently than last year's version of herself would have. The engagement had failed to happen on schedule. The marriage, someday, might succeed because of it. The town, for once, did not demand a speech to bless the possibility.

Outside, the river kept its pace, which is the same as saying the river forgave them for needing time. The loop in the shallows drank a slice of moon and did not spend it. The threshold in the south wall slept plain and available. And in the dark room with the cooling toast, Miriam let her heart be the exact temperature of a hinge in good repair warm from use, not overheated by a heroics she could not maintain.

15

JULIAN'S CONFESSION

They met at the Riverlight Café before Cedar Creek had put its hair up. The windows held the river like a postcard taped to glass; the coffee arrived with the patience of people who know mornings forgive more than afternoons do. Yesterday, she'd said "breakfast," and he'd said "yes," and now they sat in a booth at the far end where the floor slanted slightly and the sugar packets canted toward him like little witnesses.

"Order," Miriam said, because she'd learned he needed permission to do ordinary things on days when the town felt like a courtroom.

He pointed at the omelet as if choosing a defendant, then changed to oatmeal because restraint had become his version of prayer. She smiled, not as reward, only recognition. He watched the waitress go and put both hands flat on the Formica like he was swearing in.

"I've been using 'the museum' as if it were neutral," Julian said. "As if I arrived without ghosts. I didn't."

She didn't reach across. She gave him room to say the part that needed a long runway.

"My father believed that love is a kind of editing," he said. "You remove what will embarrass the people you care for and call that stewardship. His mother my grandmother taught him that. When I was little, she'd bring me to Collections and show me labels she'd rewritten how you can make a battle sound less like failure by calling it a strategic retreat. I loved the neatness. I loved how calm the world looks when every artifact sits where your hands put it."

Outside, a heron moved upstream with two beats of wings and a third that looked like it belonged to an older bird. Inside, his stomach did what stomachs do when a man is telling the truth on purpose.

"When I was fourteen," he went on, "I found a drawer in my grandmother's desk labeled 'scrap.' It held minutes from 1934 scribbles, crossings-out, drafts that didn't become the official page. At the bottom was a letter from a board member to another no signature, just initials like a handshake saying the south door should be 'temporarily sealed for better managed sentiment.' I showed it to my father. He put it back. He said, 'not everything belongs on a wall, son.' And because I wanted to be a good son, I learned to want what he wanted."

Miriam made her face into a place a man could put a memory and not have it roll off the table. "Where is the letter now?"

"In our archive," he said. "Filed as 'draft,' not as record. Accessible, but you'd have to know how to ask the room to cough. I haven't brought it out. I told myself we didn't have context, we didn't have corroboration, we didn't have a signature. All true. It's also true that I didn't bring it out because the initials were a cousin of my grandmother's. I didn't want to turn my family into a museum exhibit titled 'people who meant well and failed in public.' I resented being asked to choose."

He smiled without humor. "I also resented you," he added, quietly enough that the signing sugar packets might miss it. "Not because of your gift. Because it made my editing look small. You stood there and said, 'I dreamed a chain and a wedge,' and people didn't die of it. They didn't riot. They got better. Meanwhile, I'm over here writing protocols like a man wallpapering a flood."

The oatmeal arrived like a merciful interruption. He stirred it twice to give his hands a job while his mouth remembered how to speak without collapsing the rest of him.

"My father is a kind man," he said. "Truly. He taught me to fix hinges, the literal kind, to make doors behave. He believes in thresholds the way religious people believe in altars. But he also believes in keeping things in the house. When the south door got walled, it made sense to him: fewer drafts. The last time I argued with him about history, he said, 'son, a town needs heroes,' and I said, 'it needs neighbors.' We didn't talk for a week."

"Do you want to bring the letter out?" Miriam asked.

"Yes," he said, so fast the spoon clinked. "Because I'm tired of pretending I don't know where certain boxes live. Because I'm angry that my family taught me to curate tenderness so hard it sometimes felt like lying. Because I've been asking this town to be brave while I kept one safe drawer."

He took a breath like a man surfacing from a cold dive. "My grandmother used to say labels are love," he added. "She was mostly right. Labels help rooms not turn into weather. But sometimes labels are shame little polite squares you paste over the part of the story that smudges your spotless floor."

"It's a lot to forgive," Miriam said. She didn't mean his grandmother. She meant the child in him who still loved neatness.

"It is," he agreed. "And I think I can do it. I think I want to forgive them for not being braver and forgive myself for not being less afraid. And I want to say out loud that I resent it. Resentment is such a dishonest word when you keep it in your mouth. Saying it makes it rude and manageable."

He ate three spoonfuls, which made the room less fragile. When he spoke again, his voice had the particular steadiness it finds when he's ready to put an object on a table and let strangers decide whether it matters.

"The other confession," he said, "is smaller and meaner. Yesterday, when you and Nora were at the table, I started to say something noble 'postponement is respect' and then I heard myself wanting to be the man who makes sense in public and I hated it. I keep wanting to be the one with the sentence that moves a room. I was raised to do it. It's not wrong. But sometimes it's hungry. You keep making me do the other thing first: ask what work the sentence is for."

"You're doing it," she said, smiling into her coffee. "Asking."

"Because I want to stand next to you and know I'm not there to tidy your courage into shapes that are easier for me to label," he said, and then, because it was time, "Because I want to love you without making your river behave."

She didn't move. She did something better. She let the sentence arrive without needing to choreograph its next act. Then she gave him a single nod, not stingy exact. "Thank you," she said. "For opening the drawer. For admitting the hunger. For wanting the right kind of love."

He looked like men look when they've just discovered their lungs were bigger than they feared. "The letter," he said, returning to the object because returning to the object keeps the feelings from becoming theater. "After breakfast. We'll bring it out together."

"And read it next to the hinge," she said. "So your body knows the door it belongs with."

He exhaled like a joke had finally stopped doing the wrong kind of work in his chest. "Yes," he said. "Let's make my bones learn new manners."

They paid. Outside, the river had begun its daily rehearsal of moving forward without a fresh script. He took her hand because he had learned permission and she did not let go because she had learned receiving.

THE MUSEUM WAS empty enough to hum. Sloane's note **HINGE PROTOCOL IN PROGRESS** waited in the south window like a friendly dare. They didn't go there first. They went upstairs to the little office where the catalog terminal looks like it learned to keep secrets in 1998 and never upgraded.

He keyed in the accession number he'd carved into his memory the day he hid the letter in plain sight. The screen gave them its blue frown and then produced the map: Series B, Box 3, Folder 11, **Drafts Water Board Correspondence 1871–1874**. He pulled the drawer with two fingers and two decades of muscle memory.

"I'm not going to narrate this part," he said. "Narrating is how I keep myself from feeling."

"Okay," she said. It takes practice to say a word that short like that much consent.

They carried the box to the table like pallbearers and

new parents. The folder held onion-skin leaves with pencil sighs and a few brittle pages whose edges had taken to crumbling like old pride. Halfway down, an envelope addressed in a loop that had tried for flourishes it didn't earn. Inside, the sheet: *On account of the temper of parties and the weather ill-suited to nice observation at the slab,* Julian swallowed; Miriam did not wince *we propose to adjourn the counting 'til after the blessing, that the people may not be put out and the donors not displeased.* At the bottom, two initials in a hand that didn't plan to be famous.

He set it between them like bread. "Love as editing," he said, and it didn't sound like a defense anymore. It sounded like a confession sentence belongs in. "This is the page my grandmother would have wanted buried under the polite label: 'Draft.'"

"Drafts are the part of us that tells the truth before we've found better manners," Miriam said. "We need those."

He flipped it over. Nothing on the back but the ghost of the script showing through, thin as a fabric meant for summer. "We'll scan," he said. "We'll post a transcript, not a photograph. We'll keep initials until we have the second source."

She nodded. "Stone before steps. Method before theater."

"Us before applause," he added, then looked embarrassed and then decided not to be.

They went to the south wall because you have to do the literal thing if you want the metaphor to become a muscle. He lifted the board, and the rectangle of not-wall made its old invitation. He did not step through. He stood in the frame and put one hand on each jamb like a man consulting a friend.

"When I was eight," he said, "my grandmother set a

chair under this window and told me to write labels. I wrote: *Window: lets in light.* She crossed it out and wrote: *South window.* I said, why does it matter? She said, 'names matter when you're lost.' Then she baked a cake for a family that wasn't ours and called it *bread.* We fed people and didn't tell them we had changed the name."

"Both are true," Miriam said. "South is useful. Bread is kind. The sin isn't the label. It's what you use the label to postpone."

"Postpone," he said, tasting the word differently than the couple had tasted it in her shop. "I postponed this door because it scared me. And because keeping it closed felt like a way to keep my father safe from the kind of room where people say 'you should have' to your dead. I don't want that for him. I don't want it for me. I want the room where we say 'we didn't' and then we say 'we will now.'"

"Say it to him," she said. "Before we say it to the square."

He looked wrecked and relieved. "Will you come?" he asked, and it came naked of strategy only appetite for company.

"Yes," she said. "I am not your miracle. I am your method." She grinned. "You gave me that line."

He laughed for real and didn't disguise it as anything nobler than a laugh. He lowered the board gently back into place as if teaching his body how to close without hiding. Then he turned to her with the look that had in it the new habit he was building: ask first.

"May I kiss you?" he said, so simply the room seemed to warm in gratitude at not being turned into a performance space.

"Yes," she said, because her own new habit was being exact.

It was not a flourish. It was a hinge moving in good oil.

He touched her like he touches paper he is about to put on a scanner bed care, clarity, intention, and no fussing. She answered like someone who has learned to store weather in the right places right now, not later, not in a hidden drawer.

They stepped apart without apology. That's a skill. She rested her forehead briefly against his cheekbone, borrowing steadiness. He rested back the way men do when they do not want to say *stay* and also do not want to pretend they didn't think it.

"Tonight we tell the circle about the draft," he said. "Not as gossip. As context."

"And about your family," she said.

He flinched, then steadied. "Yes. I will say the sentence in public that I used to save for my pillow."

She raised an eyebrow.

"That I resent my family's silence," he said. "And that I understand it. And that I choose differently."

"You can do that without building gallows," she said.

"I know," he said. "You taught me how."

They ate mediocre museum almonds in the break room and felt like kings. Sloane came by with a staple gun and a grin she didn't apologize for. "If you two are going to turn cataloging into a romance, do it quietly," she said. "Also, I love you both. And also, Mayhew wants you to text him before you say *resentment* at a microphone."

"Not a microphone," Julian said. "The circle."

"Same difference," Sloane muttered, but she squeezed his shoulder in that way she has that counts as benediction.

They drove to his father's house. His father, Alan, answered with the face of a man who had taught a door to open before a knock finished. He looked at Miriam with the gratitude of a person who has watched her do work he admires even when it complicates his calendar.

"Hi Dad," Julian said, and the syllable dragged behind it thirty years of tidy love. "There's a letter I want to show you. And there's a way I want to talk about it that I haven't before."

Alan's eyes moved to the folder like a man bracing for the look of his own handwriting on someone else's mouth. They sat at the kitchen table where chairs had learned to be honest. Miriam took the fourth chair and put her palms on her thighs present, not presiding.

Julian laid the onion-skin page between them and did not begin with the charge. "I love how you kept this," he said, truthful. "You taught me that drafts matter. You taught me that kindness sometimes looks like editing. I have been using both lessons in a way that made me a little dishonest."

Alan looked up sharply, then relaxed when he saw there would be no flogging under this roof. "I taught you to be careful," he said. "I didn't mean to teach you to be afraid."

"I learned the fear anyway," Julian said. "And I aim it at other people's courage when I panic. I'm sorry."

Alan touched the margin with one finger. "My mother would have wanted this to rest," he said. "She was born in a house that believed in the short version. So was I. So were you. It takes a minute to forgive your bones for that."

Julian took the minute it took. "I want to bring it out," he said, as if asking for a tool. "Not with names. With context. Will you be angry with me?"

"I will be uncomfortable," Alan said, which is what love sounds like when it has learned not to lie. "And proud. And relieved. Bring it out. I am tired of holding weather that belongs outdoors."

He turned to Miriam with a little smile that admitted defeat to a better plan. "He listens to you," he said.

"He listens to truth," she answered. "I'm just the person who says it with him sometimes."

They left the house lighter than they'd entered. Outside, the river held its poker face. Inside him, a boy stood up off a chair in a south-window room and said *door,* and the room said, *yes.*

WORD SPREAD the way it does when a town is learning to respect information: gently, with fewer capital letters. At the circle, Mayhew spoke first to inoculate against melodrama. "We have a draft letter from the early 1870s indicating the order of the water oath was reversed for a season: blessing, then counting," he said. "We are confirming with secondary documentation. We will not weaponize initials."

Pastor Elijah followed with the part of his job that makes men forgive their fathers. "Some of us learned silence that was meant to be kindness," he said. "We will not punish people for being born in rooms where windows were myths."

Then Julian stepped forward. Not to a podium. To the edge where the rope meets the grass, because his body had learned where edges help him tell the truth. Miriam stood a yard back and to his left where he preferred her when he needed a human anchor. Sloane leaned on a coil like a guard dog with a degree in carpentry. The Adler niece held the scanning tray with her hands like someone who had finally decided her family's courage included her.

"My name is Julian Roth," he said, and his voice did not do that thing where men make it lower to sound older. "I work at the museum. I keep boxes and locks and labels. I also keep habits I'm not proud of. I've been asking the town to bring things out. I've kept one thing in."

He held up the onion-skin copy without the breathless theater of reveal. He did not read it. "This letter is part of our record," he said. "It suggests men in a hurry perhaps to be liked, perhaps to keep peace moved the order so the river's count came after the blessing. It is context for our argument, not a cudgel for our neighbors. I have not shared it before because the initials belong to my family's friends and because I was raised to call editing love. I resent that. I also honor the love that taught me to be careful. Today, I'm choosing the careful way that tells the whole truth."

Someone clapped and stopped themselves and put their hands in their pockets like adults. Mayhew nodded. Pastor said, "amen to whole truth." Sloane rolled her eyes and wiped them with her sleeve. Miriam felt the room shift the way rooms do when a man has given back a tool he shouldn't have hoarded.

A question came from the edge: "Are we going to say the name?"

"Not until we have the second source," Julian said. "When we do, we will say it in a sentence that keeps us from using it to avoid our own confession."

"Which is?" the man asked, not unkindly.

"That we haven't liked counting," Miriam answered. "That's older than any family. The stone is helping us learn."

They posted the transcript in the window with two lines at the bottom that Sloane insisted on writing: **STONE BEFORE STEPS. TABLE, NOT GALLOWS.** People read and nodded and some went home and wrote letters of their own to people who were dead and told them the short version was not a family heirloom they intended to keep.

Later, with the lanterns honest and the air gentler for having been used by better sentences, they walked to the willow. The screen did its boring work. The deputy did his unheroic vigilance with a paperback. The wedge held. The under-notch kept being exactly itself practical devotion.

"You did it," Miriam said, which contains multitudes in four syllables.

"So did you," he said. "I've been living next to a door I wouldn't open because I thought opening it would be an indictment of my grandmother. You made it a kindness to her: *look what you protected and what it cost.*"

"We're not wrong to love protection," she said. "We are wrong to make it the only face we let love wear."

He bumped her shoulder with his like a bird practicing flight. "I need you to know I won't put you on a pedestal to make my confession prettier," he said. "I'm going to keep being afraid. I'm going to over-label and then have to walk it back. I am going to want applause. And I am going to choose us over being tidy. You have permission to tell me when I'm tidying against the truth."

She laughed, the relief of not having to pretend humans don't bring their mess to the work. "Permission received. And I will keep wanting the river to do the work for me. I will keep wanting to call gifts doctrine. I will keep needing you to make me pre-register my guesses. You have permission to remind me that a vision isn't a permit."

"We're ridiculous," he said.

"We're useful," she countered.

He took her hand again because it had become a way to keep his lungs honest. They stood together, witnesses to a screen, a slab, a wedge, a town. The willow lifted its arms and put them down again like an old aunt trying to slow the weather.

"Tell me the sentence you'll put in your log," she said.

He thought, because he had learned to be worth listening to on purpose, not out of habit. "**Brought out:**

draft letter reversing order in 1870s. Resentment named in public. Family not a villain also not an alibi." He paused, then looked at her with the kind of gentleness that sounds like a plan. "And **Given: a partner who names river and record in the same breath and makes both sound like work I can do.**"

"Good," she said. "And I'll write: **He helped me make the gift into method again. He kissed me like a door opening. We will bring it out.**"

"Not up," he added, not able to help himself.

"Out," she confirmed.

They went back to the square where the couple sat on a bench rehearsing a ceremony that didn't end with rings but with a date written in pencil. The mothers talked like women who'd survived worse and were ready to admit it. Mayhew leaned on a post and let his eyes close for nine seconds, the exact amount a sheriff can afford. Pastor Elijah threatened to sing and then spared them all. Sloane pretended not to notice any of it while noticing all of it.

Julian looked at Miriam and then at his father across the green, and at the thin line the moon gave the river, and at the south wall that no longer pretended to be only itself. In another life, he would have gone home and written neat labels and put the day to bed under them. Tonight, he let the day breathe in the room with him for an extra hour. He let it mess up his desk.

"Breakfast again tomorrow?" he asked, not because he needed a reason to see her; because ritual teaches bodies to remember the order when feelings want to improvise.

"Yes," she said. "We'll eat and then open a drawer."

"And then go to the stone," he said. "And then to the circle."

"And then home," she finished, and their faces both softened around the word, each imagining a different room that might one day have the same table in it.

They parted like good carpenters leave a hinge: aligned, oiled, not forced. The town did its night work of healing without applause. The river kept its promise not to grant them spectacle. The south wall slept with its board on not to hide, only to rest. And in his apartment over the museum, Julian wrote one more line he didn't plan to show anyone right away because some confessions need a night to settle.

I loved you, and I said so, and the world didn't turn into a stage. It turned into a room where work gets done and people eat.

16

RED HERRING

By ten in the morning the square had the alertness of a dog staring at a doorknob. Confluence FM's van idled a little too theatrically; the chalk hopscotch read **AND** in a hand that had been brave yesterday and wobbly today. Sheriff Mayhew climbed the courthouse steps with a manila folder under his arm and a face he kept for removing hornets without scaring toddlers.

"I'm going to say a few facts," he told the crowd, microphone free by principle. "Then we're all going to drink water and breathe. We found, at first light, a length of clear vinyl hose under the willow. Four feet. Coupler clamp attached. Brand: Wagner Hardware." He held up a sealed bag. Inside: hose honest as sin, clamp shining with the innocence of new metal. "We also have a receipt retrieved from a trash barrel by the ferry tie-off. Time stamp: 12:11 a.m. Purchases: vinyl hose 3/4", two clamps, utility knife."

A ripple moved across the square like someone had lifted carpet and shaken old grit loose. The Adler niece who had brought onion-skin pages two days ago went pale, then purposeful. Beside her, Rosalie LeClair folded her arms as if bracing furniture. Across the green, a Cavanaugh cousin exhaled a satisfaction he did not have the wisdom to be ashamed of. People don't mean to enjoy feeling right. They enjoy it anyway.

"Before your mouths sprint," Mayhew added, "let me be plain: a receipt with a vendor stamp is not a name. Wagner Hardware sells to whoever brings money. The hose could belong to the river for all I know. We're checking cameras. We're checking hands."

Confluence's host tilted his head as if curiosity and appetite were the same noun. "Sheriff, word is a witness saw a blue truck near the willow around eleven."

"Plenty of blue trucks in Cedar Creek," Mayhew said. He kept his hands open, palms down land-this plane. "I'm not feeding you villains in a paper sack. If you came for lunch, the food trucks are that way."

The crowd half-laughed because the man had learned how to salt a sentence. Still, the facts had a smell people recognized: opportunity disguised as proof. A receipt, a hose, a rumor with a color. The square rehearsed its old choreography accusation warming up like a brass section.

Sloane, who'd been sorting stakes on the south side of the green, walked into the middle like a woman pocketing a bar fight. "We're not doing podiums," she announced. "We're doing chairs. If you want to talk, you carry one." Already the high schoolers were hauling metal folding chairs into a circle so deterministic you could have set stones by it. Geometry works. That's why mobs hate it.

"Let me see the clamp," Miriam said quietly at Mayhew's shoulder. He passed the bag to her without speechifying. She turned it in her hands like a bread roll she was deciding who to feed. "Fourteen," she murmured, reading the size stamped on the band. "That's wrong for the under-notch.

Too big. You'd use a nine if you were clever, a ten if you were in a hurry."

Mayhew's eyes flicked up. "Say it louder later," he said. "Right now, I need you and Mr. Roth to be the guardians of **we don't know.**"

Julian, who had appeared with the gravity of a well-timed cloud shadow, took the bag next and examined the coupler like a jeweler. "New," he said. "Look at the burrs sharp. Also, Wagner Hardware's hose kinks early; Sloane cusses that brand for garden work. A person siphoning with four feet would have to press the mouth well below the basin line to get head." he nodded toward the willow" doesn't give them enough drop."

"Translate," Mayhew said.

"It's the wrong length to be smart," Julian answered. "Which doesn't mean someone didn't try."

A man from the back shouted, "Bring the basin back to the steps! If they're going to cheat the river, we keep it in our sight." There it was **they** pronoun as spear. People turned their heads toward Adler faces like sunflowers choosing a different sun. The niece didn't flinch. Her mouth trembled once, then set.

"Not today," Mayhew called back. "We're sorting. We will be as boring as a ledger on purpose and we will be kind to our neighbors on principle."

Confluence FM pushed the phrase Wagner Hardware receipt to air and by noon the square had a minor riot of politeness pointed apologies, tidy sarcasm, eye-rolling at a professional level. A LeClair cousin told his boss he wouldn't work next to an Adler on the lantern crew. An Adler elder told the same cousin he'd be delighted to do lanterns with him anyway. A Cavanaugh great-aunt recited, unprompted, that she had forgiven shoes last week and would practice forgiving stubborn-ness next.

Under the willow, the deputy repositioned the canvas screen and looked like a man who had become a symbol without signing up. The rope around the river brightened in the sun like a line you draw when you decide sentences will be shorter today on purpose.

By three, a grainy still image from a shop camera on Dock Street hit phones: a blue pickup bed with a coil of vinyl and an elbow, timestamped **23:08**. The comment beneath: **Adler blue??**

"Everything looks like a Adler when you're hungry," Rosalie said under her breath.

Miriam watched the rumor climb hand over hand up the trellis of certainty and felt herself lose altitude. She could say the clamp size aloud and be right and still lose the room. Facts don't get the last word when fear has rehearsed its speech longer. She took herself away from the center because she could feel her face wanting to persuade. Persuasion is useful when it's called teaching. It turns pious when it's called I need you to stop making this hard.

"We could be wrong," she told Julian in the slim shade behind the south window, voice flat with the fatigue of a week that kept trying to move the hinge pins. "About everything. The dream. The wedge. The order. Maybe someone just cut a hose and a joke and the river is tired of our metaphors."

"You're allowed a crisis every seven days," he said. "Municipal code."

"Don't," she said, too sharp; then, "sorry. I don't want to make jokes my bandage. Mayhew is standing there with a bag and a crowd and if he blinks wrong this is a trial." She swallowed. "What if I asked the town to tell the long version, and they were just waiting for an excuse to go back to the short one with pitchforks?"

"You didn't ask them to be this way," he said. "Also, pitchforks are out of code."

She looked at him with the exasperated tenderness you give a man who has learned how to keep you on the planet and is using it. "If the hose is theirs," she said, and wished the sentence had a softer verb, "if it's an Adler, then I picked the wrong nouns all week."

"If the hose is theirs," he said, "anAdler did a foolish thing in a town full of foolishness. That's as far as it goes."

She wanted to believe him. The crowd wanted a villain. Wants are loud. She tucked herself back into the circle with a stack of index cards and a pen and told people to write their fear down instead of speaking it. They did. It helped a little laughter kept cutting in and out like radio through hills.

At five, Mayhew released a second statement: **Receipt shows late-night purchase. Camera still shows a truck with hose. We are interviewing. We are not charging. We are boring.** The square, which had been practicing boredom like a virtue, didn't quite manage it. Someone cut the rope at the west end again. Sloane tied it back without commentary and tightened it so well shame couldn't wriggle through.

By sunset, the words **red** and **handed** were stretched across a poster, and the phrase **Adler blue** had achieved the status of a color in a crayon box nobody needed. Under the willow, Miriam stood very still and felt the gift go quiet. Not gone quiet, like weather on pause. She could not tell whether the silence was discipline or withdrawal.

"We'll step back tonight," Julian said, the way you say to

a person you love *you are not in charge of the weather; your job is blankets.*

She nodded, not persuaded, only willing. Sometimes that's all the room can use.

THE TOWN'S rumor engine idled in low overnight, churning in bedrooms and group texts and beneath television anchors who longed to say a name. Miriam sat in her kitchen with the map and could not get the lines to behave. Her notebook looked like a child's dance recital every idea in a tutu, each certain it was next.

She wrote **Wagner Hardware clamp #14 (too big). WAGNER HARDWARE stamp ≠ Adler person. Four-foot hose insufficient head across grade.** Then, because the night had teeth, she wrote **unless.** She scratched **unless** out as if striking the word could make physics tender.

Her phone buzzed with a message from June Hollis, near midnight: **When the river is quiet, it is not taking your side. It is allowing you to have one without turning it into doctrine. Sleep.** She didn't. Sleep felt like betrayal when your neighbor was being gossiped into a gallows.

At two she went to the museum by the back stairs the way you do when you don't want to bump into your own better angels. The south wall waited, the board modest as reason. She put her palm on it and, for the first time since the symbol had appeared, felt nothing dramatic at all. She hated the relief of that and the panic of it simultaneously.

She lifted the board, stepped into the old rectangle, and stood. It was not magic. It was wood and air. She breathed, because that was still allowed. The words from the ledger the draft reversing the order came back as data, not thunder.

Useful. Insufficient. She closed the board gently, because failing gently is still a decency.

At the willow, the deputy read a paperback under a headlamp halo, the canvas screen humming "nothing to see" like a psalm. The water made its slow argument with stone. The wedge kept the under-notch from being eaten while the town worked through its appetite for spectacle. Miriam stepped onto the first shelf of the bank and let the chill correct her. She thought: *if I were a saboteur, would I choose Wagner Hardware hose? No. I would choose black rubber, old, unphotogenic. If I were mean, I would buy my hose at the store that would hurt the most when stamped. If I were a coward, I would leave the receipt in a barrel.*

Her mind entertained unflattering possibilities the way you welcome unhelpful guests because politeness is quicker than eviction. She pictured Adler hands old, careful, practiced at door hinges and ledger lines handling vinyl in the dark. The image would not settle. It flickered like the heron's third beat. She could not decide whether that was evidence or hope.

The next morning the bakery refused to sell a loaf to Mrs. Adler and then apologized in the same sentence. A Cavanaugh man put gas in an Adler truck without charging and called it a tax on his own pride. Rosalie posted a sign on the lantern table **NO NAMES UNTIL SOURCES MULTIPLY** and two women tried to argue with it and ended up donating blood at the pop-up drive instead because their bodies knew how to be useful even when their mouths didn't.

At eleven, Mayhew called a small meeting in the little room behind the council chamber the one with the map that still shows the creek running through three parcels that aren't there anymore. He set three items on the table: the bagged hose, the printed receipt, a still print of the blue truck.

"Camera timestamp is wrong by an hour," he said. "Owner never switched after daylight savings. Blue truck is Evan LeClair's, not Adler. He hauled folding chairs from church at ten seen parking at the square at 10:20. The license plate confirms. Hose in bed matches what he bought yesterday to fix a water line at his mother's; it was on sale."

He waited for the room to exhale. It didn't. People don't forgive misfires that fast; their mouths are left holding an unsaid accusation like a hot bowl. It burns either way.

"And the receipt?" Julian asked.

Mayhew slid it across. "Cash. The clerk stamp belongs to a teenager who admits leaving the receipt on the counter and sweeping it into a barrel at close. We don't have a buyer. We do have Wagner Hardware's shipment list twenty-four lengths of four-foot arrived Monday. Useful for tents, not siphons. Wagner Hardware sold seventeen by yesterday. Gardeners bought half."

"So the red herring is red," Sloane said from the doorway, hair tucked under a cap that meant she'd already saved three small things before breakfast. "Not a fish. Dye packet thrown in the tub to make us grab towels."

Mayhew nodded. "We're not done," he said. "Someone cut the rope twice. Someone intends chaos. But the hose and the truck and the receipt don't belong to the Adlers by anything sturdier than our desire for a tidy story."

Miriam swallowed hard the kind that rearranges a day's furniture. She had wanted so badly to be right in the direction of mercy that she'd nearly accepted being wrong in the direction of condemnation just to be done with guessing. Shame made her bones hot. She kept her mouth closed because sometimes repentance looks like letting the better fact sit in the room without turning it into a sermon about your own moral growth.

Mayhew turned to her anyway. He was kind enough to let her keep her face. "You kept a lid on the language," he said. "That helped. Say the clamp thing out loud this afternoon. Teach the room how hoses and head work. Give them a job that isn't judging."

She nodded, grateful for boring assignments. Julian touched the back of her knuckles under the table a repairman's blessing. She almost jerked away from the kindness because self-doubt wants penance, not comfort. She didn't. Discipline is letting the right help happen while your shame is still trying to audition.

At lunch she walked to June Hollis's porch because June was her designated repository for sentences that needed sanding before the square heard them. June listened without interrupting, hands in the sweater sleeves of a hundred winters.

"You're carrying the town like a sack," June said. "Put it down. If you break your back with Cedar Creek, it will not thank you. It will just hand you another sack."

"I thought I was past needing to be the hero," Miriam said.

"You are," June said. "Now you need to be the neighbor who likes the unglamorous job. Announce clamp sizes. Use the word 'head.' Tell people **AND** again until they hate you in the morning and thank you in the evening."

Miriam laughed despite herself. "Yes, ma'am."

On the way back, she passed the bakery where the earlier apology had expanded into a tray of free rolls with a sign reading **FOR MISTAKEN CONCLUSIONS** and she took one because carbs are therapy the body understands without needing a label.

By afternoon her doubt had shrunk from a thunderhead to a leaking faucet: annoying, pervasive, fixable with the right washer and a willingness to get under the sink. She went to the sink she knew **the circle** and started writing numbers on a poster board: $14 \neq 9$; 4 ft $\neq$ enough drop; WAGNER HARDWARE $\neq$ Adler. Not poetry. Plumbing. It felt like penance in the form of education. It also felt like respect.

THEY SET the chairs at dusk. The crowd arrived with the look people wear when they realize their certainty cost someone a loaf of bread. Mayhew went first always Mayhew first on days when the blood pressure of the town needed a story with small integers.

"The receipt does not name a culprit," he said. "The blue truck belongs to a LeClair who carried chairs. The hose is the wrong length and brand for siphons across that grade. We have no charges. We have a rope that needs to stop getting cut."

A low murmur of discontent anger embarrassed at being caught in its underwear. Pastor Elijah stood and did the job he seems to have been born to do: he gave people a sentence to put in their mouths that would keep their teeth from clamping down on their neighbors. "We will not let boredom feel like betrayal," he said. "We will learn the clamp sizes and go home fed."

Miriam took the middle with her poster board and did the unglamorous. "This," she said, tapping 14, "would be a sloppy choice. You could still try; foolishness doesn't check manuals. But you'd be fighting physics. This " **4 ft** " has to get you from here to here with enough drop to pull. It doesn't. It can hold a tent. It cannot run a theft." She looked up and compelled a laugh with nothing but patience. "I promise there will be cake later if we master this."

Sloane wheeled a table up with two buckets and a yardstick and let Julian do show-and-tell. He filled, dropped, lifted, demonstrated head with the precision of a man who, in another life, would have worn khaki and written lab manuals teenagers quoted back to him respectfully and with a little sarcasm. When water refused to behave at the wrong drop, the square, unbelievably, applauded. People like it when reality shows up looking like a trick it refuses to be.

"Any questions?" Miriam asked.

"Just one," a voice called from the back June's, of course. "Are we buying Adlers bread this week, or are we baking?"

"Baking," a dozen throats answered, relieved at being told exactly how to be good.

The Adler niece stepped into the circle with a pan of lemon bars that could have ended wars if wars had better taste. "We baked," she said simply. Next to her, the LeClair cousin who'd been ready to side-eye a lantern partner two hours earlier brought a stack of paper plates and didn't ask for gratitude out loud.

Miriam exhaled for the first time in twenty-four hours in a way that felt like unfastening rather than collapse. Her doubt hadn't vanished. It had been asked to help instead of perform. That is the correct demotion for doubt.

After the circle, when the kids were collecting folding chairs and Sloane was making notes for another iteration of **HINGE PROTOCOL**, Julian found her at the south wall and leaned beside the board with the ease of a man who had decided he would save his panic for fires.

"You didn't try to be brilliant," he said. "Thank you."

"I wanted to," she admitted. "I wanted a sentence that

made the square clap. June told me to bring clamp sizes. She was right. My ego's mad. It will get over it."

"It will," he said. "And when it doesn't, I'll take it for a sandwich."

She turned to him, the heat of the day's foolishness finally burning off her face. "I thought, for a minute, that I had asked the town to be brave and then handed it an excuse to be cruel."

"You asked the town to be accurate," he said. "It panicked and reached for cruelty because cruelty is in reach. You didn't put it there. You helped it reach past."

She let that sit where it needed to sit in the pocket where you store compliments you can't spend right away but will need next week during a storm. "Will you walk with me to the willow?" she asked.

He did. Under the canvas, the deputy and his paperback had promoted themselves to lantern light. The river sounded like it was encouraging punctuality. The wedge held. The under-notch looked exactly like a thing that had never once cared about hashtags.

"I don't mind if I'm wrong," she said, surprising herself with the truth of it. "I mind being wrong in a way that hurts the right person."

"You will be," he said, practical and kind. "So will I. We will apologize without a speech about how brave we are to apologize. And we will bring more clamps."

She laughed, and the laughter made room for something warmer that had been waiting all day in the truck like a well-behaved dog. "Thank you for reminding me I have a job I can do even when the gift is quiet."

"It is the sexiest thing about you," he said, which made her nearly drop into the river out of sheer relief at levity.

They stood a minute, both hearing voices from the

square detach from names and turn back into neighbor-sound. The willow shrugged its green like an old coat that has decided to keep one more winter around after all.

"May I reassure you in public for a minute?" he asked, suddenly shy, which sat gorgeous on a man as careful as he is.

"Yes," she said. "But use dull words."

He cleared his throat and addressed the deputy, who looked up, bemused. "Deputy," Julian said with ceremonial gravity, "for the record: Ms. Adler is doing her job. She is not responsible for the weather. She is kind and competent and likely to be more accurate tomorrow than we deserve. That is all."

The deputy, who had the good sense to participate in a ritual when invited, saluted with his paperback. "Noted," he said. "Now go home before I put you both on trash duty."

They walked back up the path. Near the south window, the couple sat on the steps holding hands with the peaceful bravery of people who had done an unclubbable kindness in public and survived it: **postponement** had held. The mothers were tired in the way that makes tea a sacrament. Mayhew had slumped against a post and let his hat tilt over his eyes for eight heartbeats. Pastor Elijah pretended not to notice, which is the kindest form of noticing there is. Sloane, God bless her, was labeling bins.

On the museum porch, Julian paused. "I have a confession," he said.

"We already had your chapter," she said, smiling.

"I have them in installments now," he said. "This one's smaller: when the hose photo hit, I wanted it to be true just so we could stop being tired. I wanted a villain because villains are easier to label than systems and sadness."

She touched his sleeve with the back of her fingers. "Me

too," she said softly. "Which is why we don't get to decide alone."

"We won't," he said. "That is our romance novel: **We Won't Decide Alone.**"

"That's a terrible title," she said. "But I'll read it."

He leaned in then, not for show, not to award the day a bow just a press of his forehead to hers, like the way you touch a door before you open it because the room might smell like lemon oil and memory and you need to warn your chest. The square flowed around them without making a parade out of it. That's the reward for not turning feelings into policy: sometimes the town lets you keep them.

Back at her table, she wrote three lines and did not edit them because sometimes drafts are kinder than final copies:

Red herring: hose + receipt + blue truck wrong sizes, wrong time, wrong story.

Doubt: allowed; demoted; given a job.

Reassurance: dull words, true; we will not decide alone; we will bring clamps and cake.

Outside, the river spent the moon in thin coins on stone. Under the willow, the wedge kept the under-notch from getting eaten by impatience. In the south wall, the board slept like a good boundary: not a secret, a sabbath. Cedar Creek breathed the boring air of a day that almost went wrong, then didn't. And in two apartments above two rooms with too many chairs, two people practiced the method that keeps love from becoming weather: **stone before steps, truth before theater, us before applause.**

17

THE WATER VISION

Miriam went alone. The square was noisy with its new hobby of suspicion, chairs still warm from the evening's accusations about clamps and trucks and initials. She needed something else something without paper edges or receipts. So she took the long path under cedar shade and came to the river where the canvas screen hummed like a hymn written in dull words. The deputy looked up from his paperback and tipped his chin in greeting. She nodded back, grateful for his gift of silence.

She walked past the rope, down the slope where mud still remembered being pasture, and sat on the low shelf where the water folded into itself with the patience of a mother braiding hair. She didn't close her eyes at once. First she looked. At the wedge of stone still holding its stubborn under-notch. At the symbol in the shallows, half-illumined, half-dream. At the loops of current the kids had marked with sticks the day before. Then, when the outer vision had steadied, she let the inner one come.

Her breath slowed. She folded her hands in her lap not

as prayer, not as performance, but as ballast. And the water began to speak the way it does when you let the noise in your head get tired enough to nap.

It came as a rush first a torrent behind her eyes, fast and insistent. She saw the river swollen with snowmelt, roaring past its banks, hauling branches and debris as if the world itself had lost patience. She stood in the middle of it without drowning, though her body remembered the old terror of being twelve and almost swept under by a current that didn't know her name. The sound filled her chest. She tried to speak but had no tongue in this place. Only the roar.

Then impossible as a door opening under water the current split. The body of the river divided like a curtain pulled back by invisible hands. She stood on bare riverbed, rocks slick and shining like bones under new skin. In the trough of that exposed bed lay chains. Long, rusted, tangled, their links glinting like memories too sharp to handle. She recognized them not by sight but by the ache they pulled from her chest. These were not boat chains or ferry tethers. They were promises broken and locked together, each link a moment when a hand had clutched greed, or silence, or pride instead of trust.

She bent to touch one. It burned cold, the way shame burns when you put it back on after pretending you'd outgrown it. She tried to lift it. Too heavy. She tried again, fingers straining. Still too heavy. Her lungs screamed. She would fail.

Then she heard it. Not the roar now, but a voice threaded through the river's breath: *I will bring you out.* Not shouted. Not even sung. Spoken as fact, as calm as weather that has decided to be kind. The words landed in her bones the way bread lands in a hollow stomach. She straightened. The chain in her hands snapped. Not because she was strong, but because it was time. The links shattered, pieces falling into the bed and dissolving into silt. Around her, other chains cracked like ribs opening to air, like doors swinging on hinges that had finally been oiled.

She wept in the dream. Not neat tears, but the kind that shake your whole chest with gratitude you didn't know you'd stored up. She knelt, pressing her palms into wet stone, and saw the chains vanish one by one until only the river remained flowing free, its course unchoked.

Then the current closed again. The walls of water came together with a sigh. The chains were gone. The river was whole. She was standing once more on the bank, breath ragged, heart pounding.

When she opened her eyes in the waking world, her cheeks were wet. The wedge stone stared at her, ordinary and exact. But she knew what she had seen. The mark was not about sabotage. It was about bondage. The town was chained not by hoses or clamps but by promises betrayed, by silence disguised as stewardship, by grudges polished into heritage. And the vision had said: the chains would break.

She sat still a long time, hands trembling in her lap. The deputy glanced over once, as if to check she hadn't slipped. She shook her head softly. "I'm fine," she whispered, and to her surprise, it was true. Fine not as neatness. Fine as release.

The river had taught her a lesson her mind had been too tidy to accept: this was not a puzzle to accuse with. It was a liberation to endure.

SHE WALKED BACK SLOWLY, every cedar trunk along the path looking like a sentry. Her body felt different lighter, yes, but also braced. Visions take something from you when they give. By the time she reached the square, lanterns were already strung, and the circle was forming. People's faces turned, hungry for updates, ready for gossip. She thought about staying quiet, about guarding the dream in her pocket like a jewel too fragile for daylight. But the words pressed on her ribs. She couldn't keep them.

When her turn came, she stood. "I saw something last night," she said, and the air changed. "I don't ask you to take it as proof. I ask you to hear it as you'd hear a neighbor who has lived by the river long enough to know its moods."

The square stilled. Rosalie nodded. Sloane folded her arms with deliberate attention. Julian tilted his head, worry hidden but present. Miriam breathed once and let the vision become story.

"The river opened," she said. "And at its bed were chains. Not iron to hold boats. Chains of promises broken. Betrayals that were never confessed. Pride that made us choose silence instead of repair. I tried to lift one, and I couldn't. Then I heard words words older than us. *I will bring you out.* And the chains snapped."

People shifted. A murmur ran. Some faces turned skeptical, some softened, some looked frightened by the sheer audacity of naming visions out loud. She went on anyway.

"I think we have been fighting the wrong enemy. It isn't sabotage. It isn't clamps or receipts or whose blue truck parked near the willow. It's chains. The kind we carry in our bones. The kind that make us punish our children with our grandparents' silence. The river isn't showing us villains. It's showing us bondage and telling us it's time to come out."

Pastor Elijah closed his eyes, lips moving like a man recognizing scripture hidden in modern dress. "Exodus," he murmured. "The promise to Israel: *I will bring you out from under the yoke of the Egyptians.*"

"Yes," Miriam said, voice low but clear. "Out from under the yoke. Not by our cleverness. Not by our suspicion. By the river itself calling us back to truth."

The Adler niece's hands shook where they gripped her knees. A Cavanaugh aunt began to cry quietly, no words, just water. Rosalie leaned forward, elbows on knees, as if to catch the weight of the idea before it slipped away. Julian watched with a face that mixed awe and unease museum boy torn between artifact and revelation.

Mayhew cleared his throat. "If what you say is true," he said, cautious as a carpenter testing a weak joist, "then the hose was never the story. The chains were."

"The hose was a red herring," Miriam said. "And we nearly swallowed it whole."

Silence followed thick but not hostile. The town had learned to survive silence these last weeks without making it into gallows. After a minute, Pastor Elijah spoke again, louder now: "Then let us stop counting clamps and start naming chains. Write them down. Speak them aloud. Don't hand them to your children."

He took chalk and drew a long line across the pavement. At the top he wrote: **CHAINS TO BREAK.** People hesitated. Then Rosalie stepped forward and wrote **stubborn pride.** A Cavanaugh cousin wrote **fear of losing face.** The Adler niece, hand trembling, wrote **ledger more important than neighbor.** Soon the board filled: **resentment, silence, greed, rivalry, shame.**

Miriam stood back, tears prickling. It was not spectacle. It was exodus not out of land, but out of old lies.

She whispered the phrase to herself again: *I will bring you out.* She felt it resonate not just in her but in the circle, in the cedar trunks, in the rope still humming at the willow. The town was not healed. But it had been told the true name of its affliction. That matters.

Julian came to her side after. "Chains," he said, half-dazed. "It fits. Too well. But visions " He shook his head. "Visions don't hold in court."

"They don't need to," she said softly. "They hold in hearts."

His eyes searched hers, torn between belief and defense. She didn't argue. She let the silence between them be its own promise: they would find the way to integrate both. Truth needed both artifact and dream.

THAT NIGHT, Miriam couldn't sleep. She walked again to the willow, Julian with her this time. The deputy nodded them past. They sat side by side on the bank, lantern light behind, river dark ahead.

"Tell me again," Julian said. His voice was almost reverent. "The chains. Every detail."

She did. The roar. The parting. The rust. The cold burn. The voice. The shattering. He listened like a man writing an invisible transcript, every muscle taut with the effort not to dismiss. When she finished, he let out a long breath.

"It means the symbol isn't a warning of sabotage," he said. "It's a mark of release. The past is breaking itself open."

"Yes," she said. "And that means we're not detectives. We're midwives."

He laughed, startled, and then sobered. "Which means the ledger, the draft, the board minutes they're not weapons. They're chains being named."

"And we're asked to help break them," she said. "Not to prove who cut the hose."

They sat in quiet then, both facing the water. The symbol in the shallows glowed faintly, as if approving the translation. The rope along the bank sagged gently in the night breeze, no longer a boundary but a reminder.

Miriam closed her eyes. She heard again: *I will bring you out.* This time, though, she wasn't alone. Julian's hand found hers, hesitant but steady, as if to say: if there are chains, we'll break them together.

The night deepened. The river kept moving, patient as always. Above them, cedar branches knitted the sky into shelter. Miriam felt the town behind her fractured, suspicious, hungry for villains. But ahead, in the dream-space, she felt something older: chains snapping, one by one, until the riverbed was free.

She knew then the story was about to turn. The revelation would come. The ledger would speak. The wedge would prove older than grudges. And Cedar Creek, if it chose rightly, would step out of bondage into something closer to promise.

She pressed Julian's hand once, then released it, not out of reluctance but to remind them both that liberation isn't borrowed. It's shared.

Tomorrow, the town would still argue. Tomorrow, Mayhew would still need clamp sizes and Sloane would still scold about cords. Tomorrow, the circle would still flirt with gallows. But tonight, under the willow, Miriam knew the truth: the river had already begun the work. The chains were breaking. The people only had to learn to walk out.

18

____

THE HIDDEN LEDGER

The morning after the vision, they did not chase thunder. They went upstairs to the dry hum of the museum stacks where history sits like a polite animal pretending not to stare. The fluorescent lights hummed their institutional hymn; the catalog terminal scolded in its favorite blue. Sloane handed them nitrile gloves and a look that said *eat breakfast first,* which they had. Outside, Cedar Creek was already trying to decide whether to be gentle or exciting. Inside, they chose gentle.

"We start with the drawer that has bothered me for ten years," Julian said. "Series C, misfiled after my grandmother merged two accessions to save a shelf." He typed like a man returning to a conversation he'd been avoiding. The screen coughed up an inventory line: **C-Box-14: Agricultural Ledgers & Sundries, 1870–1876. Donor: Bridger Mercantile (estate).** Below it, a line his grandmother had added in pencil, later typed by a volunteer who did not love nuance: **see also: Water Board drafts.** He looked at Miriam. "Bridger," he said. "Initials A.B. This box has been within arm's reach of the south wall for my entire life."

"Then let's reach," she said, calm making room for awe.

The box itself was ordinary gray-board with a polite lid. But lids, in Cedar Creek, have learned to hold their breath. Julian set it on the table in Collections with the tenderness of a man putting down an heirloom and a hazard. He removed the lid. Inside: two farm ledgers bound in calfskin, a slim daybook marked **accounts**, a folded map with grease ghosting its corners, a packet of receipts tied in faded blue ribbon, and because the past is never without flair a square of linen with a loop stitched in black thread, the exact curve Miriam had been carrying in her sleep.

"Why do we always tuck our evidence next to our sins," Sloane muttered, hovering at the edge like a carpenter at a christening.

Julian opened the first calfskin ledger. The ink was iron gall, browned to the color of a scar. Columns for *seed, lard, gin, salt, nails, wagon repair.* Prices in cents that made modern mouths smile and older shoulders ache. He turned pages with that museum slowness that looks like reverence and is, in fact, a learned fear of ripping. Halfway through, the hand changed bolder, less patient. A header: **WATER.** Below, a list of dates, marks, and a phrase that snatched the air right out of him:

Blessing first; counting after. A.B.

Miriam leaned in. The column widened. On the left, tallies: single verticals in runs of five, six, then seven, the seventh slashed horizontal a shade darker as if added under a different sky. On the right, notes: *low year, ditch silted, move wreath to steps to cheer the people.*

He turned the page. A sketch amateur, precise enough to try of a rectangle set into a bank, notch indicated with a deliberate V, and a loop carved across the face. Beside it, the old instruction, terrible in its cheerfulness: *If water shy, pour, then read; do not disappoint donors.* Initials again. A.B.

"Allocation stone," Julian said, his voice careful. "And the order reversed. In his hand." He looked at the header again, then at Miriam, as if asking pardon from two centuries at once.

"Keep reading," she said. The vision's certainty steadied her. The chain in her chest, named now, did not jerk at the sight of a name.

Receipts, pinned with straight pins that had thought they'd be left in cloth: two couplers from *Field's*, a tin pipe from *Ackers & Son*, wages paid for *after-sunset ditch clearing* two men, cash, no notation of cause. Then: a line entry dated late summer of '73: *Took two turns at slab; weather favored us; levee at lower bend to be mended by boys next week.* Below it, a smaller hand angrier, or embarrassed: *Boys were at school; men were at church; levee mended late.* Another page: *Prayer well received; rain praised; output held.* The ledger mixed piety and plumbing with the comfort of a man who mistrusted neither so long as he could arrange both.

Julian reached for the daybook. Less formal; more honest. Here the sentences loosened. *Elijah good sermon* sat next to *Mrs. Pike two loaves on account.* And here, the sentence that lifted itself toward the room like a confession: *Stone said no; we poured anyway. Owed half-water to Cavanaugh. Settled on paper. Rosalie's grandmother wept. Adlers promised help in winter.* Initials. A.B. Under it, a thumb-smudge where the writer had tried, perhaps, to blur his own name. The smudge had dried beautiful and useless.

Sloane exhaled an oath so tender it sounded like grace. "There it is," she said. "Not the villain. The decision. The chain."

The folded map, when spread, showed the curve of

Cedar on a day when the creek had still been learning its manners. Bridger's parcel hugged the bend like the wrist of a good friend. In red pencil, a faint line: the night ditch. It bled toward the river like an admission.

Miriam sat back. The room seemed taller. The vision's water closed above her again, but this time without fear. Here was the chain link with a date and a hand. Here was the order reversed first on paper, then in practice, then in habit, then in folklore. They had not been imagining. The stone had not been a performance. It had been an instrument for teaching restraint. They had learned to ignore it on purpose.

"Let's confirm provenance," Julian said, because bone-deep joy or sorrow never excuses skipping method. "Donor file. Bridger estate died 1891; estate cleared 1894; grandson attempted to sell shop; inventory taken. Ledger #2 described as 'water notes.'" He crossed to the file drawer, pulled a hanging folder, paged through duplicates of duplicates. "Here," he said, tapping: *Bridger Mercantile: box of three ledgers, daybook, receipts. Accepted by A. Roth, clerk; prepared by M. Adler, secretary.* He smiled at the names like a man locating himself on a map. "My grandmother filed it and then filed it again. She loved neatness so much she hid a fuse in a drawer to tidy the room."

"Scan," Miriam said. "Second source." She turned to the blue ribbon bundle, ridiculous in its daintiness. A folded letter addressed to *Friend Abner*. She read aloud because secrets rot in whisper: "*If you're moving the order, say so plain and let the women decide the soup. I'll not have boys fixing levees on Sabbath again for pride. The river counts whether you bless it or not.*" Not signed. The hand, though it was the same neatness that had scolded in the 1930s minutes. Adler allied with Field in business but not in this, or perhaps Field writing alone. Either way, someone told the truth back then like a neighbor.

Sloane set the scanner in place. Mayhew arrived with his deputy as if summoned by a hinge. Pastor Elijah came because rooms change shape when certain papers come out of boxes, and someone with a broom ought to be present. They gathered like a small jury sworn to boring excellence. The page went under glass. The light swept across ink and left a perfect ghost in pixels. The daybook went next, then the sketch of the stone. The receipts hummed into light.

"Chain-of-custody starts here," Mayhew said. "List who touched what. Video the scan. No leaks before the circle." He looked at Miriam saw the vision in her face even if he hadn't heard it yet and did not ask her to be less. He asked her to be precise. "You talk first tonight," he said. "You have the dream. He has the page. Make them friends."

Julian added a note to the Hinge Protocol board with a hand that had stopped shaking: **When mystical insight appears, corroborate; do not domesticate.** He looked at her briefly, gratitude formal and new, then back at the paper as if refusing to abandon his first love because he had discovered a second.

Miriam lifted the linen square with the stitched loop. Old needlework has a way of making a room remember women who held this town together while the men played with water and words. She turned it over. On the back, faint pencil: *Alma first year.* Alma Trigg's mother? The stitch had a learning wobble in it; the loop tilted like a young singer finding her key.

"It's all here," Miriam whispered not triumph, only relief so deep it made her feel clumsy. "Stone. Loop. Order. The man. The friends who objected. The habit that hardened."

"And," Julian said. "And the ledger that will show in the

south window, and the room that will learn to count again, and the thing I will say to my father that our family kept the box and kept the peace and kept the chain. And that we can let it go now."

They sat for a moment with the box open between them like bread.

Then they got up and went to work.

THE TOWN HAD LEARNED restraint in paragraphs these last weeks; even so, the words *we found a ledger* made people drift toward the museum in a way that would have gotten you ticketed if you were a school of fish. Mayhew put two sawhorses at the base of the south window and taped up a paper that read: **TRANSCRIPT ONLY. NO INITIALS UNTIL SECOND SOURCE.** Sloane built a stand with the speed of a woman whose prayers are made of 2x4s. Pastor Elijah stood where he stands when he needs to be visible but not focal. Confluence FM hovered like a mosquito and got swatted whenever it whined.

Miriam went first, because that was the order that would keep the room honest. Dreams before evidence, not to privilege feeling over fact, but to say aloud what had already started changing bones. She told them about the water vision and the chains and the voice. Not as proof. As frame. "I think the river is breaking something older than our current argument," she said. "The ledger we found supports that. It names a choice our ancestors made. It shows the order reversed and the cost disguised as weather."

Julian held up a facsimile of the daybook page. He did not read the initials. He read the sentence that counted: "*Stone said no; we poured anyway. Owed half-water to Cavanaugh. Settled on paper.*" He pointed to the sketch of the slab the little V nicked at the under-notch, the loop thin as a throat. He put the map under the window where the light could do its antique trick of making red pencil look fresh blood. He laid the receipts out as if dressing a wound with clean linen. "We have provenance," he said. "We have context. We are cross-checking with estate filings and council minutes from 1872 and '73. The letter we found unsigned scolds 'Abner' for moving the order. The water board draft from our other box shows initials consistent with A.B. insisting on 'blessing first; counting after.' We will confirm fully before we print a name."

A voice from the back good-natured, hurting called, "Is it Adler?" There were a hundred years of rumor in that question, and yesterday's hose.

"No," Julian said, gentle as a fulcrum. "It is Bridger."

The name, when spoken, did not land like a spear. It landed like a sigh. Bridger was a long-ago shop, a surname on a few gravestones, a road out by the old orchards. People turned the syllables around on their tongues and discovered they had no immediate enemy to assign to it. Relief, then embarrassment for having felt relief, then the long work of letting the relief become humility.

"Abner Bridger," Mayhew said, confirming in the tone he uses when he tells a room a thing it can bear. "A settler active in the 1870s. Owned the mercantile. No living family in town that we know of. If you're a Bridger in the room, we'll apologize with pie. For the rest of you breathe. We have a history to mend, not a neighbor to punish."

The Adler niece cried, and then laughed, and then clapped her hand over her mouth in apology for both, and then let both be what they were. Rosalie stood and sat and stood again, as if practicing how to carry news that wasn't about her house. A Cavanaugh uncle whispered an oh and then a thank you that sounded like a man who had been ready to hate and been robbed of the opportunity.

Pastor Elijah lifted a palm. "Hear the order, friends: confession, then blessing. Counting, then pouring. We are not here to guard the innocence of the dead. We are here to free the living from the chains of their decisions. Abner Bridger moved the order to keep peace and prestige. He cut more water than was his share. We have kept the score in our bones for a century and a half. We can set it down."

"Which means," Sloane added, because she cannot not name logistics when the Spirit is hovering, "we're changing the practice. Starting tonight: we read the slab before we light. We listen to the under-notch before microphones. The kids mark flow; the aunties count turns. If the wedge says wait, we wait. We'll make soup."

Laughter softened the corners without letting them sag. Miriam watched faces in the ring watched men who had wanted villains accept a man they didn't know as the one who had failed them. She watched women whose work it had been to keep the town fed mentally reassign that work away from soothing pride and toward teaching practice. She watched Nora and Evan stand hand in hand and lean into each other with relief that felt generational.

It could have turned, self-congratulating. It didn't. They were too tired for pride. Truth had a weight that kept them grounded.

After the formalities Mayhew's chain-of-custody, Julian's tidy footnotes on ink and paper stocks, Sloane's sharpie labels and Pastor's prayer that refused to sound like theater they opened the transcript for public reading. Not the ledger itself. The words. People lined up and took turns reading a sentence or two. The magic, if you could call it that, wasn't in the content; it was in the cadence: *we poured;*

we owed; we moved the wreath; the stone said no; low year; levee later; promised help in winter. After an hour, the town knew the sound of its original failing. It did not flinch from the echo.

Julian's father came and stood in the second circle, hat in hand. When the line thinned, he stepped forward and read the unsigned letter aloud: *"If you're moving the order, say so plain..."* He swallowed, and his son watched a chain slide off a shoulder he had loved. Alan finished: *"...the river counts whether you bless it or not."* When he looked up, he found Julian's face in the crowd and nodded once, as if to say, *we did our part, and we will do the rest.* It wasn't absolution; it was consent.

Confluence FM did its little dance and found it had fewer dramatic angles to film than it had hoped. The Cedar Creek Observer ended up using words like *historic* and *communal* and, bless him, *boring.* Cedar Creek accepted the coverage like a neighbor offering a casserole you didn't ask for but will eat anyway because you are tired.

Back in Collections, Miriam and Julian repacked the box with a new label: **Bridger, Abner Water Notes & Receipts 1871–1874.** Under it, in small letters that were part joke, part policy, they added: **Stone before steps.** They left the linen loop on the scanner table and let it dry flat with a sandwich of acid-free paper. The stitch waver looked like a child's letter learning how to be itself. It felt correct.

"Say it to me," Miriam said as they turned off lights and the stacks gave back the echoes of their own breathing.

"What?" he asked.

"That it was Bridger," she said. "That it wasn't a family we could punish in the morning. That the culprit is past, and the repair is present."

He smiled, not triumphant. "Abner Bridger moved the order because he was scared of hunger and hungry for admiration. We moved the order back today because we are scared of turning into him. And we are hungry for something better than being right."

"That's a decent liturgy," she said. "We'll test it on the square."

THEY DIDN'T SCHEDULE A CEREMONY. They did not change the poster font to something shinier. They didn't rename the festival. They changed the order, and when you change the order, everything else learns to align.

At dusk, the lantern shepherds met under the cedar like usual. The high schoolers walked their parallax lines out with the gravity of people who will be braver as adults because they practiced boring at seventeen. Sloane handed out clipboards and the word **AND** on index cards. Mayhew posted a deputy by the willow with less obligation to any microphone than to the paperback in his hand. Pastor Elijah stood at the chalk board from last night where **CHAINS TO BREAK** had been written and handed a new stick to a child who wanted to add **my dad's temper** with serious letters.

Miriam took the same shelf of bank as the night of the wedge and spoke to the water without needing it to speak back. "We will read you before we bless," she said, and if people had laughed it would have ruined something; they didn't.

Julian held the rub of the loop and the tallies and the under-notch diagram and did what he does best gave the room a job. "We're looking for a trickle under the slab at the V," he said, pointing. "If it brightens the wedge, we use half-water. If it does not, we wait and tell good stories instead."

He looked at the two teenagers assigned to write **WAIT** or **POUR** on the board. "You decide," he told them. "Not because you know more. Because we trust you to obey what you see."

They watched. The wedge glowed barely, but real. The **WAIT** went up in letters with a wobble of righteousness and a ring of cheer. A collective breath, caught. For a century, impatient men had tried to baptize the town into their timetable. Tonight, the town decided it would honor being told no.

"Soup?" Rosalie called, practical as always, and the answer was a grateful, relieved, hungry laughter. The LeClair table served. The Cavanaughs carried. The Adler niece set out lemon bars like sacrament. The bakery put up a sign that read **PAYING OUR DEBTS** and slid a tray of rolls down the table.

"Read," Pastor Elijah said softly, and the circle did. They read the chain list again out loud, unashamed, from **stubborn pride** to **fear of losing face**. Nora added **performing our goodness** in tidy block letters and then drew a tiny hinge in the corner. Evan took chalk and wrote **short version**, then crossed it out and wrote **long version**, and his mother laughed and cried and kissed his cheek with flour on her hands.

Mayhew, who cannot be seen to enjoy poetry but sometimes does, walked the perimeter with his notepad. "Rope intact," he told Sloane, mock-formal. "Bucket count: sufficient. Hose rumors: diminishing."

"Clamp sizes memorized?" she asked a cluster of men who looked properly abashed from yesterday's red herring.

"Nine and ten for siphon, fourteen for tents," they chorused, and she high-fived them like an aunt who knew the secret to civility was giving men something to prove that didn't involve enemies.

Julian's father came forward at the right moment not early, not late and put a hand on the south wall. "I would like to say the sentence out loud," he said, and the square made room. "My mother loved editing. I love it still. But I love this more: that we told the whole of it. I am sorry for the part I played in keeping the short version longer than it should have lasted." He looked at his son and then at Miriam and then at the Hilton-born ceilings of the cedar branches and added, ridiculously but correctly, "Thank you for doing my job."

Miriam read one line from the daybook *"Owed half-water to Cavanaugh"* and Rosalie answered with a simple, "We forgive," and Mr. Cavanaugh, who had an unglamorous talent for truth late in a long day, said, "We forgive back in advance for the next time your people annoy us," and the square laughed in relief.

And because Cedar Creek is a place that refuses to build altars without shelves, the night did not end with a trumpet. It ended with measurements. With teenagers teaching their parents how to read the trickle. With Sloane writing three new lines on the Hinge Protocol board under the south window:

10) **Ledger before legend.**

11) **Kids decide when eyes are tired.**

12) **Chains snap one link at a time.**

Pastor Elijah drew a tiny Exodus staff under the list and did not explain the joke; those who saw it smiled into their cups.

When the lanterns were half-down and the kids had begun their ritual of stacking chairs in pleasing geometries, Mayhew found Miriam and Julian at the willow. "Two things," he said. "One, Confluence FM is going to try very hard to make Bridger a proxy for whichever house people want to hate. Don't let them. Two, the rope is going to get cut again because old habits hate being unemployed. We will tie it back together again. That is our romance novel." He blinked as if surprised at himself for the phrase, then added, "Carry on."

"Ledger before legend," Julian said when Mayhew had ambled away. "I like that."

"Chain before clamp," Miriam answered. "We just learned to tell the parts in the right order."

He looked at her the south wall behind her, the slab before them and let his face admit love without making it into a spectacle. "You were right," he said. "The vision was not a test of our adulthood. It was an invitation to stop arguing about plumbing and begin telling the truth about our inheritance."

"Both/and," she said, reflexively, because if this town had a crest it would be a hinge and that word.

He squeezed her hand. "And," he agreed.

They walked the bank one last time, checking for mischief. A teen from the grid team saluted them with a flashlight, proud in the way a person can be when the work is delicate and recognized. The wedge caught a small starlight and held it like a coin. The under-notch did what it was designed to do: told the truth in water.

Back at her table, Miriam wrote without editing (June would be pleased):

1: **Ledger confirms loop; A.B. changed order; receipts + map + sketch = spine.**

2: **Culprit belongs to past; we refuse modern scapegoats; confession replaces gossip.**

3: **Order restored stone before steps; wait when wedge**

shines; soup when it does. Truth poured quieter than spectacle.

She set the notebook down and, because rituals keep bodies honest, lit a candle not for drama, for practice and whispered the sentence that had become a method rather than a banner: **I will bring you out.** She did not need to add *with company*. The day had proven it.

Upstairs, Julian wrote in the log he would show the circle tomorrow:

Brought out: Bridger ledger (1871–1874). Confirmed: reversed order; debt admitted on paper; chain named in dream matched by ink. Changed: ritual order (count, then bless). Hinge holds. He stopped, then added a final line, private and necessary:

We chose repair over revenge. The river approved in the only language it speaks: patience.

19

TOWN HALL CLASH

The town packed itself into the hall the way weather packs into a storm predictably and with personal flair. Folding chairs squared into rows under lights that made skin look honest. The stage was not a stage just a line of mismatched tables pushed together and covered with butcher paper so Sloane could draw diagrams if the air got ideas. On the far wall, the old photograph of the fort looked as if it had opinions about the evening and no intention of sharing them politely.

Mayhew opened the meeting without a microphone. "We'll hear, we'll breathe, we'll not shout," he said, which is Cedar Creek for *I'll arrest your voice before I arrest your body.* He held up his sheriff's note card, scrawled with reminders in a hand that had negotiated two decades' worth of drainage and drama. "Tonight is for the ledger we found, the draft letters, and the order we've changed. Not for hoses. Not for who owes whom a pie. We will be boring on purpose."

A rumble of nervous laughter scuffed under the chairs.

The room had learned a new reflex: it looked for Miriam and for Julian. When people turned their heads, they found them sitting not behind the tables but at the edge of the front row, hands visible, bodies hinged toward the room. Pastor Elijah sat three seats away like a witness you keep for the moment the air forgets how to behave. Sloane leaned against a post with a roll of butcher paper tucked under her arm and a marker like a baton. The Adler niece held a manila folder as if it were both weapon and bread. Rosalie took a spot near the aisle so she could stand or sit without asking permission. A Cavanaugh cousin had the jaw he wears for funerals and harvests.

Julian rose first, as planned. He did not perform. He held up the facsimiles: the daybook page *Stone said no; we poured anyway. Owed half-water to Cavanaugh.* The draft *blessing first; counting after* initialed in a careful, betraying hand. The little sketch of the slab with its loop and its under-notch, drawn in pencil that had outlived the man who sharpened it. "These are corroborated," he said. "Provenance: Bridger Mercantile estate, 1894. Scanned under chain-of-custody. Cross-checked by council minutes noting 'order adjusted for temper and weather.' We are not doing names at the microphone yet but you will read the transcript in the south window on your way out."

A hand went up before he could finish. "So it was Adler," a man said, practically salivating at the chance to finish last week's sentence.

"No," Julian said, patient as a good scale. "It was Bridger."

Another rumble. The kind rooms make when they're denied their favorite genre. Rosalie's mouth lifted with something like relief and grief together; the Adler niece set her folder on the chair as if her hands needed a job that didn't involve bracing. Mr. Cavanaugh's cousin made a noise, not agreement, not gloating. Cedar Creek had discovered it was capable of adult noises.

Miriam stood when the air began to thicken the moment in any meeting where a room decides if it will break or bend. "I'm asking you to listen to what the ledger is telling us," she said. "It isn't offering a villain to enjoy. It's offering a pattern to end. For a season, Abner Bridger reversed the order. He poured the blessing first and counted later because donors were bored, pride was hungry, and the weather of men's tempers felt like a Permission Slip. He wrote the debt on paper and the debt kept ourselves in chains. That's what our town has been carrying. That's what the river showed me when it opened: chains, not clamps."

A LeClair uncle stood without waiting to be recognized. "Maybe Bridger started it," he said, "but Adlers kept it tidy and the Cavanaughs liked the look of being the ones who lifted. You expect me to clap and forgive the people who turned the order into an inheritance?"

"Slow down," Mayhew said. His voice had that dry edge that could solder a wire without burning it.

From the back, Mrs. Adler's chin rose like a mast. "My family preserved records so your families wouldn't have to lie," she said, sharp as good linen. "We also enjoyed being right. Two truths. We can carry them both if we stop pretending one cancels the other."

"Two truths don't settle a bill," a young man said Evan, but he'd already learned to turn his voice into a civic instrument. "What settles the bill is turns. We've returned the order. Read the stone; then bless. We're doing it."

"Young man," the LeClair uncle said, offended by youth itself, "the ledger sits on your girlfriend's shelf like a trophy."

"It sits in the south window," Nora said, standing, no apology for standing at all. "Where everyone can read it."

Sloane stepped forward with the butcher paper and drew a rectangle with a loop and a sharp V, then a big arrow that said **COUNT - BLESS**, the arrow fat enough to be seen from the last row. "This is the order now," she announced. "Write it down. Tattoo it on your stubborn. If you want to argue, argue about soup seasoning, not this."

A woman in the aisle, cheeks damp, voice shaking with a grief that had been waiting decades for a stage, called out, "My father spent two winters angry he couldn't name. He thought the Adlers stole water. He died believing it. What am I supposed to do with the part of me that feels relieved it was Bridger and furious I didn't get to be relieved sooner?"

"Bring that to the river," Pastor Elijah said, not rising. "And write your father's name on the chain board. Then eat."

"Eat what?" a man muttered, as if the food had to prove itself now, too.

"Lemon bars, apparently," Mayhew said, which is how law enforcement does mercy when it can't think of a better noun.

Julian placed the facsimiles on the table, weighted by small rocks someone had painted with loops last summer. "We are not here to punish Abner Bridger's ghost," he said. "We are here to stop living like his decision is the only one possible."

The room shivered on its hinge. The old picture of the fort watched with its sepia seriousness. The hall had been built to hold feed auctions and prom committees and dull meetings about drainage. Tonight it was holding the first minutes of repair that could not be measured by vote count. You could tell because the bodies in the room did not look ready to storm anything. They looked ready to argue and then do dishes.

But first, they argued. Of course they argued.

"I DON'T CARE if the man's dust," Lou Cavanaugh said, standing tall in the second row like a fencepost that preferred to be a spear. "If Bridger took two turns, the shop fed on what our boys should have had in their buckets. My grandfather bundled that ache into the way he treated Adlers. That doesn't unwind with a diagram."

"Nothing unwinds without a diagram," Sloane said, drawling it to soften it, but meaning it, and the room half-laughed because Sloane had built their porches and their patience.

Mrs. Adler rose again. "We should own our part," she said, eyes level. "We kept minutes with nicer verbs than truth benefits from. We believed discretion was a virtue; we used it as a screen. It is not a sin to spare a room melodrama. It is a sin to spare it truth. I am trying to retire from that sin."

Rosalie stood no flounce, just a woman choosing to occupy her height. "LeClairs like the light," she said. "It's how we bake. We also like the sound of our names in a program. I am practicing the part where I say *we* when *we* means *we messed up the sharing.* My grandmother says we hold the flame steady and hog the attention. We can do one without the other if you all will stop flattering us for doing both."

Julian looked at Miriam this was the part where a room turns carnivorous if you let the sentences get too nutritious too fast. She nodded, and he turned a facsimile so the latecomers could see. "This isn't a trial," he said. "We're not cross-examining the dead. The record's job isn't to supply ammunition. It's to stop us from storing weather in our children."

"And yet," an older man said from the back, slow enough that people made space for what was coming, "when I was twelve, Mr. Bridger gave me licorice and told me men do what they must and boys should keep their noses in their books. I have resented Mr. Bridger for fifty-eight years without a good rebuke to use on him. Thank you for providing one."

The laugh that ran the rows was not mean. It was scapular. It sat on shoulders, took weight off spines.

Then the present mirrored the past with a speed that made it feel rehearsed. The door at the back burst open and a young man barely out of boy stumbled in with a look that had not earned the right to be called brave. "They're cutting the rope," he blurted. "At the willow."

Mayhew didn't do drama. "Deputy," he said, without turning. "Walk. Don't run." To the room: "We're not migrating. We're not feeding panic. We will be adults."

Loose air tried to spill out of the chairs. The room held. The deputy left. The boy stayed, realizing too late that delivering a rumor makes you part of it. He slid into a chair, cheeks hot. Rosalie pressed a lemon bar into his hand and said "chew," which is the most ancient de-escalation technique known to women who run festivals and families.

Miriam felt heat build in her chest and recognized it fear putting on the clothes of conviction. She closed her eyes briefly and saw again the river opening, the chains gleaming like the scalps of eels, the voice quiet and absolute: *I will bring you out.* The room tilted toward the old theater the one where men sprint toward the willow so their legs can call it heroism. She breathed. She caught Julian's sleeve with two fingers not to anchor him, to remind herself she had nothing to prove.

"Stay," she said to the room, and her voice was bigger than she felt. "If you go to the river every time the rope gets cut, you will never learn to stop cutting each other. The deputy will tie it. Sloane will tie it better."

"I will," Sloane said, fierce and content.

A Adler aunt stood, hair pinned back with a comb that looked capable of fending off a bear. "I lost my temper yesterday," she said, out of nowhere and precisely right. "At a baker who didn't deserve it. I wanted a villain. Abner gave me one tonight and I felt an ungodly relief. I repent of wanting one. If you need me, I'll count turns and keep my mouth busy with bread."

"Nora," Pastor Elijah said, "will you read the sentence from the daybook the one about owing?"

She did. *Owed half-water to Cavanaugh.* The words came weirdly tender off her tongue language that had learned to be less brittle.

Lou Cavanaugh's jaw finally unclenched. "We take half-water when the stone says," he said to Rosalie. "Not when men are putting on a show."

"Deal," she said. And if you want to know what makes a room safer, it is sentences like that said close enough to smell the other person's soap.

A teenager raised his hand, voice trying out its new courage. "My grandpa says the river's always teaching," he offered. "Maybe the rope-cutting is just somebody failing class. Can we pass anyway?"

"You pass," Mayhew said. "The cutter repeats a grade."

The deputy returned, held up a thumbs-up, and sat near the door like a punctuation mark. The room, meditative again, took in breath and released it like lungs coming off a sprint. The old photograph on the far wall seemed to sit back down.

And still there are always two or three who need theater to understand their lines.

A man in a suit that said he had more opinions than overalls stepped to the aisle and gestured at the tables. "All this dreams and ledgers and diagrams," he announced in the polished voice of people who sell things for a living. "And yet the basin ran dry. We're talking about order and truth while our town lost face."

Julian did not bristle. He held up the sketch and tapped the under-notch with one finger. "The basin ran dry to make us read this first," he said. "We are not losing face. We are learning which way to face."

The man sniffed, a sound that would have gotten him mocked in the parking lot if he weren't careful. "You're very serene for a boy with a museum job," he said.

"Thank you," Julian said, because he had decided earlier that humility was a good use of his mouth.

Miriam felt the room flicker the old desire to turn competence into a fight, to make every woman prove she deserved her verb, to make every man choose between dignity and volume. She looked down at her hands, up at the loop drawn on butcher paper, and remembered who taught her discipline: not gentleness for its own sake, but order that keeps people fed.

She stood again, not to argue, to invite. "We are not debating whether the river asked for a new order," she said. "We have documentation and a wedge that glows when we're supposed to wait. We're debating if we can live without a hero for one night. I think we can."

"That's all well and good," someone muttered, because

muttering is the last defense of men who just lost their favorite weapon.

"Name your chain," Pastor Elijah said. "Then eat."

The room inhaled as one organism made up of a hundred lungs, and chose, at last, not to break.

THEY HAD PLANNED to end with a vote. They didn't. Votes had their place roads, trash routes, whose turn it was to clean the bandshell but votes that night would have turned truth into sport. Instead, Mayhew looked at Miriam and nodded, little and decisive, as if to say, *now you.*

She stepped to the tables, palms open. The ledger lay between the rocks with its faithful ghost text. The butcher paper loop looked like a child's drawing of the town's throat. The room leaned toward her the way a barn leans toward a wind that might be strong enough to take it and also be the very thing that keeps it standing.

"I was not born here," she said, because if you lie by omission at the beginning, everything after it gets shaky. "I came because a woman I loved wrote to me from the other side of life and told me to put my hands on a wall and listen. I've listened to doors and to people. I've listened to the river. I've listened to the ledger. They're all telling me the same thing: our problem is not sabotage. It's bondage. We chained ourselves to a short version of the story and passed the cuff to our children. The river is asking us to snap it."

She looked at faces at the LeClair aunt who had apologized for greed in public, at the Adler niece who had bled paper into truth and lemon bars into apologies, at Lou Cavanaugh whose jaw had learned a new language in this very room, at Julian's father, hands folded over a past he loved and wanted to make kinder before he handed it on.

She felt her own fear the small, ordinary kind that says *don't be dramatic, don't be the woman who says river words in a room with men in hats.* She let it live for three breaths. Then she set it down.

"I know the water vision sounded like poetry," she said, and more than one person nodded, grateful for the break in tone. "The river parted in my mind, and I saw chains. Not blame to toss. Links to break. I can't break mine for you. You can't break yours for me. But we can name them out loud, and then stop pretending we're not dragging them into every argument and every kitchen."

She touched the facsimile with two fingers, respectful of the paper but not reverent toward the sin. "*Stone said no; we poured anyway.* That's what we do when we bless before we count. We pour before we read. We love being seen before we love doing right. We're ending that tonight. Not because Miriam said so. Because the slab told us how to be a town and we forgot. We're remembering."

The suited man in the aisle started to interrupt. She raised a palm without looking at him and he miracle obeyed the gesture like good choreography.

"Here is the truth," she said. "The culprit we needed was in the ledger. The culprit we wanted was in our neighbor. The culprit we have to fight lives at the intersection of pride and hunger. We can't arrest him, but we can starve him."

"How?" someone asked, plaintive, like a child. "How do you starve pride without starving joy?"

"You feed it bread it didn't bake," Rosalie said, from her seat. "And you stop handing it microphones."

Miriam smiled over at her, grateful for the friendship that arrives on time. "We do this: we practice turns. We read the wedge. We wait when it glows. We confess debts like people who learned to do math again. We let the kids write **WAIT** on a board, and we obey them because their eyes aren't tired yet. We accept that a quieter festival may be a more honest one. We take our chains to the river and name them before we bless."

Her throat tightened, but not the way it used to when she tried to make a sentence carry both conviction and apology. Tonight there was nothing to apologize for. She was telling the long version. She was doing her job.

"And I will say this," she added, because the room deserved the whole freight: "I love this town. You are my people. We are not the kind of place that needs a villain to feel real. We are the kind of place that can tell the truth and live. I promise you that as a candle-maker and a woman who puts her hand on walls for a living and as someone who heard a sentence older than all of us: *I will bring you out.* Not up. Not back. *Out.* Out of the short version. Out of the habit of blaming the nearest breathing person for a dead man's convenience. Out of the impulse to pour before we read."

Silence held. A long, working silence, the kind that doesn't demand flair to feel satisfied. Then Pastor Elijah stood, not to bless they weren't done yet but to name what had happened. "We have witnessed confession," he said. "Theirs and ours. The ledger and the room. Now we will witness obedience. We will go to the river and do the order right."

Mayhew stepped in with procedure before the moment could escalate into a parade. "We'll walk. We'll not run. We'll tie the rope if it's cut and we won't let a cut rope make us childish. Lantern crews, take your stations. Teens, you have the chalk. Sloane, you have the paper. Mr. Roth, you have the transcripts. Ms. Adler, you have the words you need and do not require our permission."

Julian moved to Miriam's side and did the small expensive thing took her hand for exactly one beat where only the front row could see, then let go with a squeeze that said *I saw you and I'm still here.* She felt the heat that goes with being witnessed lightly and did not turn it into blush. She turned it into motion.

The hall emptied in an orderly exodus, bodies making a path down Cedar Street that looked, from above, like a hinge swinging. Outside, the air had cooled enough to forgive the day's arguments. The willow waited. The wedge held its truest work. The rope had indeed been nicked; the deputy knotted it neat as grammar. Lanterns bobbed like punctuation marks in a sentence that had finally learned how to end and begin in the right place.

Miriam and Julian led not as heroes, as ushers. Behind them came the town: Rosalie with soup; the Adler niece with lemon bars and the daybook like a gospel; Lou Cavanaugh with a jaw that had decided to try being soft; Sloane with her butcher paper; Pastor Elijah humming a tune you could mistake for a breeze if you needed to. The suited man came too, hat in hand in a way that had the decency to look like thoughtfulness.

At the bank, Miriam turned and did not raise her hands like a conductor. She raised them like a woman showing a room she wasn't holding anything sharp. "Count," she said.

The kids bent to the slab, flashlights low, and the town obeyed the first children who had been allowed to hold it accountable. The wedge glimmered. The V took a seam of light as thin as a good needle. The chalk wrote **WAIT** in letters that were steadier than the hands that wrote them.

Someone sighed. Someone laughed quietly. Someone cried. None of it mattered more than the order they had chosen. The town had bent. It had not broken. Tomorrow would bring more weather. Tonight, the hinge held.

And Miriam, feeling the courage that comes after the courage you thought you needed, understood that the next chapter would not be written on the stage, but on the bank. The truth had been told. The river would answer. The basin would learn to fill on time again.

But first, obedience. First, waiting. First, the long version, spoken in a hundred throats as they learned to speak to one another without an enemy as translator.

20

DELIVERANCE AT THE RIVER

The procession wound down Cedar Street in a rhythm older than the town itself. Not a parade too quiet for that. Not a march too soft. But something that had the shape of migration, like water deciding where to fall. The town hall's lights flickered behind them; ahead, lanterns bobbed as volunteers carried them toward the willow bend, their flames little promises against the dusk. People held their breath without meaning to, as if silence itself was currency that would buy them back their trust.

At the bank, the basin waited, its rim dark with old polish, its belly as hollow as the weeks since the festival's failure. The rope had been tied again, not just once but in three places Sloane's overkill, making the knot into a sermon: *we will not break this easily.* Teens with reflective vests kept a line between the stone shelf and the gathering, their faces taut with the solemnity of being temporary priests. The slab glimmered faintly, the under-notch catching a seam of lantern light.

Mayhew stood off to one side, hat in hand. Pastor Elijah

took his place near the willow, humming a line of a hymn that might have been about water or might have been about forgiveness; it didn't matter. Rosalie held a tureen with steam rising like incense. Mr. Cavanaugh carried a bucket of sand, ready for sparks. The Adler niece clutched the daybook facsimile like a psalter. Julian balanced the ledger's transcript on a wooden stand he had built himself, refusing to let the artifact risk damp or damage. Miriam stepped to the shelf, hands open, voice steady though her ribs felt like a drum.

"We've come to count before we pour," she said, and the murmur that ran the crowd was relief, not impatience. "We've come to read before we bless. The slab said no before; we said yes anyway. Tonight we're going to hear its no. And then we'll learn its yes."

She unfolded the transcript, the paper catching lantern glow. Her throat tightened. The words weren't beautiful; that was their power. She began to read.

"*Stone said no; we poured anyway. Owed half-water to Cavanaugh. Settled on paper. Rosalie's grandmother wept. Adlers promised help in winter.*"

Each sentence landed like a bell rung without metal felt in bones, not ears. The crowd shifted. A woman clutched her shawl closer. A boy leaned against his father's knee. Someone whispered "my grandfather said this" and then hushed himself, because the ledger was saying it now.

Julian turned a page. Miriam continued. "*Blessing first; counting after. Do not disappoint donors. Weather blamed. Ledger neat.*" She stopped, swallowed, began again. "This is what we inherited not the water, not the wealth, not the steadiness. This habit. Tonight we return it."

She laid the paper down. The wind lifted one corner, as if the words themselves wanted to travel. She looked out across the faces, so many she had once thought of as strangers. Tonight their eyes shone the same color: waiting.

Julian stepped forward, voice quiet but sharp enough to carry. "We are not accusing one another. We are not applauding our restraint. We are obeying the slab. We are ending the short version. If you came tonight for a villain, you will leave with a neighbor."

Mayhew cleared his throat. "That's the only speech you'll get from me. Now do the order."

The slab glowed faintly at its wedge. Teens bent, flashlights low, and shook their heads almost reverently. One chalked **WAIT** on the board. No murmurs of protest rose. Instead, the crowd released a collective breath, relief pouring into the night like a second river. The lesson was landing: obedience before spectacle.

"Read again," Pastor Elijah prompted, and Miriam obeyed. The ledger's plain confession filled the air like incense: *we poured anyway... owed half-water... ledger neat.* No poetry, no apology. Just the weight of truth finally carried in public.

The basin, empty, waited. The people, hungry, waited too.

It BEGAN NOT with a roar but a murmur. A trickle. A sound so soft only the teens near the rope noticed first. One of them raised her flashlight, startled, and the beam caught the shimmer of water seeping back into the basin from the under-notch. Gasps rose. Then silence, absolute, as the town strained to hear stone and water negotiating.

The seep became a pour. Clear stream flowing where dry walls had mocked them days before. It filled the basin slowly, no hurry, as if water was taking its time to prove its point: restoration comes patient. The surface rippled under lantern light, mirror and flame together.

Miriam felt her knees weaken. She pressed her palms together, not as prayer, as ballast. Her vision of chains, the ledger's plain confession, Julian's meticulous care all of it braided into this single sight: the basin alive again. The town leaned forward as one body. Some wept. Some laughed. One man muttered "well I'll be damned" and then crossed himself, covering his bases.

Pastor Elijah's voice threaded the hush: "*I will bring you out.*" He didn't raise it. He didn't need to. The phrase had already taken residence in their ribs. The Adler niece whispered it under her breath. Rosalie echoed it softly. Lou Cavanaugh, stubborn jaw finally surrendered, said it loud enough for two rows to hear: "*I will bring you out.*"

The basin filled to its rim. No hands touched it. No hoses forced it. Nature had responded to truth. The wedge glowed brighter, not blinding, but steady a light you could follow without burning your eyes. Sloane wiped her face roughly with the back of her wrist and said, "Well, it passed inspection," which was as close as she would come to awe in public.

Julian leaned close to Miriam, voice shaking with a reverence he tried to mask with reason. "Ledger confirmed the habit. Vision named the chain. And the river " He broke off, unable to finish.

"And the river agreed," Miriam whispered.

Mayhew gave one curt nod, the sort of gesture you make when the world has just confirmed it is larger than your badge. He turned to the crowd. "Nobody touch it. Nobody bottle it. Let it sit."

For the first time since the basin had run dry, the people of Cedar Creek stood not as rivals, not as suspects, but as witnesses. Witnesses to a healing that wasn't their performance. Water had chosen them again.

THE SOUP CAME OUT FIRST. Rosalie and her cousins ladled it into mismatched mugs and handed it down the rows. No speeches accompanied it; no one wanted to break the hush with performance. The Adlers carried bread baskets. Cavanaugh children passed apples polished bright. People ate as if food could anchor them to the moment, as if chewing was the safest ritual for awe.

After the meal, Pastor Elijah motioned to the chain board someone had carried from the square. Chalk words stared back: **pride, silence, greed, rivalry, ledger more important than neighbor, fear of losing face.** He handed chalk to the nearest child. The boy added **short version** and underlined it. Laughter rippled, gentle, and applause followed not for eloquence but for accuracy.

Miriam stepped forward one last time. "We came here divided," she said, "hungry for culprits. The ledger gave us history. The river gave us mercy. Tonight we practice the long version together. We will argue again, because that is what families do. But we will not hand our children chains when we could hand them truth."

Rosalie stood. "LeClairs forgive debts," she said. "That's our part." Mr. Cavanaugh raised his mug. "We forgive grudges," he said, and his voice cracked. The Adler niece lifted the daybook. "We forgive discretion," she whispered. The crowd murmured approval, the ritual complete in its imperfection.

Julian took Miriam's hand not hidden, not staged. Just held it, fingers woven, lantern light dancing on the gesture. Murmurs spread but no one jeered. The sight of it felt like punctuation, like the basin filling, like the wedge glowing: confirmation that truth and companionship belonged together.

The teens erased **WAIT** from the board and chalked **YES** in large letters, not because the slab had changed but because the town had. For the first time, the order was obeyed not by accident or desperation but by choice.

They carried lanterns to the edge and let them float, one by one, flames gliding across water that had decided to return. Each lantern mirrored itself, twin flame above and below. It looked like a town doubled one in flesh, one in reflection both learning to be honest.

Miriam whispered the words once more, the phrase that had steadied her through visions, ledgers, and arguments: *I will bring you out.* And when she turned, she saw the words written not on stone or paper but in the faces of her neighbors. They had been brought out of blame, of silence, of bondage. They were beginning, at last, to walk free.

21

JULIAN'S HAND

The lanterns had begun their slow drift, each flame a small sentence let loose upon the river. People lingered, because leaving after a miracle feels like walking out before the credits finish thanking everyone who held the light. The basin, full again, kept its steady hush. The wedge held. The rope hummed, newly tied, chastened. Miriam stood on the bank with the ledger transcript folded against her palm, the paper warm from her hand and the night.

Julian came up beside her, not theatrical simply present, like good lumber. "The water didn't ask for commentary," he said.

"It never does," she said.

They stood without the frantic appetite of before no sprinting to stop rumors, no choreography to keep a square from boiling. Work had been done; the room had obeyed. The river, patient as a teacher who loves her students enough to be boring, had answered. Miriam let herself be still long enough to notice her own body: the tired calves from holding a line, the breath that no longer hurried to the next sentence, the tremor in her fingers that wasn't fear anymore; it was unused celebration.

He looked down at her hand then, that small tremor, and asked the question like a man who's learned to name hinges before he moves them. "May I take it," he said, "here?"

Here meant the river. Here meant within sight of people who kept minutes and memories. Here meant not backstage or behind the south wall or in the hush of an office with the catalog light blinking, but on the bank where Cedar Creek had decided to become honest again.

"Yes," she said. She wanted the yes to be unambiguous, a word you could build a table with.

He slid his palm against hers. No flourish. No flutter. Just the way one worker passes a tool to another with the quiet knowledge that the job is shared. Warmth. Weight. A living yes. She felt the day settle inside her like a bowl set right.

Someone noticed. Of course. It was a small town with excellent peripheral vision. But the noticing didn't feel predatory. It felt like a room recognizing furniture that had always belonged there and was finally put where the sunlight could find it.

Sloane raised her chin from the coil of rope she was pretending not to pet and gave them a look that translated to *about time* without resorting to punctuation. Rosalie, ladling soup to people who didn't need it but did, flicked her eyes at Miriam's hand and then back to her pot, a grin tucked into her ladle. Mr. Cavanaugh nodded once, the solemn benediction of a man who knows a good lift when he sees one. The Adler niece, still tucked behind the daybook, mouthed **yes** like the chalk had taught her. Even Mayhew, hat tucked under one arm, cut his gaze over and then away as if to spare them ceremony and give them privacy in public the highest courtesy Cedar Creek could offer.

"Feels like we moved a door," Julian murmured.

"We oiled a hinge," she answered, and the old language one they had built together out of wood and stone and weather settled around them like a quilt.

A few feet away, two teens from the parallax crew leaned on their stakes. "You gonna tell them we wrote **YES** before they held hands?" one whispered.

"History's about sequence," the other whispered back, smug with a new power accuracy.

Miriam laughed, and Julian's thumb to his own surprise brushed once across her knuckles. If there had been a microphone nearby, it would have missed the sound that their two bodies made: a quiet exhale that told the truth without needing adjectives.

"Tomorrow," he said, "we'll wake up, and the basin will be just a basin again."

"Tomorrow," she said, "we'll count first."

"And then," he added, eyes still on the water because he did not want to turn this into theater, "I'll walk you to breakfast and sit on the side where the floor slants so the sugar comes to me."

"You like a predictable physics," she said.

"I like being handed what I can't reach without moving," he said. "It feels like grace."

She could have kissed him then. The river would have allowed it. The town would have pretended not to see. But restraint had become something other than starvation for them. It was form. A way to make the feelings last long enough to grow into practice. So they stood and let the hand be the whole sentence.

Pastor Elijah drifted over, a human barometer whose

reading was *safe.* "Congratulations," he said, mild. "On your continued adherence to the order."

"What order is that," Julian asked, humoring him.

"Count," Elijah said, pointing at the hand. "Then bless." He tapped the basin with two fingers. "You did both."

They laughed, and the laughter didn't flip into performance. It stayed where it belonged in their chests, warm as soup.

Behind them, Confluence FM's camera lifted, sniffing for romance with a lens. Mayhew took half a step sideways into the shot and admired his hat with great interest until the camera lost the line. Even the station had learned. You don't turn neighbors into content on the night the river gives you back your water.

"Come on," Miriam said. "Let's let the basin be admired without us standing next to it like two people who built it with our bare hands."

"We did not," he said.

"We did enough," she said, and tugged lightly and he followed with pleasure and they made their way up the bank through a crowd that seemed to know how to part without turning the aisle into a parade.

If anyone whispered, the words were small. If anyone gossiped, the gossip had the softness of a blessing that still wanted to check your resume. Around them were the sounds that made a town: spoons against paper cups, the creak of someone's good knee, teenagers practicing not to stare, a woman telling a man he had done enough for one night. The river kept talking to itself like a friend you trust to fill the pauses.

They didn't let go until they reached the south window. He set the ledger transcript into the cradle. She set the daybook beneath it. Both looked through the glass at the empty hall, remembering the fights that had tried to grow there and failed to thrive in the new air. Then they turned toward Main together, not heroes, just people who had learned to carry a basin without sloshing.

Morning brought the particular flavor of whisper Cedar Creek keeps for the day after joy: not sharp, not sugary. Coffee-scented, chair-scrape gentle. The square was a series of little circles instead of one big one. People gathered to retell the thing they had seen to prove to themselves it wasn't just air and night. The basin had stayed full. The under-notch was mundane as ever. The wedge still a wedge. That was the point. The miracle had been order, not spectacle.

Miriam and Julian arrived separately because they had jobs. She had cinnamon buns to accept and pay for, candles to trim. He had a lines-long email from a regional archive that had, predictably, woken up to Cedar Creek's usefulness. They met in the middle only because the day folded them into the same crease.

They did not announce anything; they didn't need to. Their hands found each other by habit, not hunger. The gesture wasn't an argument. It was a statement like a well-written label: **Object: Partnership. Provenance: Practice. Condition: Sound.**

Sloane called across from a stack of folding chairs she was moving for no reason other than that stacked chairs made her blood pressure behave. "If you're going to make this official," she barked, "I'll need your names for the label maker. I'm not putting 'misc.' on your bin."

"Put 'and,'" Julian called back.

"Punctuation bins are full," she shot, then winked, then

went back to arranging the physical world the way the rest of them were struggling to arrange the invisible one.

At the café, Rosalie set a plate in front of Miriam, an extra grapefruit spoon on the side, because love is competence dressed like breakfast. "I heard a rumor," she said. "Two adults held hands where God and Mayhew could see."

Miriam glanced down at their fingers. "It was very irresponsible," she said gravely.

"You'll set a precedent," Rosalie said, leaning in. "Next thing you know, Mr. Cavanaugh will pat Mrs. Cavanaugh's elbow in front of the courthouse."

"I did," Mr. Cavanaugh said behind her, affronted. "Once in '83. After the baby parade."

"Exactly," Rosalie murmured, and slid another spoon onto the saucer. "We are all simply trying to survive the romance."

The Adler niece wandered in behind a stack of freshly printed transcriptions and caught sight of their hands. She didn't clap. She didn't squeal. She did something kinder: she put the pages down and took the seat across from them like family. "I prayed last night," she said without preamble. "Not for the basin. For your restraint. I wanted you to kiss in front of the willow. It would have been pretty. But this is better."

"This is the long version," Miriam said. "It ages well."

Mayhew appeared with a to-go cup and the expression of a man who refuses to be accused of sentiment. "You two are violating no statutes," he said, as if replying to a complaint nobody filed. "Carry on."

"Sheriff," Julian said, deadpan.

Pastor Elijah tipped his hat from the door without interrupting anyone's breakfast with a parable. The teenagers from the grid team slid past with a rolled-up **YES** sign and tried very hard not to comment and failed. "We made a new board yesterday," one confessed. "It says **COUNT THEN BLESS** and **NO GRANDSTANDING** and also **NO PDA** but we were outvoted."

"By whom?" Miriam asked.

"By me," the other teen admitted, unrepentant. "Some things belong in the square."

Not everyone approved. Two women at the window bar put their heads close, the way safety used to require secrets. "It's quick," one said. "They're quick." The other shook her head. "They're slow. It looks like quick because they're steady."

Miriam heard it, because she is built to hear, and filed it where it belonged: under **People Practicing Accuracy.**

Julian's father, Alan, showed up as if he were running an errand and had accidentally found himself in a conversation he'd secretly dressed for. "I brought the south-window key," he said. "Miriam, would you keep a copy, for nights when the town needs the ledger and my back is in rebellion?"

She took the little brass and felt the unfamiliar ease of what the key meant: not permission; belonging. "I'll return it when I'm old and tell you you're not," she said.

"Deal," Alan said, and, banking a lifetime of tidy affection into one casual sentence, added, "Thank you for the way you hold my son."

"Mostly he holds me," she said, but the fairness of it pleased all three of them.

At noon, Confluence FM tried to make a segment about "The Woman Behind the Water." Sloane wandered into frame and installed a sawhorse by accident between the camera and Miriam. "We're allergic to behind," she told the producer. "She's beside." The segment turned out to be about clamp sizes, Mayhew's rope knots, and a teen explaining head pressure with a cracked garden hose. Which is to say: it was perfect.

All afternoon, Cedar Creek practiced its new sport: quiet approval. Mrs. Adler bought two candles and said, "For your shop and for my temper," and slid a recipe card for lemon glaze across the counter like a treaty. Mr. Cavanaugh's cousin came in to ask if candles came in *forgiveness,* then bought unscented because his wife was sensitive. The LeClair aunt from the peas gave Miriam a jar of preserves with an air of pretending she did this for everyone and failing to hide her pleasure.

Every approval was small on purpose. The town refused to inflate them into parade floats. That restraint gave Miriam something she had not known she needed: a relationship not as decorations for the town's story, but as proof the town had learned new manners.

In the late afternoon, when the light through the south window turns the floorboards into old honey, Julian leaned across the counter in the shop and asked the softest kind of practical question. "I'm going to the stacks at six," he said. "Should I meet you here after, or there?"

"Here," she said. "So we can walk together where people can see us not make a scene."

"And in the alley," he added, conspiratorially, "I will attempt to put my arm around your shoulders. For practice. For science."

"You will succeed," she said. "Because consent is a better physics."

They grinned like teenagers and then, because they were not, went back to work.

.　.　.

EVENING SLIPPED into the square like a neighbor forgetting why she crossed the street and deciding to stay because the porch light was kind. The festival had resumed its useful hum fewer speeches, more pie. Miriam did what she always does when the day asks how it can be of help: she put her hands to work. She lit wicks. She accepted payments and apologies. She wrote names on brown bags in a hand that had learned to be legible for other people's sake.

But the air around the work was different. People called her "Miriam" without the clause of curiosity that used to attach to her name. Invitations landed like birds that had finally discovered which tree was theirs. "We're short a person at the booth tomorrow," a young mother said. "Do you...?" "Yes," Miriam said. "I do." "Do you emcee the kids' stage?" a teenager asked. "No," Miriam said, "but I will make you a sign and teach you how not to shout." The girl nodded solemnly, as if this were a secret only adults knew how to modulate.

At the museum, the south window glowed like it had been waiting for this kind of night its whole life: not a crisis, not a closing, just people reading. Alan had posted the latest transcript with Sloane's flourish: **STONE BEFORE STEPS**. Two middle-school boys stood tracing the little V with their fingers on the glass. "It's just a wedge," one said. "Everything is just something until you obey it," the other answered. Miriam loved the second boy immediately and without caution.

She and Julian walked the loop from the shop to the window to the willow and back again, like ushers at a wedding that lasted a week. Their hands made a line between them that did not cordon anything off. It invited traffic.

Mayhew, circling with the unhurried wariness of a man

who had decided to trust people until they made him regret it, tipped his hat and said, "You ever going to make this official?"

"What would official be," Julian asked.

"Paperwork," Mayhew said, disgusted. "Don't do that to me."

"We'll make it official by showing up for trash duty," Miriam said.

"That, I can file," Mayhew answered, pleased.

Pastor Elijah stopped them only once. "A blessing," he said, raising a hand as if measuring a doorframe. "May your sentences continue to be dull and true."

"Amen," Miriam said, sincere.

Rosalie posed without asking, "Who's cooking for whom?" the nosy aunt role she had been born for and had perfected but her eyes were kind. "Both," Julian said. "Alternating turns." "Count, then bless," Rosalie murmured. "Marital advice."

They took the alley on purpose. He did what he said he would: rested his arm across her shoulders, weight precise, not possessive. She fit her palm against his back in the place men forget to stretch. Two teenagers walked by and pretended to pat each other's shoulders as if it were a barbaric ritual they could not believe grown-ups tolerated, then laughed too hard and ran. The alley smelled like yeast and lemon oil and the kindness of old wood.

"Do you feel different?" he asked.

"Yes," she said. "Like my name has stopped being a question."

"And mine?"

"Like your voice learned to be a room other people can stand in when they're tired," she said.

"Ambitious," he teased.

"Accurate," she corrected.

When they came back into the square, Alan was on the steps of the south wall, laughing at something Sloane had said about screws and repentance. He saw them and, with the same easy logic he'd used to hand her the key, lifted his palm in a small salute that translated to *my son is visible, and I am unafraid.* It undid something in Miriam's chest she hadn't labeled yet an old conservation of self that had kept her half-packed for years.

She realized then that belonging is not the town's opinion of you. It's the town handing you an ordinary chore and trusting you to finish it without applause. It's Mrs. Levine at the bakery asking you to unlock the back door at five because your hands are good with stubborn latches. It's a teenager rolling her eyes at your joke and still bringing you a clipboard because you are, infuriatingly, correct. It's a sheriff telling you to leave the paperwork alone and keep the rope tied. It's a pastor blessing you with dull words and meaning them. It's a man taking your hand in front of people who might misunderstand and trusting them to practice understanding anyway.

Miriam tucked that definition into the place where she keeps instructions for all the doors she's ever listened to. It would be there when she needed it tomorrow, or when the bell failed to ring and the river asked for new obedience, or when silence tried to braid itself into a virtue again.

They sat on the museum steps because sitting is a luxury in a town that believes in standing. The basin murmured its soft approval down the bank. The chain board leaned against the willow, chalk dusty from fingers smaller than the sins they named. The evening settled into the kind of ordinary that earns the right to be called peace.

"Tell me your sentence for the log," she said.

"**Hand taken in public; town practiced quiet approval; no casualties; rope intact.**" He thought, then added, "**South window key shared. Ledger read like prayer.**"

"Mine," she said, "**Name returned to me by use; belonging measured in chores; love practiced without theater.**"

He leaned his head to hers, not a kiss just the pressure of a man taking the measure of a threshold and finding it level. "Tomorrow we rehearse again," he said.

"We always do," she answered.

Down by the water, two boys knelt, matching the lanterns' drift the way children try to keep time with music. Up in the square, a woman made change and a man carried a chair for someone who had taught him how to count. Somewhere between them, Cedar Creek slipped its old chain, link by link, and let it fall harmlessly into silt. Miriam felt it the looseness and knew it was not a trick. It was the long version finally having its day.

Julian squeezed her hand once an amen. She squeezed back, then let go, because you can tell the truth and still save the last step of the night for your own door. They stood, they worked, they locked up what needed locking, and as they crossed the square toward closing chores and clean counters, the town did what it had learned to do best: noticed, approved without clapping, and made space. The river kept its promises in its one fluent language. Above it all, the cedar canopy held, old and generous, and Miriam, at last, felt held by more than branches. She felt held by *place*.

22

RECONCILIATION FEAST

They set the tables in a long curve under the cottonwood, a crescent that faced the river as if even furniture knew to turn toward water that had kept its word. Sloane and three teenagers strung bulb lights from trunk to trunk, and when dusk slipped in they clicked on like a row of quiet yeses. Folding chairs multiplied the way chairs do when a community refuses to let anybody stand. The square hummed not nervy, not performative just the steady domestic sound of a town that has decided on soup over speeches.

"Seating chart," Sloane announced, slapping a butcher-paper diagram against the south wall like a general briefing troops for hospitality. "Alternating. No clumps. If you find yourself next to somebody you enjoy arguing with, consider it a sacrament."

Rosalie arrived with casseroles that could comfort cities. Mr. Cavanaugh wheeled a grill that had seen weddings and near-wars and, healing being healing, one of each in the same season. The Adler niece set down a platter of sliced roasts with the air of a woman who had retired from curating minutes and decided to curate meat instead. Pastor Elijah rolled out a chalkboard, wiped last night's **CHAINS TO BREAK** with the side of his hand, and wrote **TURNS TO SHARE** in clean, steady letters. Under it: **bread, stories, work, water.**

Miriam came with baskets of bread and a crate of plates borrowed from the museum's stubborn cabinet white with an honest chip here and there. She set the bread at the table's seam, the place where LeClair met Cavanaugh met Adler, and felt ridiculous for how moved she was by the sight of simple crust beside simple crust. The basin murmured from the bank like a bowl content to be what it was. The wedge held its coin of light. Somewhere a teen in a reflective vest practiced telling an uncle **we wait** just because you'd had a miracle didn't mean you forgot the order.

Julian stood beside Miriam, thumb still carrying the faint ink of the ledger's transcript, a badge as accidental as dignity. He had built a low stand for the daybook and set it on a side table next to Sloane's diagram. People could read a sentence and then pick up a fork. That was the design: truth as a condiment, not an entree you had to pretend to like.

Mayhew showed up without a hat and with a pie, which caused such a stir that Rosalie had to clap for quiet. "The sheriff has baked," she said. "All charges dropped against the evening."

"Rhonda baked," Mayhew corrected. "I am in charge of the delivery chain."

"Chain," Pastor Elijah repeated, letting the word do a small work in the air without locking it to its former use. "We have better chains now."

The first awkwardness came on schedule and in a familiar costume: a man who preferred to hold plates as shields. He hovered near the roasts and said to no one in particular, "Feels quick." The Adler niece, who had chosen to be brave in public three days in a row and discovered she could survive it, answered without blinking. "It is quick," she said. "We practiced too long the other way."

Lou Cavanaugh, jaw less militant than yesterday, held up tongs like a man raising a white flag. "I'll serve Adlers first," he said. "Just to confuse my grandfather's ghost."

"Serve LeClairs first," Rosalie countered, "to confuse mine."

"Alternate," Sloane said, because she refuses to let punchlines outrun policy. "Left, right, left, right. No one invents a parade."

They obeyed. It was odd, and then it wasn't. A plate went to a woman whose mother had once told her to avoid Adlers at fundraising tables because they counted your cookies with their eyes. A fork scraped against porcelain and made the sound of someone learning a new habit in their mouth. A boy passed bread across a seam in the table as if it didn't exist. Someone said grace in a voice that hoped forgiveness came in family sizes. Pastor Elijah nodded and did not monopolize the blessing. Cedar Creek did the thing that tests a vow better than an anthem: it chewed.

Miriam didn't sit at once. She moved down the curve with a basket, accepting thank-yous as if they were coins to distribute later. When she reached the center seam Adler on one side, LeClair on the other, Cavanaugh further down she paused and listened to the undertow of voices. There were the sighs that follow relief. There were the scraps of old rumor retold now as jokes that had earned enough humility to be harmless. There was the raw sound of two cousins realizing they'd built a decade on a story that had run out of plank. There was laughter, the dull kind that refuses fireworks and settles for sturdiness.

Julian claimed the chair at her left with the ease of a man who has learned not to announce his anchor. He set his plate down, not touching her, touching the table as if connection is a layout first. "I made space," he said, and it was true: he had placed a second plate, a glass, the fork she prefers because it sits right in her hand.

"Who taught you to read the geometry of dinner?" she asked.

"Stacks," he said. "Shelves. This is just history lying down."

They sat. The ledger's line *owed half-water to Cavanaugh* floated up from the side table and settled above the roast like steam. Mr. Cavanaugh himself arrived with a platter of corn and laid it down in front of the Adler niece because choreography is the truest apology when words are too shiny. She blinked tears back and reached for a spoon like a woman taking a vow.

"Say something," Julian murmured, voice low enough that only the plate could hear. "Your sentence."

Miriam glanced down the table at faces that had learned to be brave and then tired and then brave again. "**Stone before steps**," she said, and tore a piece of bread in two, handing him the larger half.

The town began to sound like a family that had chosen a good argument: who makes the better pie, how early is early when you say you'll show up, whether the river will accept a new banner or prefers dull rope. Mayhew walked by with a pitcher of water and topped off cups without standards and without preference. Sloane collected empties with the focused glee of a woman whose love language is not having to ask.

By the time the first plates cleared, the night had learned the new order: counting in public, blessing in turn, passing across seams as if they were seams because they were, not because they were borders. The feast had the feel of a town standing up from its own table and finding, to its surprise, that its legs still worked.

It TURNED out forgiveness sounded like utensils and paper napkins and a few necessary sniffles. It looked like people doing chores for other people whose names they had used as punctuation in stories about their own virtue. It tasted like bread you didn't bake and soup you didn't season and lemon bars you didn't slice, sweet with a glaze that might break your teeth if you tried to chew it as symbol.

A lull arrived, as lulls do, offering a soft space for something important to try standing. The Adler elder rose with the uncertainty of a man whose joints had opinions about how fast truth should move. He tapped his cane against the grass once gentle, attention without demand. "I kept minutes," he said to the table more than the crowd. "I thought I was preserving. I was preserving. I was also curating. If preservation without confession is a sin, I have practiced it well." He set his hand on the daybook, reverent not toward the sin but toward the record of it. "I ask pardon. I promise help in winter."

Across from him, a Cavanaugh aunt one of those women with a voice that could direct a barn raising by pointing stood as if her chair had asked for relief and she had given it. "I liked the look of my boys lifting," she confessed. "I may have enjoyed it too much and too long. I ask pardon for the part where we made heroism our hobby."

"We forgive," said Lou, jaw set gently. He said it without

theater and sat down too fast, like a man embarrassed by his own competence at mercy.

Rosalie took her turn without rising, spoon still in hand. "We LeClairs enjoy the sound of our names on a program," she said, grin trying to be humble and managing it. "We will continue to be excellent at food and lighting and enthusiasm. We will practice not turning it into a weather system."

"We forgive," the Adler niece said, and if it caught in her throat on the first syllable, the second came easy.

Miriam sat very still and tried not to ruin anything by narrating it. This is what forgiveness looks like, she thought, watching Mr. Cavanaugh slide a bowl to a Adler child as if he'd always meant to. This is what letting go sounds like, listening to two LeClair cousins decide to carry the trash together even though they could move the world with an eye-roll. This is what coming out feels like: not trumpets forms. Schedules. A chalkboard under the stars with the word **TURNS** written by a pastor whose handwriting made everything look gentler than it was.

Julian brushed her sleeve not a claim; an alert. He tipped his chin toward the end of the table where two women were doing the delicate work of turning an old grievance into a story that could be handled. "Listen," he whispered, and she did.

"My mother told me your mother kept the good candles for your table," one woman admitted.

"She did," the other said. "Because she was afraid of spilling wax on the mayor's wife's dress."

"She told us Adlers thought we were clumsy."

"She told us LeClairs thought we were stingy."

"Were we?"

"Sometimes."

They sat with that for a moment, the way you sit with a

small truth you had to build up to like a hill. Then the first woman shrugged. "Pass me that salt," she said, and the second did, and their hands did not burn upon touching.

The teenagers, possibly confused by a night with no villain to aim their burgeoning drama at, invented hoops out of extension cords and challenged Mr. Cavanaugh to shoot pie tins at the trash bin. He did, and the pie tin arced toward the target like a fact finally reaching the room it belonged in. Sloane shouted, "No performance art," and then applauded, hypocrite and community builder, perfectly both.

Mayhew sat against a tree and wrote nothing in his pad for a long time. Pastor Elijah wandered, refilling people's water the way a man does when he refuses to let liturgy leave just because the choir went home. Alan Roth told a boy the story of a door that used to stick and the day he learned to lift and push at the same time; the boy filed it away where he keeps the knowledge that adults are mostly just kids with better tools.

Miriam realized, in the middle of the clatter and the mercy, that her shoulders had dropped two inches and might never go back up. She put her palm on the table and felt the wood's good weight and had the sense, sudden and entire, that her great-aunt would have approved of the evening truth read in public, soup when **WAIT** is written, forgiveness practiced without allowing it to turn into a brand.

"Say your sentence," Julian murmured again, as if keeping the log of the heart could prevent it from forgetting itself in the next storm.

"Debts converted into chores; tenderness measured in portions; the ledger read like grace," she said.

He looked at her like a man who would spend the rest of his life refusing to be less accurate than that.

The old ache still made appearances memory doesn't roll the credits just because you've chosen a better ending. A woman excused herself from the table to cry by the willow about a father who had died with a villain in his mouth. Rosalie followed with a lemon bar and no wisdom; they stood, one handing sugar, the other handing tears, a fair trade. A man muttered, "We gave too much," out of habit, then realized no one had asked and swallowed it with his last bite of corn. Miriam made a tally in her head: **remnants** present; **resentment** diminishing; **recipes** exchanged.

Then came the quiet ritual that no one planned and everyone needed. Pastor Elijah walked to the chalkboard and, under **TURNS TO SHARE**, wrote **talking/listening**. He drew a line through **talking** and wrote it again after **listening**. The town laughed, and the laughter had learned its manners.

Miriam waited for her own turn to say a sentence to the room. She didn't stand on a bench. She didn't ask for attention with her palms. She simply rose and spoke a sentence to the length of the table, letting it travel like a loaf: "If you think of a story too short to be true, you can bring it to the south window and help us make it longer."

The Adler elder patted the daybook as if patting a small animal that had finally learned not to bite. "We're learning," he said. "Despite ourselves."

"Because of ourselves," Lou countered, and his jaw, lately converted from weapon to hinge, opened into a smile he must have inherited from some aunt who had loved good practical jokes and accurate ledger lines.

Forgiveness, Miriam decided, is not a mood. It's a seating chart, a serving order, a plank laid over a ditch you misjudged. It's the set of small actions that make it possible to be in the same place as the person who reminds you of your former self without setting either of you on fire. It looks like bread. It sounds like let me. It tastes, tonight at least, like lemon and relief.

BY THE TIME plates had been scraped and stacked and Rosalie had bullied three teenagers into washing spoons as if spoons were a path to heaven, the feast had turned into the sort of evening that lets romance be real because it is not the point. Music started because someone forgot to forbid it. A fiddle found its way under somebody's chin. A guitar failed to be tuned and still behaved. Two Cavanaugh cousins danced like men trying to remember their own knees, and a Adler aunt clapped off-beat with determination, which counts.

Miriam and Julian did not perform a waltz for the square. They didn't owe the town theatrics and the town didn't ask. They sat together, hips nearly touching, at the seam between families, the place they had learned to favor because seams are where strong things live. The ledger's stand held steady on the grass. The south wall glowed from within like a house light left on for the sake of arriving truth.

Alan wandered over, wiped his hands on a towel that clearly belonged to Rosalie from three kitchens ago, and set two cups on the table. "Seltzer," he said. "With that syrup Nora made that tastes like blackberries and apologies."

"Thank you," Miriam said. He didn't leave at once. He looked at their hands, at the way Julian's knee found her knee in the square root between bold and polite, and, after a beat, delivered the sort of blessing men of his generation believe in most: logistics. "I'll inventory the storage tomorrow. If you want to turn the south window into a rotating case for the ledger and the loop, I'll build the mounts. And " he hesitated; the old conservation inside him had to be paid its due "I'm glad you're here."

"Me too," Miriam said, and did not make it larger than it needed to be.

Mayhew came by with a trash bag and an eye on a cluster of teenagers testing a rope for acrobatic properties. "No circus," he said without stopping. "You two" a nod at their hands "carry on."

Pastor Elijah ambled in the opposite of a hurry and offered them both that dull true benediction he had perfected: "Your restraint is blessing us."

Julian smirked. "We are very boring," he told the pastor.

"Boredom," Elijah said, "holds marriages together."

"Are we " Julian began, more to tease than from fear.

"Not my department," the pastor said cheerfully, and floated off to refill a grandmother's cup.

Miriam leaned her head against Julian's shoulder, a brief resting, purchased with consent and without parade. The publicness of it didn't make the private part smaller; it made it steadier. The town noticed and did nothing fancy about it. A LeClair child asked if Miriam would judge the pie contest tomorrow with Mr. Cavanaugh; Miriam said yes and pretended not to see Rosalie scowl in satisfaction at the fairness of it. The Adler niece pressed a recipe card into Julian's hand for lemon glaze "because she'll make it better than I do and I need someone to compete with" and he promised to mess it up at least twice before achieving competence.

Sloane dragged a long bin over and slapped a masking-tape label on it: **MIRIAM & JULIAN EVENT SUPPLIES.** She wrote it big enough to feel like graffiti and official enough to survive the next storm. "I'm not walking back to the museum every time you two decide to be useful," she said. "Put your things in here. This is what belonging looks like in my language."

Miriam touched the tape, surprised by how seen she felt by adhesive. "We'll earn it," she said.

"You already did," Sloane replied, which is the kind of sentence you tape into your chest for later.

There was a moment because there always is when an old reflex tried to surface. A man in a jacket that said he loved committees more than people lifted his chin toward their joined hands and murmured to his neighbor, "Fast," the way a critic murmurs to the stage. The neighbor shook her head. "Long," she corrected. "We're just seeing it now." He shut up with enough grace to qualify for a second slice of pie.

Under the cottonwood, children began a game of **AND** with chalk, writing it between two names, then another two, drawing lines and loops and hinge marks until the grass looked like a map of how neighbors are meant to function. Miriam watched them and felt the future tap her shoulder not a warning, just a reminder: tonight is feast; tomorrow is work again; soon, another mystery will tap the bell and ask you if you're paying attention. She felt the familiar readiness rise and was relieved to find that it did not come at the expense of her ease. She could carry both now: belonging and alertness. She could count and bless.

"Walk?" Julian asked.

They took the path to the willow the way couples take vows after they've already lived them for a year without ceremony, with reverence. The basin gleamed in the starlight. The wedge kept its thin coin. The rope had not been cut since the town ate together. Miriam put her palm on the south wall in passing habit, not superstition and felt no new thunder, just a purr, the way wood hums when it is part of a structure doing its job.

"Tell me what you keep from tonight," Julian said. He'd been asking all week, ritual turning into romance turning into ritual.

"That forgiveness is a seating chart," she said. "And that love is a bin with our names on it."

He laughed, and the sound filed itself neatly into her memory under **reasons to stay**. "My turn," he said. "That truth tastes better when you eat it with soup. And that the town learning to approve quietly is the best gift I've ever been given."

They turned back toward the tables because that is what you do when you belong: you return for the last stack of plates, the last string of lights, the last kid whose parents forgot to collect them because talking had, for once, turned into listening and no one wanted to interrupt the conversion.

At the end, when the bulbs clicked off and the chalk lay spent and the chain board leaned forgotten against the trunk, Miriam stood in the emptying square and tested her new weight. It held. Julian's hand found her hand; she didn't flinch at the publicness of it; the town did not either. She squeezed, he squeezed back once, twice, count then bless and they walked the last stretch toward the shop together, the sound of chairs folding like pages turning, the night carrying them with the same gentle insistence the river had used when it refilled what pride had emptied.

Cedar Creek exhaled a feast-sized breath. The basin, sated, kept its quiet. The long version of love, of truth, of us had been spoken with forks and plates and yeses. Miriam unlocked her door, flipped the sign to **closed**, and knew with the deep restfulness of a person finally home that nothing important had ended. It had taken a seat.

23

A WALK AT DUSK

They took the river path they'd worn into the week past the south window that glowed like a low lantern, past the chalkboard where **COUNT THEN BLESS** had been smudged by small hands and rewritten in fresher chalk, past the willow that had learned to be the town's living pulpit. The festival ran behind them like a happy engine laughter, a guitar attempting competence, the thin metallic applause of forks. Dusk collected itself along the bank in soft purples and the river took the color without comment, because water doesn't have to describe what it is doing to do it well.

"Walk slow," Julian said. "My day is still taller than I am."

She matched his pace. "Mine's the right height," she said. "It just keeps trying to wear a hat."

They didn't hold hands at first because restraint had become a pleasure and because people who trust a thing to last don't always hurry. They matched steps, left and left, right and right, the cadence of bodies that had spent an uncommon number of days choosing not to perform what they felt. The basin murmured behind them. Ahead, reeds made the kind of sound that proves you're not alone even when the footpath tells you you are.

"Did you eat?" he asked.

"Soup and a lemon bar and a compliment from Mayhew," she said. "Which counts as protein."

"Mayhew complimented you?"

"He said, and I quote, 'your restraint is blessing us.'"

Julian laughed, light and incredulous. "He's been reading Pastor Elijah's pocket-sized book of benedictions."

"I hope there are diagrams," she said. "Otherwise Sloane will write her own."

A breeze came up the seam and tilted her hair against her neck. He noticed because he always does, because his attention has learned to be helpful and not hungry and reached into his pocket for the elastic she always forgets to remember. He held it out on his flat palm the way you offer a skittish animal a treat without turning it into a command. She took it, brushed her hair back with both hands, and made a loop that would hold through wind and laughter. It felt like the way they were with each other tension that didn't bite, a tie that could be undone without drama.

"Does this count as the romantic interlude the town keeps wanting?" he asked, faux-solemn.

"This counts as us being competent in public," she said.

A pair of teenagers skittered past like swallows, giggling into sleeves, one of them whispering a story to the other that had the new embarrassments of the day in it, softened already into legend. They waved at Miriam with an ease that would have pierced her a month ago and now warmed without injury.

"Do you know what I wanted at the feast?" she asked after they'd passed.

"What?"

"To kiss you under the lights, so the town could practice not turning it into a parade. To give them muscle memory for minding their own joy." She smiled at herself. "I didn't because the soup was hot and because you and I have made a sport out of patience."

"We can always rehearse the kiss," he said, mouth quirked.

She pretended to consider it and then decided, more honestly than coyly, to step closer until their shoulders touched. Her skin registered him the way a door registers the turn of a key: not shock. Fit. The sound that rose out of both their chests wasn't dramatic enough to insult the river but it was real enough to move their blood.

They rounded the bend where cedars lean into the water like tired men who finally found the right place to rest. The path narrowed and the festival sound bent with it laughter becoming music becoming breeze. Miriam turned and so did he, their bodies aligning by accident and intention both. His hand found the back of her neck and paused, a courtesy more electric than urgency could ever be. Her breath came in a quiet yes that wasn't a word, and that would have been enough.

But the town, keeping its feral right to interrupt, did what it does when too much tenderness gathers in one spot: it sent a chorus of laughter from the picnic lawn, bright and irresistible, a whoop of triumph as Mr. Cavanaugh sank a pie-tin shot into the trash bin and Sloane, her contradictions top-coated in competence, booed and applauded in the same breath. The sound arrived at the river like children rushing into a room: we're here; we're uncontained.

Julian's hand stayed at the place where her neck held her pulse. They did not pretend the interruption hadn't come; they let it fold into the moment like steam. They almost kissed. They didn't. The almost was not a failure. It was a promise they had decided to enjoy with the care of people who know an orchard is not ruined because you wait for the pears to sweeten.

"Saved by trash," Miriam murmured against his shoulder.

"Story of Cedar Creek," he said, and eased his palm away with the kind of reluctance that respects as much as it desires.

They walked on, not to escape the laughter, but to find the kind of quiet where a different talk can grow the kind without windshields or witnesses.

THEY STOPPED where the path forgot to be a path and tried out being a patch of flattened grass. The river worked in small syllables there, consonants against stone, vowels over a smooth run. Fireflies began their unscientific charting of the air. The willow leaned a little lower as if eager for over-heard sentences.

"What's the word for what we did?" Julian asked.

"Which part?"

"All of it," he said. "Ledger. Feast. Restraint. Rope. The basin refilling without our hands on it. What do we call that in a log that has to be read by a person who didn't stand here?"

She thought about her notebook, the way some pages had started to look like a kind of scripture and some looked like the world's most precise grocery list. "Healing," she said. "But not the kind that erases the scar. The kind that learns the story of it and decides not to reenact the injury."

"Specific, please," he said, because he knows that she curates words and he prefers labels.

She took her time. The dusk gave her the space to assemble sentences without panicking. "Healing is a seating chart," she said. "It's Sloane taping names to chairs so you sit next to someone you've practiced avoiding and learn you can survive soup with them. It's the chalkboard that says **TURNS TO SHARE** and the teenager who crosses out **talking** and writes it again after **listening**. It's Mayhew tying the rope without telling us what a hero he is for doing it, and Pastor Elijah pouring water without calling it sacrament. It's the river saying *wait* and us saying *okay*. And it's us taking each other's hand where God and Mayhew can see."

He nodded slowly, like a man translating a good paragraph into the language of shelves. "So in my log I write: **healing = order + humility + soup.**"

"And," she said.

"And," he repeated dutifully, smiling.

He kicked off his shoes and put his toes at the edge of the water like a person negotiating a treaty with a truth that will get his cuffs wet one way or another. "I always thought healing would feel like fireworks," he said. "A show. A crescendo. Instead it feels like a lot of unpopular verbs: return, admit, wait, carry, count."

"And bless," she said. "Eventually. But not as a performance. We bless by telling the long version and by changing the order and by writing clamp sizes on poster board. Blessing is dull when it's true."

He sat. She sat. Grass leaned in all directions as if attempting to be helpful. The basin's faint syllables made a backdrop to silence that didn't need to be rescued. After a while, he told her something he hadn't told her because some things earn their audience slowly.

"When I was a kid," he said, "I thought the south wall was a secret passage. I'd pull the board and stand there and hope for a door to open to some story that would make me brave. It never did. Tonight I realized it did exactly what it was meant to do it kept a room square and reminded me to listen. I don't need a portal; I need a boundary that tells the truth."

She didn't say *same* because she has learned that the way to love a confession is with a second truth that's not just a mirror. "I came here with a letter," she said. "I expected thunder. I got chores. And I think that was mercy."

He looked at her with the unobtrusive wonder that belongs to men who never expected attention to be reciprocated and have realized it might be. "Do you still feel the chains?" he asked quietly.

"Lighter," she said. "But not gone. You don't snap a century without it echoing. Tonight I could hear people naming them without throwing them. That's new. And the river "

"Approved," he said, finishing for her without stealing.

She leaned back on her palms and let the willow make a ceiling out of the evening. "You asked for a word," she said. "Maybe it's *out.* We were in something habit, rumor, image. We walked out. Not back. Not up. Out. And the out is not a single step; it's the path you redraw every morning."

He made a sound under his breath that belongs somewhere between agreement and gratitude. "Out," he said, like he was filing it on a shelf by itself. "We can keep that one near the door."

A gust of laughter came again from the square smaller this time, not intrusive, like a house telling another house goodnight across a lawn. They could have gone back. They stayed.

"Tell me what you're still afraid of," he said, because intimacy isn't just revelations; it's inventory control.

"That I'll enjoy being believed too much," she said. "That I'll like the power of being right about the river and use it like a weapon when I'm tired." She exhaled. "And you?"

"That I'll hide behind provenance," he said. "That I'll say 'source' when I mean 'shield.' That I'll use the label as a way to keep from feeling what the artifact is trying to teach."

"Then we'll watch each other," she said. "Not to police; to remind."

He smiled toward the water. "We're becoming a very boring romance."

She liked the sentence too much to let it go unblessed. "It's the kind that has a calendar," she said. "And bins."

"Right," he said. "Bins labeled **US**. Sloane already made one."

They laughed, easy now in a way that let the heat between them be a low steady thing rather than a flare. She turned toward him again, the twilight making the edge of his jaw a soft line. He tipped forward, not hurried. She did too. It would have been the perfect place for the kiss, and probably the willow would have rustled in approval.

From the direction of the fort, a bell rang once thin, like a spoon hitting a jar and then stopped as if it had thought better of speaking. Both of them started involuntarily at the oddness of it, at the way sound can trip.

"That was... wrong," he said.

"It was," she agreed, her body filing the detail before her mind decided whether to let it matter. The near-kiss retracted without injury. They waited for a second strike. None came. The river pretended innocence. The festival laughed again, oblivious. The evening developed a seam.

"Probably a kid," he said after a beat. "Climbing."

"Probably," she said. She did not add that *probably* is a word that often precedes history taking a turn.

THEY FOLLOWED the sound they hadn't heard toward the fort, which had been a palisade and a school and a museum and always a rumor. The path pitched up; the cedar gave way to thinner shade; the fort's outline cut itself out of the sky with that prim insistence old buildings have when they've survived more weather than most families. The door stood open the way Alan leaves it those evenings when the air needs to learn how to move through old wood without hurting it.

Inside, the south wall held its posture. The board fit. The room smelled like catalog ink and lemon oil and the sensible part of memory. The staff desk lamp was off; the emergency light washed everything in a modest theater blue. Julian's keys were warm in his palm. He didn't use them. The door had been left ajar on purpose; trust is a muscle you practice or you lose.

They climbed to the loft where the bell rope came through the ceiling. Miriam's hand found the banister, traced the gouge a hundred littler hands had made near the third post where fear becomes a pressure and then a groove. Children had braced here, brave and sweaty and impatient to ring something older than their names. Tonight the banister seemed to prefer their company to the quiet. She let her palm say *we remember you too.*

At the landing, they both stopped. The bell rope hung properly, its fibers oiled in the way Alan taught docents to prevent splinters and stories. But near the knot where the rope meets the ceiling, a pale thread of ribbon was caught, frayed to almost nothing, the color of something that used to be white on purpose.

"Wedding ribbon," Miriam said before she could stop her mouth.

"Or a bookmark," Julian said, kind to coincidence.

She reached and freed a piece the size of a thumbnail, weightless, like a breath someone forgot to have. It had the faintest dusting of glitter, the cheap kind you only notice after you've already hugged the bride and have committed yourself to wearing celebration for three days. Her stomach tightened as if the room had shifted. The bell rope, undisturbed, made the smallest sound a creak like a throat deciding.

"How long do you think it's been there?" he asked.

"Hours," she said. "Or a century." She glanced up at the belfry. Through the hatch you could see the bronze lip dreaming in darkness, the clapper a silhouette. A swallow's nest tucked into one corner held the soft insistence of other lives. Outside, the night pressed its ear to the gap and listened for how people in Cedar Creek would behave next.

They moved back down the stair and out into the yard. The fort's bell tower faced the square and the river both, a referee with equal affection for music and patience. They found the rope's lower loop and stood several feet away like people visiting a grave that belongs to someone they haven't met yet. Julian put two fingers on the line, no pressure, and then let them fall. "We'll leave it," he said, and she nodded **count, then bless,** even here.

Over the rail of the porch, the square's laughter canted toward them and then away as a gust rearranged everyone's sentences. Miriam turned her head. The basin showed itself through the trees like a wide eye doing what it's meant to do:

taking in light. The river made its old simple verbs. Life resumed its ordinary. And yet.

"Say your sentence," Julian said, ritual returning to her like a field returning to wheat after a year of barley.

"**Near-kiss; laughter; bell misfired; ribbon caught; keep watch,**" she said. "Also **we are not out of work.**"

"Mine," he said, "**healing feels like chores; desire is patient; noise interrupts; I remain grateful. And listen for the bell.**"

They closed the fort door gently. He settled the latch with the care he uses for artifacts and other people's secrets. Outside, the first star that could handle being called such appeared in the low west. The willow's silhouette accepted its job as chapel without asking for permission. Mayhew's hat moved across the square, gravity with ankles. Sloane wound a last cord and labeled it with tapes that will outlive fashion. Pastor Elijah walked a grandmother to her car with a paper plate held flat like an offering. Rosalie extinguished her last flame with the casual piety of people who believe fire belongs to neighbors.

"Shall we try the kiss again?" Julian asked, not to rush, just to let hope have a joke.

"Yes," she said, and that would have been enough, and maybe the bell would have kept its mouth shut out of courtesy and maybe the river would have applauded beneath its breath and maybe the square would have taken up its professional talent for noticing without clapping. But two children tumbled laughing down the path from the square, each convinced the other had cheated at some unimportant game, and the moment leaned and then righted itself and then decided to live for another day.

They laughed with the children, because you do; you

honor interruption when it's alive. She put her hand in his without revising the night into either story failure or triumph. It was just the long version doing what it does: taking its time, collecting evidence, making a case for good.

As they walked back toward the shop, the ribbon scrap slept against her palm like a tick of time. She resisted the urge to file it under drama and filed it under **note for later** instead. Healing had not ended the world's appetite for mysteries; it had simply strengthened her patience for them. The fort's bell hung silent behind them, but the air around it felt attentive, as if a room were clearing its throat before speaking.

Tomorrow would bring chords and chores booth schedules, a boy who thought the wedge was boring and would be seduced by its logic, a woman with a memory that needed a chair, a sheriff with a rope to tie and untie and tie again. It would also bring, she suspected, a new question rung in metal, a sound that didn't sound right and would ask them to learn again the difference between rumor and truth.

They reached the square. The festival laughed them in. The south window put a soft square of light on the ground, and they stepped into it as if it were a porch. Julian leaned closer, forehead to hers, and let the contact be the whole kiss. When he pulled back, he looked as proud as a man is allowed to look in public without Sloane teasing him for it.

"Tomorrow," he said. "More walking. More counting. More blessing."

"And," she said, because if they had a crest it was punctuation.

"And," he echoed.

The river lifted its plain hymn and carried it along. Above them, in the belfry, something adjusted swallow, rope, weather. Not a peal. Not yet. Miriam felt a brief thread of cold lace the warm air and didn't fear it. She only noted it, like a dutiful neighbor, and turned with Julian toward the work of closing the night.

24

PASTOR ELIJAH'S WARNING

He asked to meet where the town doesn't perform no dais, no chalkboard, no camera trying to turn neighbors into content. The parsonage study had a door that stuck in winter and a window that preferred spring, and shelves that had learned the precise weight of hymnals, minutes, and casseroles delivered to the wrong address and eaten gratefully anyway. The room smelled like paper that had kept its manners and lemon oil with an honest job.

Miriam arrived with the ribbon scrap in her pocket and the aftertaste of the river still steady in her mouth. The basin had slept full; the wedge had kept its coin of light; the town had gone back to the dignified labor of washing spoons. Pastor Elijah poured coffee and didn't apologize for the bitterness; he trusted his guests to know how to sweeten their own.

"Sit," he said, and when she did, he didn't smile first. He indexed her face the way an old tree reads wind. He had been kind all week sturdy kind, with nails and rope but today he was something weightier: the kind of kind that presses warnings into your hand the way a mother slips a card with a phone number into a teenager's pocket before a dance.

"You did good work," he said.

"We did good work," she corrected, because she is allergic to hero myths and because the river had made its feelings on order known.

He let the correction stand like a sign on a path: **this way is safe.*" Then he set his cup down and folded his hands where men fold them when they are about to say sentences they will later wish they had said more carefully. "Truth has a long tail, Miriam," he said. "We've been stepping on it all week and it's been mostly polite. That makes people reckless. We are about to forget that truth, when cornered, sometimes kicks."

"From whom?" she asked, not to deflect, to understand where to brace.

"Everyone," he said. "The families who didn't get the villain they trained for. The businesses that learned the town prefers a ledger to a headline. The station that came for spectacle and left with clamp sizes. Even the parts of ourselves that learned to like being right about the river and will try to eat that pleasure like dessert for breakfast."

He leaned forward, elbows on desk, posture already a sermon. "When you open one door, the house remembers every other door it padlocked. The water oath was one door. We opened it and the room filled with soup. Somewhere else in this town, another door is now restless."

She felt again the spoon-on-jar *ting* from last night, the near-kiss that had stepped aside for laughter, the ribbon dusting glitter onto her palm like a secret that wanted to be touched and not yet told. "You're thinking of the fort," she said.

"I am," he admitted. "And of the bell. And of the way vows echo in metal longer than they do in human throats."

He picked up a paperweight that had been a river stone before it decided literacy might be a good second act. He turned it once, as if weighing which sentence to throw into her evening. "You were given a gift," he said. "And a job. The gift is hearing. The job is deciding which truths belong in daylight and which ones need dusk. I am, by trade and temperament, a man who invites truth to potlucks. But there are truths that ruin tables if you open them like a casserole. They need plates, and names, and privacy, and sometimes a season of silence before a sentence."

"Are you warning me off?" she asked. She kept her tone light on purpose; the weight would come whether or not she invited it.

"I'm asking you to count before you bless," he said, which was their shorthand for *do the order and survive.* "I'm asking you to hold the bell with both hands when the town tries to ring it like a doorbell."

"And you're not telling me something," she added, because if they had a sacrament, it was naming the long version out loud.

He allowed the smile then, rueful and warm. "Authority gets hungry when it knows more than it says," he confessed. "I've been trying to starve that hunger all week. I will not put you in a position where you have to walk into a room armed with my rumor. But I will say this: when bells falter in Cedar Creek, they are not broken. They are bargaining. Something wants witness."

He reached behind him and took down a book that wasn't a book more a ledger pretending to be a hymn. Its spine was cracked in the place a town would crack it if it kept the long story open on its lap while it learned to take responsibility for its verbs. He opened to a page that had been touched more than others faint skin oil turning paper into a kind of cloth. "Marriages," he said. "Dedicatory rings. Rations in old flood years. And a note two generations after Bridger about a bell that skipped its own joy."

He didn't let her read it yet. Not because he was hoarding. Because he was about to say a sentence he needed her to hear with empty hands. "You showed us what to do with a river's *no*," he said. "Be ready to show us what to do with a bell's *silence*."

"Is it that bad?" she asked.

He shook his head. "It's that tender." He slid the ledger across the desk. "Read. Then walk. Then decide your next door."

Miriam let the pages find their own speed. There were names, tidy and proud, the way names learn to be proud when the town agrees to say them correctly. There were dates next to small blessings and next to griefs with stubborn birthdays. Midway down one column a line she didn't expect: *May 19, 1911 bell fell quiet at blessing; ribbon tied, bride took breath, groom spoke slow; vows postponed at river; Pastor Thomas wrote: sometimes love requires a wait.*

She closed the book like a woman putting a lid on a pot that isn't done and nodded because there were no fancy words at the bottom of the page to help her. Elijah tapped the cover with the tip of his finger. "Risk," he said. "Not danger like cliff edges. Danger like altitude clear air that can starve you if you sprint. Walk slow, Miriam. There are people in this town who will slap a story onto silence to keep themselves from having to listen to it. I need you to hear the silence before anyone names it."

He stood and the room stood with him; some men are like that because they've practiced being careful for years and their furniture loves them for it. He reached for his coat, paused, then folded it back over the chair. "Julian can help you with provenance. Mayhew can hold the rope. I can pray like a man who believes the God he's invoking thinks rivers are classrooms. But the first step belongs to you."

She slid the ribbon scrap onto the desk. It flashed cheap glitter, poor as truth, bright as it needed to be. "This was on the rope last night," she said. "Caught near the knot."

He studied it without touching. "Then whoever's knocking has been patient enough to leave a calling card where only people who know where to look will find it."

"Bride," she said, not as drama; as diagnosis.

He nodded, and she saw beneath the pastor's polish a man who had stood near ugly vows and better ones, and knew the bell keeps score where he refuses to. "Or someone who loves a bride," he said. "Or someone who lost one."

He didn't bless her. He didn't send her. He simply opened the door and stood out of the way so she could practice being the person who decides which direction to walk.

She walked toward the fort because sometimes obedience is a direction rather than a feeling. The square had thinned to the sort of people who stack, sweep, hum. The south window put honey on the pavement. Sloane nodded from a ladder and didn't ask where Miriam was going because Sloane trusts people who walk like they know why even when they haven't told their feet yet.

The fort yard held its hush. The cedar threw a long shadow like a helpful sleeve. Alan had left the porch light the color of old beeswax and a note under a chipped sugar bowl on the stoop: **rope's oiled; key where you expect; count, then bless A.** She smiled under her breath at the kind of love the note represented: one man's decision to make a room's work easier because a woman had decided to take it on.

Inside, the south wall did its good square work. The cases slept with their mouths closed. She didn't turn lamps on. Some rooms behave better when you approach in twilight. She climbed to the loft the way you climb toward a mouth you intend to hear, not force. The bell rope hung, more patient than it had any right to be after a century of children and pandemics and fundraisers and weddings and one war nobody in Cedar Creek felt necessary to name because the names they gave it didn't make the houses warmer.

Up close, brass has a smell metal and old rain and Sunday clothes. She breathed it in. The ribbon scrap in her pocket answered, the way two things from the same story call to each other without permission. She didn't touch the rope. She put her palm against the stout post that accepts its weight and listened with the body part that hears better than ears when the town is about to start telling on itself.

Her head filled with that river-silence the kind that isn't empty. Behind it a moth's frantic geometry tapped against a window. Beneath, the boards murmured the thousand shoes that had hurried across them in the name of joy and casseroles. In front of it all, the air lifted once and settled, exactly like a person trying to speak and choosing not to and then regretting the choice.

She set the ledger Elijah's ledger on the loft stool and opened it to 1911. The script tilted as scripts do when the writer wants to be calm and can't stop their hand from telling the truth. *Bell fell quiet at blessing.* She traced the words with a finger the way you trail a current at the dock when you're trying to tell if the river is turning.

"Help me hear," she said not to the bell, not to God specifically, but to the job. "Not so I can be right in public. So I can be useful in private."

A small draft came from the tower mouth, cooler than the room. It carried the scent of feathers and the clean penny tang bells wear when they want you to stop referring to them as if they were merely instruments. Miriam closed her eyes, not to make the room more holy, but to give her mind fewer excuses. The dream of water rose and did not claim the space. Instead, what arrived had edges timbers, a cord, a loop knotted by hands confident in their apprenticeship.

She saw not with asleep-sight but with the little theater behind her eyes that honest rooms lend you a woman's hand tying ribbon to rope. White once, then cream because time always wins. The ribbon caught twice; someone another hand steadied it. Laughter came up the stair, ordinary and bright, the kind of laughter that will break your heart twenty years later because it didn't know it needed guarding. Then a sentence she could not hear mouthed across a shoulder, soft, specific and the bell's throat closed the way a throat does when it doesn't trust the words it's supposed to carry into the world.

Miriam's eyes opened. She was alone, unthreatened, ankle-deep in a new beginning she knew better than to call mystery yet because that's how you make mysteries theatrical before they've earned their stage. She sat. She let the not-quite picture sit in her lap. The ribbon in her pocket pressed the inside of the fabric like an idea that needs a pen.

"Some things live better at dusk," she told the bell. "We're at dusk now. I'll come back when it's morning. We will count. Then bless. And if you decide to say nothing, we will practice that too."

It felt absurd to speak to bronze. It felt correct. She wrote three words in the margin of the ledger because writing makes you accountable to yourself: **wait with.*" She did not add *me* because this wasn't a romance with an artifact; it was a covenant with a sound.

On the way down the stairs, she passed the gouge near the third post again and smoothed it with her palm. I know you, she thought at the wood. I know what fear does to grain. I know how hands teach timber to be more human than furniture. The banister hummed with the satisfaction of being recognized.

She stepped outside into the yard and the world performed being ordinary: Sloane swatting a mosquito and missing because competency has limits; Mayhew dragging a bin and pretending he liked it; Rosalie telling a child *two more minute* swith the tone that says *I will sell my soul to silence for five.* Over all of it the river practicing yes, no, maybe, in water. The bell did not ring. But she felt watched in the clean way you feel watched when a job has started in a room and the room is waiting for you to be punctual.

HE WAS WAITING at the south window because that is where men who have learned patience stand when they don't want to interrupt you and want to be exactly where you can find them once you're ready to be interrupted. Julian had one hand on the sill, the good hand that steadies artifacts before daylight teaches them they are fragile. He didn't ask *news?* with his mouth. He asked it with his shoulders.

"She warned me," Miriam said.

"She?"

"History," she said, deadpan, and then smiled because he makes her braver with accuracy.

He fell into step and they made the small pilgrimage to the willow. The basin wore starlight. The wedge held its coin. Someone had left the chalkboard leaning against the trunk, **COUNT THEN BLESS** re-written by a child with letters that looked like they had been carried in careful hands.

"Pastor Elijah said truth has a long tail," she told him. "We're about to step on the part attached to a bell."

Julian squinted toward the fort as if squinting could make the night identify its intentions. "We heard something last night," he said, and the *we* landed like a present on the table. "One note, then silence. A misfire. I told myself swallow, rope, weather. Then I found the ribbon on the loft."

She touched her pocket and felt the scrap approve of being admitted to the conversation. "White," she said. "Cheap glitter."

"Bride," he said, in that same diagnostic tone she had used with Elijah.

"Or loss," she countered. "Elijah wouldn't say. He asked me to count before I bless."

"He would," Julian murmured with a fondness that made Miriam want to keep the pastor safe by telling him less and telling him sooner in equal measure.

They sat on the dock and let quiet be half the dialogue. The river did its even breathing. A frog regretted something loudly and then forgave itself. The fort hunched into loyal silhouette. Miriam slid the ribbon scrap onto the dock boards between them and it looked, in the low light, like a piece of day that had forgotten to turn in its work.

"Do you want me to climb with you?" he asked.

"Yes," she said. "But not tonight. Tonight the bell owns its silence. Tomorrow, we listen with daylight ears."

He nodded as if to a colleague outlining a method. Then he did a thing that was both priestly and amateur and exactly correct: he pulled a notecard from his jacket the kind he uses to label boxes people will be too tired to remember the contents of and wrote, **IF THE BELL IS SILENT.** He slid it into an envelope, sealed it, and handed it to her. "Open if," he said.

She laughed softly at the ceremonial gravity. "We're going to become insufferable," she said. "We'll have protocols for romance."

"We already do," he said. "Count, then bless."

Behind them, pastor's steps made the sound of a man measuring a threshold. He didn't join them. He stopped in the place where men who lead without crowding stop a respectful radius from the center of the next story. "The bell has two jobs," he called mildly. "To gather and to warn. When it fails one, respect the other."

Miriam turned, heart tipping toward him with gratitude and mischief. "That's almost a riddle, Reverend."

"It's a budget," he answered, and kept walking because he knows when to stop being quotable.

A breeze ran up the seam from river to fort. The belfry gave the smallest metal breath the sound bells make in sleep when their dreams roll over. The three of them heard it and none of them said **ah** or **omen** or **oh God.** They said nothing, which in Cedar Creek is how you keep from summoning the wrong kind of story.

In the shop later, Miriam set the envelope beneath her notebook and wrote a line for herself because this book had taught her she has to write down the verbs that keep her honest or the day will edit them into gossip. **Watch the bell.**

Wait with it. Refuse the short version. She added, almost shyly, **Tell Julian everything.** Then she added, in smaller letters because you don't taunt fate: **Ask about the bride.** She did not commit to sorrow as theme. She committed to listening.

In his apartment over the museum, Julian opened the log and wrote with the neat hand he uses when he wants to make it easier for a tired future to be responsible. **Fort bell gave one note, then withheld. Ribbon found at loft cheap glitter. Pastor advised: count first. Prepare south window for marriage ledger rotation.** He paused, tapped the pencil against the margin, then added: **Do not let station invent a ghost.**

The town slept as only towns sleep that have been generous all day with their breath. In the loft, the bell stood over its own throat like an old king considering abdication. In the belfry, a swallow adjusted in its nest and decided anyone who would ring in the middle of the night must be either foolish or in love. On the dock, the ribbon scrap remembered being tied with hope and felt the strange electricity that runs through objects right before stories use them.

Miriam woke once, at a sound that might have been a dream practicing, and listened to Cedar Creek rehearse being ordinary. She did not fear the next door. She felt the hinge oil already in her pocket. Morning would bring booths and bins and a boy who thought he could make the wedge into a meme and would be rescued by science. It would also bring a bell that might choose silence and require a town to treat quiet as instruction.

Pastor Elijah would keep his caution close enough to be useful and far enough not to own her verbs. Julian would bring his keys and his careful and his ands. Miriam would carry the envelope and the ribbon and the prayer the river had lodged in her bones. And when the question came as it does from bronze, from vows, from rooms that have seen more than the people who linger inside them she would not flinch. She would count. Then bless. And the next book would open its mouth.

25

COMMUNITY RENEWAL

Morning reached the square the way it prefers to arrive in small towns on the soles of people who carry things. Before the sun cleared the courthouse roof, Sloane's crew was already unspooling cords with the choreography of a pit team, and Rosalie's ovens had confessed enough warmth to perfume the street in statements no politician could out-argue. The chain board leaned against the cottonwood with **COUNT THEN BLESS** rewrite large by a child whose A s had antlers. The basin murmured at the willow bend steady, satisfied as if the river had chosen to be a metronome.

Miriam woke to it all as to a hymn that hadn't required rehearsal. The key to the south window sat cool in her pocket. Under her arm: the volunteer clipboard; over it: the bin Sloane had labeled last night in tape and certainty **MIRIAM & JULIAN EVENT SUPPLIES** already gathering the sort of ephemera that proves a life: extra chalk, a roll of butcher paper folded like a flag, three pens that worked and one that insisted on naps. She set the bin on a table, took a breath that didn't snag on anyone else's expectations, and went to find the line that needed her first.

"Kids' stage," a teenager announced, skidding up with the urgency of a person entrusted with power and glitter beads. "Can you " She didn't finish the sentence because Miriam was already moving in the direction the girl's hands had drawn.

The stage was a wagging platform of plywood and good-will. A boy in a cape argued with a girl in a tutu about whether magic came before ballet or ballet before magic. Two microphones sprouted from the front like badly planted saplings. The sound board operator was eight.

"Count," Miriam said, kneeling to the kids' eye level. "Then bless."

The tutu frowned, doubtful but willing. "Counting looks like…?"

"Point once at the person who goes first," Miriam said, "twice at the one who goes second, and then you both take a breath as if the audience is fragile and you've been allowed to hold it." She pointed at the cape once and at the tutu twice and both children, gloriously obedient to order when order is kind, inhaled, exhaled, and took their turns. The sound board operator gave Miriam a thumbs-up with the solemnity of a knight, then pretended to adjust a fader so adults would feel useful watching him.

At the pie tent, Mr. Cavanaugh stood beside a table of rounded truths, his jaw unusually gentle, his hands lifted in benediction over rhubarb, peach, and one lemon curd that had ambitions. "Judge with me," he said when he saw Miriam, and she obliged, because why else live in a town if not to risk an opinion with a neighbor and survive it?

"Criteria?" she asked.

He pointed to the chain board as if it were a culinary

rubric. "Count: crust, filling, courage," he said. "Bless: whoever fed more people while pretending this was a contest."

They ate. They murmured. They argued quietly about the correct shade of golden that means generosity instead of vanity. Lou wandered by and without his habitual armor asked if anyone needed coffee. Rosalie appeared with two mugs at exactly that moment, invented a smile that made her look guilty of being on time, and pressed one into each judge's hand. "This is an ethical bribe," she declared, "and also breakfast."

Mayhew patrolled with the benevolent boredom of a man whose town has chosen to be predictable for a day. His hat stayed on. His notebook stayed shut. He stopped only to help a grandmother unfold a chair without turning the act into a spectacle and to tell two teens politely that their slingshot looked like a metaphor begging to become a problem.

In the south window, Alan had rotated the ledger facsimile and pinned a new line from the daybook in place beneath it. People stood with paper plates in hand and read the sentence while chewing. A boy, still small enough to press his face to glass without leaving shame behind later, traced the wedge with his finger again and asked his grandfather, "Why does a V mean wait?" The grandfather answered, "Because the river said so," and the boy decided this was better than science because it was science plus someone who loved him telling him how to survive it.

By midmorning, the square was noisy in a way that made Miriam's bones feel unlonely. She corrected a banner that had tried to call the festival **RIVER FRIST** and delighted the boy who'd done the letters by making him add a caret and fix it publicly, because humility practiced on a signboard ages well. She taught a small girl with stern bangs how to cut wicks and not cry when the first one curled wrong. She took a complaint about booth placement, wrote **thank you for saying it out loud** on a sticky note, and taped it under the map where only complainers would notice and feel privately recognized.

"Ms. Adler," petition man called not a petition in sight, only a clipboard and a sunscreen stripe unmixed on his cheek. "We need your ruling on the dunk tank Cavanaugh versus Adler first turn."

"Coin," Miriam said. "Count then bless."

He had a coin, of course. He flipped. The coin obeyed probability; Adlers went under first; Lou clapped as if fairness were his favorite flavor of cold, and an entire row of children learned that adulthood is worth aspiring to if it includes losing on purpose without turning your face into a weapon.

Julian arrived with the kind of quiet competence that folds itself into the work without requiring anyone to clap. He handed Miriam a bottle of water and a fresh marker, kissed her on the temple in the air public without parade and slid an index card into the bin: **extra cord at museum desk; sign-up forms under south window; remember to eat something not made of sugar. J.** She read it twice because attention feels like nourishment and because his handwriting made lists look like a promise.

They moved through the square like two people who had practiced not tripping over each other's verbs. He fielded questions about exhibit hours without becoming a TED talk. She calmed a girl whose ribbon had come untied by making the retie feel like a sacrament. When they reached the chalkboard, a boy with serious eyes had added a line below **COUNT THEN BLESS CLEAN THEN DANCE** and the square, recognizing a leader when it sees one, adopted the doctrine wholesale.

"Cedar Creek looks good in its own clothes," Julian said.

Miriam nodded. Joy had acquired the sound she trusted: a thousand small chores done without complaint. No speeches, no sirens. Not even a microphone. The basin said yes in its language. The wedge glowed its coin. The town, at last, seemed content to be itself without performance.

IT IS A PARTICULAR SWEETNESS, in a town that prides itself on memory, to hear your name called correctly from multiple directions without anyone needing to check their notes. Miriam discovered that sweetness before noon and then kept discovering it until dusk.

"Miriam, can you hold the clipboard while I un-knot this cord?" Sloane asked, thrusting the volunteer sign-up at her like a relay baton. "If anyone tries to put 'TBD' in the three o'clock hole," Sloane added, "give them a broom as penance."

"Miriam," called the Adler niece from the south window, "will you look at the caption before we print? We're avoiding nouns that make people itchy."

"Miriam," said a boy at the kids' stage with the bravery of someone asking to be seen gently, "I practiced breathing like you told us. Do I still yell when I say my poem?"

"Only if you want Pastor Elijah to confiscate your adjectives," she said. "Let your words do their own work."

"Miriam," Mayhew said, surprising them both, "someone turned in this wallet. You know the grandmother who puts a rubber band around her bills so tight it's practically a felony? If she's within earshot, she'll come for me. I'd prefer to be elsewhere when that happens."

She did know. She took the wallet, found the grandmother, returned it, and accepted a lemon cookie as both thanks and currency in a small economy that runs best on fairness and sugar.

At the pie tent, Mr. Cavanaugh leaned back in his chair and called across the aisle, "Miriam, tell them we're not rejudging at noon."

"We're not," she said without stopping. "We are however eating again at two."

Rosalie sent a runner with a plate and the kind of note you get from people who have decided you are theirs: **you likely forgot to sit; this counts; if anyone argues, send them to me. R.** The plate held chicken salad that could end wars and a small square of something which, upon eating, proved to be a treaty between lemon and mercy.

In every exchange, she felt the calibration shift the town adjusting its sightline. She wasn't the woman with the mysterious aunt and the patience for doors. She wasn't the candle lady you consult when you want your tables to smell like vanilla. She was a person whose name you said when you needed fairness, when a stage required a calm hand, when a key had to live in a pocket that wouldn't wander.

Alan arrived with a crate and set it under the south window as if installing a habit rather than delivering wood. "For rotating displays," he said. "Kid-proof. Sloane-proof." He pointed to a corkboard where he'd pinned a schedule: **LEDGER/LOOP 10–1; MARRIAGE NOTES 1–4; SETTLER MAPS 4–close.** Next to it, a handwritten line: **MIRIAM HAS KEY. SEE MIRIAM.**

"Are you certain?" she asked. "That's a lot of see Miriam."

"Yes," he said. "It is."

Mayhew, passing, added, "If anyone needs to see me, too

bad. See Miriam." His mouth betrayed a tug toward a smile. "And for God's sake, make them stack the chairs right."

Even the Cedar Creek Observer and Confluence FM, chastened by the week found her to ask what story they should tell. "Talk about the kids' stage," she said. "Talk about the rule **CLEAN THEN DANCE**. Talk about the dunk tank choosing fairness." The producer blinked, relieved to be spared a metaphor, and then did a neat piece on broom choreography that made half the county tune in and say, tenderly, *those fools are okay today.*

Belonging never arrived in a parade. It leaked in through tasks. When a string of paper lanterns indulged in a minor collapse, three teenagers shouted "Get Miriam," and then "Get Julian," and then, in a choir of competence, "Get rope," and the problem solved itself while she handed a mother a chair and listened to a girl tell her she had written her first poem without shouting. When the generator hiccuped, a plumber said, "Miriam's lane ends before electricity," and fetched Sloane instead. It was a glory to be unnecessary at the right moments.

Near the willow, a young couple she didn't recognize drifted toward her with the tentative courage of people ready to ask for help. "We heard you did " the woman began, and then laughed at herself. "This is a festival. I'm not going to say *ministry.* I'm going to say *lists.* We're getting married next spring. We don't want to... you know. Rush the bell. We want to count first." Her fiancé squeezed her fingers as if to say *I am here for this order even though I had no idea it existed yesterday.*

Miriam felt the ribbon scrap in her pocket as a cool declaration and answered the only way she could without stealing the next book's thunder. "Come Tuesday," she said.

"We'll walk the fort and the river. We'll name the steps. We'll practice not letting guests perform your vows for you."

"Thank you," they both said, and a little weight in Miriam's chest shifted, not heavier, just seated more properly. Guide, not stranger. Not guru. Not gatekeeper. A woman with a key and a broom and a hand that knows where the wedge glows.

Pastor Elijah drifted through with his water pitcher and an expression that suggested his job had shifted from triage to maintenance. "The joy is sturdier today," he told her. "It tolerates ordinary bumps."

"That's healing," she said. "Joy that doesn't need theatrics to prove it counts."

He nodded and moved on, and Mayhew followed him, not because pastors need sheriffs, but because sheriffs need pastors when a generator hiccups and you're tempted to shoot it.

By late afternoon, the festival had found its lazy rhythm. Tables acquired ring stains that will never come out and will be mourned by no one. Children discovered that chalk tastes awful and decided to use it on pavement instead. A Adler aunt asked a LeClair cousin for a recipe without making a face about it first. That was belonging: recipes offered without bracing.

Miriam took her turn at the information booth and fielded questions that used to be warnings disguised as curiosity: *Are you from here? Are you planning to stay?* Today the questions sounded like inventory: *Where do we put this? When does the kids' stage start again? May I borrow your tape?* She answered them like a person whose *we* no longer required translation.

. . .

EVENING PUT honey in the air and shadows where chairs wanted company. Clean then dance, the chalkboard instructed, so Miriam cleaned. She stacked chairs properly by fours, then a gap, then fours because Sloane had trained them out of towers that become lawsuits. Julian appeared with a rag in his back pocket and a face that suggested he had successfully convinced a third grader that provenance can be fascinating when accompanied by jelly beans. He set a tray on the table in front of her: a burger split in half, a modest pile of chips, a small container of something green that turned out to be loyalty disguised as parsley sauce.

"Count," he said, and she did two bites of burger, three chips, one confession: "I thought belonging would set off a firework in my head. It's just... quiet."

"Quiet," he agreed, "with paperwork."

They walked the loop they always walk south window, willow, kids' stage, pie because ritual had become their way of telling the town *we're not going anywhere*. Between each stop they did the tiny public acts that make romance durable in a place that sees you: he plucked foam from her coffee before it thought about mustaches. She straightened his lanyard so **JULIAN ROTH MUSEUM** faced the right way and the town didn't have to crane. He wiped lemon glaze from the corner of her mouth with his thumb and then, because their restraint is not a religion, didn't laugh when she blushed anyway.

At the kids' stage, the tutu and the cape had become an alliance. They tried to recruit Julian into a finale that required him to pretend a coin had disappeared from his ear and reappeared in his pocket. He obeyed with academic rigor, then labeled the trick **CLIPBOARD MAGIC** on a note card because every good illusion deserves a file.

"Are we a spectacle?" Miriam asked him later, half-teasing, half-caution.

"We're a lesson," he said. "Count, then bless. Act, then label. Hold hands, then let go to carry chairs. Dull verbs, hot heart."

They reached the willow and stopped the way people do at places that hold their yes and their not-yet without flinching. The basin lifted lantern light to the underside of leaves. The wedge kept its coin, neither needy nor shy. They stood shoulder to shoulder and let the river say its simple sentence in a language their bodies had learned to translate.

"Tell me a plan for tomorrow that feels like a life and not a festival," he said, because intimacy isn't only petals; it's calendars.

"Breakfast at Riverlight Café," she said. "You take the slant, sugar slides to you. I'll bring the envelope."

"The envelope," he repeated, and that was enough to turn romance into partnership again without requiring either of them to disguise their wanting.

"After breakfast, the fort," she added. "We'll listen with daylight ears. We'll not invent ghosts to satisfy the part of us that misses theater."

"And after the fort," he said, "we'll check on the south window and the kids' stage and show up at the dunk tank when Lou decides he's a target again."

"And," she said.

"And," he echoed, and the word sat between them, familiar as the bin label, sacred in its smallness.

They moved back into the square as dusk finished reading its line and stepped down. Sloane had declared it dance time and enforced her doctrine by confiscating three brooms and turning them into batons. A fiddler started something that sounded like knees remembering how to be equipment, not evidence. Partners found each other the way magnets do quietly, accurately. Miriam didn't expect to be asked. She had a chair to move, a cup to toss, a boy to shoo off a rope.

Julian offered his hand anyway and did not make a face when she refused. He turned the refusal into the smallest spin of her wrist so it felt like choreography rather than decline. Later, when the chairs had been stacked properly and the cups had found the bin and the boy had chosen a less dramatic rope, he offered again. She took it. They did not waltz. They did the sort of dance people do when they intend to avoid spectacle but are not opposed to joy: four steps, laugh, two steps, apology to a neighbor they nearly grazed, pause because Mayhew had decided to cross the floor with a lemon bar at precisely the wrong time, resume, count, bless.

"Are we terrible at this?" he asked, stepping on nothing and being proud anyway.

"We are excellent at not falling," she said. "That's the Cedar Creek metric."

He grinned and leaned his forehead to hers the way he had at the end of last night, letting contact do the work that language would oversell. Rosalie whooped, not because she wanted a show, but because she recognizes good form when she sees it. Sloane shouted, "No performance art!" which is how she says *carry on, I love you all,* while pretending to police.

The stars agreed to be ordinary. The fort was a square of honesty against the darker sky. The bell kept its pact with silence no misfires, no spoiled omens just a weight above town that did not yet ask to be carried. Miriam felt its watching the way you feel a neighbor's lamp in a second-floor window: not invasive, but present. She filed the feeling beside the envelope and the ribbon under **tomorrow's verbs** and let the square have the rest of her attention.

When the song thinned and the fiddler's elbow gave up within the bounds of dignity, Miriam and Julian made the last loop south window, willow, kids' stage, pie tent closing things with hands that have learned latches better than arguments. At the board, the child's amended doctrine had acquired an addendum in uncertain script: **LISTEN THEN RING.** Someone had added a small and beside it: **AND ASK.**

She touched the chalk lightly so as not to smear the fierceness of a child who had decided to help name the future. Julian took a picture for the log and promised to transcribe it into the file called **LITURGY OF COMMON SENSE.** They laughed; they meant it.

On the way to the shop, a woman Miriam didn't know stopped her with the urgency that used to mean rumor and now meant gratitude. "I moved here last year," the woman said, breathless. "I haven't belonged anywhere in a long time. Today I did because a stranger handed me a plate and didn't ask for my story before trusting me with a seat."

"Keep the plate," Miriam said, and when the woman looked horrified at the idea of stealing crockery, added, "I mean keep the seat."

"Right," the woman said, and laughed, and the laugh had a Cedar Creek vowel already.

They locked the shop. They stood in the square with the feeling of having finished a day that mattered without wringing it for applause. The river made the decent noise that helps people sleep. The south window gave its small, faithful light. Mayhew tipped his hat as if counting people home. Sloane scolded a cord into behaving. Rosalie stacked pans like trophies and turned her face to the sky to let herself be tired out loud. Pastor Elijah walked by and said, "Joy plus chores equals endurance," and kept moving before anyone could accuse him of poetry.

"I like us like this," Julian said.

"Like every day is a rehearsal," she said.

"For what?" he asked.

"For the long version," she said. "Of everything."

They took each other's hands with the casual accuracy of people who have decided *ours* is a word the town can hold without making a genre out of it. No one who noticed clapped; everyone who noticed made space. They crossed the square at a pace that let them point out the hinge they'd oiled and the rope knot that had held and the bin that had found its proper corner. Above them, the bell kept quiet and the stars tried not to show off. Cedar Creek practiced sleeping without bracing for a fight. And Miriam guide now, not stranger felt the sensation she had once thought shut behind a door in another town open right here, in plain sight: home, spelled with chores and counted with gratitude, blessed without trumpets, alive.

26

EVENING IN THE SHOP

Dusk came in like a sensible friend no drama, just hands already full of night. Miriam propped the door of the shop half-open to let the festival air rinse the day off the shelves. In the front window, three lanterns burned down at the same patient rate, the way good habits do. She swept, not to chase perfection but to reset the room to useful. The square's music ghosted in fiddle, a mild drum, laughter with the edges rounded off by fatigue. The key to the south window sat beside the register as if it had always belonged to that square of wood.

On the counter lay the bin Sloane had labeled with cheerful authority: **MIRIAM & JULIAN EVENT SUPPLIES.** It had already begun to gather their life chalk, a coil of twine, envelopes, three pencils with the softness of a well-used voice, a folded program with **CLEAN THEN DANCE** underlined twice in a child's bright hand. She tucked a roll of labels into the side pocket because labels keep neighbors from arguing about which drawer the tape lives in. Then she flipped the sign to **OPEN IF YOU WANT A QUIET PLACE** and meant it.

Julian tapped the doorframe with the back of his knuckles his version of knocking at a room that was half his by practice. He came with two items in hand: a paper sack that promised dinner and a cloth-wrapped parcel whose shape announced itself to anyone addicted to paper. Museum tissue, tied with red string. You could smell the book from three feet away. Or maybe that was just the way Miriam's brain received good news.

"I brought you something rare and something practical," he said.

"Which is which?" She took the sack and inhaled lemon and garlic and a rumor of dill. "Rosalie's?"

"Left on my desk with a sticky note that said, 'Don't let scholarship starve your girlfriend.'" He reddened, then laughed. "Sloane probably forged that word to save time."

"Eat before you say anything you want to keep," she told him, because the week had taught them both that calories prevented theological errors.

They ate at the counter, a dinner that would scandalize restaurants and please saints bread broken with fingers; chicken salad that insisted on courage; cucumbers derailed by vinegar; two cookies because mercy rarely travels alone. He refilled her water from the little shop carafe without being asked. She plucked a lemon seed from the corner of his mouth because restraint is not a religion.

Only when the plates were guiltless did he set the parcel down and untie the string with the care of a man who believes knots have feelings. The cloth came away: a small, older hardcover, plain brown boards, gold-stamped title almost given up by time.

"From the back cage," he said. "I think it was cataloged once and then forgot to insist on itself."

She read the cover aloud, tasting each word like a liturgy.

"*Campanile & Covenant: Country Bells and the Common Life.* Reverend E. T. Thomas. 1909."

"Thomas," Julian said. "Two years before the ledger note about the bell that fell quiet in 1911. Likely the same family as Pastor Thomas who wrote, *sometimes love requires a wait.* If not, at least a man whose sentences wear similar boots."

He opened to the flyleaf. A name in old ink, careful hand: *Eliza Adler, 1910.* Below it, a later pencil line: *loaned to Nora/returned.* The graphite had thinned to silver, the way the present does when it agrees to become the past.

"Of course Eliza had it," Miriam murmured. "The Adlers collected nouns. Nora's grandmother?"

"Probably," he said. "Your diner will have ancestry."

"Next you'll tell me the lemon glaze has provenance."

"It does," he said, deadpan. "Cross-referenced under *Citrus, weaponized.*"

They smiled into the little stupid joy of it the world doing them the favor of being specific. It was a relief after a week of elemental verbs. They leaned over the book together, shoulders almost touching, the rail-light bright enough for reading but not for judgment.

The first page still smelled faintly of ink and coal. The paper had that soft roughness that allows a pencil to feel useful. She ran a thumb under the date line and it offered up a fleck of dust as if grateful to be touched by someone with decent intentions. He set a note card by the spine his habit, his altar. On it he wrote a title: **BELL & VOW.** Then he looked at her hand without making a show of it.

"Ready?"

"Count," she said.

He turned the page.

The chapter headings made promises about small things doing large work. *On the Stewardship of Sound. On the*

Bell as Table. On Waiting and Witness. The sentences were compact, unshowy, somehow both theological and practical, like instructions for how to make soup without lying.

She snorted at a footnote where the reverend criticized modern bell ropes for being "too cottony, encouraging lazy hands." He caught it. "My people," he said, "have strong opinions about twine."

"Strong opinions are just muscles without rest days," she answered. "Let's not injure anything."

He laughed, and it wasn't awkward laughter meant to fill dead space; it was the laugh of a body that had finally learned what to do with relief. They read in turns, each of them taking the paragraphs most likely to make the other person happier. He gave her the stories and kept the specifications. She took the metaphors and surrendered the metallurgy to him like a gift, not a defeat.

When the shop bell chimed for a late customer, both of them looked up automatically, then relaxed as Mayhew stuck his head in long enough to say, "Carry on," and left with a jar of matches and the expression of a man who appreciates a scene and refuses to wreck it by lingering.

"Romance, sanctioned by law," Julian murmured.

"Do not draft the sheriff into our genre," Miriam said, mock-stern.

They read until the festival noise thinned and the world outside became more porch than stage. When the book's string-tied envelope fell out the sort of thing people tuck against a pastedown for later they both froze like two librarians discovering a rare marginalia in their cereal.

"Prayers and Addenda," the envelope announced in the reverend's hand. He slid out two papers: a printed errata slip and a narrower ribbon of note in pencil, Eliza Adler's steady hand again: *Ask about the bridal loop; she knows where it began.*

Miriam traced the letters with a fingertip, a faint current running from the graphite to the ribbon scrap in her pocket. The shop felt crowded suddenly not with ghosts, but with proper nouns Eliza, Lenore, Thomas people who had loved a bell enough to argue with it. She met Julian's eyes. He was grinning like a man who has been given permission to care about the exact right thing.

"Tomorrow," he said.

"Count first," she said.

"Then bless," he echoed.

They placed the note card under the loose note so it wouldn't blow away from their small life. Then they did the most romantic thing either of them knew: they took turns washing the two dinner forks in the back sink, dried them thoroughly, and put them in the bin under a masking-tape label she wrote just then: **US FORKS.**

THEY PUSHED two stools together at the counter, bringing the book into the wedge of warm light like a guest. Julian angled the lamp so the gold of the title would catch and hold; Miriam poured water and added a strip of lemon rind because lemon made everything behave. The window stood at two fingers open, letting in that night breeze Cedar Creek uses to carry news to people who can be trusted to sleep on it.

"Read me the part about witness," she said.

He did. The reverend's words landed like fence posts: honest, spaced for weather. *A bell is a steward of time and event. It rings not merely to gather bodies but to divide before and after. Therefore it must abide an order. First the counting of guests, of dowry, of consent then the blessing. Where witness is disputed, the bell may fail of its office and keep itself from sound until the house has its truth.*

"Fancy way of saying wait," she said softly.

"Fancy way of giving *wait* dignity," he countered. "I have never met a sentence so patient with the town's tendency to rush."

She took the book and read aloud from a later chapter, *On Knots and Conscience.* The reverend cataloged the proper ways to tie the lower loop of a bell rope: sailor's coil, farmer's tie, bridal loop. He described the bridal loop without romance: *A nail-head of ribbon is sometimes affixed a hand-span above the lower knot, that the bride may take hold and add her consent to the congregation's pull.* Then, in italics the reverend's concession to emphasis *Let no man take the loop for himself.* In the margin, a sensible hand Eliza's had written: *and let no congregation swallow her.*

Miriam closed her eyes a second, accepting that small ghost of tenderness and charge. "Eliza was busy," she said.

"She was," he agreed. "Busy telling us not to ruin things."

They found a plate illustration at the center an engraving of a fort bell nearly identical to the one that slept above the museum. The captions pleased him; the shading pleased her. At the bottom edge, a tiny maker's mark had tried to hide behind the border. "Voss & Hale, St. Joseph, 1890," he read, satisfied. "That tracks with our bell's weight. And " His finger paused at a second line no one had bothered to translate into the catalog. "Look. *Brake pin optional; see page 116.*"

"Brake," she said. "As in... stopping sound."

"Not a brake exactly," he said, flipping, already alive with the pleasure of being tasked. "A check. A clapper check. You install it for storms, silence hours, or to protect the bell from misuse."

His voice trailed because page 116 had been turned down Eliza's doing, likely and under the diagram someone had penciled initials in a blocky, hand-forged script: **A.R.** Next to it: *installed after the May incident.*

They both went very still. He didn't say it. She didn't either. *A. R.* could be anyone. But the town had a Roth, and in families, initials tend to behave.

He exhaled. "My great-grandfather was Abel. He did iron work. Doors. Latches."

"Then the check might be Roth-made," she said gently. "Installed because a bell needed gentling. That isn't sin. It's stewardship."

He turned his head and from that angle he looked like Alan when he tells a joke nobody gets until the next day. "I know," he said. "I also know the station will want it to be villainy. And that I will need to not let them."

"We won't," she said. "We'll count, then bless. And if the check is there, it might be the necessary silence that saved someone's hearing or heart."

They kept reading, a rhythm so good it felt inevitable: one of them taking text, the other harvesting footnotes; notes migrating to notecards; notecards stacking with the neatness of a mind that intends to leave a breadcrumb trail for its future tired self. They laughed twice at the reverend's cranky footnotes (he had strong emotions about ringers who sweat on ropes), and once at a typo *campanile* misprinted as *companion* that, in context, felt like a disclosure rather than a mistake.

At the back, tucked against the pastedown, they found a narrow strip of stiff paper that had once been a ribbon spool label the sort of thing a person saves because they prefer having proof of choices. Someone had written on it in pencil: *If bell declines, consult brides. The rope remembers hands.*

"'Consult brides' is either a festival committee rule or a theology," he said.

"Both," she said. "If the loop is theirs, their story is witness."

They rested their heads briefly together, a contact more restful than heat. It felt like what the town had been practicing all day intimacy as competence, not spectacle. He kept reading. She kept listening. He translated bad Latin for her and confessed to a childish affection for engraved horses on printer's ornaments; she admitted that sometimes she picks up a candle wick just to enjoy how a small thing behaves when it knows it must be trimmed to serve.

"And here," he said, catching at a paragraph that bore the tint of local. "*In Cedar Creek County (cf. post), a fort bell once declined to sound at a wedding blessing, remaining still until a matter were put right.* No details. Just that *cf. post.* Which isn't here. Either the reverend never wrote it, or he did and Eliza didn't get the pages, or " He shrugged. "The post went missing in the post."

She put Eliza's envelope back into the book and smoothed the edge of the paper that had sheltered it for a century. "We have enough," she said. "A brake check. An initial. A question Eliza asked. And the thing Pastor Elijah warned: truth has a tail and bells bargain. It's not a scandal. It's a calendar. We keep it."

"Keep it," he agreed.

They closed the book like laying down a tool. He wrapped it again in tissue not because he was finished; because it needed to be safe when they weren't using it. She slid a note card under the red string before he tied it, not with any flourish, just her small handwriting: **tomorrow**

bridal loop A.R. He smiled, then reached for the pen and added his *and* beside it: **brake check / p.116.**

The two lines, stacked, looked like a plan that could survive sleep.

NIGHT FOLDED INTO ITSELF OUTSIDE; the last of the chairs across the square made that scrape that is not angry, just tired. Miriam locked the till and dimmed the front lights until the room was more home than shop. The lanterns in the window found their low flame and held steady no performance left in them, just clarity.

Julian checked the bin as if it were a patient. "Forms, tape, forks, rope, pencils, envelope," he inventoried. "Room for tomorrow."

"Good," she said. "We are trying to become people with a room for tomorrow."

He leaned elbows on the counter, palms open, posture that said he could stay or go and would be happy either way. "Tell me your sentence for the log," he said, because the day had taught them to speak their verbs out loud before sleep could edit them into something tidy and false.

"Evening: ordinary, held; book: witness; initials: A.R.; plan: ask brides; feeling: quiet not empty."

He wrote it on a card without correcting her punctuation. "Mine: **found the brake; do not let the story become a weapon; laughter felt like proof of life; US forks labeled.**"

They grinned at that last one and then let the grin fade into the kind of silence you earn by doing things in the right order. She reached for the shop bell with two fingers and made it speak once no trill, just the smallest confirmation. The sound hung a second and then folded itself into the night outside, obedient to private air.

"May I try something," he asked, "without Mayhew writing me up?"

"You may try almost anything," she said. She respected the *almost*. It kept them from breaking good things.

He came around the counter and took her hand as if he were handing her a tool in a room where both of them were responsible for the floor. He didn't kiss her. He put her palm on the red string of the wrapped book, then laid his own over hers. Two hands, one package, one history. No audience. No river. Just a table. Just a plan.

"This is what I want," he said quietly. "To put my hand where yours is when it's on something the town needs."

"That's lust, in Cedar Creek," she said, straight-faced.

He laughed the way a person does when relief splits its lip and doesn't even mind. Then the laughter softened and he did kiss her briefly, accurately, in the middle of a sentence they had already decided to keep writing. It felt like the bell might not mind.

When they parted, she breathed out and heard maybe from outside, maybe from the room itself that thin not-quite-sound the fort bell had made last night when it thought about speaking and thought better. It could have been a truck a block away. Or weather. But it brushed her ribs in a way ordinary noise doesn't.

"Did you " he began.

"Yes," she said. "But I'm not inventing a ghost. Tomorrow we listen with daylight ears."

"And Pastor Elijah?" she asked.

"We'll tell him after we've counted," he said. "Let him bless what needs blessing. Keep the station thirsty and far away."

She took the ribbon scrap from her pocket the one that had clung to the rope and slid it beneath the red string like a bookmark. It looked casual there, then purposeful, like a piece of punctuation accepting its fate. The glitter caught a little of the lamp and threw it back as if to say, *I was not expensive; I was important.*

"Foreshadowing," he said lightly.

"Inventory," she corrected, because she refuses to live in a book that is only genre and not town.

The shop bell chimed again dentist's office soft and Sloane stuck in her head, hair pulled back, shoulders loose the way they get when she's finally satisfied nothing will explode in her absence. "I am confiscating the two of you," she announced. "Or rather, I'm evicting you from the work for the evening. Off-duty. Close the shop. Go home. Be boring aggressively."

"Noted," Julian said.

Sloane stepped inside, rapped the counter with her knuckles, and squinted at the wrapped book. "Is that our next mess?"

"It's our next *order*," Miriam said, and Sloane, satisfied with the word, left without a rejoinder.

They finished the closing smalls: wicks snuffed; back sink wiped; register balanced; the little rug straightened so morning wouldn't immediately trip over evening's carelessness. Miriam turned the sign to **CLOSED SEE YOU IN THE LONG VERSION** because she'd written it on an impulse and nobody had made her take it down yet. They stood at the door, looking out at a square that had finally learned what to do with its breath.

"Tomorrow, then," Julian said.

"Tomorrow," she echoed, and the word felt like a room with a table already set.

He kissed her again at the threshold the kind of kiss that blesses the door rather than claims the person standing under it and stepped into the summer night. She watched him cross to the south window and rest his palm on the glass, a habit he had stolen from her with no intention of returning. The fort sat beyond, considerable, square. The bell forgot to misbehave. The river hummed what it always hums when a town is trying to become honest: count, then bless, again.

Miriam locked the door and stood in the soft hush a moment more, the wrapped book on the counter, the ribbon caught under string, the bin labeled **US** with forks shining like small, silly vows. The room felt pleased to be trusted with sleep. Her body felt the same.

She killed the last light, pocketed the key, and stepped into the dark air. It held. The night did the decent thing and left them alone. Somewhere above the museum, a swallow shuffled in its nest. Somewhere in the bell throat, a metal part dreamed of movement and refrained. Tomorrow would have work. Tonight had enough.

27

———

DREAM OF THE BELL

Sleep didn't take Miriam gently. It came like a hand on the back, pushing her over a threshold she hadn't chosen. One moment she was lying in her narrow bed, the ribbon scrap from the book still tucked under the lamp base, and the next she was standing in the fort courtyard as if time had lost its hinge.

The night sky above was split by a tower's silhouette dark, square, inevitable. The bell hung there, heavy in its frame, a mouth waiting to speak. Except it didn't.

A crowd pressed in around her, clothed in generations. Some wore shawls, some coats with brass buttons, some dresses that looked borrowed from daguerreotypes. All eyes were lifted toward the tower. Waiting. Expectant.

Then it came: the tug of a rope pulled by unseen hands. The wheel turned; the clapper should have swung. But the bell refused. The iron mouth stayed clenched. The silence wasn't simple absence. It was a weight, an active denial, like a throat closed in grief.

Miriam felt the silence strike her chest harder than any

sound could have. The people in the dream looked at one another with panic barely disguised as patience.

And then she saw her: a bride in white, no veil, hair pinned but not adorned. Her face was pale with the shock of public humiliation, but her eyes were bright with something fiercer accusation, sorrow, maybe both. She gripped the lower loop of the rope, the bridal loop the reverend had described in the book. Her hand shook with effort. She pulled. Again the wheel turned. Again the bell withheld its voice.

The silence became unbearable. It drowned out breath, drowned out birds, drowned out even the river. The crowd began to shift, the way crowds do when shame is hunting for a victim. Miriam felt the bride's gaze travel across the decades and land on her.

"Do you hear me?" the bride whispered. The words were soundless, carried on the lips, but they pierced anyway.

Miriam wanted to say yes. She wanted to ask what had been betrayed, what oath broken. But her own voice was stolen by the silence. She opened her mouth and nothing emerged.

The bride's grip slipped. The rope burned her palm red. A single tear cut through her powdered cheek and fell into the dust. The bell loomed overhead, mute, as though it had judged the town unworthy of its note.

A gust of wind came up, sudden, rattling shutters. Miriam tried to step forward but her feet stuck fast. The bride mouthed one more sentence *the bell remembers* before dissolving into shadow. The rope fell slack. The wheel stopped turning.

Miriam woke with her throat raw, as if she had been shouting in a room that refused to echo.

· · ·

THE DREAM CLUNG like wet cloth. She sat up, sweat chilling her skin, the lamp still burning low beside the bed. For a long moment she could only press a hand to her sternum and feel the silence lodged there like a stone.

The bell remembers. The phrase refused to fade. It carried the same gravity as the wedge glowing at the basin, as the ledger's confession, as the chains snapping in her vision of the river. Except this symbol wasn't about water or liberation. It was about voice, about absence, about a covenant broken in sound.

She rose, feet bare on the wood floor, and went to the window. Cedar Creek slept, lanterns guttered down to embers, the river hushing itself against the banks. Above the museum roof, the fort's square silhouette cut the horizon. She could almost see the bell's weight inside it, even without light. She could almost hear the refusal again, that silence that was louder than a toll.

Voice withheld is not nothing, she thought. It is punishment. It is protest.

Her mind wandered back to the reverend's note: *Where witness is disputed, the bell may fail of its office and keep itself from sound until the house has its truth.* The bridal loop. The initials *A.R.* scrawled by the diagram of a brake check. The silence in her dream had not been mechanical; it had been moral.

And yet, it was also personal. She could still see the bride's eyes. Young, humiliated, furious. A woman bound by covenant and betrayed by silence.

Miriam leaned her forehead against the cool glass of the window and let the ache settle. She thought of Pastor Elijah's warning: uncovering history has costs. The ledger had broken the basin's drought, but the bell... the bell might choose a harder lesson.

Symbolism layered itself thickly, almost suffocating. The basin had been about bondage broken. The bell was about a voice denied. The first mystery had ended with water flowing, a yes after confession. The next would demand reckoning with a silence that wanted to be explained, if not avenged.

She whispered into the empty shop below, into the shelves and wicks and windows that had become hers: "I hear you." Her voice cracked, but the sound at least carried. "I hear you."

The phrase wasn't meant only for the bride. It was for Cedar Creek too. For all the women whose stories had been shortened or swallowed. For the town that had learned to thrive on *the short version*. The bell's silence was a record of one such short version, one that had left a woman voiceless at the threshold of her vows.

The dread she felt wasn't the dread of failure. It was the dread of inheritance. The basin had already proved the town's capacity for fracture and renewal. The bell would prove something else that the cost of silence is borne not only by the one who holds the tongue, but by all who wait to hear it.

Miriam turned from the window, heart pounding with the certainty that she had been drafted into another story.

Sleep was out of the question now. She lit a single candle on the counter and opened her notebook. The ribbon scrap lay beside it, flattened under the book parcel from Julian. She wrote quickly, hands trembling:

Dream: Fort courtyard. Crowd waiting. Bell refused. Bride pulled rope. Rope loop bridal. Bell silent. Bride

wept. Words without sound: "the bell remembers." Meaning: covenant broken. Voice denied.

She underlined *the bell remembers* three times, then sat back. Her pulse slowed, but the dread remained, quiet and coiled.

What would Julian say? He would frown at the dream, sharpen his pencil, look for a historical record. He would insist that brakes and checks, not ghosts, explained silences. But even he could not ignore the phrase *the bell remembers.*

She imagined telling him. He would resist, as he always did, but he would stay, as he always did too. Their partnership had become a weave of doubt and belief, each pulling against the other to create a pattern strong enough to carry the town. She trusted that when she told him of the dream, his doubt would not diminish her vision. It would sharpen it.

Still, the emotional stakes chilled her. The bride's sorrow had been thick as tar. It carried the weight of all the town's unfinished confessions. The basin had required truth to refill. The bell would require courage to unseal silence.

Miriam pictured the next days: climbing the fort tower with Julian, brushing dust off iron fittings, searching for initials and brake pins. Talking to Theo at the café, coaxing stories of Eliza Adler's question about the bridal loop. Listening to Pastor Elijah, who already seemed to know the outlines of what was coming. And she pictured herself standing before the town again, ledger in one hand, vision in the other, voice trembling but clear.

The dread became a vow. Whatever the bell's silence meant, she would not turn away. She would not allow Cedar Creek to inherit another century of mute stone.

Her candle guttered low, wax pooling into its dish. She closed the notebook, slid the ribbon scrap back under the string around the book parcel, and whispered once more into the empty shop:

"I will hear you."

The flame flickered, as though some draft had answered, and she felt the dread shift into resolve.

The bell had fallen silent in her dream. In waking life, she would not.

28

JULIAN'S QUIET CONFESSION

Riverlight Café opened at six because history wakes hungry. By ten minutes after, the bell on the door had trained itself to ring softly so it wouldn't shame latecomers. Miriam took the booth she always pretended was an assignment the one with the slight slant that made sugar packets migrate to the far corner like opinions.

She had slept in fragments dream shredded, breath up against the edge of panic and then backing off. The ribbon scrap lay in her pocket the way a sentence lives under the tongue when you're not ready to speak it. The fort's silhouette still sat behind her eyes, bell heavy and unspeaking. *The bell remembers.* She held coffee with both hands because heat counts as mercy.

Julian arrived with the second pot and a look that said he'd brought himself on purpose. He set a napkin on the table and then, with the precision of a man who cleans glass before mounting a photograph, set a small envelope dead center: the one he'd written last night **IF THE BELL IS SILENT.** He didn't push it toward her. He just let it be ready.

"You look like you wrestled a hymn," he said gently.

"It won on points," she answered. "But I lodged a formal complaint."

Theo slid plates down with the tenderness she reserves for people who don't realize yet that food outruns most metaphors. "You're getting eggs," he informed Miriam. "And toast. And you" to Julian "are getting your usual, because routine keeps men from inventing weather."

"We believe in weather," he said.

"You needn't marry it," Theo said, writing something no one could read on his pad and leaving them with the kind of care that pretends not to be watching.

They ate first. It was their rule count then bless even here. Miriam's fork found yolk and decided not to preach. Julian tore toast in half and buttered both pieces in equal measure like a man training himself to share without accounting. They talked about nothing loud. The sugar slid toward him; she let it; equilibrium is a romantic act when practiced in small public rooms.

When the plates were honest, he reached across the table, not for her hand the diner was a parish; they didn't need to turn prayer into pageantry but for the envelope. He tapped it once, then left it there. "I need to tell you something," he said, and his voice had the clarity good glass has. "And I need to say it plain so you can carry it without having to translate."

She sat straighter without making a scene. "Say it."

"I'm afraid," he said. No throat clearing, no scholarship. "Afraid of losing you to a story. Afraid of losing you to the part of the town that prefers theater to truth. Afraid of heights, a little" his mouth bent, wry "and of brake pins that might not have been installed as well as my great-grandfather believed. Afraid of history's appetite for heroes and martyrs. I trust you more than I trust my fear. But the fear still lives with me and some days it takes up more furniture than it should."

The sentences sat between them like dishes you don't rush to clear because what's on them matters.

"I know the work," he went on. "I believe in it. The ledger, the wedge, the basin. But last night when I lay in bed I thought about you on the loft stairs, the gouge where hands grab when they're frightened. I kept seeing that ribbon on the rope and your hand reaching for it. And I felt " he paused, ruthless enough with himself to find the exact noun "the old Roth thing in me. To fix it. To tie something down. To put a lock on the door and call it stewardship when it's fear."

He folded his fingers together the way a man folds maps when he's trying not to boil the road down to a line. "I don't want to be the person who silences you in the name of safety. My family carried that sin far enough. I also don't want to clap from the square while you fall off a ladder I should have held."

His eyes met hers. Brown in daylight, steadier than the coffee, honest in that quiet way the museum teaches keepers to be when they sign for something that can't be replaced. "I am asking not to own the choice. To share it. If we are going to walk into the bell, into whatever it's guarding, I want to be the hand at your back and the one on the rung and the one that refuses to let the town turn you into a symbol it can consume."

Miriam didn't touch him. She heard him. There's a difference, and it's the only reason people survive love and work at the same time.

"I dreamed the bell refused," she said, not to trump him, to tell the truth fully. "A bride, the loop, the wheel turning without sound. The silence felt like a verdict. It told me, *the bell remembers.*" She gave him the dream without decoration. She watched his face not for belief but for the thing she values more: attention.

He didn't roll his eyes. He didn't consecrate it. He nodded once, the way you nod at a witness who has earned the stand. "Then that's a lead," he said. "And a hazard."

"Both," she said. "Pastor Elijah warned me about truth's tail. I'm carrying the warning in one pocket and the ribbon in the other."

"Good," he said, and exhaled like a man who has been allowed to be afraid out loud and discovered it didn't cost him his competence. "Then here is my quiet confession, complete: if I ever ask you to slow down, it's because I can't imagine a Cedar Creek where your voice goes quiet. Not because I doubt what you hear."

She smiled, crooked and grateful. "Permission to say the corny thing?"

"Please."

"Love and truth walk together," she said softly. "If they separate, we wait until they can hold hands again."

He laughed relieved, foolish, reverent and then let his face settle into the seriousness that makes her trust him near ladders. "Deal," he said. "I put that on a label, I swear."

He reached into his jacket and produced a length of flat webbing, rolled neat. "Harness," he explained. "From the theatre days in college. Adjustable. Tested. We use it on the loft ladder. I called Mayhew. He has a second. He'll grumble and show up anyway."

"Count, then bless," she echoed. "And clip in."

"Clip in," he said, and the phrase felt like a vow nobody would clap for, which made it more real.

Theo brought a second pour and because God loves

comic timing two lemon wedges on a saucer. "No speeches," he said, "but I enjoy the look of agreement on people. Wear it in public."

They did.

THEY CROSSED the square with the ease of people who've started measuring errands as courtship. The south window held its polite light. Sloane shouted at a cord from three tents away and blessed them with a wave that meant *I see you, don't make me see you more than necessary.* Mayhew materialized near the museum steps, hat already skeptical, a coil of rope on one hip and the world's least romantic carabiners on the other.

"Your harness," Mayhew said to Julian, holding up the hardware as if offering a boutonnière to common sense. "Your harness," he said to Miriam. "Free with admission."

"Clip in," Julian told him.

"Don't invent a ceremony," Mayhew warned, but he was smiling the way a man smiles when his community insists on being safer than it used to be.

In the museum foyer Alan had set out a stack of cones with a note that read **no heroics; also no radio stations.** A He handed them one, then another. "Put one on the porch and one at the stair," he said. "I am not burying either of you when I have other shelves to catalog."

Julian buckled into the harness like a man reconciling two kindnesses: fear, and the permission to walk past it. He checked Miriam's buckles and asked, "May I?" before pulling a strap snug. She nodded and let him be meticulous. He looked at her like a thing he intended to keep safe without making a museum out of her.

On the loft stairs the gouge near the third post waited, a

familiar bruise on the building's body where hands grip without asking. Miriam touched it with the reverence of someone greeting an old teacher. "We'll put a brass plate there one day," she said. "Not to pretty it up. To tell the truth: *here is where fear holds and does not fall.*"

"Plate after investigation," Julian said, and then because rituals are weapons if you don't keep them humble tapped the rail twice. She matched him. Two taps: still with me. They climbed.

The bell rope hung true, loop knotted competent and old. In daylight the ribbon scrap would have looked foolish cheap glitter on the sacred but it wasn't there now, tucked under the string on the wrapped book back at the shop. Instead: fibers worn by a century of hands. A grayness you only learn to love once you've been trusted with ropes long enough to understand what they've carried.

Julian anchored their lines to the post he'd inspected twice and judged older than his grandfather's pride. "Bend-fast," he murmured, admiring the joinery. "Abel's generation. Or the same school."

"You and your families," she teased.

He didn't apologize for loving the honest parts of his line. He clicked her carabiner into place soft metal kiss and gave it the gentlest tug. "Okay?"

"Okay," she said, and meant *I accept your fear as a form of love.*

They moved slow. Up close, bells smell like weather and weddings. Miriam put her palm near the rope and felt not memory, exactly, but that quiet gravity rooms give off when they've been used for both joy and lesson. She breathed. The dream's silence didn't flood her. Instead came a steadier instruction: listen with daylight ears.

Julian worked practical: lamp up, bracket checked,

clapper examined. He unrolled a cloth and laid out tools that looked more like conversation than surgery: brush, dental mirror, a small flashlight with a beam that respects artifacts. "Brakes first," he said.

At the throat of the frame, half-hidden under a lip of iron, a small dark piece sat like an old idea. He used the mirror and the light and then made a sound so small she almost missed it a pleased exhale, a grief. "There," he said. "Clapper check. Not engaged. But present." He tilted the mirror so she could see: a simple pin with a collar, neatly fitted, not crude. The initials were faint, but not coy.

"AR," Miriam read, heart tugged not by melodrama but by the miracle of accuracy.

"Abel Roth," Julian said, and didn't run from the truth. He used the brush on the space around the pin like a man cleaning his own name. "Installed after a May incident," he murmured, remembering the note. "It doesn't silence the bell by itself. It keeps it from ringing if someone sets it. The story isn't *villain made silence.* It's *someone asked the bell not to speak that day.*" He sat back on his heels. "Maybe the bride. Maybe the pastor. Maybe the sheriff of 1911. Maybe... the congregation."

"We won't guess," Miriam said. "We'll ask. *Ask brides.* We'll read the minutes without using them like weapons. We'll collect witness like plates. We'll set a table with it. Then " she gestured gently at the bell " we'll see if she has anything else to say."

He nodded, grateful not to be judge and keen to be steward. They took measurements, logged photos, wrote **do not engage** in block letters in the notebook as if they were speaking to their own worst impulses. They lowered the lamp's brightness and stood in the dusky loft together, clipped side by side, ritual invented: two taps on the rail, I'm here. Two taps back, me too.

"This is the part where I apologize for my fear," he said finally, voice small in the best way. "But I won't. I'm not sorry for loving you in the direction of caution. I am sorry for every time that love will feel like a slowing you didn't want."

She turned so their shoulders met, the closest thing to a kiss the loft had authority for. "I'll take the slowing," she said. "If we do it together. If slowing doesn't mean swallowing. If waiting is an agreed hour, not an indefinite sentence."

"Deal," he said. "You'll tell me when the hour is up?"

"Yes," she said. "And you'll tell me when the ladder needs another hand?"

"Yes," he said. "And when the town needs me to be less museum and more neighbor."

"Good," she said, and they stood letting the sound of not-sound teach them whatever lesson it was in charge of.

They descended as carefully as they'd gone up. At the bottom, Mayhew unhooked them with a tenderness he would deny under oath. "Alive," he said, a verdict he prefers. "What's the word?"

"Check present," Julian answered. "Not set. Initials: AR."

Mayhew's mouth pressed toward a line. "We'll keep that in the circle. Not on the radio."

"Count then bless," Miriam said.

He tipped his hat in the direction of the south wall. "And don't forget to eat lunch before you decide anything."

Outside, Cedar Creek kept doing the decent work of afternoon. The square looked like a sentence convinced of its own grammar. They walked toward the shop at a pace that let the future keep up without having to sprint.

.   .   .

BACK IN THE SHOP, shade fell across the counter in stripes, like the room had put on a cardigan. The wrapped book lay where they'd left it, the red string taut, the ribbon scrap tucked under like punctuation behaving itself. Miriam opened her notebook to the morning's dream lines and added new script beneath: **loft: check. AR. do not engage. Ask about bridal loop. brides as witnesses.** She drew a small bell and put a square around it because she refuses to be embarrassed by how her brain needs symbols to sit still.

Julian washed his hands at the back sink, then stood in the doorway drying them on a towel that had learned to live at the museum and moonlight in her shop. "I want to say the second part," he said. "The part that lives behind the fear."

She turned, hinge inside her easing love was an old door and he had learned where to push.

"I'm not only afraid of losing you to danger," he said. "I'm afraid of losing you to the story. I watched my father get swallowed by the museum once by the idea that the object mattered more than the person holding it. He called it duty. My mother called it *being married to shelves.* I'm afraid I will love this work more than I love you. Or that you'll think I do when I'm just bad at telling you the order of my loves."

Miriam leaned her hip against the counter and let the confession be heavy enough to change the furniture arrangement. "Order them," she said, not as test, as invitation.

"You first," he said, because he knows she asks to learn, not to grade.

"Truth," she said. "Then people. Then the story. Then the objects. Except when people have to come first so truth doesn't kill them. And except when the story has to be told before the object makes sense. It's a circle, not a stack."

He exhaled, smiling like a man who's been handed a draft that saves him from defending the wrong sentence. "Love," he said then. "Then truth. Then town. Then history. Then me again, so I don't forget I exist inside the list." His smile crooked. "And lately, *us* sits like connective tissue through the whole thing."

"Us is the and," she said, and wrote it on a label and stuck it to the bin because labeling doesn't make a thing truer; it makes it easier to remember when you're tired. **US = AND** in her neat hand looked ridiculous and perfect.

He came around the counter, left hand open not a performance, an offering and placed it on the book's string where her fingers already were. They stood like that, touching the pack of pages that had made this week honest and complicated, forming a shape that only held the two of them because it didn't ask for more. She felt the ground under both their shoes the literal wood and the longer thing steady.

"Practice," he said. "If you go toward a door, you say, 'I'm going toward a door.' If I think the door shouldn't be opened this hour, I say, 'I need more hands and daylight.' If either of us is tempted to do the other's job for them, we go get Sloane and accept our punishment."

"Which will involve cords," she said.

"And labels," he added.

"And possibly a lemon bar," she said.

They both laughed, there at the counter where the town had brought so much of itself to be blessed and counted.

"Tell me your sentence for the file," he said.

She looked out at the square, through the south window where people drifted by as if the museum's glass were part of their natural habitat now. **"We walk together into risk; we don't rush silence; we prefer safety that doesn't lie; we**

choose each other before headlines; we will not permit the bell to be used as theater; we will listen to brides."

He wrote it down, not as law but as a working document. Then he made his own: **Fear named. Harness clipped. Check found. Ask Eliza's line. Ask Mayhew about 1911 sheriff. No radio until circle.** He added, stubbornly, **Do not lose Miriam to the work.** He underlined it once, then put the pencil down like a man refusing to pretend known things are complicated.

She told him the rest of the dream, line by line, without ornament. The rope burns on the bride's palm. The single tear. The wheel turning without sound. The sentence *the bell remembers.* He listened the way he listens to fragile paper: head tilted, breath low, disrespect nowhere in him.

"We'll seek her," he said when she finished. "Not to expose her. To ask what she needs to be remembered for. If truth and love walk together, then witness is their child. We raise it. We don't parade it."

"Say that again," she said, because sometimes repetition is the only way to keep a sentence from slipping off the table.

He did, and it held.

The shop bell chimed lightly and Pastor Elijah leaned in not all the way, just the shoulder and the smile he uses when he's checking pulse, not doctrine. "Mayhew swore, which in my line means good news," he said. "You climbed. You breathed. You came down."

"Check with initials," Julian reported. "Engaged only when somebody decides to. We decided not to."

"Stewardship," Elijah approved. He glanced at their hands on the wrapped book and nodded once, relieved that intimacy had found a way to be practical. "Remember the two jobs of the bell," he said, backing up already. "Gather

and warn. Don't let one job steal the budget from the other."
Then he was gone, as pastors are when they trust you more
than they trust their need to keep talking.

Afternoon slid toward the soft hour that makes Cedar
Creek look like it's been polished with kitchen towels. They
did small chores with large consequences. Miriam labeled a
folder **BRIDAL LOOP**, and tucked Eliza's pencil slip inside.
Julian drafted a sign for the south window: **NEXT
EXHIBIT: MARRIAGE NOTES & WITNESS.** He made the
font boring on purpose; truth doesn't need fancier clothes
than clean.

They ate an apple between them, alternating bites as if
measuring fairness. He traced a thumb over the place her
hair tucked behind her ear, a touch so matter-of-fact it felt
like part of the room's architecture. She tugged his lanyard
until his name faced forward; he tugged her sleeve down
where the cuff had folded; the romance came on like breath,
not fireworks.

Before they locked up, he said the line he had been
saving without realizing it: "If I have to choose between the
story and you, I choose you every time. I just need to build a
life where I don't have to choose."

"You just did," she said. "With a harness and a sheriff
and a pastor and a bin with our name on it."

"And," he said.

"And," she echoed.

He kissed her then, not like a man auditioning for
legend, but like a partner signing a document. It landed and
held. No bells tried to steal the moment. No river interrupted with a sudden moral. The shop approved by staying
as it was shelves, wicks, a ledger of small sales and larger
yeses.

Outside, Sloane's voice lifted in bossy blessing;

Mayhew's hat crossed the square at an angle that meant nothing was on fire; Theo wiped a counter with the ferocity of a sacrament. The fort watched, square and patient. In the loft, the check waited for instruction that would not come from ego. In Miriam's pocket, the ribbon scrap warmed like a clue content to take its time.

They turned the sign **CLOSED SEE YOU IN THE LONG VERSION** and stepped into the evening, shoulders touching, pace matched. They didn't sprint. They didn't dawdle. They walked like people who had given fear a job and love a schedule. The town, tuned to notice and then mind its business, made a little lane for them without applause.

"Tomorrow," Julian said, that gentle promise at the end of the day.

"Breakfast first," Miriam said. "Ask Theo. Then the circle. Then the bell if it wants us."

"If it wants us," he agreed, and reached for her hand because some choices are supposed to be easy once you've done the hard part of telling the truth.

29

FESTIVAL CLOSING

By the time the sun pressed itself into the far line of firs, the square had gone quiet in that charged way crowds go quiet when they know they are about to witness something worth saving. Booths folded down to skeletons, tables wiped and stacked, music equipment wrapped in blankets like sleeping children. Only the lanterns remained, lined up in tidy procession along the bank, each one painted, carved, or tied with scraps of fabric in some family's hand.

Miriam stood near the water's edge with Julian beside her, their shoulders lightly touching. The town had been noisy all day with reconciliation, with apologies rehearsed and spoken, with cautious laughter over meals. But now the hush ran down the bank like a rumor that everyone wanted to believe. Even the children hushed themselves, wide-eyed at the glow about to be released into current.

Pastor Elijah said nothing at first, only lifted a hand as if directing silence to its proper place. Then, with voice low enough to require leaning in, he gave the only instruction:

"Carry your light with both hands. Offer it to the river, and to each other."

The line of families began. Cavanaughs first, then LeClairs, then Adlers, as if order had been quietly negotiated without needing Mayhew's hat to enforce it. Each household lowered its lantern into the water, steadied it until the current claimed it, then let go.

The lanterns took to the river like stars that had been waiting all day to find their reflection. They bobbed at first, awkward as calves, then steadied into glide. Dozens, then hundreds, drifting in slow procession toward the bend where the current would gather them into one long ribbon of fire.

Miriam held her breath. Not because she feared the lights would falter they didn't but because she felt the weight of what they meant. The ledger had been read. The symbol had glowed. The quarrels had bent toward forgiveness, even if not fully yet. And now the river was saying what no speech could: *take light into dark and let it move of its own accord.*

Julian's hand brushed hers, tentative, then firmer, until their fingers laced. He didn't look at her. He looked at the water, as if the gesture belonged more to the town than to them. She squeezed once her yes and kept her eyes forward too.

Children's laughter returned, soft first, then bolder, as the lanterns caught in small eddies and spun like dancers before rejoining the flow. The old folks murmured names of the dead as if this too were an altar.

Miriam felt the cool grass under her shoes, the river's breath on her face, Julian's steady warmth against her palm. The night was not spectacular. It was steady. That steadiness was its own kind of miracle.

The water took its light and promised to carry it farther than anyone in Cedar Creek could follow. And somehow that was enough.

WHEN THE LAST lantern was set afloat, Pastor Elijah stepped down from the bank, lantern unlit in his hand. He knelt and dipped it directly into the basin at the river's edge the very basin that had drained dry days before. This time, it brimmed full, fed by both stream and seep, water bright with reflection. He set the lantern there, and it caught flame as if sparked by nothing but readiness.

The crowd inhaled in unison. Miriam felt it ripple through her ribs, a single great body recognizing the basin's answer. Where before it had refused, now it blessed.

"The basin speaks when we are honest," Pastor Elijah said. "Tonight it speaks yes."

It wasn't thunder, but people cheered all the same. Not the cheer of victory it was gentler than that. A cheer of release, of relief. A sound that said *we survived our own story and chose to tell it whole.*

Julian turned slightly toward Miriam. His eyes shone, not from the lanterns but from something closer. "It's not just water," he whispered. "It's witness."

She nodded. "The river remembers. And forgives."

The lanterns flowed on. Couples leaned into each other, not in romance alone but in solidarity neighbors leaning neighbors. The rival families watched their lights merge on the current, indistinguishable once afloat. For the first time in memory, no one argued about placement, timing, or weight. The river had equalized them all.

Mayhew, arms crossed, tried to pretend his throat wasn't thick. Sloane openly wept, muttering something about *damn extension cords of the soul.* Children jumped and clapped as if the river itself had given them permission.

Miriam felt tears sting, uninvited but correct. She let them fall, not hiding. Julian squeezed her hand again. His thumb traced a line over her knuckles like a signature.

The symbolic closure was unmistakable: betrayal confessed, truth spoken, basin refilled, lanterns carrying forgiveness downstream. And yet Miriam sensed something unfinished too, a silence coiled in the fort bell. But for now, she let the water write this chapter's end. The river had said yes. Tomorrow could wait to ask new questions.

THE CURRENT PULLED the lanterns farther, the ribbon of light bending toward horizon. Miriam and Julian stood until most of the town had drifted back to the square, unwilling to step away before the last glow left sight.

Julian's hand stayed firm in hers. Not nervous, not claiming, just steady. She realized with a start that it had become natural so natural she almost forgot how much courage it took to begin.

The water sparkled as if blessed, lantern reflections dancing across the ripples. Miriam thought of the bride in her dream, the rope in her hand, the silence that had thundered. She whispered inwardly: *I will not forget you.* The lanterns felt like a promise to her too.

Julian glanced down, finally letting his gaze break from the river. "We'll remember this night," he said, voice low, private.

"Yes," Miriam answered. "Because it wasn't just ours. It belonged to everyone."

Still, she felt the belonging deepen inside her. Weeks ago she had been outsider, widow, stranger on the edge of

Cedar Creek's stories. Now she stood on the riverbank, hand in hand with the town's historian, entrusted by the river itself.

The romance of it wasn't in stolen kisses or dramatic declarations. It was here in being seen, in standing together, in holding light and letting it go.

As they turned back toward the square, laughter spilled from ahead families sharing pies, teenagers sneaking cider, Mayhew telling a story too tall for its own hat. Miriam leaned into Julian just enough to feel his shoulder brush hers with every step.

The night closed like a book that knows it will be opened again. The basin full. The lanterns afloat. The lovers walking home, hand in hand, the town finally beginning to believe in its own healing.

Tomorrow, she thought, would bring the bell. But tonight belonged to the river, to the lanterns, to the unity their light carried into dark.

30

THE SILENT BELL

Miriam woke to the gray edge of dawn, the kind that turned the shop windows silver before the sun had chosen a side. She rose expecting the steady reassurance that had marked every morning in Cedar Creek the toll of the fort bell cutting through mist, a sound so habitual it stitched the hours together.

But no sound came.

She stood barefoot in the middle of her shop, apron still slung from yesterday, and listened hard. The silence was not absence; it was deliberate, coiled, waiting. It felt too heavy to be natural.

The town stirred restlessly outside. Doors opened sooner than usual. Men leaned on railings, frowning into fog. Women gathered shawls tighter, waiting for what should have been the first note of the day. And when it didn't arrive, the square itself felt unfinished, like a sentence left hanging.

Julian appeared at her door, jacket thrown over one shoulder, eyes wide. He didn't have to say what they both knew: the bell had failed. The bell that had always rung, through snow and storm, through births and funerals, through every Rivers Festival since memory.

He looked at Miriam, and for a moment the whole town's unease passed between them. She remembered the dream the bride gripping the rope, the silence louder than any toll. She remembered whispering *I hear you.*

Now the silence was real, and so was the dread.

They didn't speak. They didn't need to. He nodded once, and she nodded back. The river had spoken and been answered. Now the bell was silent, and another story was demanding to be told.

BY MID-MORNING, the square looked almost normal. The festival booths were open again, pies laid out, children chasing each other with leftover lantern stems. But beneath the chatter lay a nervousness too deep to ignore. People asked one another with forced casualness: *Did you hear it? Maybe we missed it. Perhaps it rang softer today.*

But no one had heard it.

The sheriff checked the bell tower himself, returning with a shrug that convinced no one. Pastor Elijah walked the green with hands folded, murmuring prayers that sounded suspiciously like negotiations. Theo muttered that silence can be a curse or a cure, depending on how you listen.

Miriam tried to steady herself by serving tea in her shop, but her hands trembled each time she set down a cup. Julian arrived near noon, his expression somewhere between scholar's curiosity and a man bracing for grief.

"It isn't mechanical," he said quietly, leaning close so customers wouldn't hear. "I checked the wheel, the clapper, the pin. Everything's intact."

"Then it chose not to ring," Miriam whispered. The words chilled her even as she said them.

Julian frowned. "Bells don't choose."

She held his gaze. "This one does."

The silence pressed harder, not just from the tower but from their own history. They had stood together at the river when the basin refilled, hand in hand while the lanterns drifted. That had been a yes. This was a warning.

He brushed a hand over hers on the counter, only for a moment, but enough. "We'll face it," he said. "Whatever it is."

And she believed him. Still, the unease deepened. The town had only just healed one wound. Now it was as though the past refused to let them rest.

DUSK CAME EARLY, the kind that painted the fort tower black against a lavender sky. Miriam walked with Julian toward the green, lanterns in townsfolk's hands flickering like small rebellions against gathering dark. Everyone had turned their eyes upward, waiting half hoping the bell might yet change its mind, half dreading what it meant if it stayed silent.

The mayor cleared her throat for a speech, but no one listened. All ears strained for the iron mouth above them. Seconds stretched, then minutes. Still nothing.

And in the moment when they all knew it would not come, a murmur rippled outward like water disturbed: *Why? What does it mean? Whose fault this time?*

Miriam felt the dream bride's eyes on her again, the weight of unfinished vows pressing against her ribs. She turned to Julian, searching for an anchor. He met her gaze with the same mixture of fear and resolve she carried.

"This is only the beginning," he murmured.

She reached for his hand, not in public declaration this time but in private pact. "We'll find the truth," she whispered.

Above them the bell loomed, mute, a shadow against fading sky. Its silence was not emptiness. It was testimony.

The town shifted uneasily, whispering, suspecting. Miriam felt it in her bones: they had been delivered from one wound at the river only to be summoned into another in the tower. The river had given them water again. Now the bell was demanding voice.

And as the last light faded from the square, she knew with certainty: the next chapter had already begun.

The bell had chosen silence. And silence was never empty. It was a door.

Julian squeezed her hand once. Together, they stepped into the hush, knowing they were crossing a threshold.

The mystery of Cedar Creek was not finished. It had only deepened.

AFTERWORD

It began with *The Thirteenth Petal*. She saw herself then, cautious and uncertain, holding her aunt's manuscript like a shield. Cedar Creek had seemed foreign, half-ghosted by old stories and whispered suspicions. The thirteenth petal was still hidden then, its mystery unsolved, its promise untasted. She had been an outsider, searching the past for answers to questions she had barely begun to ask herself. Yet even then, the land had whispered to her, the river had tugged, and the petals of prophecy had begun to stir.

Waters of Redemption rose in her memory next—the basin running dry, the first covenant tested. She recalled how frightened she had been by the silence of water, by the possibility that her search was folly. But she also remembered the strength she found in listening, in daring to stay rather than flee. That was when Cedar Creek first began to claim her, when she learned that redemption was not about possession but about presence.

Then came *The Silent Bell*. Miriam saw herself again standing beneath the old tower, hearing absence louder than sound, sensing that silence was itself a summons. It had been a season of division, fear, and mistrust. Yet within it, she had heard something more: a call to endure, to wait, to stand even when answers were withheld. Julian had drawn closer then, his loyalty steadying her steps even when her own faltered.

The memories folded into *The Fifth Cup*, when the goblet gleamed and the town's faith was tested by falsehoods and shadows. She remembered how she had nearly lost her trust in herself, in the manuscript, even in the possibility of belonging. But the fifth cup had reminded her: covenant was not about certainty, but about choosing to lift the cup even when hands shook. That act had prepared her heart for deeper mysteries still to come.

The arc curved forward into *The Bride's Lantern*, when love and sorrow mingled on the riverbank, and the grief of generations still pressed upon the town. Miriam remembered how she had felt that sorrow in her bones, how it had nearly undone her. But the lantern's glow had also shown her a way through—how grief could become light, how remembrance could become release. And in that glow, her heart had turned more fully toward Julian, not as ally only but as beloved.

And in *The Rose Reborn*. She saw it all as if laid upon the window: the manuscript sealed and then opened, the prophecy spoken aloud, the carving uncovered, the pendant glowing with memory, the council divided and then healed, the people fractured and then mended. She saw her own fear of leadership, her hesitation to love, her doubt that she could belong—and she saw how each had been answered, not by spectacle, but by covenant kept through trial.

THE SILENT BELL: BOOK 3

Cedar Creek Legends, Book Three: *The Silent Bell*

When the dawn bell of Cedar Creek fails to toll for the first time in living memory, a town built on its music falls abruptly uneasily silent. Baker and antiques-shop owner **Miriam** feels the hush like a hand on her spine; museum director **Julian** hears it as a puzzle rattling inside history's locked drawer. What begins as a technical glitch quickly exposes a century-and-a-half-old wound: in 1846, a bride was abandoned at the chapel and the bell stopped speaking the same day.

From the café's rumor mill to the church's guarded ledgers, **The Silent Bell** unfolds as a lyrical small-town mystery where every clue is tactile: a frayed rope, faint initials carved into bronze, a torn diary page, a wedding ring that never reached an altar. Miriam's second sight half intuition, half mercy pulls her toward the lost bride's story; Julian's reverence for artifacts keeps the investigation honest and humane. Together they comb attic boxes and archive stacks, scale the bell tower's dust-bright stair, and listen for truths in the spaces where words once failed.

As whispers swell into debate, Cedar Creek teeters. **Pastor Elijah**, part guardian, part gatekeeper, warns Miriam not to "meddle with the silence," even as his own family line knots into the legend. A young engaged couple, rattled by the omen, falters in public mirroring the town's fear that vows mean less than the stories we inherit. The square becomes a battleground of nostalgia versus repair: replace the bell or restore it? hush the past or tell it?

Miriam chooses the harder verb **tell** and the town follows. A bride's journal emerges from the chapel rafters, naming betrayal instead of crime. A carved inscription reveals the groom's other promise. False leads fall away. In midnight dreams the bride whispers, *"Tell my story,"* and Miriam wakes with the courage to do exactly that.

What makes **The Silent Bell** irresistible isn't just the puzzle; it's the way solving it changes everyone who listens. The investigation becomes communion: handbells passed from neighbor to neighbor, apologies rung before they're spoken, a festival where Cedar Creek learns a new grammar of sound one tender toll at the precise right moment. The community begins to heal not by forgetting, but by **remembering well**. And in the quiet between revelations, romance finds its truest pitch. Julian lets Miriam all the way into his grief; Miriam lets joy move back into the room. Their partnership intellectual, spiritual, and deeply felt rings as surely as the tower itself.

With sumptuous sense detail, wry humor, and a faith in ordinary kindness, this third installment deepens the series' signature alchemy of heart, history, and hush. Fans of contemporary, character-driven mysteries with a luminous thread of the mystical will savor every scene: the attic dust motes that behave like clues; the ledger of "heard apologies"; the cracked forgiveness bell passed to anyone brave enough to use it. By the time the restored tower speaks again once, perfectly readers will feel the note settle in their own ribs.

And just when Cedar Creek breathes easy, the museum's ceremonial goblet Elijah's Cup begins to gleam of its own accord. Light writes an unfinished sign along its silver band, and a new invitation stirs: **redemption.** The bell has delivered the town from silence; the cup will ask it to settle old debts with grace. In a final, luminous tease, Miriam and Julian stand before the glass and feel the future lean in the fifth place at a table set for four.

The Silent Bell is a complete, satisfying story of truth told, love risked, and a town remade by gentleness. Perfect for readers of small-town fiction, soft-mystery romance, and redemptive legends that feel as real as your own front porch.

ABOUT THE AUTHOR

Jordan Jace is a Pacific Northwest author whose mysteries and heartwarming tales are set against stunning landscapes. With a deep connection to the PNW region's natural beauty, Jace infuses each story with the magic of misty mountains, lush forests, and tranquil coastlines. Jace believes that joy can be found in the smallest moments and the most unexpected places. When not writing, Jace is exploring the world, seeking inspiration in every corner for the next unforgettable story. Discover more at jordanjace.com

www.ingramcontent.com/pod-product-compliance
Lightning Source LLC
Chambersburg PA
CBHW030056310726

48970CB00004B/1033